THE TRAP

TABITHA KING

THE TRAP

MACMILLAN PUBLISHING COMPANY   New York

Macmillan Publishing Company
866 Third Avenue, New York, N.Y. 10022
Collier Macmillan Canada, Inc.

Epigraph for Part One from *The Oxford Self-Pronouncing Bible*,
Red Letter Edition, Authorized King James Version, Oxford University Press.
Epigraph for Part Three from "The Woes and the Furies," *Five Decades:
Poems 1925–1970* by Pablo Neruda, translated by Ben Belitt,
Grove Press, 1974. Used by permission.

Printed in the United States of America

Quality Printing and Binding by:
ARCATA GRAPHICS/KINGSPORT
Press and Roller Streets
Kingsport, TN 37662   U.S.A.

0-025-63140-3

for G. W.
"by any other name . . ."

THE TRAP

PROLOGUE

ONE AFTERNOON, while Travis and Sarah and Pat all slept naked under a blanket of August heat, Liv took a plastic bucket that once had held two pounds of Shedd's peanut butter and walked the half mile to where the road ended at Helen Alden's driveway. While out walking with her children in June, Liv had noticed the blackberry bramble so thick with white blossom it looked, at a distance, as if it had been snowed on. She had been waiting since for the fruit the flowers foretold. On first meeting Miss Alden she had asked permission to pick there. Miss Alden seemed pleased she had bothered to ask. Most people wouldn't, wild berries on anyone's property being widely, if not universally, deemed a kind of free fall to anyone with sufficient initiative to glean them.

Wearing a long-sleeved cotton shirt and jeans to protect herself from the brambles, never mind the heat, and an old straw fedora to shade her face and protect her head from the sun, she walked down the dusty dirt road listening to the insects, which seemed to be the only living things besides herself abroad.

She saw at once she was not the first to pick here; there were many empty calyxes in each bunch. Whoever it was—Helen Alden, perhaps, with her companion, Miss Betty Royal?—had picked their berries a few days previous, for a quantity of berries had ripened since then on the same branches. Not that what they had taken, or what she was going to take, amounted to more than a dent in the crop; the thicket was enormous, spreading back into the woods, and laden with enough to feed the whole neighborhood. As far as she was concerned, the thorns were entitled to their tithe of flesh and blood.

Hardly feeling them scratching her hands and face and hooking her clothes as she went deeper into the thicket, Liv quickly forgot almost everything—the fretful worry that had possessed her all this first summer in Nodd's Ridge that Travis or Sarah would wake up unheard, Travis climb out of his crib, Sarah at seven become overconfident and enter the water alone, one or both children somehow slip out and drown in the lake, perhaps while Pat was napping, too, and she was out berrying—she almost forgot even that, everything except the clusters of berries with their fruity smell. The path she made for herself, carefully pinching branches between thorns and moving them aside, hooking them onto other branches, sometimes stepping on them, particularly if they were barren or old, closed up behind her until she was in the heart of the thicket, enclosed in a wall of thorns. But she was entranced and did not notice.

The bucket grew heavy. She wished she had brought two and then smiled at herself. Whatever would she do with a gallon of berries, let alone the two quarts she had already picked? The berries would be ripe and ripening for another two weeks. She would come back. Her straw hat was hot on her head. The straw even smelled hot and dusty. She took it off and fanned her face, then put it back on again. She was reaching into the brambles once again when she heard voices.

She stopped and listened. She could not make out what they were saying, but they were male, and sounded boisterous. And they were coming her way, up from the lake, through the woods. Making noise enough to alert the whole town. Feeling stupidly guilty, as if she were a thief caught in the act, but equally irritated at the interruption of her pleasureful solitude, she prepared to smile and be neighborly. And the voices died away.

Relieved, she fell to picking again.

"Fuck," said a voice that seemed to be at her elbow. "It's a fucking cat."

Liv froze.

Other voices chorused *goddamn, shit,* and *fucking cat.*

She sorted out three voices. Locals, by their accents. The first voice was the deepest, the most authoritative—the voice of a grown man. The other two seemed younger. One was a nervous Yankee tenor, high and light, vague with swallowed syllables and air. The third, who spoke the least, was much like the first voice, but more adolescent, thinner, less resonant. They were not really at her elbow, but only yards away, on the other side of the thicket, in the woods. The first man had sworn loudly, and some trick of the still air had made him sound closer than he was.

The obvious, sensible course was to announce her presence, step out of the brambles. Only then did she realize that that was not as easy as it looked; she would have to make a new path out. And spellbound by the violence of those first obscene words, she kept still, holding her breath.

There was a faint, wet, mewing sound. The cat they were cursing. It sounded hurt. She began to be angry.

"Hey," said the tenor giggling. "It's not dead yet."

"No shit," said the other two simultaneously. The younger one was interested. The other, older voice of the first speaker announced he already knew it.

"What do we do?" the tenor asked.

"Kill it, you asshole," said the arrogant first voice. "What do you think, we're going to nurse it back to health?"

The tenor giggled again.

"Let's leave it on the old dyke's doorstep." It was the third voice.

They all laughed.

The cruelty of their proposed prank shattered Liv's trance. She began to struggle out of her prison, trying to do it silently, without dropping her bucket. She went in the direction of the voices, away from the road. She was furious. Nobody was going to kill any injured cats and leave their corpses on Helen Alden's doorstep or anyone else's if she could put a stop to it.

The thorns tore at her and she staggered. "Ow," she said involuntarily, and tore herself free.

Ahead of her there was sudden watchful silence, a cessation of movement. She had revealed her presence to the men. A wash of fear weakened her resolve only for a fraction of a second; she meant to declare her presence anyway, to stop them. All she had lost was the element of surprise. She broke through the edge of the brambles, which were taller than she was, and found herself on a ledge overlooking a little gap in the woods, where the granite rose too close to the surface, the soil too much to hold any green thing except the most tenacious moss and fungi. The three men were just below, a few feet away, staring at her. Husky young men. One was bareheaded, one wore a Boston Red Sox cap backward. The third wore a head-band, a leather strip like a phylactery around his head, tied over his right ear with a bundle of feathers and beads hanging down.

At their feet they had uncovered a trap, and a big old gray cat, badly wounded, in it. The cat was in fact nearly dead, its eyes glazed with shock and pain. Its fur was matted with blood. Bone and torn flesh and ragged fur were in the teeth of the trap.

"Oh my God," she said, and slid down the ledge in a crouch, reaching out instinctively with her free hand toward the mangled cat.

She saw the blur of movement out of the corner of her eye but could not avoid the man who grabbed her wrist. His foot was sud-denly behind her heel, his hand around her wrist, as hard as a mana-cle. He jerked her backward. She lost her balance and flipped onto her back onto the rock-knobby ground, the breath knocked out of her. The pail flew up out of her grasp, raining berries as it arced over them and hit the ground with a thunk. What remained of her patient work spilled onto the mossy ground around it. For a moment she was stunned and disoriented. Gasping for breath, she managed to refocus her vision; above her was a ragged canopy of trees under the white hot sky, and the man, like the trunk of a tree, who had decked her, staring down at her. His eyes were the color of spit. The short cut of his blond hair emphasized the squareness of his jaw. He showed a quantity of carnivorously healthy white teeth. His lips were thin and the upper one was flawed just off the center as if someone had taken a stitch there. He stepped over her, one foot on either side of her knees, and crossed his arms.

"Who are you?"

Liv recovered her old fury with her breath. She sat up. He stepped back in surprise.

"Who wants to know?" she snapped. "And what the hell are you doing?"

The man laughed. He bent over her and offered her a hand.

She looked at it, then scrambled to her feet on her own.

The other two men stood staring at her. The one with the head-band was a smaller, slimmer version of the man with the crooked lip, with the same blond hair, grown long. Most likely his younger brother. The other was shorter, round and stupid of face, heavy bodied. Very pink-skinned, he had small blue eyes and a snub nose, so he looked like a pig in overalls, especially since he wore no shirt under the bib. Wisps of rusty hair showed at the edges of his backward baseball cap, sprigged behind his ears, and matted the back of his neck; on his bare arms and chest where the overall bib did not cover; and bunched from his armpits, even when they were not open.

"Look, lady," the man with the crooked lip said. "This goddamn cat blundered into our trap. We have to put it out of its misery."

She looked at the cat again. Its bloody bib heaved with an involuntary effort to take breath. She could see there was no hope for it.

"Okay," she said, though there was nothing okay about it. "How are you going to do it?"

The men exchanged amused glances.

"We don't happen to have a gun with us," the one with the headband said. "Do you?" He seemed to think this was very funny.

She looked at him in disgust. "This is your fault to begin with. You set the trap."

"Fuck you, lady," he said.

The man with the crooked lip interrupted. "We have permission to trap here. It's not our fault you summer people don't keep your cats in."

She glared at him. "I can't believe Helen Alden gave you permission to trap on her land. I heard you talking about leaving the cat on her steps. That doesn't sound like you're on very great terms with her."

The pink boy in overalls giggled.

The headbanded blond stared at him. "Shut up, Gordy," he said.

"Who the fuck are you?" the man with the crooked lip challenged her.

"None of your business," she said. "But I do have permission to be here. To pick berries." She looked at her pail on the ground, the berries around her feet.

"Sure," he said.

It occurred to her then that she was a woman alone with these men who were strangers to her. There was the sudden rush of the apprehension any woman feels alone in the midst of men she does not know. Until then, the adrenaline of righteous anger had carried her. She felt herself paling, and cursed herself.

The eyes of the man with the crooked lip glittered. Calmly, he stepped away from her, and without looking at it, still staring at her, he stomped on the cat's head.

"No!" she wailed, and felt her gorge rise. She turned away, and his arms clamped around her waist. She vomited into the bramble patch. Spitting the evil taste of her own bile, she jerked away from him. He tightened his hold. The pressure on her diaphragm made her feel ill again. She closed her eyes, fighting it. Then she drove her elbows backward into his diaphragm and he released her, swearing at her.

"Don't you call me names," she hissed. "You bastard!"

And the three men laughed.

She stood there with her fists clenched tight enough to cut the skin of her palms, panting.

"I know who you are," said the man with the crooked lip. "Miz O-liv-i-a Russell. Seen you at the post office. You never seen me, though. I'm just a local. Have to work for a living summertimes."

"Is that what you call working?" she snarled, gesturing at the dead cat.

He looked at the cat with mock surprise. "That? That's a mercy, ain't it, O-liv-i-a? What you wanted?"

"Get your goddamn trap and get the fuck out of here!" she shouted.

The three men looked at one another.

"Don't get your crack in an uproar, O-liv-i-a," said the man with the crooked lip mildly.

"Get the trap, Gordy," the one with the headband said.

"Do I have to?" Gordy whined, but he was already doing it, freeing the grisly remains of the cat from the metal teeth.

"Just don't get your pecker caught in it," the man with the crooked lip said.

Gordy snickered.

"Nice meeting ya, O-liv-i-a," the man with the crooked lip said. "Take care now."

He sauntered into the woods, followed by Gordy, who swung the bloody trap. The headbanded one idled behind them. He peeked at her from under womanishly long, nearly white eyelashes. He looked over his shoulder to see if the other two were out of sight yet. Then he unzipped his jeans, reached into his fly, and drew out his penis. Fine blond pubic hair threaded out onto the metal teeth of the zipper.

"Oh for Christ's sake," Liv said.

He grinned and wagged his penis at her. "Hope we meet again, Miz Russell," he said.

He tucked his penis into his pants, zipped up, and ducked into the woods, following the others.

Liv shuddered. She looked at the cat and felt sick at her stomach again. She *was* sick again. When she stopped shaking, she found some sticks and nudged the body into some bushes. The soil here would be too thin to dig a grave, assuming she had a tool besides her hands to do it with. The plastic pail would never do. She would have to go home and come back with a plastic garbage bag and a spade and take the carcass to the apple orchard behind Helen Alden's house to bury it. She would tell Miss Alden what had happened. Miss Alden ought to know.

Liv picked up her berry pail and emptied out the last few berries. Her pants legs were stained with the berries she had knelt in, and more berries were crushed into the treads of her sneakers. Her hands were stained with them where she had supported herself, regaining her feet. From the splotchy sensation of wet on the back of her shirt, she knew there must have been some under her when she hit the ground. The berries were black, but when they were crushed, they bled red. Her scratches were beginning to sting. She trudged off around the thicket, feeling defeated.

Miss Alden was not at home when Liv finished burying the cat and knocked at her door.

She decided not to tell Pat anything about the incident. She didn't want him using it as an excuse to dislike Nodd's Ridge, to find it unsafe. It was supposed to be a refuge. She needed it, time away from her pottery business, which had become such a success since her sister Jane had joined her and taken over the marketing. Pat had gone along with the summer house because she had wanted it so badly, and she had paid for it, after all, with her own hard-earned money. But he was a country boy himself, raised in the grimmest kind of rural poverty. He brought a cynical eye to the beautiful countryside, quick to pick up the rusted-out automobiles, the shacky trailers, the galled and beaten curs. It made her uneasy to keep anything from him, but she didn't want to see the twitch of his mouth, the tired unspoken I-told-you-so-babe in his eyes. She didn't want him going all grim and male and rushing off to get the shit beaten out of him in the name of her honor and his. They were new people in Nodd's Ridge, and she didn't want trouble right at the start.

A week or ten days later a starveling gray kitten appeared on the Russells' doorstoop and they put out some milk for her. Of course, she would not leave then, and they gave up and took her in. The vet shook his head over her and muttered uncomplimentary things about summer people who kept a cat for the season and then, come Labor Day, turned it out, along with its kittens. Though, he admitted, he usually didn't start seeing the feral survivors until late in September. Liv did not tell him she thought she knew what had happened to this kitten's mother.

By then, in the store in the village, she had encountered the three men again in the presence of an older man who looked too much like the two blonds, balding and too fat, to be anyone except their father. They were extravagantly polite to her, and laughed as if at a dirty joke as she was walking out. The next time she was in the store, she asked the storekeeper who they were. He told her the brothers were Rand and Ricky Nighswander and the other boy, in overalls, was their stepbrother Gordy Teed. The older man, their father, with his military haircut and surly expression, was Arden Nighswander.

George Fogg leaned confidentially across the counter, over her milk and eggs and orange juice. "I don't like to say it, Missus Russell," he had said in a low voice, glancing around nervously, "but I wouldn't take that fellow's check. And I wouldn't leave nothing lying around loose either."

Part One

Deliver me, O Lord . . . from the violent man;
which imagine mischiefs in their heart;
continually are they gathered together for war.

—PSALM 140. 1, 2.

. . . the dark places of the earth are full
of the habitations of cruelty.

—PSALM 74. 20.

CHAPTER 1

FIREFIGHT

Rough Cut #1

Here in a patch of jungle, blasted and torn as
by enormous machines, a terrible battle has been
fought. The jungle is winning now: a ruined
bulldozer, seemingly big enough to clear a
runway for a jumbo jet all by itself, rusts on
its side like a huge ugly sculpture; a
helicopter troop ship, stripped and savaged, is
smashed into the smooth boles of trees only
yards away. Vines are groping over both
machines. Soon they will no longer be visible,
even from each other, yet both bear a military
insignia that is still identifiable. It is an
open mouthful of canine teeth outlined in red
that has faded to the color of dried blood. A
lurid tongue lolls over the bottom row of
incisors. Block letters—US XIIITH CAV—
identify the symbol like a studded collar.

Against the background of the jungle,
uncorrodible green against the rusting
mechanisms, a man in a camouflage uniform marked
with the same insignia as the wrecked dozer and
chopper stands like a totem in the clearing.
Pocked and seamed, his face is that of a Mongol

warrior. Under his visored cap his coarse,
straight black hair whips cruelly into narrow,
slanted eyes that show no white or anything
except their own black fire. He stares at the
body of a woman, tied to the rotor blades of the
Huey, a razor-edged catherine wheel. The
mottling on the blades may be rust—or blood. The
woman's body is pallid blue. Her face is a Noh
mask, pouting open lips black against her
bloodless skin. She is an Oriental, almond-eyes
blank. Dust motes have settled on the silvery
black irises like tiny grains of snow. Her black
hair is plastered to her finely shaped skull.
The delicate bones of her face are disappearing
as her tissues swell and tighten the mask of her
skin. A fly lands on her cheek and crawls across
it. For a long time. Someone has scrawled a
symbol on her naked belly, in her blood. It is
the same symbol the man wears on the shoulder of
his uniform, the jaws of a ravening beast.

Then she is gone. The jungle becomes a rainy
city street at night. Streetlights reflect over
the wet surface of the pavement like the glaze of
dead eyes. The red fangs of the XIIITH CAV
insignia, just seen on the dead woman's belly,
bubble in lurid neon over a honky-tonk bar
across the street. The barbaric-looking man
cradles a shotgun. He watches the bar, people
going in and out. Mostly men, a few women. The
women are cheap and whorish-looking and drunk.
The men wear bits and pieces of military
uniforms with their civilian clothes, as if
unable to give up their military identities.
They are young, tough-looking, drunk or stoned
or both.

A camouflage painted Trans-Am, jacked, with
a glass-packed muffler, screeches around the
corner and brakes violently in front of the bar.
Its front grill and bumper have been transformed
into a mouthful of canine teeth.

A lanky blond man, with the small but
prominently boned features of Appalachia,

unfolds himself from the car. He is drunk, staggers, stops to piss on the front wheel. Kids in a passing car jeer at him; he tosses off a clumsy bird at them.

Then, for a moment, the street is almost silent, even the drunken hilarity in the bar seems muffled. The two men have the street to themselves.

"Jackson," the man with the shotgun says clearly, flatly.

The lanky man looks up, too drunk to be startled. "Huh?" He squints into the night but can make out only shadows in the glare of the street lamp and the neon.

There is no answer. Jackson shakes himself off, zips up.

"Jackson," the man with the shotgun says.

Now Jackson sees him, and terror flashes across his face. He tries to disguise it.

"Hey, old buddy," he says, his accent now clearly border-southern. "Long time, no see."

"This is for May," the man with the shotgun says and raises it.

"I didn't have nothing to do with it," Jackson cries. He begins to back away, holding up his palms in self-defense.

The man with the shotgun is silent.

Jackson laughs a high nervous laugh. "You got me all wrong, buddy. I tried to stop it," he says.

The man with the shotgun sighs. "You never could bluff for shit," he says, and pulls the trigger.

The lanky man screams and is blown against the side of the Trans-Am and up over its hood by the force of the gunshot.

THE PLAY BUTTON popped up. Pat Russell reached over and depressed Rewind.

He got up and opened the curtains that covered the window wall, admitting the mellow light of late afternoon reflected from the lake. The back of his neck was stiff with tension.

Liv felt an impulse to get up and hug him. Travis was half in and half out of her lap.

Pat continued to stare out at the water, but he wasn't seeing it. He patted his breast pocket idly, reassuring himself his cigarettes were still there. Then he went through the nervous ceremony of scraping the pack out of his pocket, shaking out a butt, inserting it between his lips, locating his lighter, lighting the cigarette, inhaling it. All to put off the moment when he would have to face them and gauge their reactions.

If she dumped Travis out of her lap and jumped up now, she would be putting herself between him and his cigarette. So she just waited.

"Well," he said, "what do you think?"

The setting sun caught a few silver strands in Pat's hair and shone in Travis' fine spun mop. Liv, in dark shorts and a halter that were too big for her now, sat on the big comfortable sofa she had covered herself in a high-spirited pattern during their first summer on the lake. Travis had been sitting in her lap through the several minutes of the rough cut from Pat's movie. Now he lounged against her thigh, playing with several of his G.I. Joes, the miniature soldiers that had become his favorite toys in the past year. Sarah, her round face flushed with excitement, sat cross-legged on the floor near her mother's bare feet.

"It's great," Sarah said. "It's fantastic. Isn't it, mom?"

Liv smiled. "It looks good. It looks like a real movie."

"What did you think, Trav?" Pat asked the boy.

"Is that guy a Bad Guy?" he asked.

"The one that got blown away? You bet," said Pat.

"No, the Kung Fu guy," Travis said. "Was he a Bad Guy?"

"Ah," Pat said. He stared at his cigarette with distaste and then abruptly ground it out. "As usual, Travis has gone to the heart of the movie."

"I think he wants to know which side he was on—was he Cong or American?" Liv said.

"Oh." Pat shrugged. "U.S., of course. Didn't you see the patch he was wearing on his shoulder, Trav?"

"Yeah," said Travis. "But he looked like a Cong."

Pat chewed his lower lip. "Do you think maybe Travis has identified a serious problem with this picture?" he asked Liv.

"No," she said. "He only knows Kinsella from that Kung Fu flick you took him to see. He was a Good Guy then, but he was also a Chinese warrior or something, wasn't he? I don't think all those millions of Kinsella fans out there will have any trouble recognizing he's One of Ours."

Pat chewed his lower lip. "He does look awfully Oriental. Actually he's just another Mick. Like me."

"Well, the girl's a Cong, isn't she?" Travis asked.

"Not exactly. She's a friendly," Pat said.

"Who killed her then?"

"That guy Jackson that Kinsella blew away, and some other guys. Some other Americans," Pat said.

"Why?" Travis persisted.

"Because they're Bad Guys."

"But they're Americans, you said they were on Our Side!"

Liv reached out and pulled Travis, still clutching his brace of G.I. Joes, into her arms. The hard plastic of little hands and boots and heads pinched her breasts.

"Sometimes guys on Our Side are bad, too," she said. "Sometimes they do bad things."

Pat paced. "Was this a mistake," he said to Liv, "letting Travis see this clip?"

She shrugged. The question had occurred to her previously, if it hadn't to him. It had seemed important that he know what his daddy's work was, what Pat had been doing during the long absences. "He has to find out sometime the world is not black and white." But she didn't really know if now was the right time. It was a distinctly doubtful proposition.

Travis pushed out of her arms. "I'm not a baby."

"That's why you sat in your mother's lap the whole time?" Pat said, taking the cassette clip out of the VCR.

Liv winced and started to rise. The degree of hostility, real jealousy, in his tone of voice shocked her. "Pat," she said.

Pat jumped at her touch. He stared at her, suddenly conscious of how tight the skin over her high cheekbones had become. The skin looked fragile, as if it might split if he dared to touch her.

Travis elected his only defense—direct denial of the truth. "I did not," Travis said. "I did not."

"Did," Pat sang. "Did. Beeg Guy."

"Jesus," Liv muttered. She shook her head wearily and passed a hand through her hair.

"Did not!" Travis screamed.

Pat stood stock still, his face open with surprise as he realized what he had provoked, then quickly closed with guilt.

"Don't scream at me," Pat said in a low voice. "Don't you scream at me, mister."

"I hate you," Travis screamed. "I hate your stupid movie! Go away! Leave me alone!"

Travis' lips were blue, his skin livid. His fists were clenched like little maces, parts of the G.I. Joes extruding between his fingers.

"That's enough," said Liv, and picked Travis up. "No more," she said softly to him, and carried him out of the room.

Pat sank into a chair and looked helplessly at Sarah.

"What did I do?" he said. "What did I say?"

Sarah, her face pale, shook her head.

"You still love me, don't you?" he asked, and held out his arms.

She came to him at once and hugged him, then bounced out of his embrace, blushing. He felt immediately worse, recognizing the incest taboo had at long last fallen between them. It might be years before they would be able to embrace each other comfortably again. Along with everything else, he appeared to have lost his daughter this summer.

"Sure, daddy," she said. "The movie's going to be super. Don't worry about it."

Then she was gone, no doubt to the safe haven of her bedroom, papered with Springsteen posters.

"Jet lag," he said out loud. But he was too nerved up to sleep. He decided to take a walk.

The lake was suddenly quiet, all the water skiers and boaters gone home to slop up martinis and scoff barbecued steaks. The smell of charring meat in the air made him hungry, and a little sick to his stomach. He wandered toward the woods, thinking if he had to toss his cookies, he might as well be discreet about it.

He found himself on the meandering track that he thought of as the Path of Least Resistance, like something out of *Pilgrim's Progress*—not planned, just a convenient way people had taken over from the wild things. He didn't like the woods very much. They were wall-less, unpaved, and full of untamed unpredictable creatures.

Dark had already gained ascendancy in the woods. The thick-trunked, middle-aged trees towering over him made him feel like a little kid again in a world of giants. The thick fronds of the evergreens not only spread their fans between him and the light of the setting sun, they actually seemed to absorb it, from green tip to palmlike black midrib. Tree roots extruding through the soil felt as hard and sharp-edged as stones through the thin soles of his shoes. And as suddenly, as it always did, Liv's studio emerged from the shadows.

It was the biggest reason they had chosen this particular summer house. During the late sixties, when flower children had bloomed even in such obscure corners of the world as Nodd's Ridge, the teenage son of the previous owner had built it as a place to paint, and as a refuge from his indulgent but hopelessly obtuse parents. So the old caretaker, Walter McKenzie, had told them. The kid had had some fey talent, for he had built, from scrap lumber and old windows retrieved from the town dump, a one-room gingerbread cottage replete with the peculiar feature of a glass roof. The cheap colors of the original paint had faded, so it seemed as if the little house had stood there a very long time, longer than the house at the other end of the path. It really only needed an old witch to make it complete.

It was unlocked, as usual. Pat let himself in, thinking about the kid who had built the place. The flower child. By now he would be about their age, early thirties, and perhaps struggling with his own teenage children, if he had any.

Like a stage set, the gingerbread house was all outside. The interior was unfinished, uninsulated, un-Sheetrocked bare bones of framing exposed like the inside of a barn. The time-grayed boards of the wall were decorated with plastic-sleeved family photographs, pictures Liv had cut from magazines or picked up in junkstore rummages, and odd objects she fancied for their shape or texture or color—feathers, leaves, swags of pine cones and pine needles, birds' nests. And among them, fine-meshed metal sieves, brushes, trivets, tools, ready to hand. Rocks and pebbles and bits of polished glass lined the windowsills. The unpainted wood floor, much worn now, was dusty and stained with the ghosts of old paint, with Liv's clays and glazes. All of the meagre furnishings—shelving for supplies; an old, much-painted and chipped kitchen table; a high, three-legged stool; the cupboards—were of wood and, like the battered slate sink and its slate counter that Liv used as a wedging bench to prepare her clay, had been salvaged from junkstores like Linscott's in Greenspark, or the town dump. Except the wood-firing kiln, which she had built herself. It renewed her, she said, to go back to basic techniques every summer. The place had a decidedly seedy air, but it was full of chemical and earthy smells he associated with Liv at her happiest.

He walked around the room, poking into open boxes, opening the cupboards where Liv stored carefully labeled glass jars of prepared glazes, dragging other boxes out of the corners into which they had been shoved. From the shelf set aside for Travis, Pat took down the Tupperware container and smelled the sweaty lump of multicolored clay Travis had probably played with all summer. A flat plastic box held little clay figures he had constructed—neat little army men in battle poses. They all had distinct faces, eyes and noses and ears and mouths and beards, shaped out of tiny balls of clay Travis had added on and incised with one of his own small plastic tools. Not bad at all for a little kid. Those fat little fingers were surprisingly nimble.

In his childhood, Pat's mother had hidden the few Christmas gifts she could afford—mostly sweaters and socks and mittens that she made herself and that he needed anyway, but always a few toys, secondhand things she picked up at yard sales and in junkstores—in the back of her closet. She painted and repaired her finds late at night, like the cobbler's elfin helpers, a profligate investment of time and energy that Ellen Russell, who supported herself and Pat as a practical nurse, could afford as little as she could afford new toys. He was about seven when he discovered her hiding place, and one afternoon when school had been dismissed early because of snow, and he was home alone, he wriggled to the back of the closet and peeked into each and every carefully wrapped present. He never knew whether she noticed the packages had been disturbed, but she never said anything. She was a wise woman; perhaps she knew that after the wild excitement of his peeking, there was a letdown he would never forget. There were no surprises that Christmas, and that was more than punishment enough. And he had never peeked again. Like that naked Christmas, there was shockingly little to be discovered in Liv's workshop where in previous years there would have been dozens of pleasing little surprises. The disappointment and guilt that he felt were the same as he had known then, creeping away from his mother's closet with burning cheeks, sick stomach, and tight throat and on Christmas morning, opening the presents he had opened before. Like a sin of omission, what counted was what wasn't there. Not even a barrel of failures, for Liv was catlike in her neatness. What didn't work was smashed to bits and either buried or reused.

He even looked inside the dehumidifier, an electrified tin breadbox, that Liv used as a drying cupboard. Of course, it was empty. This late, she wouldn't have anything half-finished sitting around. And then, idly, reflexively, he looked in one last cupboard. His heart actually raced for a moment with relief and joy. Three or four pieces huddled in the shadows as if they were waiting for him. A small amber-glazed bowl incised with a swirling pattern clearly related to her current style. A pitcher with a sleek iron glaze like woman's skin. He took it out and felt of the curving female lines, and smiled. Behind it, almost invisible in the shadows, was a tall vase, twice its size, shaped like a shield. The glaze had been dripped irregularly over the surface to repeat, wavering, the shape of the piece. In some areas, the glaze was so thin it was almost matte, and in others it had been built up to the gloss of the pitcher with its silky iron finish. The uneven color, shiny black and dull black, was sooty and glinted red and purple as he turned it. It was something entirely new. And last of all, tucked in the very back, a football shape the size of a human head, with a gaping mouth in the top seam. The outside was bisque-colored and unglazed, the inside a thickly, unevenly glazed purple red. He pushed it back quickly. There was something unsettlingly organic about it.

Surely it was a good sign that she had done these difficult things, and to his eye, not hers or even sister Jane's, to be sure, but humbly educated by propinquity if nothing else, she had done it very well. Only the bowl and the pitcher seemed remotely commercial, but that didn't matter nearly as much as that she was working again, and apparently very creatively.

He sat down on her stool and handled the clean, almost surgical instruments she had left in their tray. He spun her throwing wheel idly. This place had always had such an extraordinarily empty quality—perhaps because no one had ever really lived in it. And when Liv was not in it, the emptiness was underlined by all the evidence of her sometimes presence. But he was comforted when he sat where she sat and when he touched what she touched, especially that, because her sense of touch was so extraordinary. He supposed in a literal sense she was very thin-skinned, and if it made her frequently hard to live with, it also made her a top-notch potter.

The room had grown very dark, almost darker than the world outside. If he didn't leave soon, he would have to turn on the lights. So he closed everything he had opened and went out.

He sat down on the cottage stoop to have a cigarette. It was true, he decided, she had enough sensitivity for them both. He didn't know how she endured the constant assault of life on her fine-tuned sensibilities. She didn't smoke, do dope, and drank so rarely she might as well not drink at all. Maybe with her system so virginal and clean the aspirin she'd been taking all summer was like real dope. Maybe it hit really hard for her. He hoped so.

On his last trip home but one, he had found out. He had come in from the road and despite his best intentions, no doubt because he was exhausted and jet-lagged and strung out, launched into a recitation of all his vexations and troubles with the movie.

Liv sat at the table in the kitchen, as the clock ticked toward midnight of a day that must have been as long for her as it was for him, and with little prospect of sleep that night, and sipped some herbal tea that smelled like wet weeds from the side of the road, and listened patiently. Or seemed to. She cocked her head to one side, her eyes stayed on him, she nodded now and then, but she didn't say anything. She seemed drawn, but it was late. He noticed her look at the clock once and then a few minutes later, glance at it again.

Boring her, he thought, boring her titless. But she surprised him.

She stood up abruptly and crossed to the sink, drew water, and tapped aspirin from the bottle she kept on the windowsill, and knocked back the tablets.

It hit him then that she had been waiting for it to be time, sitting there holding on, waiting. When the bottle said take the medicine every four hours, the pharmacist's daughter never took it until every minute of the four hours had been counted off.

He saw as if for the first time the depth of the smudges under her eyes, as dark as the woods in which the gingerbread house–studio stood, the gauntness, the tension in her jawline, and knew everything he had said had flowed over her like a cold rain. Maybe she had absorbed some of it through her pores, enough to make her shiver uncomfortably, but she had not actually heard a word. She had just endured it. She had been waiting. That was all she could do just then.

He had shut up then, and put his arms around her, and she had cried, his woman who never cried. And he had it out of her, how the goddamn tooth hurt all the time so she couldn't sleep or eat or do anything, and it had been root canalled a half dozen times and been anesthetized to a faretheewell, and it still *hurt*, her whole face and head hurt past thinking around or about. He shouted at her out of his own unspeakable guilt, so she had stopped crying, which made him feel even worse. And the next day he had made her promise to have the goddamn tooth out and had gone back to the movie set because he had to, and with guilty relief because he couldn't look at her without feeling like a total shit.

And then when he was supposed to be working, he couldn't think about anything else except Liv, and every night he called home and then he called the airlines to book a flight home, and then didn't take it, and when he did come home again, she was visibly recovering, and he was so relieved, he stayed an extra day, and went back to work half-convinced it had never been as serious as it seemed.

The heat of the late summer day is as ephemeral as summer itself. All of a sudden it was getting colder as well as darker, and he was hugely empty. Pat ground out the cigarette with his heel and started back to the house.

Clearly, they had been apart too much. He would have to try to make it up. Liv was getting stronger, she was working again, she would be all right, but it would be an enormous relief to have her back in Portland, with her family to keep her company and keep an eye on her. It wouldn't be long now and the movie would be finished, would make it or fail on its own, and they would all be back together again. It was just a matter of a lot more hugging and kissing so both Liv and Travis knew how they stood with him.

When he glimpsed the light of the house through the trees, he stepped up his pace as much as he dared through the unreliable undergrowth, thinking of how a little icy gin would set him up. They would all feel better with charred red meat and Liv's Caesar salad and some baked potato in their stomachs. A prescription of which both his late mother, the everloving Ellen Russell, and both of Liv's parents, Doe the pharmacist and Marguerite the smiling dragon, would have approved.

" 'And that was the end of him,' " read Liv, and closed the book.

Travis shuddered a long, satisfied sigh. Bedclothes clutched tight under his chin, he pressed his head back into the pillows.

Liv kissed his tear-swollen eyelids in quick succession. Giggling, Travis curled up against the sudden onslaught of affection.

The bedroom door opened. Pat peered around its edge. "Ready, babe?"

Liv glanced up at him. "Right with you," she said.

The door closed.

It was too much to hope that Travis hadn't noticed his father hadn't even looked at him, much less said goodnight. The boy flopped onto his belly to hide his face in his pillows.

Liv smoothed Travis' hair. Gradually, he relaxed.

She heard the screen door slap shut behind Pat and then the suck of his lighter from the stoop. In the dark beyond Travis' screened window, she could see the flame flare in Pat's face before it went out. The occasional red coal of his cigarette marked his position as he loitered restless in the yard, waiting for her.

Liv tucked in the bedclothes, picked up Travis' discarded jeans, T-shirt, socks, and Underoos, and dropped them into the laundry bag in his closet. Not the night to hassle him about picking up his clothes. She switched off the bedside lamp, leaving only E.T.'s heartlight glowing from his nightlight. She bent over Travis to kiss him again.

"Goodnight, baby," she whispered.

He was asleep.

Hand on the door, she was startled by the perfume of marijuana coming in through his window.

Suddenly her teeth hurt. She ducked into her bathroom. The top shelf of the medicine cabinet was lined with prescription bottles of narcotics. She hardly even noticed them anymore. She took two extrastrength aspirin. Gripping the basin with both hands, she tried to relax the reflexive tensing of her facial muscles against the pain. There was nothing she could do about the pallor that yellowed her skin to the color of a faded bruise. At least it was dark of night and everyone would be drunk. She picked up her cardigan on the way out.

In the living room, Sarah was ensconced in front of the TV, watching a taped movie while listening to Bruce Springsteen through the earphones of her new Walkman. Liv knew it was Springsteen even though only Sarah could hear the music. Since Pat had given her her first Springsteen record the previous Christmas, she had listened to no one else. Pat had grown so bored with "Born to Run," he had composed an obscene parody to sing along with it. With the Walkman, Sarah could listen to Springsteen by herself. It was a coming home present as much to Pat from Pat, as to Sarah from Pat.

Liv touched Sarah's shoulder so as not to startle her, and then pressed the mute button to make herself heard over the music.

Sarah blinked at her.

"Trav's out," Liv told her. "We're going."

Sarah nodded and blinked again: Message received. Over and Out. Her eyes glazed over.

Liv released the mute button, feeling disconcertingly as if she were turning herself off.

It was only necessary, of course, that Sarah be able to hear

Travis and the telephone. Liv couldn't be sure Sarah would hear Travis if he cried out for her, but there was no doubt she could hear the phone ring over the sound of the Walkman. It was actually un-wise to stand between her and a ringing telephone. Off to camp at the beginning of the summer still just a big kid, she had come home two weeks previous a full-blown teen. And since then, the phone had jangled constantly for Sarah, rarely for anyone else. Boys with voices that ranged two octaves in three words, girls who could hardly talk for giggling. They all used to be cute little kids. Now they were like some species of visiting aliens.

Liv picked up a flashlight and fled.

Pat jumped up from the lawn chair he had come to roost in, tossing away the end of the joint. The roach flew like a miniature falling star, scattering an arc of bright ash over the lawn.

Liv bit her lip. It was not the time to brace him over smoking dope around Sarah.

"Trav okay?" Pat asked.

Liv looked back at the summer house. It was a child of the fifties, a crackerbox on its side, the victim of a series of do-it-yourself-ers. The original back porch had been enclosed to make a new kitchen; the master bedroom, bath, and study tacked on and new decks built on the lake side of the house. Without character or recog-nizable style, it was comfortable, just the right size, like the Three Bears' house. Its one point of beauty was the fieldstone fireplace in the living room. Travis' window showed a dim rosy glow set like a jewel into the shadowed clapboard siding. From the backdoor spilled a tall, bent oblong of yellow light onto the porch. Tinted by the TV, a bluer light from the glass-walled living room that overlooked the lake backlit the house, rendering it shallow as a facade. Trees loomed over it like big, dark ghosts.

"Sure."

While she tied the cardigan around her waist by its sleeves, Pat shook a cigarette, a legal one, from a crumpled pack. He didn't seem particularly stoned, or even very mellow.

"I didn't mean to make him cry. I was just teasing." And then, hopeful of exoneration, "Is he going through some kind of crybaby stage or something?"

Liv flicked on the flashlight, catching the cat, under the station wagon, in its sudden beam. They had named her The Poor for her tenacious adoption of them, after the biblical class that is promised always to be with us. Her eyes were luminous ectoplasm reflecting the light. Liv swung the flashlight hastily away, feeling as if she had inadvertently surprised someone naked.

"You've been away," she said. "Trav's gotten used to a different status quo. Your coming home means a readjustment."

Pat's lighter sucked the air repeatedly, angrily. "That makes me feel great."

Liv shrugged. "Nobody's trying to make you feel guilty. That's just how it is."

She played the light over the driveway, picking out the brush at its shoulders and the woods around them, in patches like the cutouts hidden behind little doors in Travis' favorite storybooks. It was her idea to bring the flashlight. Pat would have felt his way along by memory and the borrowed light of houses and cottages along the way. But she didn't feel that brave. It was not anything in the dark she feared, but a misstep, a twisted ankle, wrenched knee, or fall.

"Travis needs some time to get used to you being home again," she said.

"Well, he'll get that," said Pat. He blew smoke between them in an angry stream. "You cried, too," he accused her. "You went into his room with him and you cried, too."

Liv said nothing. She was very close to tears again, and she could not allow herself to give way, not now. There had been too much crying.

"That means you don't want me home, either," Pat said. "I'm just upsetting you all."

"No," she cried. She hugged herself tightly. "We do want you home. For Christ's sake, don't take it all so personally. It's just a readjustment, that's all."

She hated the tremor in her voice and felt a sudden flash of anger. She was trying to make it easier and he wouldn't leave it alone. How could he possibly expect to walk back into things exactly as he had left them? He wanted Father Knows Best. Everything hunky-dory in thirty minutes. Not an unhappy four-year-old, a self-involved adolescent, and a sick wife.

Pat put an arm around her shoulder and drew her close.

"Okay," he said, but he sounded weary of it and as if he were reassuring himself.

They started up their driveway. In the quiet of the summer night their sneakers rattled the gravel. The cat stalked them soundlessly. By daylight, The Poor was a staggering derelict that no amount of overfeeding, vitamins, or expensive consultations with the vet would ever make sleek and elegant. By night, she came into her own; she was a spook, a killer, lurid death in the dark. They hardly noticed her, not because she was so seamlessly a part of the night, but because they had grown used to her. She hunted each and all of them ceaselessly, as if she were afraid of being abandoned in the forest, which she had been, of course, when they took her in. They reached the cottage road that served their house and their neighbors, connecting them with Dexter Road, which led to Route 5, the main road through Nodd's Ridge.

"Listen, babe," Pat said. "If this is a real horror show tonight, we'll come home early. We can always say Trav wasn't too happy about our going out the first night I'm home."

It bothered her that he didn't seem to realize the convenient social lie was true: Travis had been disturbed to find out they were going out, even if it was after his bedtime. Or else Pat attached no importance to it. Nor did she want to respond to the hint of sexual approach in an early home. It seemed perfunctory on his part.

"I really wouldn't mind an early night," he said. He looked at her closely. "You okay? You look great."

Liv nodded absently. The aspirin had silenced the pain in her teeth. "Thanks," she said.

"You really do," Pat insisted. "A lot better than the last time I was home."

She gritted her teeth. It was past and done with. Talking about it wasn't going to change anything.

"Thank God you finally had that fucking tooth out," he said. "Should have made you have it out months ago. I could kill that fucking dentist."

"It wasn't his fault," she said automatically. He was confessing, she knew, asking forgiveness, but managed to sound offensively proprietary. She had not done a proper job of taking care of herself, and because she was his, his responsibility or his property, it amounted to the same, it had rebounded on him. The absentee landlord—who didn't care enough to do the job himself but was mad as hell when somebody else didn't. "It's done, anyway. It wasn't fatal."

"It could have been," Pat said. "I feel guilty about that, too. If I'd been here, or you'd been on location with me, you never would have gotten so sick."

"Just what you needed," Liv ran down the list of reasons, as much for her sake as his. "A sick wife. You didn't have time for that, and you know it. And you had to be there, you had a contract. What would you have done with Trav?" *And me.*

"Taken care of you," Pat said, as if he had heard the unspoken part of her question. "I would have found a way." He fumbled for her hand, found her wrist, and grasped it tightly, as if he feared her escape or sudden disappearance. "You should have told me."

She knew that now. But she hadn't. And she had survived. They had all survived. The summer was over.

"Water under the bridge," she said.

Pat let go of her wrist and flicked away his cigarette. He shoved his hands into the back pockets of his jeans and looked around at the seemingly scenic dark.

"I can't believe I missed the summer here."

Me, too, she thought. *I missed the summer, too.* But she said, "It was just like every other summer." *What a lie.*

Still she deprecated it. "You'll hear all about it at the party. The entire summer, condensed into pure gossip."

Pat laughed. "I doubt there'll be anything very pure about it. Probably it'll sound more scandalous than it really was. No-holds-barred, as soon as everyone's loaded." He put his arm around her waist. "You seem jittery. What you need is a drink. To start, anyway."

CHAPTER 2

LIGHT showed through the trees ahead of them. Faint party sounds, music and a babel of voices, were audible. There were vehicles parked on both sides of the road, late model Cadillacs and Lincolns, Mercedeses, BMWs, expensively outfitted four-wheel-drives like the Breens' Ramcharger, and fat-assed station wagons, all bearing out-of-state licenses—Massachusetts, Rhode Island, Connecticut, New York, even California. In silence they strolled down the narrow lane, between the parked cars, to the pair of wooden rain barrels planted with nasturtiums and the rustic sign nailed to a battered pine that marked the Winslows' driveway. On each barrel a reflector glowed the same dim dirty orange as the nasturtiums. Plastic Japanese lanterns that had seen two decades of Labor Day partying hung like faded fruit in the trees. All the lights of the cottage were on so it glowed like a Hollywood spaceship taking off. A floodlight over the garage door provided additional outdoor lighting.

The party had spilled out of the cottage and surged around an enormous barbecue pit presided over by Len Winslow, his saturnine face, red as the devil's below a tall, white chef's hat, glimpsed amid clouds of roast pig–flavored steam rising from the pit like steam from a volcanic vent. People clotted around improvised sawhorse picnic tables schooled on the levelest portion of the lawn, or at the bar, a regulation redwood picnic table forested with bottles, jugs, and plastic cups. The still night air was heavily laced with cigarette smoke.

At the sight of new guests, Claire Winslow flushed like a quail from the cover of the party. Two small dogs that looked like Chinese temple dogs whipped around her small feet, which were crammed into even smaller, glass-stone studded sandals.

"Pat! Liv!" Then she seemed to run out of things to say. Claire wrung her hands uncertainly. Worry moved the mask of her makeup in subterranean faults and waves. "I didn't think you two would make it this year." The dogs yapped and clawed at Liv's legs.

"Surprise," said Liv, and laughed, surreptitiously kicking away the dogs.

Claire seemed not to hear her or notice the bad manners of her pets. "Why, I haven't seen you all summer." The dogs bounced away, yipping.

"I've been away," Pat said. "Shooting a movie in Louisiana."

Claire's eyes widened, threatening cracks at the corners. "Oh, my!"

"Actually," said Liv, *"I've* been here the whole time, with Travis. And Sarah's been home from camp for two weeks."

"And I haven't seen you anywheres about," Claire exclaimed. "Isn't that the oddest thing?"

Pat looked thoughtfully at Liv. "Yes, it is."

"It certainly is," Liv said quickly. "I saw you the day before yesterday at the post office. You were talking to Walter McKenzie."

The two dogs were suddenly underfoot again, worrying their ankles. "Oh, indeed I was," Claire said. "Listening to one of his yarns, if I remember it correctly. Never even saw you." Her mouth crumpled in consternation. "And you alone all summer. You must think me a perfectly dreadful neighbor."

Liv suppressed the desire to tell Claire not to fuss. She was *grateful* Claire was a dreadful neighbor. The last thing she wanted to do with her summer was listen to Claire's dramatic monologues on her bitch's female problems.

Instead she did some more lying. "Of course I don't," Liv reassured her. "Travis and I just had a very quiet summer. You know how it is with a four-year-old."

Claire, who had never had children and hadn't the faintest idea how it was with a four-year-old, nodded wisely.

"I can't believe you manage this party every year and still stay calm," Liv continued.

Claire smiled contentedly with the stroking—and a generous quantity of gin and Valium.

Liv felt Pat's curious eyes on her and looked around quickly. Terry Breen, six-foot-five and tonsure gleaming, was easy to pick out of the herd. She elbowed Pat.

"There's Terry. We'd better go say hi."

"Excuse me," Pat said, and abandoned Liv.

Liv squeezed one of Claire's plump hands in hers. "Thanks for having us," and followed Pat.

Claire fluttered vaguely, her dogs pogoing around her ankles, and drifted back into the general melee.

Liv found herself alone in the crowd. After three years' summering on Nodd's Ridge, most of the faces were familiar to her. She had begun to match the faces with the names on the sign at the junction of the cottage road and Dexter Road. But she didn't really know any of them. The season was too brief. People didn't neighbor all that much. Why should they? They came here to get away.

It was a largely middle-aged to elderly population, with the Russells, the Breens, and the Spellmans representing the first infiltration of the Baby Boom. The three younger couples drifted together, though they saw one another only occasionally during the short summer.

Liv groped her way to the table the Spellmans and Breens had claimed. Arriving earlier, they had eaten their fill, evidenced by a minor wasteland of paper plates, napkins, and plastic utensils on the table. The two wives had settled, deep in conversation, at the end. Pat joined Mike Spellman and Terry Breen.

Mike hugged Liv eagerly. A Californian who brought his deep tan with him to Nodd's Ridge each summer, he had been through several kinds of sensitivity encounters between divorce from his first wife and his current marriage. His enthusiasm for hugging and touching was always disconcerting to Liv, who had grown up among people embarrassed and afflicted by feeling, who rarely touched one another, except in anger. She had come to be able to touch her children and Pat, but was still profoundly uneasy at the casual touch of acquaintances and strangers.

Terry paused long enough in demonstrating his backhand to Pat to smile and say hi. His wife, Linda, and Mike's wife, Barrie, heads bent close, glanced up together. They fluttered fingertips and made ephemeral, embarrassed smiles at her, and with undue haste resumed their interrupted conversation. Mike frowned at them, cast a worried, apologetic smile at her, and turned back to Pat and Terry.

Liv sat between the men and the women, at the unoccupied end of the table. She wondered what weighty subject enthralled the other women—children? Barrie had a two-year-old girl by Mike, and her stepchildren, the teenaged boys Mike called the Twinkies, every summer. Terry and Linda had a fifteen-year-old girl. Or perhaps they were discussing career-wife-motherhood conflicts. They both worked with their husbands: Linda a senior attendant training new stews for the airline whose wide-bodied jets Terry flew; Barrie the head surgical nurse in the university teaching hospital where Mike was head of pediatrics. It might be anything—antiques, prevention of massive coronary in type-A males, the total famine of designer labels in any shop within fifty miles of Nodd's Ridge.

Pat's hand fell on her shoulder. "Want a drink?" Before she could answer, he squeezed her gently and disappeared in the direction of the bar. Terry Breen went with him, talking excitedly and laughing a lot.

Mike sat down next to her. "How are you, babe?" he asked, and squeezed her thigh. It was his bedside manner, intimate, total concentration on the patient, but distinctly Papa Bear, warmth without sex.

"Just fine," she said easily, and squeezed his thigh. "What about you, doc?"

Mike glowed, delighted at being answered in kind.

Liv was embarrassed at herself for mocking him. She ought to know better by now. Mike Spellman didn't have a sarcastic bone in his body. She was almost sure he didn't have any sense of humor either, which unexpectedly didn't make him grouchy or gloomy, but rather curiously, almost relentlessly cheerful. She didn't hold it against him. Her own sarcastic streak brought her little pleasure. And she had begun to think she had lost what little sense of humor she had once possessed. At least Mike had a sunny nature by way of compensation.

"We've been worried about you," Mike said.

"Oh?" Liv braced herself.

"Yeah. I tell you it was a real relief to see you two here tonight. Is everything okay again?"

Liv was excruciatingly aware that Mike's hand had fallen over hers on the table.

She summoned up a smile for him. "I don't know."

His hand on hers tightened and his face sobered appropriately. "Jesus," he said. "If there's anything I can do, just call. It helps to talk sometimes. I know, babe, I've been there. You want to talk to Uncle Mike, you just say so. We'll take a canoe out on the pond and have a picnic, a nice bottle of wine and some cheese, over on the island. How's that sound?"

"You're sweet," Liv said.

Mike looked up and beamed. "Pat!" he said. "I've been making a date with your wife."

"Can't trust that man a minute," Barrie said cheerfully.

Terry Breen, juggling a stack of paper plates loaded with roast pig and potato salad, a nosegay of plastic forks in his breast pocket, roared delightedly. Linda forced a constipated smile.

Pat, drinks in hand, inserted himself between Liv and Mike. "Better rush it, then," he said. "We're out of here Sunday afternoon."

"Shit," said Mike. "How about Saturday?"

Liv shrugged apologetically. Mike was downcast.

Terry Breen slid a paper plate of greasy meat in front of her and handed her a fork.

"Thanks, Terry," she said automatically.

He winked at her. "Struck out, hot shot?" he asked Mike.

Mike patted Liv's shoulder. "You get a minute, call."

Nodding agreeably, to close the subject, she tasted the drink Pat had given her: white wine, tepid and oversweet. She put it down. The combination of wine and aspirin would keep her up all night. She had enough problems sleeping.

"So what kept you from paradise all summer?" Mike asked Pat.

Barrie looked up at Liv and just as quickly looked away, Linda just straight through her, as if she weren't there. Liv felt a sudden, surprising surge of amusement.

"Work," said Pat. "What else? Shooting a movie."

Respectful silence indicated he had impressed them all.

"L.A.?" Mike asked. He was comically surprised when Pat answered, "Nope. Louisiana."

"Louisiana?" Terry repeated. He loomed over them, a beer in

one hand. Splaying one big hand on the table, he bent over it to shove his face into Pat's. "You spent the *summer* in *Louisiana?* Louisifuckingana?"

Heads turned in the crowd around them. Linda hissed softly at Terry. He ignored her.

Liv wondered when Terry had gotten started and how much he had had.

"Louisifuckingana," he said again, in wonderment.

Pat laughed. "Yeah. Louisifuckingana. Down in the Bayou. Which had the juicy role of the Big Bad Jungle. Bayard Rohrer's the director. Scott Kinsella is the male lead." He dropped the names casually.

"Scott Kinsella!" Barrie Spellman squealed.

The table had become the center of a larger group. People around them were listening avidly.

By herself at the edge of the crowd was Miss Alden, of an uncertain age, a little stooped but not enough to perceptibly diminish her six feet of height. At last year's Labor Day barbecue, notable for her absence, Pat had remarked that Miss Alden, who held the Douglas MacArthur Chair of Military History at Harvard, had apparently inherited the General's wardrobe as well, for she habitually wore riding boots and crisp khaki trousers and shirts and did not vary her costume for social events. A measure of contempt showed in the stance she assumed: hipshot, with her gnarled hands clasped over the gold head of the cane planted directly in front of her. She did not seem to really need the cane; Pat insisted that, like her military-style clothing, it was a prop. But tonight, Liv thought, Miss Alden was really leaning on it. Her large head was thrust slightly forward of her body, like that of a predatory bird. Dark, feverish eyes outlined in kohl dominated her pale, nearly fleshless face despite the prominence of her nose—a haughty, exotic beak. Her skin seemed hardly more than a layer of paint and powder over the mask of the petrified bone. Her skull was turbaned, like a gypsy's, in a black silk scarf, showing enough forehead and temple to suggest severe loss or total absence of hair.

"What's it about?" Terry asked.

Pat grinned at them boyishly.

"It opens in 'Nam," Pat said. "Americans trapped in a firefight calling fire in on themselves."

Liv studied the bugs swimming in her paper cup of wine to hide
the irritation she felt with Pat for using 'Nam, which implied the first
name familiarity of those who had been there. Bayard, the director,
did, too. All the men associated with the movie did. The only one of
them who had actually served there was Jesse Rideout, the sound
man, who had been a medic. He was a big gentle black man, who
favored faded MASH T-shirts and sung scat under his breath while
he worked. He was a Coptic Zionist who smoked marijuana, which
he called Ol' Red Eye, like it was tobacco. It did not seem to affect
him at all.

During her single, midsummer visit to the set, Liv heard him
talk about Vietnam only once, and that was after hours, in the motel
bar that had become a crew hangout for the duration. Scott Kinsella
and Pat had gotten into an argument about the war, one of those
futile expositions of cliché to which Liv had listened for years.

Kinsella rapped the mug of his beer chaser on the table. "We
were never allowed to fight to win," he declared.

"Eisenhower warned us not to get into an Asian land war," said
Pat. "That kind of war can't be won. The Chinese have been trying
and failing to subdue Cochin China for a thousand years. The Japanese couldn't do it. The best French forces got their asses whipped
there, too, you know."

Kinsella dismissed the history of Cochin China with a shrug of
his meaty shoulders. "The Frogs haven't won a war in a hundred
years," Kinsella said. "Hitler rolled right over 'em, didn't he?"

Jesse Rideout, who was half-Cajun French, laughed softly.

Liv Russell recognized Jesse Rideout's laugh. It was the amiable
rueful sound her father made when he had to suffer a fool.

Though it hurt to talk, sudden rage loosened Liv's tongue. "We
dropped eight hundred thousand tons of explosives on South Vietnam in one year, the same amount of explosives we dropped on the
entire South Pacific during World War Two," she said bitterly.
"That's what you call holding back?"

Kinsella looked at her from across the table. "We should have
nuked the little bastards," he said.

"Come on, Scott," Pat protested.

"He means it," Jesse Rideout said. "He don't know what it
means. But he means it."

Scott glared at Jesse. "Goddamn right I mean it."

"When you there?" Jesse asked softly.

Kinsella looked uncomfortable. "I was exempted," he said.

Too old, Liv thought, looking at the creped skin around Kinsella's eyes that was always made-up for the camera. She smiled.

Kinsella turned on her.

Pat jumped in to defuse the tension. He leaned across the table, his eye alight. "What was it like, Jesse?"

Jesse was quiet a moment. "The people was real little, like kids," he said. "I always felt like Uncle Jesse. I could understand 'em on account of they spoke French, not just like Cajun French, but close, you know, with a real pretty accent. That way I picked up Vietnamese. It was a lot like home, like here. I liked it. Met my wife there."

No one had known about the Vietnamese wife. Pat and Liv exchanged uncomfortable glances, both wondering if this movie was in some unspoken way offensive to Jesse. How had he felt seeing the Japanese girl, Terry Shore, who played the doomed May, naked and seemingly dead upon the chopper's rotor blades?

Kinsella snorted, reaching for his whiskey. "Maybe you should have stayed there, you felt so at home."

Jesse smiled at him. "Maybe I should have, Mistah Kinsella," he said, and there was the faintest mockery in his voice. He got up out of his chair with a measured grace that made Scott Kinsella flinch for an instant, as if he thought Jesse was going to reach across the table and take him by the throat and shake him. But Jesse only looked at Kinsella with scornful, bloodshot eyes, and turned his broad back to leave.

Liv and Pat went back to the depressing little room in the cement block motel that had been Pat's home all summer. On the inadequate bed, with its worn acidic green whipcord spread and broken-backed mattress, they made love for the first time in several weeks, though Liv was in the last day of her period, and she bled, inadvertently and to her deep embarrassment, upon the sheets. Naked in the suffocating heat of the Louisiana summer night, they tried to sleep, but the bed seemed to grow smaller as they shifted and turned, trying to find the right position.

In place of sleep, Liv imagined that this was how Jesse Rideout's nights in Saigon had been. The heat of the night tenting the whole world, the night sounds of the city coming in through the

louvers at the glassless windows from the street below, the Vietnam-
ese-accented French of the bar girls going home in the pre-dawn,
something like the French she heard outside their door in the morning, when the motel maids began their day's work. She imagined
Jesse Rideout and his Vietnamese wife, as small as a child, asleep on
whatever passed for their bed, a mattress on the floor, or perhaps
they had a real bed, left over from the colonial days, with a mosquito
net like a cloud of marijuana smoke over them. Perhaps there was a
darkening spot of menstrual blood diluted with semen on the sheet
beneath them. Though the sun had not yet risen, the new day's heat
weighed on her when she rose to take her fifteenth and sixteenth
extrastrength aspirin in twenty-four hours.

If Kinsella was over age, Bayard the director, all the young
actors who played vets (including Pat, who as well as writing the
screenplay had taken a cameo role and died early in the movie), half
the crew, in fact, were in the right age group for Vietnam service.
But they had all been safely tucked away in college. As she had. It
was a war she had hated, hated still, but she felt, a decade later, an
unexpected burden of guilt because working-class kids had died there
while she and her friends, white and all right, smoked dope, screwed
each other enthusiastically, and took their moral pulses daily.

'Nam. She knew it wasn't guilt that suddenly blossomed into
'Nam flashbacks for every name male actor in every action film made
in the last few years. It was just macho convenience—real men had
been, *of course,* to 'Nam, been scarred, and come back home. To
smoke dope, screw endlessly and to no end women who had never
been where *they* had been and so could never understand, the sexual
intimacy not just nullifying but actually widening the wall of experience between them. Their moral pulses were stopped at the instant,
flashing back on them while they slept or tried to screw or encountered stress; they remembered, or almost remembered, the terrible
things they had witnessed. Witnessed, never done. In 'Nam. In the
movie 'Nam.

"Incredible losses, but there are survivors," Pat continued.
"Some of the survivors think they were set up by the Vietnamese
girlfriend of their sergeant, who was badly wounded in the firefight.
They execute her. The rest of the movie is ten years later when the
sergeant, who knows it wasn't his girl and wants to avenge her and
the guys who got killed, stalks the survivors all over the country to

execute them. 'Course they're all combat vets, trained killers, and they've stayed in touch. He only gets one or two before the others are alerted. Then they fight back."

Pat stopped to sip at a can of beer. Everyone was quiet, waiting for him to go on.

"Do you want to know what happens next?"

They all groaned and there was a chorus of "Yes, yes!"

"Well, that would be telling," Pat said. "You'll have to go see the movie."

There was another explosion of laughter and protest.

"Jesus," Terry Breen said. "That was great."

"What's it called?" Barrie asked.

"Firefight."

"I love it," Linda said.

"Me, too," said Barrie.

"When's it out?" Mike asked.

"Christmas, I hope," Pat said. He stood up and stretched.

"What was it like working with Kinsella?" Barrie wanted to know.

Pat launched into a story about the actor that Liv had heard in a previous, cruder version earlier in the summer. Pat had revised it to make Scott look cleverer and himself more the butt.

Liv toyed with the strips of cooling meat on her plate. A hard clawlike hand dropped on her shoulder.

"Room for me?" Miss Alden asked.

Liv nodded and moved over. Disposing her cane crisply to one side, Miss Alden lowered herself onto the bench next to Liv. At the other end of the table, Linda and Barrie shot uneasy glances.

"How are you, Helen?" Liv asked.

Barrie and Linda looked at each other. No one ever addressed Miss Alden by her first name.

"Still in the land of the living," Miss Alden said, and sounded as if it were not so much a privilege as a sentence.

She peered into Liv's plastic cup. "What's that?"

"White wine."

Miss Alden looked down her magnificent nose. "Jug swill."

Mike Spellman leaned over to ask what he could fetch for her.

"I expect the scotch will be drinkable," Miss Alden told him. "A double on ice, please."

"I'm not fussy," Barrie said. "I'll take another glass of the jug swill, Mike."

"Linda?" Mike asked.

"Jug swill for me, too," she said.

"All those years of med school," Barrie said, "and he goes to work as a waiter."

"The tips are better," Mike said.

The younger women laughed. Miss Alden smiled thinly.

She turned to Liv. "How are you, my dear?"

Barrie and Linda arched carefully shaped, penciled, and significant eyebrows at each other.

"Much better, thanks," Liv said. She touched Miss Alden's hand lightly. "You were a lifesaver, you know. And Travis and I had a wonderful time at our tea party."

"What's this?" Pat asked, slipping back onto the bench on Liv's other side. His hand covered hers on the table. "What's this about tea parties? Have you been leading Miss Alden astray, Liv?"

"Helen helped me change a flat tire one day," Liv said. "Then she had Travis and me to tea. Ask Travis." To Miss Alden, "He still talks about it. He's always wanting to have a tea party."

"We'll have another," Miss Alden said. "I'm afraid it will have to be next year, though. The summer's gotten away from us."

"I'd like to come," Pat said, "if I wouldn't be intruding."

"Oh, I expect we can handle it," Miss Alden declared. "An old maid I may be, but it takes more than a mere man to turn my head."

"Shucks," said Pat.

Mike Spellman appeared with the assorted drinks on a tray and a dish towel folded over one arm.

"Madame," he addressed each woman as he placed her drink before her.

"Mademoiselle," corrected Miss Alden.

"*Mais oui,*" Mike said. "I'm sorry."

"I'm not," Miss Alden said.

Barrie Spellman shrieked with laughter.

Pat raised his beer can in a silent toast to Miss Alden.

Miss Alden addressed Liv. "Have you been able to work?"

Liv shrugged. "No. But I've been having ideas."

"Good," said Pat lasciviously. He squeezed her. "So have I."

Everyone laughed, except Miss Alden, who looked as if lewd ideas were exactly what she expected Pat to have.

"Perhaps a vacation is just what you needed," Miss Alden said to Liv. "Fallow time."

"I hope that's what it was," Liv said. "I'll feel like I salvaged something from this summer, then."

Miss Alden patted Liv's knee. "I know just what you mean. I think I'd go mad without work."

Quite visibly, Barrie Spellman elbowed Mike, who had taken his seat next to her and was eavesdropping, like the rest of the table, on the conversation.

"Then again," said Miss Alden, looking at Barrie, "I'm sure some people think I'm raving anyway."

Mike elbowed Barrie back, and said in a low voice, "I guess she told you, babe."

"I think you're the sanest person I know," Liv said.

"Well, thank you," Miss Alden said. "I appreciate the vote of confidence. I expect you're wrong, my dear. I'm as crazy as anyone else in this insane world."

"Isn't there an argument that insanity is the only defense against reality?" Pat said.

Len Winslow sat down opposite them, clutching his chef's hat in one hand and a drink in the other. "Mind if I join you?" he asked in a perfunctory way. "I'm about ready to fall down if I don't sit down. I'm getting too old for this show."

Breathing heavily, nearly purple in the face, he did indeed appear about ready to collapse.

He gulped from his drink. "What I want to know," he said, "is why the goddamn thieves don't ever take my barbecue spit. They steal every other thing that isn't nailed down. They took the goddamn thing, I could switch to hot dogs and live a little longer." He looked around guiltily. "Don't tell Claire I said that. She's thought a pig on a spit was the only thing for it ever since we honeymooned in Hawaii."

Liv felt Miss Alden tense. "I'll leave 'em a note, Len," Miss Alden said.

Several people laughed.

Pat looked puzzled. "Sorry, I missed something."

Miss Alden looked at him. "They've hit me three years running."

There was head-shaking and commiseration.

"You're not alone," Len Winslow said. "And Walter McKenzie told Claire just the other day he's stumped."

"Walter McKenzie is an old fool," Miss Alden said. "I fired him after the second break-in. What goddamn good does it do to pay a caretaker if he can't take care of a place? Walter's too old for the job. If he had any sense left, he'd retire."

A general silence followed. On this side of the lake, Walter McKenzie had been everyone's caretaker forever. There had never been another caretaker. No one could imagine who would take his place.

"It's true," Pat said. "Walter's getting on. What's he now, seventy-five?"

"Eighty-three," Miss Alden said.

"Wow," said Mike Spellman. "I had no idea. He sure doesn't look it, does he?"

Miss Alden ignored Mike. "Pity Joe Nevers is gone. I'd've hired him in Walter's place in a minute. Nobody ever broke into one of Joe Nevers' places."

"Joe Nevers wouldn't have taken the job," Liv said.

Everyone looked at her.

"This is Walter's side of the lake," she said.

They did not seem, any of them, to understand. Nor did she really expect they would.

"Wait a minute," Pat said. "I'd like to know why no one's ever broken into one of Joe Nevers' places."

They all looked at Liv, who had inadvertently revealed an unexpected fund of knowledge about Nodd's Ridge.

She blushed. "Respect. There was too much respect for Joe Nevers." She looked into her cup of wine. "And a measure of fear. But mostly," she said with a smile, "I believe it was because he used to pay off the likeliest villains."

Everyone laughed, except Helen Alden. And Liv, who was surprised they found Joe Nevers' sensible arrangements amusing.

"How do you know all this?" Miss Alden asked.

"I used to run into old Joe once in a while," Liv admitted.

She wasn't going to tell them the whole story. She already felt as if she had lost something valuable to them.

"Ho, now," Joe Nevers said when she came up silently under his line and tugged it gently.

She kept the tension steady but light, so as not to break it, and rose with it at the rate he reeled it in.

"A mermaid," he exclaimed, as he always did when they played this game, as her head broke the surface. "I'll be goddamned."

And they shared a soft, smothered chuckle.

" 'Morning, Missus Mermaid," Joe Nevers said.

" 'Morning, Joe Nevers," Liv said. "Guess you've got three wishes."

"Ah," Joe Nevers said. "Much obliged. I think first off I'd like a smoke."

And he set aside his rod and took out a cigarillo, politely first offering her one, which she just as politely refused. One hand light on the skiff, she trod water, waiting on his little ceremony.

And then he talked. She asked questions now and again to clarify matters, but otherwise was content to listen. He seemed not to expect anymore return from her than that. She had heard stories from him she suspected no one had ever heard, not even his cronies at the post office or the diner or the town office, or even his sister Gussie, who had been the town librarian for years before she retired to Florida.

One day she asked him about Arden Nighswander.

"Arden Nighswander," said Joe Nevers, and rolled his cigarillo in his hand.

"I'm afraid of him," Liv said. She trod the water of the lake, and moved her arms lazily, rippling the water in swirling, curving arcs. The water glistened pinkly in the rosy spill of sunlight coming over the wall of the mountains and staining the wisps of mist over the water. "I don't know why. He's so polite, he's greasy. But he smiles like a shark. Gives me goosebumps."

Joe Nevers shook his head. "Just shows your good sense." He extinguished the butt of his smoke into the lid of the mayonnaise jar which he carried for that purpose, and returned the lid to his kit bag before shaking out a new cigarillo. Bending over with a little grunt, he struck a wooden match on the sole of his shoe, a dexterous motion for an elderly man sitting in a boat. He took off his cap and scratched behind his clean pink ear.

"I hear," he said, sucking at the cigarillo, "that fella is the kind that makes a career of being a nuisance. Lives off what he nuisanced outta the govamint, don't you know he's s'posed to be 'disabled' on account of his war wounds." Joe Nevers grunted. "It's his back, a course. Saddle sores or hemmerhoids from sitting at a desk, I imagine. With the taxpayer feeding and housing him, he's free to develop his full potential as a deadbeat son of a bitch. When he ain't being sued by somebody he's suckered, he's suing one of his neighbors over a propitty line or a cross look, it don't matter. When court ain't in session, he's a common thief, whelping thieves and vandals. That I know for a fact. Don't leave nothing lying around loose, missus. Them boys, Ricky and Rand. He's got 'em trained like hunting dogs to smell out opportunities."

"Are they some of the people who do the breaking in?" Liv asked.

"They're all of 'em," he said. "Do it as a regular thing. Closest thing to pros. Most of the rest is just boys been drinking. Just need a taking down. Give 'em a good scare and sober 'em up, then slip 'em a five spot to keep a eye peeled for the wrong truck on the wrong road. Generally, that's the end of it. But since the Nighswander boys been around, the trouble's gotten seriously ugly." He shook his head. The water lapped against the sides of the boat in little shivers.

Liv tipped her head back and her feet up, floating briefly on the surface of the lake. Along the backbone of the mountains the sunrise was still bleeding but directly overhead, the white bowl of the sky was bluing, the mist burning off. "They're not from around here," she said.

That cheered Joe Nevers right up. "No, they ain't. New Hampshire, I expect. Nighswander talks like it. Probably seven years ago, the year Gussie went off to Florida and come back married again, surprised the hell outta me, I'll tell you, that was the winter Ola Whicher died and in the spring, Nighswander showed up to claim her propitty. Ola was his great-aunt, married his grandmother's, on his father's side, brother. Ola never could stand sight nor sound of her husband's kin, but he died young of consumption and they never had no children, and she just got old up there, all by herself, on a piece of land that wouldn't grow rocks it was so poor. Took in cats and dogs and all kinds of creatures and after a while she took a pittance from the town and was listed as the animal control officer. Everybody figured her to pass away in the night and be discovered when the cats and dogs were yipping and yowling around her corpse, but actually she took it in her head to fix her own roof and killed herself falling off of it when she was eighty-seven. Big fat woman, she landed on her neck and broke it. Otherwise, she might've lived another twenty years." Joe Nevers looked aggrieved. "Any one of us would have been happy to fix them shingles, if she'd just ast. Wouldna charged her nothing, either. She was always poor-mouthing, but folks used to say she actually had quite a lot of money tucked away in shoe boxes. No doubt that's the biggest reason why Nighswander bothered to lay claim to her propitty, aside from it was someplace to go because where he was was getting too hot for him, one nest fouled beyond even what he could stand, so he moved on."

"Guess he didn't find any shoe boxes," Liv said. She touched the edge of the boat lightly and held onto it, resting.

Joe Nevers grinned. "Don't guess he did. 'Bout the only treasures Nighswander dug up on the Ridge was Jean McKenzie and her boy. Leastways with Jeannie, Nighswander got somebody to cook and clean for him and the boys. And not just Jeannie to beat, but the boy, too." Joe Nevers grew gloomy, and fidgeted as if the subject were uncomfortable. "The boy—Gordy—'s worse 'n useless."

"Is there something wrong with him?" Liv asked. "He seemed like he might be a little retarded to me."

"Well, Gordy's never had much to start with, worst of both parents, Jeannie's looks and Harry Teed's brains," Joe Nevers said, "and living with the Nighswanders, what brains he's got has been turned right around, being pounded against walls, and with drink and filthy habits and worse language. No, poor Gordy's just like one of their cur dogs they've made half-foolish and dangerous, torturing 'em and encouraging the worst part of their natures. Someday he'll have to be put down." He ground out the butt of his second smoke and put the jar lid away.

Liv shivered, the water suddenly very cold.

The red of the sunrise had faded to a thin mauve line marking the edge of the planet, where the glacial bones of the mountains peaked. She let go of the boat, and pushed herself backward. "Time for me to go," she said. "What about your other wishes?"

He thought a bit. "Well," he said, as the ritual required, "I wish you a fine day. That's number two. And I wish we meet again. That's number three."

Without a word, just a smile, she slipped beneath the surface and swam away, not coming up again to breathe until she was some distance away. By then, Joe Nevers had put away his rod and was pulling for the Narrows.

"Oh oh," said Terry Breen.

"What's that supposed to mean?" Pat asked.

Terry grinned lasciviously. "You've been away too much, old buddy. You must not have heard how old Joe went."

Linda and Barrie giggled in chorus.

Pat's eyebrows made gull wings and he assumed both a mock cigar and a Groucho accent. "So tell me, how did he go?"

Terry sniggered. "You could've watched it, you'd been here. Right across the lake from your place. The old goat was in bed with the widow Christopher, you remember her. Little red headed woman with a .44 caliber tongue and a taste for scotch. Both of 'em older than King Tut."

Helen Alden's mouth pursed. "She was my age," she said. "Riddled with cancer. Passed away last fall." And then, in a softer voice. "She was a friend of mine."

Terry Breen rolled his eyes and looked uncomfortable.

Pat touched Miss Alden's wrist. "I'm sorry," he said.

"He was a nice old man," Liv said. "I miss him."

Barrie Spellman twitched and fidgeted. "The only thing you can do is lock up, and don't leave anything around that's worth stealing," she said, as if she had missed the entire conversation about Joe Nevers and the late Mrs. Christopher.

"I don't know what people expect," Linda Breen put in. "The people here are poverty-stricken. It must be very tough for them to see the luxuries some of us just leave here all winter."

Liv laughed. "The ones who do the stealing use snowmobiles,

Linda. Snowmobiles start at over a thousand dollars. How hard up are you if you do your stealing with a thousand-dollar toy?"

Linda reddened.

"There's always insurance," Terry put in. "You can protect yourself against the potential losses. The premiums don't cost that much."

"They do more than steal," said Miss Alden. She looked very grim. "They are vandals, barbarians. They destroy. They break windows. They slash upholstery. They do terrible things."

"Well, we know you've had some bad luck," Mike Spellman said.

"Luck!" Miss Alden exclaimed. Her face was hectic, mottled bright over her cheekbones. "Luck has nothing to do with it. This is not random, Doctor Spellman. They have chosen me as their victim. I know what they think of me. They wrote on my walls that I am a filthy, cuntlapping old dyke. They wrote it in shit."

They were all frozen, horrified.

Liv touched Miss Alden's hands, clenched on the table. "I'm so sorry, Helen. How can people be so awful?"

"They are mistaken if they think they will get away with it again," Miss Alden said.

"What are you going to do?" Pat asked.

"Go home," Miss Alden said. She groped for her cane and stood up. "I'm getting on myself. Too old for all-night partying. Thank you, Len. Why don't you just misplace the spit? Or bend it accidentally beyond repair?" She turned to Liv, cocked her head, and with both hands gripping the cane, declaimed, " 'A prince being thus obliged to know how to act the beast must imitate the fox and the lion, for the lion cannot protect himself from traps, and the fox cannot defend himself from wolves. Therefore be a fox to recognize traps, and a lion to frighten the wolves.' Frighten the wolves," she repeated, and took a deep satisfied breath. She looked at Barrie Spellman scornfully. "Niccolò Machiavelli," she trilled. Then she nodded at Liv. "Goodnight, my dear."

"Take care," Liv said.

Miss Alden straightened herself to her full height and left them, bearing down on the cane every few steps, stiffly, as if she hated the unmistakable revelation of weakness. The crowd parted for her passage, and closed behind her, buzzing.

"I don't believe it," Linda Breen said, just loud enough for them all to hear. "Did you hear what she said they called her?"

Barrie giggled like a cheerleader at a dirty joke.

"She's quite remarkable, really," Pat said to Liv. "You didn't tell me you'd made friends with the formidable Miss Alden."

"She helped me out of a tight spot. No way in hell was I going to find anyone to change a tire for me on a Sunday afternoon. If she hadn't come along when she did and stopped, Travis and I would have had a long walk home in the heat and been without a car until Monday. What would I have done in an emergency?"

"Called the Rescue Squad," Pat said. "But she was a trooper to help you out. Where'd you get the flat?"

"I hit that rock at the first bend in the road. The tire just seemed to explode. I went out Monday and painted the rock orange to warn people to look out for it."

"Oh," said Pat, and dropped the subject.

CHAPTER 3

FIREFIGHT
Rough Cut #2

The neon outside washes red over the narrow
interior of the bar. It bleeds over the faces of
the clientele, already high colored with drink,
the exertion of dancing to the music blasting
from the juke, the lack of oxygen, hustling each
other for drinks and sex, the determination to
have a good time if it kills them. The crowd,
rowdy, suffocating, crammed into too little
space, is neither young nor middle aged, but in
that no-man's-land between. The men signal
their military service with bits and pieces of
old uniforms, or psychotically sentimental
T-shirts that advocate killing everyone and
letting God sort them out. The women have bad
teeth and play country and western music when
the men give them quarters for the juke.

A very large man taps beer into glasses and
flicks them down the bar with intimidating
control. Even when he is not laughing, as he
often is, he bares his fine, small, white teeth
in a grin that despite its constancy is not
reassuring. His is the face of a satyr, as
sketched in white or red on the black ground of a

Greek vase of great antiquity. Though set in a
web of laugh lines, the blue eyes are small and
melancholy. Tight curled coppery hair covers
his large skull and beards his chin, but his
upper lip, under a long and beautiful nose, is
clean-shaven. His body though is not satyric;
not half-man and half-horse, but rather
entirely bull: from the thick column of neck
widening into massive shoulders and deep broad
chest, matted with red hair showing at the open
neck of his white shirt, torso widening in turn
into a bulge of belly that shoves out his shirt
so he looks to be in the seventh month of a
healthy pregnancy, and blooming, and despite
the belly no bottom to speak of but heavy
muscular thighs, a little short and thin in the
calf, an elegant almost female turn of ankle,
and small, wide, stubby feet, the next thing to
cloven hooves, in leather sandals.

The sound of the shotgun freezes them all
like a spell in a fairy tale. The bartender's
head comes up; his ears all but stand up to catch
the noise: *ka-boom*. And under the explosion, the
scream of the man being murdered, and then the
thud of his body against metal, a hollow
thumping and low pop of sheet metal such as might
be heard from a hit and run, except this time it
is the man hitting the automobile, not the other
way round. And at once, the bartender goes over
the top of the bar on his gorilla arms, an
amazing, Olympian defiance of gravity, the
customers diving left and right out of his way,
beer mugs breaking, spilling, so the top of the
bar is instantly slick and dangerous as a wall
topped with broken glass, but he is already over
it and across the room, knocking down the many
who are not quick enough to get out of his way,
and hitting the row of light switches next to the
door, bringing down in an instant the limbo
state of After Hours not only inside, but
outside. The neon sign disappears amid the
shrieks of the women and not a few of the men

frightened by the sudden dousing of the light.
Someone strangles the juke by unplugging it. And
then there is a ripple of nervous laughter.

"Shut the fuck up," the bartender says.
Though his voice is low, it carries through the
room, and they do.

Neither total dark nor total silence, but a
limbo state like an ambush waiting to happen in
the jungle. The streetlights outside spill thin
yellow light like moonlight into the room; the
drizzle reflects it like sleazy sequins on a
stripper's G-string. A keening sound grows
louder, the police arriving, quickly
obliterating the stertorous breathing of three
dozen frightened, less-than-sober people. When
the blue lights wash the room, like ghosts of the
red neon, the bartender switches on the lights
again. He stands by the door, staring out, as
policemen spill out of cars, clot around the
body, which has come to rest on this side of the
Trans-Am, driven over the hood and upside down
by the force of the load, flipped over the
farside and curled up on itself, head down, like
a baby being born, in a puddle of gore that the
rain dilutes but does not wash away, and then the
cops are flowing toward the bar, toward him. In
the blue light, the bartender's face seems
bloodless, as if he were one of the walking dead.

When a cop asks him if he knew what had
happened, he moves his head from side to side.
The cop reads this as a negative signal, but it
could also mean simply that the bartender is
denying what he sees. When the policeman asks
him if he knew the dead man, the barkeep's eyes
fill up with tears. "Jackson," he says. "His
name was Jackson. We were in the same unit. He
survived hell for this. That's all I know about
it."

And then there is total dark and total
silence, and out of him erupts an agonized
scream, not unlike that of the man being

murdered, and the bartender sits up in his bed,
his face wet with sweat and tears.

A hand grasps his arm gently. "Paul, my God."

And then the other, a shadow in the dark,
fumbles for a bedside light, and the bed is a
field of light no fiercer than candlelight, and
the other is revealed, a young man, slim and as
hairless as Paul the bartender is hairy. His
eyes are wide and naked-looking; he fumbles for
a pair of glasses, and once they are on, he looks
dressed, even though he and Paul between them
have but the sheets. He is turning back to Paul
even as he pushes his glasses up his nose,
reaching to embrace him.

"It's all right," he says.

"No," Paul answers, staring into the dark.
"No."

The young man sighs, squeezes Paul, then
releases him. He untangles himself from the
sheets, and gets up.

Paul reaches after him anxiously. "Where are
you going?"

The other giggles. "To piss. I'll be right
back." And then bends over Paul. "You'll be all
right, won't you?"

Paul nods.

The young man flicks on the bathroom light,
closes the door behind him.

Paul looks at the door, slips out from under
the sheets. He opens the drawer of the
nightstand. Inside is a gun. Paul hesitates,
then removes it. He puts it in his mouth. He
closes his eyes. A tear leaks out and slides down
his cheek. Beyond the closed door the toilet
flushes. He pulls the trigger.

WHEN the right front tire blew, with a wumping sound like
the distant explosion of a bottle rocket, the Pacer slewed
sickeningly. Liv fought the steering wheel. She knew what
it was, of course—an encounter with a nasty outcropping of rock as

she swerved too far to the right to avoid Linda Breen. There was no place to pull off the single lane cottage road as it passed between a narrow corridor of trees, so she limped onward to the turnoff around the second bend. Patched with blueberries and poison ivy, it was a far from ideal place to stop, and what the blowout had left of the tire was destroyed by running the car on the rim, but there was nowhere else to go. Linda kept right on going in her Ramcharger.

"Fuck," said Liv.

Travis hung over the back of the front passenger seat, a G.I. Joe in each fat fist. "What's wrong, Liv?"

"We just blew a tire," she said. "Stay in the car while I look and see what the damage is, okay? There's poison ivy here."

"Okay," he said. He had experience with poison ivy. He went back to his G.I. Joes. "Be careful, Liv," he said.

"Sure," she said.

Sometimes he was such an old lady.

The air was so thick and still with the heat that she could not smell the cool water of the lake, less than a quarter of a mile away. It was like being inside a plastic bag. The only things moving were the bugs. Immediately they were all around her, a fierce, localized little storm with her at its eye. She flicked her hands at them impatiently, wishing she had remembered the bug repellant. Usually the little bastards left her alone. Perhaps it was nervous sweat drawing them, or the scent of old blood in her mouth. She hauled out the jack and the spare and the beach blanket that was in the back of the Pacer. Folded into a pad, the blanket was something to crouch and kneel on, as well as insulation from accidental contact with the poisoned ivy while she struggled to remove the nuts from the ruined tire.

Half an hour later she was bug-bitten, soaked with sweat, and had succeeded in removing only three nuts and several samples of her own skin, blood, and nails. On top of her toothache, from the tooth extracted day before yesterday, she had a throbbing headache from the sun.

Travis hung out an open window of the Pacer. "I want to go home, Liv," he said, for the fourth time in seven minutes.

"Shit," said Liv. She threw down her wrench. "So do I." She wiped one hand across her brow. "Let's leave this and walk it, okay?"

"Is it a long way?" Travis asked.

"Less than a mile. You can do it."

He opened the door and climbed out. "Will you carry some men?"

"Sure."

They stuffed the pockets of their shorts with G.I. Joes. Liv put her tools inside the car, heaved the spare into the back end, unrolled the windows an inch or so, locked the doors and the hatchback, and pocketed the keys. They left the newspaper they had been out to pick up on the backseat.

"Okay," she said. "Let's go."

Travis walked very slowly. She tried to keep him in the shade of the trees on the sides of the road, but the annual brush clearing party had left long stretches open to the sun. The bugs had a feast. Travis slapped at them and scratched at the bites and worried out loud about poison ivy.

"I wish we were home, Liv," he said. "These bugs are *killing* me."

"Walk a little faster, Trav," Liv said. "Maybe they won't catch you so often."

"They're faster than anybody," Travis said. "Faster than a speeding bullet."

"Well, pretend you're in a war and you're wounded," Liv suggested.

He was too. Ragged spots of drying blood and red swellings marked his neck, his hairline, his ears, his arms and legs, everywhere his fair skin was exposed. She had more bites than she could remember having at one time since she was a kid. But worse, her head was threatening to explode from the sun.

"I wish I was home," Travis said miserably.

"So do I," said Liv. She slapped viciously at her own neck. "And I wish all these shitting bugs were in hell."

Behind them, the sound of an automobile grew louder. Liv took Travis' hand and drew him well off the side of the road. Two cars had passed them already: a white Lincoln Continental, gray with road dust, driven by Claire Winslow, who waved and simpered from behind her sequined sunglasses. Claire's dogs hung their triangular little heads out an open back window in the slipstream, pointed little tongues flicking. They yapped and yipped hysterically, their bright stupid little eyes permanently frantic. After coughing and choking on

Claire's exhaust, Liv and Travis turned their faces away from the road when they heard the approach of a vehicle. Then Barrie Spellman's bottle-green BMW passed. Barrie kept her eyes firmly on the road ahead.

A little later there was another coming their way, and they ducked off the road again, hugging each other, holding their breath. Liv was surprised to hear the car slowing. She turned her face back to the road and tried to smile.

Miss Alden rolled down the window of her old Plymouth Fury. She was wearing a straw Panama tied under the chin with tulle or some other fine netting. One hand on the steering wheel, she drove with her browned, muscled forearm out the open window, touching the roof of the sedan with strong, blunt fingers. Her nails were rippled and thick; if they had been pointed they might have made real talons, but they were broken and ragged-edged by work. She was known to chop her own wood and do her own maintenance. She brought the car to a stop.

"Mrs. Russell," she said, "isn't that your vehicle back there, with the flat?"

" 'Fraid so," Liv said. "How are you, Miss Alden?"

"Quite the same as ever," she answered. She paused. "I called at your house earlier this year. You weren't in. I wanted to thank you for the card and the potted plant you sent Betty. The pot was lovely. Your own work, I think?"

Liv smiled, and squeezed Travis' hand. He looked up at her, worry huge in his eyes, and drew a little closer. He had heard from Sarah that Miss Alden was an old dragon.

"I hope she's better," Liv said.

"She won't ever be," Miss Alden said, "but thank you all the same. Now why don't you get into this car and out of the sun and away from the bugs. I'll take you straight home, if you like, or we can go back and I'll help you change that tire. Got a spare?"

Liv didn't hesitate. "God bless you. I do." She opened the front door. "Hop in, Travis," she said.

He hesitated. Liv patted his bottom. "Come on, you want to be eaten alive?"

He got in, keeping a nervous eye on Miss Alden, and sitting as far from her and as close to Liv as he could manage. The first sight of Miss Alden's gold-headed cane, on the seat next to her, seemed to reassure him, as borders are meant to do. It was not impassable, not an unencroachable, inviolable Wall, but a signal, a flag planted to claim territory for oneself: This Is Mine; That's Yours.

"You've met Travis, haven't you?" Liv asked her.

Miss Alden nodded vigorously, and they started off down the road.

"Quite a long time ago, I'm afraid," Miss Alden said.

"Do you remember Miss Alden, Trav?"

Travis looked at Miss Alden wide-eyed and nodded his head. "What happened to Miss Betty?" he asked.

Miss Alden looked at him, a surprised smile curving her thin lips. She didn't answer him at once but turned left into the Spellmans' driveway, looked back over her shoulder and backed out on the road, reversing directions to return to the Pacer.

"You remember Miss Betty, do you?" she said at last.

Travis seemed to relax. He took out one of his G.I. Joes and examined it carefully. "Sure," he said. "She gave me those cookies, what do you call 'em, Liv? The ones with tops and bottoms and insides?"

"Oreos," Liv said. She was surprised Travis remembered Betty Royal offering him cookies. That day seemed such a long time ago now, though it could only have been the beginning of last summer. Travis, not quite three, had been teething, and had made an outrageous mess of himself. Liv had had to dunk him in the lake to clean drool, chocolate cookie crumbs, the gooey cookie filling, and a sprinkling of sand from his face, out of his fine colorless hair, and even out of his ear.

It was one of the few occasions on which Liv had met Betty Royal, Miss Alden's companion of many years. She remembered it herself not so much for the mess Travis made, he was always a mess then, but because Miss Royal had, after conversing pleasantly and quite rationally about minor things, the way one does with a new neighbor one barely knows, advised Liv calmly to look out for the wires growing out of the walls. Her condition deteriorated over the summer and she was hospitalized in late August. Miss Alden did not attend the Winslows' annual Labor Day party. Later, Liv heard that Miss Royal might have Alzheimer's disease, and that Miss Alden had been forced to institutionalize her. Liv had sent a postcard with a picture of Nodd's Ridge on it and a plant in a pot she had made herself and received a handwritten thank-you from Miss Alden.

"Betty cannot write for herself. I'm afraid she does not remember who you are. But she looks at the picture and touches both the ivy and the pot you sent it in and they make her happy. For that, I thank you very much."

Miss Alden pulled off the road next to the Pacer. Her hand fell automatically upon her cane.

"Husband still away?" she asked Liv as they got out.

"Yes," Liv said.

"They do come in handy for changing tires, don't they?" Miss Alden observed.

"Some do," Liv answered.

Liv unlocked the hatchback. Miss Alden surveyed the tools and the spare Liv had thrown into the back of the Pacer, poking them with the cane.

"Got started, did you?"

"Couldn't get all the nuts off," Liv said.

"And the shitting bugs wouldn't leave us alone," Travis said.

"Travis!" Liv exclaimed.

Miss Alden threw back her head and laughed.

"You said it, Liv," Travis said.

"Well, I did," Liv admitted. "They are shitting bugs." She smiled and blushed at the same time.

"Let's get to it, then," Miss Alden said. "Maybe there'll be something left of us besides hamburger when we're done."

Travis squatted in the shade of Miss Alden's car to watch. She handed him her cane. He grinned, handling it as if he thought it might break. She seemed not to need it, striding easily around the car.

The two women looked around for a patch free of poison ivy and heaved the spare out onto it. They jacked the car again, and Miss Alden squatted, shoulder to wheel, to remove the nuts with the wrench.

Liv was not surprised at the older woman's strength. Miss Alden had a military posture, was browned from working in the sun, and brooked chivalry from no man. Working with her hands herself, Liv noticed other peoples' hands. Miss Alden's looked strong, and were. She had no trouble with the nuts at all, only grunting with satisfaction when she had one off, as if she were a dentist pulling a tooth. When she was done, she made quick work of removing the flat. Liv rolled the spare up and was allowed to help put it on. Miss Alden squatted down a second time to replace the nuts.

Miss Alden threw down the wrench and settled onto her haunches like an old Indian.

"There," she said.

Liv thanked her. "I couldn't have done this myself."

"Bosh," Miss Alden said. "You had those nuts all loosened up for me."

Miss Alden rose, one hand on her hip, as if her joints were a little sore, and helped Liv lower the jack and replace the tools in their kit.

"That rock at the bend?" Miss Alden asked, as they threw the flat into the back of the Pacer, not bothering to put it into the spare tire recess.

"Yes."

"Ought to be marked."

"Oh yes," Liv agreed and made a mental note to paint the rock orange in the morning.

Miss Alden wiped her hands on her khaki trousers. "You look peaked. Care for a glass of iced tea at my house? Or are you in a hurry to get home?"

Miss Alden held out her hand to Travis, and he presented her with her cane. She accepted it with a grave little half-bow, then leaned on it casually.

"I've got some toy soldiers Travis might like to look at," Miss Alden went on.

"Oh, please, Liv," Travis said quickly.

Liv nodded. "Thank you. You're so good to us, Miss Alden."

"Don't be silly," Miss Alden said gruffly. "And call me Helen, will you?"

"If you call me Liv," Liv said.

Miss Alden led the way. Liv rolled up the Pacer's windows and turned on the air-conditioning. Travis settled down next to her in the front seat.

"Reach me the aspirin, will you, darling?" Liv asked.

Travis popped open the glove box and extracted the plastic bottle.

"Got a hurt, Liv?" he asked sympathetically.

"Headache," she answered.

"Does aspirin work for bug bites?"

Liv chewed the aspirin and thought about it. "Ought to help, some. You want one? Have to chew it."

Travis thought about that, then extended a not very clean palm. She shook out a single aspirin with one hand. Grimacing, he chewed it thoughtfully and swallowed hard.

"Yuck," he said.

That seemed to settle the subject.

The road rose to their own driveway, and once past it, dipped again and leveled, as did the land itself. Miss Alden's house was the last on the road, and the oldest as well. Hers was the old Dexter place, a farmhouse that had been for a hundred years the first and only habitation at the north end of the lake. Unlike the cottages and summer houses of her neighbors, built on slices of shore frontage, Miss Alden's house stood alone, separated by thick woods and some twenty acres of the original Dexter holdings. Much closer to the lake than any of the late-comers, its broad, screened porch, shaded by the big old trees, gave onto a much-envied sand beach, built in the twenties before such tinkerings with the shore line were regulated. Lowbush blueberries bound the sand in place. On the far side of the house, the soil was just fine, and supported lawn aplenty, patches of flowers and a garden. A little ways away, gnarled apple trees still bore edible fruit. It was always a cool and beautiful spot, smelling of green things growing, and the baptismally clear water of the lake.

Liv rolled down her window and breathed it in. The aspirin was easing her headache, and her toothache.

The old house was built of stone, with thick walls and a slate roof. Its design was plain, a simple rectangle with the second story tucked under a hipped roof. In the twenties the porch had been added to one of the short sides, and though roofed with asphalt and floored with wood, its arched pillars and foundation piles were also of stone. Ivy had taken hold of the stone so many years ago that the vines were woody and as thick as electrical cable. Around the stone foundation the vines had recently been cut away, so the stone looked exposed. Narrow cellar windows squinted blankly out of the naked stone. But the glass, caked with dirt, had been taken out, perhaps for cleaning, and stood leaning against the stone. Fresh red caught Liv's eye and when she craned, she saw a new course of bricks laid behind the sill. Miss Alden was bricking up her cellar windows.

Miss Alden was slow leaving her car, stopping to check the set of her hat in the rearview mirror and collect her cane, so Liv and Travis gained the porch, and waited for her at the top of the steps. At one end of each step cacti grew in large clay pots.

"The door's open, go in," Miss Alden called to them, climbing out of the Plymouth.

Travis pushed open the screen door, and Liv followed him in. It seemed at once much cooler than it was outside, and quiet, the way library vaults and churches are. Threadbare pillows smelling of eternally damp feathers cushioned wicker chairs, rockers, a porch swing. At the far end of the porch, a hammock hung limp as a flag without a breeze. A single window opened from the porch to the interior of the house.

Miss Alden's cane stumped up the steps behind them and across the porch. She bustled past them, a ring of keys in her hand. "Come in, come in."

The door, like its frame, was a new-looking modern one, custom-made of thick solid pine to fit the opening, but hung on old-fashioned wrought-iron hinges, perhaps the original hardware. It offered an iron latch instead of a doorknob, incongruously topped with a brand new mortise lock. Beyond it, the house was one large, low-ceilinged room. The stone walls of the house had been plastered and wainscoted. Instead of the more-common narrow, vertical strip pattern, the white-painted, waist-high wainscoting was paneled like a door, or the mahogany library paneling of the Neal Street Victorian townhouse in Portland that was the Russells' home in the winter. At the far end, the wainscoting framed the fireplace, leaving only the stone mantel and the granite stiles exposed. Travis' fingers twitched nervously at Liv's trousers at the sight of several trophy animal heads on the walls: a lion, a buck with an awesome rack of antlers, a coyote. Their glass eyes, dusty and dead, did not render the lion and the coyote, with their fierce displays of yellow teeth, less fearsome, but rather more so. The fireplace looked as if it could easily handle the roasting of a big game animal, or Len Winslow's pigs. Wood for a fire was laid on wrought andirons, and more wood was neatly stacked within reach against the paneling. Handy to the fireplace, a brass box screwed to the wainscoting held wooden matches. The floor was of wide pine planks, bare of paint and aged to a warm, translucent beer-gold, on which Miss Alden had placed the animal skins as rugs. A coarse-haired zebra skin at the door, a bear rug, head and all, before the fire, the headless lion at the foot of the couch.

The long walls were pierced twice each with small, many-paned windows hung with plain white net curtains. The light admitted was not great and the room, despite the reflective white surfaces of wall and ceiling, was dark and cool. Miss Alden flicked a light switch, illuminating a big wrought-iron wagon wheel chandelier suspended from the exposed beams of the ceiling. Its watery light reminded them of the brilliance of the day outside and the impermeable thickness of the stone that walled them in.

"Make yourself at home," Miss Alden said. "I'll be right back." She disappeared up the steep stairs that rose on the right of the door, working the cane ahead of her a little like a mountain climber's piton.

The room had been furnished with the sort of cast-off pieces relegated to a summer place when they had lost their first charm but were still too good to throw away. They were old and comfortable, and a little smelly, not only with the accumulated scent of the people and pets that used them, but of cleaners and polishes, their own aging fabric and of damp and long periods of disuse. On the stone hearth, a blue bottle that had once held a quart of Swedish mineral water was filled with black-eyed Susans, daisies, and the first Queen Anne's Lace that signals summer's end and promises snowdrifts where its own white drifts billow on the high weeds of the fields.

A spinet piano graced the long wall opposite the stairway. Liv wondered how it stood the damp, the freezing cold of winter, and why the vandals had not destroyed it. Closer, she could smell the finish and see the grooves scarring the wood, like a network of roads going nowhere plowed through deep snow, that no amount of refinishing could ever repair. The thieves that had broken in—that must be why she was bricking up the cellar windows.

Travis slipped his hand into hers. She squeezed it and led him to the sofa, which creaked in a friendly way when they sat down. There was a big wicker basket of needlework handy to it; Liv remembered Miss Royal bundling her needlework back into the basket, rising from the very corner of the sofa she was now sitting in to meet the new neighbors, the only other time Liv had been in this house. Her other encounters with the two women had been at the post office in Nodd's Ridge or walking on the cottage road, on the beach, or berrypicking in nearby fields. For three summers Miss Alden and Miss Royal had remained just the two elderly lesbians who lived next door.

Miss Alden came stumping downstairs again. She still wore her khaki safari shirt and trousers tucked into high black boots, but she had changed her Panama for a black silk scarf tied gypsy-style around her head, and she had freshened her red lipstick. She carried a leatherbound wooden case the size of a large breadbox in her hands, and her cane under her arm.

"You might be interested in this," she said to Travis. She held the case out to him.

Wide-eyed, Travis accepted it, settling it on his knees. He pried off the lid. Inside, three-inch-high lead soldiers in blue uniforms were ranked in alternate rows with lead soldiers in gray uniforms. Some stood straight to attention, their rifles held across their bodies, and others knelt to fire. They were beautifully detailed: blue-eyed or brown-eyed; blond, brown, black, and even a couple of gray-haired ones who wore officers' insignia. One wore glasses, several sported beards or mustaches or sideburns, and three of the lowest rank were black. They all bore markings of rank: two colonels, four captains, six lieutenants, ten sergeants, twenty corporals, one hundred privates, and two resplendently uniformed generals.

"Wow!" Travis breathed in awe.

"Travis!" Liv exclaimed. "Miss Alden! They're marvelous."

Miss Alden chuckled. "When I was six, I wanted those soldiers worse than anything. It was quite unsuitable, of course. But I summoned up my courage and asked for them anyway. They were given to my brother for his birthday, which followed mine by three days. He was the best of brothers, Travis. His name was Emmet. He gave them to me, in front of our parents, because, he said, 'Helen didn't cry, even though she wants 'em so bad.' I gave them back to him, years later, when we were grown up and he had a little boy. And then, they came back to me. Emmet's son died, and Emmet couldn't bear having them around."

Travis grinned at her. "Can I play with them?"

"Of course," Miss Alden said. "That hearth over there makes a bully battlefield."

He looked at his mother. "What's bully, Liv?"

"Super."

Travis slid off the sofa, clutching the case fervidly. His cheeks were flushed with excitement.

"Bully," he muttered thoughtfully, as he sank onto his knees at the edge of the hearth.

Miss Alden watched him, her hands on her thighs just above her knees, and showed her large, yellowed, and rather fiercely crooked teeth, right to her gums, in a stiff smile. Like the box of toy soldiers, her smile seemed taken out of storage, wrinkled and faded, like something that had been folded away in damp and dark for a long time, in an attic or cupboard under the eaves. Abruptly, she stood up.

"I expect you'd like that iced tea I promised. I know I would," she said.

"Could I do anything to help?" Liv offered.

Miss Alden looked closely at her. There was nothing unused or retired in her bright eyes; they saw everything. "No, no," she said. "You look done-up, if you'll forgive my saying so. Are you in pain?"

Liv colored. "Just a headache. I took some aspirin in the car."

Miss Alden was silent.

It occurred to Liv that Miss Alden must have listened to a thousand student lies in her day.

But the tall old woman merely nodded. Leaning on her cane, she stalked to the old refrigerator.

"Wow!" Travis breathed. He looked over his shoulder at her, his face shining with excitement. "Look at this, Liv." He held up a cannon. He had ranked the soldiers on the hearth and discovered a second layer in the box, of artillery and cavalry horses.

"Fantastic," Liv assured him, but he was already rapt again.

Miss Alden settled a tray on the coffee table.

"Much as I hate to disturb Travis' maneuvers," she said, "perhaps he'd like some rations."

"Travis," Liv said.

Travis looked up again and saw the tall glasses of tea and the plate of Oreos on the tray. He grimaced, then carefully deposited the two horses he was holding on the hearth and scooted up to the coffee table.

"Sugar?" Miss Alden asked.

"Yes, please," Travis said. He wiped his brow with a grubby hand, leaving a smear like ashes. With the other hand, he accepted the glass.

"Cookies?" Miss Alden asked.

"Yes, please."

Concentrating intensely, he made short work of the snack. He drained the glass with an audible rattle.

"More tea, Travis?" Miss Alden asked.

He looked at his mother hopefully.

Liv nodded.

Miss Alden poured another glassful from the pitcher on the table. She bent over Travis to give it to him.

"Can you be trusted with a secret?" she asked him.

Travis' eyes widened over the rim of his glass. He shook his head solemnly.

Miss Alden held out her hand.

Travis placed his glass carefully on the table, then climbed off his knees and took it.

"This house has a lot of secrets," she said, casting a proprietary eye around the room. "For instance." She rose and went to the nearest window, and drew wooden shutters rattling across it. The shutters slid out of the thick stone walls like the blades of a rusty guillotine.

Travis grinned at Liv. His eyes danced.

"Built right into the walls," Miss Alden said. "Indian shutters."

She held out her hand again, and Travis jumped up to take it. She led him at a processional pace to the fireplace.

"This house is the oldest house in all of Nodd's Ridge. It wasn't the first one built, but it is the oldest one still standing," she told him.

Travis looked up at her, waiting for the secret.

"It's so old that the man who built it, Stephen Dexter, who was my great-great-great granduncle, was afraid the Indians might attack it and kill him and his family."

Travis caught his breath.

"So he built a secret hideaway that would keep his family safe even if the Indians burnt the house down around them. Nothing like that ever happened. The Indians all died from cholera, along with Stephen Dexter's first wife and three of his children. But the secret hiding place is still here."

With that, Miss Alden reached forward with her cane and pressed a piece of molding on the wainscoting to the left of the brass matchbox. And a section of the wainscoting, about as big as a china cupboard door, opened up.

Travis gasped. Liv came to her feet in surprise.

Behind the door was a dark hole tunneled in stone, the very wall of the house, and the fireplace. Miss Alden swung the secret door open and stepped up to it. Travis, still clinging to her hand, followed her. But he looked back over his shoulder at Liv, and she came to him at once.

Without so much as a backward glance to see if they were coming, Miss Alden stooped into the darkness. They could hear the hollow tap of her cane on the stone.

Travis and Liv, hunching her shoulders instinctively, followed her. It was immediately cooler. The light behind them showed them the rising steps of a very steep, stone stairway. The passage was so narrow they could not help touching its rough, cold, raw walls every time they moved, not just with their hands, but all over, so it seemed as if the walls were reaching out to touch them. Travis tightened his hold on Liv's hand, and she assumed he was tightening it as well on Miss Alden's, who was a dark shape, like a shadow in thick woods of a cold dark winter night, above them. His breathing had quickened, and so had hers. Behind them, the door in the wainscoting swung slowly shut.

Travis jumped, and dug his nails into Liv.

Miss Alden turned and whispered, "Don't be frightened. You're safe as houses in here."

And with a tug of Travis' hand, she led them upward in the blind dark. Every once in a while, it seemed as if the gold head of her cane flickered, reflecting a minuscule quantity of light seeping from some unknown source, perhaps around the edges of the secret door. It seemed possible at the time that it flickered on its own by magic. Their eyes had just begun to adjust to the lightlessness when Miss Alden stopped. Here the passage seemed to widen as it turned.

She tapped the wall on the right. "Three and a half feet of stone wall between us and the fireplace." She swung the cane to tap the left-hand wall. The sound of the cane was wood on iron. "Here's the gun rack Stephen Dexter built into the wall."

Miss Alden groped with her free hand to find Travis' in the dark, and helped him feel of the iron bands that formed the gunrack. Then it was Liv's turn. Liv winced at Miss Alden's rough, callused, almost cruelly tight grip. At once the old woman let go of Liv's hand, releasing it onto the crude iron of the rack. Liv was astonished at the coldness of the shotgun muzzles as she felt them blind.

"How many are there?" she asked.

"Eight. It's only part of my collection. The rest I keep in Wellesley. They come from several sources. My father and Emmet and my own acquisitions. Stephen Dexter had no intentions of sharing his weapons with the Indians, so he placed his rack here. The thieves have never found them." Miss Alden chuckled. "Perhaps they'll have the luck this year."

Then Miss Alden's cane tapped higher, on stone. "Three feet on this side, part of the exterior wall." She started up again, and shortly they reached the top of the stairs. Miss Alden thrust with her cane into the darkness ahead of them, and there was a thunk as it solidified and became a door, the twin to the one by the fireplace, opening before them. They emerged into a bedroom under eaves.

Blinking, they turned to look where they had been. The secret exit was closing. Miss Alden tapped it lightly with her cane and it lay flush against the wainscoting around the bedroom fireplace. She turned to them, smiling broadly. Her eyes were alit with a fever of excitement.

"How about that?" she asked Travis.

"That's some secret," Liv said, and let out the breath she had not realized she had been holding.

"Far out," Travis said. "Really awesome."

Liv shot a rueful smile at Miss Alden.

Miss Alden laughed. Then she was suddenly very serious. Bending to meet Travis, eye to eye, she sealed her lips with a forbidding finger. "Remember now, it's a secret." She crossed her bosom in a familiar childish gesture. "Hope to die if I should tell," she said.

Travis crossed his bosom in solemn imitation.

"Shall we go back down?" Miss Alden asked.

"Please," Liv said.

"The conventional route or the secret way?" she asked.

"The secret way," Travis said, his voice high and squeaky with excitement.

Miss Alden bowed slightly to them, gesturing to the secret door. "Find the key, Travis," she said.

Travis stepped up to the wainscoting and studied it fiercely. He began to slide his fingers along the molding, pressing as he went. He felt something give under his probing, and the door began to swing open. He looked up at them, face shining. Then he bowed slightly, gesturing toward the door.

The two women ducked into the darkness and he followed them.

"Thanks," he said to Miss Alden, when they were back in the living room again and the secret door had closed behind them so that no one would ever suspect it was there.

He drank off his second glass and with a quick look at his mother for permission, snatched another cookie from the tray and stuffed it into his mouth. With his cheek still lumpy, making crunching noises as he chewed, he slithered back across the floor to the hearth.

Miss Alden picked up her tea but did not sit down with Liv again. She walked stiffly, using her cane again as something besides a prop, to the piano. Setting her glass of tea on the top, she opened the piano and began to play a rousing medley of marches.

Travis looked up and grinned. He marched a pair of mounted cavalry through the air in time to "The Yellow Rose of Texas." Liv could not help laughing.

And then Miss Alden shifted to slower, more soothing music, movie scores and love songs of modern composition. Travis grinned at Liv when he recognized "Chariots of Fire." The old woman's ungainly hands with their broken nails moved over the keys with predictable authority but with an astonishing feminity. For the first time Liv could imagine the sexual relationship between this woman and the afflicted Betty, and it did not seem grotesque at all. It seemed a romance, and like all true love had come to a tragic end.

Miss Alden began a new song, a piece Liv had never heard before. Almost at once it was unbearable, suffocating. It seemed to vibrate in Liv's teeth and bones. She covered her eyes, and to her own horror, began to weep silently, but quite uncontrollably.

The music stopped. There was a brief silence and then Miss Alden exclaimed, "Liv!"

Reaching for her cane, propped against the piano, she knocked it with a clatter across the floor. She did not stop to pick it up, but stalked, rather stiffly, to the sofa, on which she collapsed awkwardly and gathered Liv against her bony collarbone.

Miss Alden fumbled a large cotton handkerchief from her breast pocket and thrust it into Liv's hands.

"There, there," she said briskly, as she must have said numberless times to undergraduate women in the throes of love or academic failure or menstrual cramps. "Get it all out."

Liv sniffed and snuffled and fought to regain control of herself. She peeked anxiously at Travis.

He seemed not to have noticed, too wound up in the war he was fighting across the hearth, to his own sound effects, soft explosions. "Ptuiee! Pkoo!"

"What is it?" Miss Alden said, brushing Liv's hair out of her eyes. "What's wrong?"

"I don't know." She fumbled. "The music, the song. It's the saddest song I've ever heard. I feel so stupid, crying over a song."

" 'Elise,' " Miss Alden said. " 'Für Elise.' "

The old woman came to her feet quickly, rubbing her hands together.

"I used to play it for Betty," she said distractedly. "Elizabeth, you know. Elise."

Liv blew her nose violently in Miss Alden's handkerchief. "I'm sorry to be such a baby. I don't seem to have any stuffing anymore," she said.

Using the back of the sofa as a crutch, Miss Alden retrieved her cane, returned to the piano, and closed it carefully. She took down her glass of tea and came back across the room. The ice tinkled delicately in the glass in response to the irregular rhythm of the cane. She sat down in a wicker chair arranged at an angle to the sofa.

"How's your headache?" she asked.

Liv sat up straighter. "Better, thanks. All gone, really."

A moment's silence marked a new tension between them: Miss Alden had touched Liv in a familiar way, and was afraid she had offended her; Liv was conscious of Miss Alden's discomfort and equally embarrassed, but by her own emotional display, not because she had been hugged by an elderly lesbian. She tried to think of a way to tell Miss Alden she had taken the hug for what it was, comfort, not a cheap feel or a come on, without making her feel like a bigger fool than she already had.

Miss Alden sat straighter, too.

Liv admired the old woman's unflinching courage even as she dreaded the questions she knew Helen Alden was going to ask her.

"What's really wrong?" Miss Alden asked.

"I've had some teeth capped. One of them abcessed. I've had it out, but now I'm having something called 'ghost pain,'" Liv told her. "It's supposed to go away anytime. I really do believe it's fading."

Miss Alden nodded. "Is that why you've lost so much weight?"

Liv grinned. "You don't miss much, do you?"

"When I'm paying attention. But I've been distracted. Now I feel rather self-indulgent. Here you are, clearly not feeling very well, and haven't been for some time, and could have used some help or some company," Miss Alden said. "One ought to be a better neighbor."

Liv felt a rush of guilt and compassion. Miss Alden's sin was her own. Miss Alden, too, had been lonely and unhappy, and had had no one when she needed someone.

"Oh, Miss Alden," she said (she would never be able to use Helen without a conscious effort), "if only I'd known." Then embarrassment overcame her. She lapsed into confusion. "I didn't want to be a burden on anyone."

"That doesn't surprise me," Miss Alden said. "We're much of a kind, I'm afraid." She did not disguise her curiosity. "And you've been keeping this from your husband as well?"

Liv smiled. "I tried. He knows now."

"But he's not here. You're still alone."

"I'm okay now. My worst problem is insomnia. I can manage. He has a contract to meet."

Miss Alden slapped her big hands onto her thighs. "I'm being nosy."

Liv shrugged and smiled shyly. "I invited it, bawling my head off, didn't I?"

Miss Alden stood up. "If you need help again, you will call me, won't you?" It was not so much a question as a statement. "For now, why don't you put up your feet and rest? Travis is having a fine time. It would be a shame to interrupt him. It's cool here, and I'll leave you to yourself. I've some work to do in my shop downstairs, but it won't be noisy."

Liv opened her mouth to make a conventional protest. Travis looked up at her, beaming. She shut her mouth. As she was taking her sneakers off, Miss Alden disappeared through a door under the stairway, and Liv heard the cane tapping on the cellar stairs, then movement in the cellar below. There was a smell of hot metal, as from a soldering iron, and clanking noises.

Miss Alden in her cellar chamber, thought Liv blearily. Bricking up the windows. Or someone. *The Cask of Amontillado.* It was enough to make her giggle. But the smells were wrong. Forging something. Down there in hellish heat, fire reflected in her eyes and in the bloody smoke she wears like a cloak. Metal fangs to close on some pitiful half-wild creature. Crushing and rending the fur and flesh and bone. There would be a dreadful shriek and dust settling like smoke on glazed eyes. Something she was supposed to tell Miss Alden. But Miss Alden already knew. It was no longer necessary to struggle against the lid of darkness. She closed her eyes and fell heavily asleep almost at once.

When she woke the room was shadowed with the advance of the sun over the house. Miss Alden and Travis were sitting cross-legged on the hearth together, in earnest discussion. Travis was showing her his G.I. Joes, identifying them for her and acquainting her with the contents of their personnel files, which he had memorized from the dossier cards Liv had read him from the backs of their packaging. Miss Alden was relating rank and speciality to the toy soldiers, who were being replaced, one by one, in their packing box. Liv listened to them drowsily a few minutes before struggling to her elbows.

"Sleeping beauty," Miss Alden said to Travis, gesturing toward Liv.

Travis laughed. "Liv," he said, "you were *snoring.*"

"Thanks for telling me," Liv said. "We'll have to tape record the next session and see if we've got a hit record."

"Actually they were quite ladylike snores," Miss Alden said. "Now *I* am a great snorer, Travis."

Travis looked up at her.

"Why I've blown down trees," she boasted.

Travis giggled.

"A tent, too, and it wasn't any little Boy Scout one, either. It was a circus tent."

Travis hooted.

"And once," Miss Alden said darkly, "I blew down a whole house."

"Nooo!" Travis squealed.

"I did," she insisted.

He considered this cynically. "Sounds like a tease to me."

Miss Alden glared and arched one eyebrow. "Well," she said, "a little. Tease."

Travis snickered.

Using her cane for support, Miss Alden clambered to her feet. "I rather like little boys," she said to Liv. "It's when they get their growth I can't stand them. Do me a favor, Travis." She ruffled his hair. "Don't grow up."

Travis grinned. "I *have* to," he explained cheerfully.

"Ah," said Miss Alden. "That's the rub."

"I'm afraid so," Liv said. "Say thanks, Trav."

Travis did and they took their leave, both of them sneaking quick looks at the secret door panel, trying to remember just where it was. And then at each other. They really had seen it and not imagined it. Hadn't they?

They took Miss Alden's unlisted phone numbers, for both the Dexter house and her home in Massachusetts, with them, and her stern injunction not to be strangers. Liv went away feeling almost decent for the first time in weeks. The visit had been therapeutic, whether because she had talked to someone, or cried, or napped, she could only guess.

Next day she took over an orange date cake, but though the Plymouth was in the yard, Miss Alden did not answer the door. The cake, left on the porch, was acknowledged with a rather coldly polite postcard, and Liv decided Miss Alden had repented of her neighborliness. Somehow it wasn't surprising. But she had a persistent sense of unfinished business. There was something about which they should have talked, something from which she had been distracted.

CHAPTER 4

NO SOONER had the light and noise of the party diminished behind them, as if it were in another zone of night, than The Poor emerged from the brush to trot almost soundlessly by their sides all the way home. By the time they were home, Pat was almost sober. The cat twisted between his feet as they entered the house, and he scrambled, cursing, to keep his balance. The Poor shot into the interior darkness. Pat disappeared toward their bedroom.

Liv stopped in the kitchen to read the notes pinned to the refrigerator door. They were pinned under magnets that looked like real food, but which functioned as a form of editorial comment by Sarah.

A slice of bacon underlined: "10:37 Bayard called. Said he would be up late, please call back."

Under slice of dill pickle was: "9:05 Your mother called. Will call again tomorrow." Sarah and her grandmother had never been *simpatico,* not even in Sarah's infancy when she never failed to spit up or wet through her diapers onto Marguerite Dauphine's tailored silk suit. Marguerite in her turn seemed always to encounter Sarah at her worst—sullen, whiny, or in a tantrum. Now that Sarah had arrived at adolescence, Marguerite was in a constant state of barely restrained disapproval. And Sarah had taken to reminding Liv just who was responsible for inflicting stiff-necked, impossible Marguerite on her by referring to her grandmother always as "your mother."

A slice of tomato, redder and juicier than any supermarket tomato, pinned: "8:50 Jane called. Catch you tomorrow." No messages from Sarah about Travis or herself. She had left snack dishes in the sink. Liv cleared them into the dishwasher and turned off the lights.

She went not to her own bedroom but toward the children's, on the opposite side of the house.

Sarah sprawled open-mouthed on her bed, in a T-shirt and bikini underpants printed with blue whales, still wearing the Walkman's earphones. Liv found the cigarette pack–sized tape player half under Sarah's pillows and turned it off. She pulled up the top sheet and kissed Sarah's forehead, just as she always did. In her sleep, even with a mouthful of braces and earphones for a headdress, Sarah was already a beautiful woman. A twenty-first-century woman, barbaric with her wired mouth and skeletal electronic diadem.

Travis was curled up in the glow of the nightlight, with his thumb in his mouth. His fine hair was matted darkly to his skull with sweat, the pillow under his head, damp with both sweat and drool. He drew a deep sobbing breath around his thumb. Very gently, Liv tugged the thumb from his mouth. Travis turned onto his back. Liv drew his top sheet lightly over him, and kissed him, too.

On the way back through the house, she found The Poor curled up on the couch. Picking her up gently, Liv took her to the back door and put her out.

When she came in, Pat was still in their bathroom. She heard the sound of vigorous toothbrushing, which meant he still wanted to make love.

Though he had grown up poor enough to have used salt to brush his teeth, he was casual to the point of benign neglect in their care. The well water he had drunk as a kid had been naturally fluoridated, enough to discolor his teeth to some degree and leave him entirely without cavities. For him it was sufficient to have his extremely sound, if somewhat crooked, teeth cleaned of nicotine stains twice a year. He seemed mildly amused at the fuss she made about the kids' cleaning their teeth, the fluoride drops when they were babies, the regular dental exams, or her own compulsive flossing and brushing. Seeing that on the same diet and with the best home hygiene she required more dental care than he did, he had come round to the idea she might indeed be cursed by heredity with soft, cavity-prone teeth. But he retained a child's attitude of footdragging suspicion of the dentist. The dentist was a fabled monster who never failed to hurt the helpless victim in the chair. More important, Pat had never had a toothache in his life.

But she had made it clear when they were first lovers that she found the taste of his cigarettes on his breath unpleasant, and so he brushed his teeth and used mouthwash faithfully before lovemaking. It had become a reliable signal between them.

Liv shucked her cardigan, T-shirt, and bra, and pulled a light summer nightdress over her head. She unzipped her jeans and dropped them to her ankles, then stepped out of them. Tossing them into the hamper, she reached for her hairbrush, part of a silver-backed set her parents had given her for her sixteenth birthday, when her initials had still been OAD, for Olivia Anne Dauphine. The OAD were traced on the silver in a pattern so elaborate it was nearly abstract, like the swirling, curving forms on Persian carpets that had been vines and leaves in their ancestral designs. Sometimes similar forms turned up as designs on her pottery, frequently skewed and chopped into further abstraction. The brush and comb were in their usual place on her vanity, but her hand mirror was not. Before she had a chance to wonder where she had left it she saw Pat open the bathroom door behind her, in the oval mirror of the dresser.

"Don't stop," he said. "There's nothing I'd rather watch than you brushing your hair."

"Bayard called," she said. "He'll be up late if you want to call him back."

Pat started to reach for the bedside phone.

"Why bother?" she asked, putting down her hairbrush. "He can't possibly want anything that won't wait until tomorrow. Or that you could do anything about until then."

Pat's hand hovered over the phone, then went to his shirt buttons. "Right," he said.

Liv went into the bathroom to brush her teeth. Her hand mirror was on the counter next to the basin. After she had brushed her teeth, washed her face, had had a pee, and washed her hands, she stared down into the hand mirror. It was glass side up. She picked it up and blew off a few fine grains of white powder. She carried it back to its place on the vanity.

Pat had undressed and was sprawled naked across their bed, smoking a cigarette. She was conscious of him watching her as she moved about their bedroom, folding her sweater and putting it away, putting their sneakers into the closet.

"Lady," he said, "come to bed."

She sighed. Afraid to look straight at him, she walked to the bed like a woman pushing a wire basket in a supermarket, her mind full of the ripeness of avocados, her shopping list, the sheaf of coupons in her handbag. No seductive twitch, no heat under her lowered eyelids. Standing over him, she pulled her nightdress off, over her head.

He held up his arms to her.

God knew she was horny, had been a long time without sex. Not a very noble motive, but she was not going to kid herself it was not important to her.

He seemed to have no sense of how terribly angry she was with him. She wanted to beat him with the bed pillows and scream at him. But she had never denied him love in a fit of anger. Sometimes the only thing that had kept them from irrevocable words was lovemaking. When all else failed them, in the lee of lovemaking they had always been able to talk again, to bridge the gaps between them. This time it might be the last chance, their last stand together.

She lay down next to him.

He drew her close. "God, you look good."

There was a dot of white powder on his right nostril.

She laid her head on his chest and bit her lip. His heartbeat under her ear was thudding like the footsteps of a heavy man running up a flight of stairs.

He tucked his hand under her chin and tilted her head to him. She shuddered against him, and he hugged her very tightly to him.

The act was quick, and elementally violent, as it often was for them after periods of abstinence or separation. She climaxed twice and could have gone on, but when he asked if it was all right with her if he came, she consented, relieved to think he, too, was horny enough not to be able to sustain a longer act. It meant, she hoped, he had done without the past few weeks.

Almost as quickly as it was done, Liv slipped from the bed and went into the bathroom. She turned on the shower.

Pat stood in the bathroom door.

"You okay?" he asked.

"Yes," she said. She reached into the shower to test the water temperature.

"It was okay for you, then?" Pat asked, leaning against the doorframe.

"Sure. How was it for you?" Liv asked. "I know you were in a hot hurry to get laid. Wanted to find out how it was to fuck your wife on a rush of coke?"

Pat froze. "What?"

"Maybe I'm jumping to conclusions," Liv said. "Maybe it was the first time you ever fucked *anybody* on blow."

Pat reached out and grabbed her arm. "I don't believe what I'm hearing."

"Look in the mirror," Liv said softly.

Pat looked over her shoulder, peering into the bathroom mirror. He touched his nostril, and reddened.

"Jesus Christ," he said, still extravagantly injured. "Bayard laid a little coke on me before I left. Christ, it's nothing. Two lines. It was in my shaving gear, and it spilled, that's all. I didn't want Mrs. Parks to find it."

"Pardon me," Liv said coldly and stepped into the shower. She pulled the shower door tightly shut behind her and thrust her head under the shower.

When she turned her back to the spray of water, Pat's shadow on the glass door was gone. She laid her head against the tiled wall and wept under the screen of the water. She was not sure why she was crying. She was angry, not afraid. This was only a fight, not the end of the world. But she was overwhelmed with a rush of black inexplicable grief.

Pat was sitting in their bed smoking a cigarette with the sheets pulled up to his waist when she came out of the bathroom. He shot an angry, guilty glance at her.

"There hasn't been anybody else, with coke or without," he said. "Let's make that clear. I resent that nasty little implication. I really do. I don't deserve it." He sucked at the cigarette. "Because it hasn't been easy."

Liv picked up her nightdress. "I'll accept that, for the moment. I apologize if I accused you wrongly."

"Accepted," Pat said, and reached for his ashtray. "I feel like I've been hit with a hammer right between the eyes, Liv. You were the girl that wrote the letter to the college paper advocating the legalization of pot. When did you go straight on me?"

"I've always been straight," she said. She turned back the sheets on her side of the bed and climbed in. "I never smoked the stuff. I just didn't think it was any worse than alcohol and I still don't. In a rational society, people would be encouraged to substitute pot for alcohol. But it's intellectual principle with me, not self-interest. When have you ever known me not straight?"

Pat smiled. "Never, I admit it. Except for booze. I've seen you tie one on now and then."

" 'A little wine for thy stomach's sake,' " she said.

"But the Bible doesn't mention coke, right?" Pat said. "Anyway, you haven't been to church in years."

" 'Consistency is the hobgoblin of little minds,' " Liv said.

"I'm not worried about your mind," Pat said. "I'm worried about your increasingly tight ass."

She arranged her pillow and turned on her side, away from him.

"The shit's illegal, Pat," she said wearily. "You'd better know right now if you get caught, it's *your* ass. I won't bail you out, and I won't defend you to your kids."

"Thanks a lot, babe," Pat said. She heard the hard clunk of the ashtray as he set it down on the nightstand. "I love the feeling that you're behind me all the way."

"Don't ever make love to me again after you've used that shit. I'm not just another cheap thrill," Liv said. "I'll leave you if you do."

"Jesus Christ," Pat said. He threw back the sheets. "Since you seem determined to piss me off, I'm going to have another beer and call Bayard. We're both too tired to make sense right now."

He stood by the bed a few seconds, waiting for her to respond.

"All right," he said. "This has been a bitch of a summer. On me, too, babe. But it worries the hell out of me that suddenly we're so far apart on this."

She curled up on herself and waited for sleep. She heard Pat leave the room and pick up the phone in the study next to the bedroom. The tick of dialing carried through the bedroom extension a few feet away from her, the muffled conversation and laughter between him and Bayard was audible through the wall, which on her side was the closet and on his side was floor to ceiling bookcases. She rolled onto her back and stretched, then composed herself in what she thought of as her corpse position: flat on her back, body straight, hands folded just below her breasts. Eyes closed, she breathed evenly, simulating sleep, hoping to fake her way into it.

But her mind was restless, full of her anger with Pat, her anger at herself for letting him screw her when she knew what he was doing. And for fucking him because she wanted fucking that badly. Every act of copulation between them could not proceed entirely from love; there were inevitably elements of compromise, the times when one or the other of them was less than wholehearted, doing it because the other wanted it, the times when selfish desire, the need, was more important than who their partner was. But if it was true that the very habituation to each other's bodies achieved over years together produced reliably easy good sex, that good fucking they got from each other reminded them how good it could all be, and brought them back together. And it *was* still good between them. She did not believe, though, they could go on long fucking each other merely because the other was there to be fucked. At least she couldn't.

Maybe she had been unfair to accuse him of cheating. Either she was being realistic, accepting the worldly wisdom that these things happen, meaning grown people couldn't keep their pants on, or she was being cynical, refusing the possibility that Pat was keeping the promise to have no other. It was a curse of the times. The old rules had been abolished to no tangible improvement. Love had been reduced to a crap game. Sometimes you got lucky. Mostly the house made money off the suckers.

When she heard the click of the phone being hung up, she realized she had been holding her breath. Her stomach was queasy. She was, she realized, enraged again, as enraged as she had been at Pat for coming to her for the first time in weeks with cocaine up his nose. Having fulfilled his connubial obligation, he had then rushed to phone Bayard—to whom he had talked for half an hour before they left for the party, as well as been with every day of the last six weeks on the set of *Firefight*.

Pat would tell her she was not to take any of it seriously, yet he lived and breathed it. He had never really left acting behind. Unconsciously, he picked up the voice, phrasing, idiom, gesture of whomever he was with. He had come back to her talking and walking like Bayard Rohrer, reminding her with whom he had filled the last six weeks of his life.

Pat was on the deck, she could smell his cigarette smoke, see the blue of the buglight, hear the zap and sizzle of insects dying fiery deaths in it. He coughed and cleared his throat now and then. She

felt disgusted with herself for the rush of spleen that had overwhelmed her, and was enormously weary. What did it all matter?
She closed her eyes and listened for the rending shriek of the loons.

The birds must have gone to bed for the night. She was still
awake when Pat came to bed, but she pretended sleep. Sometime
later she got up to take aspirin and drink warm milk. Sometimes it
helped. She slipped into a doze, waking with a start around three-
thirty. Her usual hour. She collected a blanket from the closet and
left the bedroom. In the kitchen she made herself a cup of camomile
tea, and carried it and the blanket to the deck, where she lay down
on a chaise lounge. The lake mirrored the sky, which was clear and
white with the false dawn. Only a jagged black line of trees on the
opposite shore, the mountains gray ghosts behind them, defined air
from water. Overhead, the trees were inky, jagged-edged Oriental
brush strokes. The loons began their morning noises, raising goosebumps on her arms. Curled underneath her blanket, she listened to
them with her eyes closed. Hours later, just before the sun's first
tentative warmth touched her face, all the other birds went at it at
once in a raucous chivaree. Suddenly the world was soft and clean,
all new again. Another day.

She went back to her bedroom to put on a bathing suit. As she
reached for her beach cover-up in the closet, her knuckles rapped
against something hard in the pocket of Pat's sports coat, the one he
had been wearing when he arrived home the day before. Slipping her
hand into the pocket, she gingerly passed the tips of her fingers over
it. It was a small glass bottle, the size of the ones in a child's chemis-
try set. Attached to its ribbed plastic cap by a short chain was a tiny
spoon made of a bead and a tube of metal flattened into a spoon at
the end. The tiny bottle was half-filled with white powder. She didn't
have to be a weathergirl to know which way to blow that kind of
snow. Just a few lines someone had slipped him, no doubt. She
dropped it back into the pocket and closed the closet door on it.

The pond was a cold shock, the slipstream of the angelic sword.
She felt it from the roots of her teeth. Her skin reddened in protest.
But the water was also silky, caressing her as she moved through it.
After a few laps, it began to seem actually warm, though really it was
only her own body heating itself with exertion.

She came out of it feeling reborn. Stripped of her bathing suit, curled up in her cover-up under the blanket on the chaise, she fell deeply asleep at last.

"What's left?" Sarah said, wiping her hands on her jeans.

Liv looked around the gingerbread house–studio. "There isn't much."

It always looked naked and abandoned at the beginning of the season and at the end, when everything was packed away. She never left anything behind except a few cheap and simple tools and her old-fashioned kick wheel, locked in a cupboard. The kiln, now cold and swept clean, was built in.

Travis sat in the middle of the floor, playing with a lump of clay. His face and hands were very dirty, and the clay stained his white T-shirt. But he was sweaty with happiness. Liv had given him clay as soon as he was old enough to hold it, just as she had given it to Sarah when Sarah had been the baby toddling around her studio. But Sarah had never taken to it the way he had.

Liv indicated the small stack of boxes by the door.

"You weren't kidding," Sarah said, for once too genuinely surprised to be cool.

Liv tried not to notice, as her daughter really looked at her for the first time in weeks. It occurred to her then that Sarah's self-absorption had at least had the effect of preserving Liv's privacy.

"I've had some good ideas," Liv said. "I'm ready to really work again."

Sarah picked up the first box and carried it out, her face closed again.

Working on what her mother could have done with the summer, Liv thought. There should have been a dozen cartons to take back, not three.

She squatted down next to Travis. "It's time to go," she said.

He sighed. "Good," he said.

He climbed to his feet, and put the clay in its Tupperware box. When the cap was firmly on and burped, he joined her at the door. She looked around once. The air already smelled stale and empty. She closed the door and locked it.

Pat was putting the last of the perishables in the station wagon.

Liv went into the kitchen and checked to be sure everything was gone. Then she went through the house, locking windows and doors. She stopped on the back porch, trying to commit how it all looked just then to memory. She always did. But her mind was too full of closing up and what she had to do when she was home again, and she felt not the moment of cherishing she wanted but only mechanical emptiness. Like the house itself, a shell in which nothing lived, except small creeping things and insects, until spring came again. All she got was a bad photograph in which everything would be flattened, small, indistinct, and ordinary.

"Pee?" Pat asked, as she came out the back door.

Sarah groaned. "Daddy!"

"Well?" he insisted and was answered with a chorus of yeses.

"Move 'em out," he said.

Liv took the wheel of the Pacer, Travis sitting beside her. From the back, The Poor yowled miserably from her cat carrier. The air was already fierce with the stink of cat piss.

Pat leaned in at the window. "See you when we get home," he said. "Be careful." He kissed her forehead. Straightening up, he looked around sadly. "It's all over again, babe."

Liv watched him get into the station wagon with Sarah. Already rock loud enough to deafen was pouring out of the wagon's windows. She started the Pacer.

"Summer's all over," she said to Travis.

"Good," he said. He was lining up G.I. Joes in a troop transport truck on the seat between them. "I don't like this house."

"Why?" Liv asked.

"Daddy's never home, and you cry all the time," Travis answered matter-of-factly.

Shit, she thought. You can't hide anything from them, no matter how hard you try. They always know. "We'll come some weekends this fall," she said. "Gather pinecones like we always do. And when the snow falls, we come skiing, and sliding. That'll be fun, won't it?"

Travis was more interested in battling G.I. Joes over the terrain of his ragged blanket than in weekends in Nodd's Ridge.

Putting it into words, she realized how unlikely it was, unless she and Travis came by themselves. Sarah had games and practices every weekend and no enthusiasm for parting from her friends even for forty-eight hours. Pat would be away most of the fall and would not want to leave Portland when he was home.

Maybe it was just as well. Put the summer behind them. Maybe everything would be better next year. She had to hope.

CHAPTER 5

FIREFIGHT

Rough Cut #3

Frowning slightly, a woman in a gold-lamé halter and a pair of very short black shorts paints her nails. They are excessively long and luridly red. Teenage girls often affect such nails, part of a natural experimentation with sexual display, but in a grown woman, such nails are either a holdover, an indication of immaturity, or a narcissistic statement that she does not work with her hands, which implies some kind of kept status, of which she is proud. They may also be a lie, as well as poor taste.

She glances up as the man entering the room passes between her and the television screen a few feet in front of her. He drops onto the couch next to her and drapes an arm around her shoulders. She had not taken her eyes off him, though her hands are held rigid to protect the wet glaze. She squeals softly when he hugs her and pulls away, holding her nails in front of him to show him why.

He sits back and pops a can of beer. A small, lithe man with arresting dark eyes and curly black hair, he is not just handsome, he is

beautiful. And he knows it. There is a swagger in
the way he tosses his head back, in his self-
satisfied smile.

"Whatcha watchin'," he asks the girl.

She flicks a wrist at the TV. "Nothin'."

She is taller than he is, bony-thin, but with
disproportionately large breasts threatening
to spill from her gold-lamé halter. Her pale
skin is freckled, and fine hair glints on her
forearms, as if they had been dusted with gold.
Her abundant hair is an artificially white-
blond, and floats loose over her shoulders,
occasionally veiling her face when she bends
forward over her nails.

The man stares at the TV. The evening news is
on. It seems to cast a spell over him, without
his showing any interest or reaction to it.

She continues to flick glances at him. It is
clear there is a high sexual charge between the
two. What is also apparent is that for both these
people, most of sex is in the display, the
innuendo of glance and stare and grab. They have
nothing much to say to each other beyond double
entendres. It is what has held them together as
long as it has: The best part of their lovemaking
is in suggestion. It is how they assure
themselves not only of their desirability but
their sexuality.

As if a scale were lifted from his eyes, the
man changes. Abruptly he comes out of his
lounging, his nose going up in the air like a dog
pointing, and he is on his feet, facing the door
to the apartment. Even from his television
trance, over the noise of the telecast, he has
heard something.

She follows him with her eyes, puzzled, then
hears the footsteps on the stairway. He is
moving to one side of the door, positioning
himself.

She sighs, inserts the applicator back into
her bottle of nail polish, and screws it tightly
shut. There is a tentative knock at the door, and

she rises to answer it. The black shorts expose
more of her bottom than they cover. The man is
behind her, ready to peek through the crack of
the hinges.

Leaving the door on the chain, she opens it
wide enough to see the visitor. Eyebrows raised
high in question, she asks, "Yes?"

Even as she does, the man moves out of hiding,
and nudges her aside.

"Let 'em in," he says, and turns his back, an
insult the woman reads if not the visitor.
Whoever the stranger is, her man is not afraid of
him.

It is the young man who was with Paul Taurus,
the bartender, when he shot himself. His eyes
behind his thick glasses are pale and nervous
and frightened, but there is a countermanding
determination in the thrust of his chin. He
peers around the room, at the gaudy woman, and
then at the man who has returned to the couch and
is slumped there, staring at the TV.

"Denny," he says, and approaches the couch,
his hand extended.

Denny ignores the hand. He sits up. "Barbie
Sue, go wash your hair or somethin'."

Barbie Sue blushes. She is not the kind of
woman that blushing flatters. She crosses her
arms, being careful of her nails.

"You can't order me around," she snaps.
"There ain't anythin' I can't hear you say to
this fruit."

The young man puckers his lips at her. "Same
to you, sweetheart," he says.

"Both of you shut up," Denny drawls. "You
watch how you talk to her," he says to the young
man.

Barbie Sue preens victoriously. That's all
she really wanted, just to have her sexual
dominance acknowledged. "And you," he says to
Barbie Sue, "I don't need your troublemakin'.
Get the fuck outta here."

Barbie Sue slams out of the room.

The young man loiters in the middle of the floor, evidently on the verge of bolting.

Denny settles back on the couch.

"You ain't here on a social call, are you?"

The young man looks around nervously, and then pulls a straight-backed chair around, and sits down in it.

"Paul's dead," he says in a low voice.

Denny sits up, his eyes glittering. "Goddamn," he breathes. "What happened?" His eyes narrow. "It wasn't that fucking AIDS, was it?" He is already rising, his hands raised before him as if to ward off the dread disease.

The young man's jaw drops loose and he stares at Denny. "Jesus," he says. "Sweet Jesus."

"Well, was it?" Denny demands.

"No!" He cannot keep the disgust out of his voice. "You ignorant redneck."

Denny flies at him, catching him by surprise, knocking him out of the chair and onto the floor. The young man's glasses fly off. Once there, Denny quickly has him by the throat. Denny slaps him across the face, splitting his lip.

"How?" Denny screams at him.

The young man wipes his bloody lip, smearing blood across the back of his hand. His naked face is drained of color, taut with shock. "Shot himself," he said.

Denny releases him abruptly. "Goddamn," he says and gets up, walking away into the kitchen as if he were just taking advantage of a commercial break.

At first the young man does not move. Surreptitiously he wipes a tear from the corner of one eye, then he begins to grope for his glasses. He fumbles for a pocket-handkerchief to mop his mouth.

Denny comes back, carrying a bottle of vodka and two grimy juice glasses.

Pouring with one hand, holding the glasses in the other, he half fills each glass. He puts the bottle down on the TV and offers one glass to the young man, who has gotten to his feet and righted the chair.

"Here's to Paul," Denny says, and raises his glass.

The young man takes the glass and raises it, then knocks back a mouthful with alacrity. He winces at the sting of the alcohol in the split of his lip. Denny watches him, eyes bright, and Hollywood-white smile beaming.

"I always liked Paul," Denny said. "Even if he was queer."

The young man looks morosely into the empty glass. "He didn't like you," he said.

Denny shrugged. "Not his type," he said, and laughed. "Hit ya again?"

The young man accepted the refill. "Paul said you were the toughest one. He usta call you Killer."

Denny sucked at his glass of vodka. "Paul talked too much. All you queers do."

The young man put down his empty glass. "Look, I thought maybe it was worth something to you to know."

Denny nodded. "Made a special trip, didya?"

The young man put his hands in his jacket pockets. "I couldn't stay there. I didn't know who would be next."

Denny frowned. "I thought you said Paul shot himself."

The young man smiled. "He did. It took him a week to make up his mind."

Denny reached out and caught the young man's shirt and jerked him close. "Quit teasin' me, you cunt. What do you want?"

"To see your face, Killer," the young man said. "I want to know what you guys did that Paul couldn't stand living with. You don't have to tell me now. I can guess. At least you'll get yours, too."

Denny shook him and thrust him away. "You tell me, you whore. Why did Paul do it?"

"Because a week ago somebody blew Jackson

away right in front of Paul's bar. And somebody
called him every day for a week to say they were
going to get you all."

Suddenly Denny looked sick.

The young man laughed.

BAYARD ROHRER, the director, sucked his cigarillo and
stared at the moviola screen. "I like it," he said.

Over the director's shoulder, Pat nodded. "Blows me
away."

Bayard spun his stool to face his assistant director, Mickey Cahill. "What do you think?" he said around his cigarillo.

Mickey scratched under his chin. He was growing a beard in
imitation of the director's, except Bayard Rohrer's was the neat,
glossy Vandyke of a man vain both of face and mind, and Mickey's
crinkly reddish hair was too anarchic and untameable for that style.
Mickey's beard wanted to grow like a mountain man's or a biblical
prophet's and promised to look sparse no matter how wild and long
it might eventually be.

"We might have a problem with Gay Rights," he said.

Bayard snatched his cigarillo from his mouth and spun anxiously toward Pat.

"Look, all the homophobic stuff comes from our certified bad
guy, or his moll," Pat said. "I don't think it's a problem."

"Maybe we'll have a problem the other way. The fundamentalists will think we're promoting homosexuality," Bayard said. He
hopped off the stool. He was very short, about five-foot-three, with
very white, arsenical skin and lustrous black hair. Someone had told
him that swimming lengthened the muscles and stretched the spine,
so he swam faithfully each day, but did so secretively, because he was
embarrassed by the almost total hairlessness of his body. When on
location and forced to use a motel pool or a local Y, he wore one of
his collection of silk kimonos right to poolside and donned it again as
soon as he had swum his mile, to minimize his exposure while maxi-
mizing his display. Bayard spent phenomenal sums of money on
tailor-made clothing that in their very perfection of proportion only

emphasized his smallness. And like many small men, his head was quite large, so he looked dwarfish when he wasn't.

Pat laughed. "Fundamentalists love war movies, Bayard. I don't think they're going to read Denny's homophobia or his sleazy girlfriend as evidence of character defects, if they notice them at all, which I think is the likeliest scenario."

Bayard laughed. Scenario was one of his favorite words. Delicately, he removed the cigarillo from between his thin lips and admired it. There was a sign on the door of the editing room that clearly said NO SMOKING. It was obeyed by everyone but the director.

Pat itched for a cigarette himself. He wondered if the smoke from Bayard's little cigars was damaging the film, which naturally led to speculation about what would happen if Bayard accidentally ignited something with one of his butts, how many seconds it would take before the room, walled with shelves lined with film canisters, and hung with pieces of film like flystrips, was an inferno. Fortunately, Bayard was moving toward the door.

"I want some coffee," he said.

Mickey Cahill jumped to open the door for the director. "What about Dian's top?" he asked. "She's really falling out of it."

Bayard laughed again. "She did, once. You missed it, Mickey; you were with the second unit."

"Some set of garbonzas, huh?" Mickey asked. "Are they real?"

The director leered. "Ask Pat."

Pat, bringing up the rear, wanted to duck. He settled for a noncommittal shrug.

Mickey dropped back a step to interrogate him. "Come on, man, let's have it."

"She dropped 'em on me a couple of times," Pat said. He was blushing, and the knowledge he was blushing made him blush even more. "Fell into me, you know. That's all, honest."

Mickey chortled. "All right! So are they real or not?"

Pat shrugged. "No. I don't think so."

Mickey pressed him. "What did they feel like?"

They arrived at the staff room. Pat skipped ahead to open the door for Bayard, who grinned at him wolfishly in passing. He was enjoying Pat's discomfort, as well as the opportunity to tease Mickey.

The director picked out a comfortable chair while Mickey fetched the coffeepot and cups. Pat slumped onto the institutionally fucked-out sofa, a blue-green horror that must have been acquired at a discount furniture store close-out around about the time of the Korean police action. Mickey perched next to him, still breathing hard on the track of the evidence.

"Well?"

Pat reached for his coffee but stopped just short of touching it. Maybe it wasn't a good idea this late at night. "I don't remember," he said.

Mickey howled. "You had 'em in your hands, and you don't remember?"

"You want to know so bad, why don't you find out for yourself?" Pat snapped back.

The wind went out of Mickey. "I've tried," he admitted. "How come she's hot for you? They're always hot for married guys."

Bayard tasted his coffee and smiled omnisciently. "Mickey, *that's* why."

Mickey got up and slunk off to the bathroom, lost in the conundrum of women who only wanted what they couldn't have, and Pat who didn't want what Mickey couldn't have.

The director took a vial of coke and a polished slice of stone from his breast pocket. He spilled a little powder onto the stone, took out a minuscule gold razor, and cut the coke into lines. He produced a tiny gold straw and offered it to Pat.

Pat hesitated, then shook his head no.

Bayard raised one eyebrow, and shrugged. "More for me," he said gleefully, and vacuumed the stone clean through the straw. Afterward, he sat back with an air of postcoital satisfaction. "I admire your discretion," he said, "in the matter of Dian's extravagant tits."

"There's nothing to be discreet about," Pat said. "But thanks."

Bayard's eyebrows rose and fell in a gesture of have-it-your-way.

"I thought she was rather obvious," he said.

Pat shrugged. "She's a nice girl. I like her. I won't say it wasn't attractive. But once she got the message, we got along fine. Better than we would have if I'd taken her up on it."

"You were heroic," the director said. "Jesus God, Pat, are you the last faithful husband in America?"

Pat laughed. "I don't cheat, no, but I'm sure I'm not alone." Sometimes he felt like he was. It was always oddly embarrassing to admit to monogamy. There was always the temptation to make a joke of it, and if he did, he felt shitty about doing it. Unfaithful in spirit. But if he said it straight, he felt like a Boy Scout. When had fidelity become embarrassing? And why?

"I must confess," Bayard said, examining a fresh cigarillo, "I have a hard time imagining what it would be like to have sex with the same woman for so many years, and with no one else." He laughed, seemingly a little embarrassed himself.

Suddenly conscious how tired and headachy he was, Pat said, "Sometimes monogamy is like a pair of cement boots," and at once regretted it.

Bayard roared with delight.

Pat shrugged. "We have our dull times, and I think we're done up, and then all of a sudden it gets glorious again. It's like interest accruing, or something."

Bayard, for once, seemed taken aback. "Really?"

Mickey Cahill shuffled out of the bathroom. He nursed the end of his nose with a large, dirty cotton handkerchief. His eyes were watering. The consolation he had indulged in the bathroom was not of the same high quality as the director's.

Pat was relieved not to have had to turn down Mickey's shitty coke, too. Mickey was more likely to feel personally rejected, but it surely wouldn't have been worth it.

"Oh man," Mickey groaned.

The director shrugged at Pat. "You can't give a man advice he won't take."

It was raining hard outside. Between the door to the studio and his rented Audi, Pat was soaked to the skin. He sat there shivering for a minute, waiting for the defroster to clear the windows. The effort it took just to shiver made him realize he was desperately hungry. It was eleven, nearly everything would be closed. Except McDonald's. If he had to eat another McDonald's hamburger, he would puke. But he had to eat something, so he headed there.

It was just like the night he had gone home to see his mother, after the March on Washington. He had hitchhiked from the interstate exit to her small isolated home in Winthrop in a cold hard rain. Ellen Russell worked as a night nurse, eleven to seven shift, but he had managed to get home before she left for work.

She had opened the door in response to his banging, and her face lit up like Christmas at the sight of him. "Look who's here," she had said, and chuckled, way down in her throat, the way she did, all hoarse from her three-pack-a-day habit. "Kill the fatted calf," she had said.

"Ma," he had said, and dropped his sopping backpack in the shed and hugged her.

She was tall as he, though hardship had worn her thin and gray; she hugged him back hard enough to hurt.

"Well, get in outta the rain," she had scolded. "I heard a car, and saw the lights in the driveway, I thought it was someone lost, turning themselves around."

"Deke Utterback picked me up in Augusta," Pat had said. "Told me I needed a shave and a haircut," and she had laughed. Actually, what the selectman, whose boys had been Pat's buddies in grade school, had said, was "Why do you want to cultivate on your face what grows wild on your ass, boy?"

"Have you eaten?" she wanted to know first off, and while he changed into dry clothes, worn shiny trousers that were too short in the leg and balky in the zipper, a shabby iridescent shirt that had once seemed daring and suave and now looked gauche to him, two pairs of holey mismatched socks for his poor tired blue-to-the-bone feet, she made him a supper of canned stew and toast and cocoa, and stuffed his wet boots with newspaper to dry on the furnace grate in the hall.

He wolfed the food while she chatted about the neighbors and her job and smoked and drank coffee.

Then Ellen asked him, "What brings you, Pat, on a night like this?"

"I was coming back from the demonstration in Washington," he said. "It's been a long time. Just thought I'd like to see you."

She had snorted and laughed. "Well, good," she said. "I guess I ought to be touched, you tramping through this nasty rain."

He shrugged.

"You thumb the whole way?"

"Had a ride with a friend."

"Couldn't bring you right to the door, huh?"

She had a sixth sense about what he didn't want to discuss with her. "My friend was a girl. We had a fight, okay?"

His mother rolled her cigarette between her fingers and her mouth twitched. "She put you out on the highway. In this rain. Musta been quite a fight."

"She wanted to bring me here. I wouldn't let her," Pat said.

What went unspoken between them, because it didn't need to be said, was the core of their family history: Ellen Russell had put his alcoholic father out, pushed him out of the pickup truck in the middle of downtown Lewiston late one night, after bailing him out of jail yet again. Pat had been seven then, and while in time he came to appreciate the peace that descended once the family was sundered, once his father disappeared into the no-man's-land that is the true country of the winos, he still felt, though he knew otherwise, that she was responsible for his fatherlessness.

"Ah." Ellen Russell let him eat a while, but she was not finished. "Why not?"

"Why not what?" Pat responded, deliberately obtuse.

"Why couldn't she bring you here?"

He wiped his mouth with a paper napkin and grinned. "Ma, you got it backward. *I* couldn't bring *her* here."

But, of course, that didn't end it; it only made Ellen want to know more.

"Why?"

He sat back. "Ma, this is what set us off the last time I was here."

Ellen shook out a fresh butt and lit it. "You mean, your Private Life."

"Yeah, ma," Pat said. "That's right."

Ellen sat back and blew smoke out her nostrils. Pat coughed and waved it away. She tossed him the pack and waited for him to light up in self-defense.

"I've been thinking about it," she said. "I've had time enough."

Pat waited. He was supposed to be feeling guilty about not having been home in seven months, and he was. He was also getting pissed at being jerked around.

"All right," she said. "Hot shot. You're right. I'm not ever going to let you shack up under my roof."

Pat raised his hands in surrender. "Up to you, ma."

Her flat, white-uniformed bosom rose and fell in a great sigh. "I don't understand you kids, the way you act like trash. But," she said, and leaned across the table toward him, "you *are* a grown man."

"Right on," Pat muttered.

"Just," she said. "Mister. Just."

"Ma," he said.

She held up her hand. "I hate the thought of my son using girls like whores."

"I'll leave that up to you, ma," Pat said. "That's what you're doing when you tell me there'll be no fornicatin' under your roof. You're callin' my girlfriend a whore."

"No," she said. "You're wrong about that. My house is my house. I make the rules here. What I'm saying is, I can't stop you screwing around. Just you doing it here. What I am asking you is, be responsible about it. It takes two to make a whore, Pat."

She had taken him by surprise. At the time, he had thought she had dragged the conflict off into irrelevancy. But what she'd said kept popping up at odd times in his life, forcing him to meditate on the whole thorny business of responsibility, and what the hell she had meant exactly by the word *whore.*

So more than a decade later and a continent away, he sat in a rented car in pouring rain thinking of his mother, who was dead because of a drunk driver. Who might have been his father, had not his father died of pneumonia in an alkie ward in Bangor a few days before her. He ate as much of the Big Mac as he could before it turned utterly tasteless and began to choke him. Then he headed for his hotel room, to call Liv.

It was three hours earlier there. Travis had gone to bed, but Sarah was still up. She had been waiting for him to call: that afternoon, she had made the winning basket for her team. As he listened to her bubbling over, he felt as he had when she took her first steps.

At last she careened to a breathless stop, and said, "Well, you're not saying anything. Don't you care?"

He laughed. "You didn't give me the chance, kitten. I'm just stunned with the glory of you, that's all."

She giggled and gave up the phone to Liv.

"It's raining hard here," he told her. "I got soaked."

"Oh, Pat."

"Hey," he said. "I flashed on that time we were coming back from Washington and we had the fight and you put me out on the interstate."

She said, "You went to see your mother."

"Yeah." Pat fidgeted, hauled the blankets up to his chin. "I had a kind of fight with her that night."

"About girls," Liv said. "You told me. She wouldn't let you bring me home."

"Not exactly. She didn't want me sleeping with you in her house."

"Different generation. She did the best she could. She was more accepting than my mother was," Liv said. That's what she had said then, too.

Marguerite had refused to meet him at all until after they were married, had even stopped talking to Liv for several months. It was Doe who had quietly slipped them money without being asked, and who came around to see Sarah.

It was weeks after that visit to his mother before Liv told Pat she was pregnant. Only then, counting back, had he realized she had known or suspected, had been in the grip of her own panic and confusion, and that the fight, ostensibly over an old girlfriend's attentions, had happened because she didn't want him to feel bound to her. Sarah became a test: He had to choose Liv because he wanted her, not because he had impregnated her and had some kind of duty toward her and the baby.

Somehow, Ellen found out. He'd always suspected the fine and steely hand of Marguerite Dauphine in that. She waited a while for him to tell her, and then took matters in her own hands and turned up at their door, to claim her granddaughter and have a look at Liv. She went away carrying a piece of the soap that Liv used to bathe Sarah, to remember the way the baby smelled, satisfied that Liv was a good mother, though frankly puzzled at her refusal to do what Pat was willing to do, which was to make it all legal and proper.

The wedding had been in Ellen's house, and without Marguerite.

Ellen took Pat aside. There had been no shortage of cheap wine, and she was not entirely sober.

"I confess," she said, leaning on him rather heavily. "I thought it was funnier than hell."

"What was that, ma?" he asked, putting an arm around her waist to steady her, and because he was tight, too, and if they couldn't be affectionate on his wedding day, with a skinful, when could they?

"That girl of yours," she said. "Making you eat the cake you baked."

"Whoa," he said. "One of us is drunker than I thought."

She poked him playfully. "You got already to do the right thing and she wouldn't have you," Ellen said, and snickered.

It took him a minute to work it out, but once he got the joke, he laughed, too, and every time they looked at each other for the duration of the party, they were reduced again to red-faced giggles.

"I miss her," Pat said.

"I do, too," Liv said.

"I miss you," he said.

"When are you coming home?" she asked.

"Day after tomorrow," he promised. "Break for the weekend. It's looking good."

"I'm glad to hear it. It would be great to be looking at you."

"You will be," he said. "It won't be long, now. Halloween, maybe."

Of course, he was wrong, but there was no way of telling that then.

"So tell me what you saw today," Liv said.

With her father as her silent partner, Liv had acquired the building, which had been a multibay garage, when the oil embargo had forced its independent owner into early retirement. She had the gas tanks out front removed and replaced them with her own hand-made sign, which served in season as a freeform plant box. Inside, the hydraulic lift had been taken out, and the pit enlarged into a proper cellar. The interior had been gutted and rebuilt into the pottery proper, with two large kilns, one of which was adaptable to wood in case of fuel shortage, or for purposes of special firing that could only be done properly with wood; a shipping and storage department, and a tiled shower and locker room, for the work was grubby. She employed two proficient and experienced women, and a recently hired male apprentice, as well as herself and her sister Jane. Liv shared office space, which was a narrow mezzanine overlooking the main floor, with Jane. At the end of the day, the place was noisy, because of the blowers which recycled the excess heat generated by the kilns and kept the air clean. They all wore Walkmen clipped to their pockets and earphones so they could listen to music if they wanted, or just to block out distracting noise.

Liv, her earphones around her neck like a punk choker, left her apprentice, Misha, wedging porcelain clay, and trotted up the iron stairs to the office.

Jane glanced up from the tiny patch of open floor space when Liv opened the door. Squatting by a large cardboard shipping carton, she spread her hands over it, and groaned theatrically.

"I told them to wrap the damaged pieces separately!" she said.

Liv stooped over the carton to see for herself. "Shit," she said, "there's at least five pieces in there." She flicked the top of the carton. "It's not even our carton. What do they think we go to the expense of our own cartons for?"

"They didn't send the tearsheet from the invoice either," Jane said.

"Wonderful." Liv poked among the shards in the box. "I think there's two large bowls and three dinner plates in this mess."

"Yeah," said Jane, picking up a clipboard and making notes on it. "Me, too."

Liv straightened up and stretched. She glanced at the clock. "Hallelujah, it's quitting time."

Jane jumped up. "I'll say goodnight to the crew." She slipped out.

Two desks had been crammed into the narrow office, and every available wall space covered with shelving or cupboards. The room was piled with boxes, every surface cluttered and heaped with paper, files, color chips, manufacturers' samples of earths, glazes, the myriad tools and substances that went into making pottery. Liv took a bottle of wine from a cupboard and two plastic coffee cup holders from a drawer. She dropped clean plastic cones into the holders and opened the wine. She was pouring it as Jane's steps could be heard clanging on the iron stairs.

"I locked up," Jane said.

Liv handed her a cup of wine. She pushed a book off her desk chair and sat down in it.

Jane sank cross-legged to the floor and sighed happily.

Liv raised her cup. Jane did the same.

"Another day," Liv said.

"Ayuh," Jane drawled.

Liv threw back her head and laughed.

Jane was the eldest of Marguerite's and Doe's children, six years Liv's senior. Jane's hair had grayed prematurely, and she refused to dye it, wearing it in a Gibson girlish upsweep. Her fragile porcelain-clear skin was delicately furrowed from the outside edges of her nostrils to the corners of her mouth and across her brow. Old-fashioned wire-rimmed glasses obscured her dark eyes. She favored huge flamboyant earrings, low-cut peasant blouses that exposed her rather bony freckled décolletage, and tight blue jeans. It was a look declaring an unconventional, possibly artistic soul that caused people to mistake her for the potter. She liked that, for in the years of her first marriage, she had been the image of a banker's wife, wearing silk blouses with ruffled fronts and discreet pearl earrings. Since her husband had left her seven years previous, she had come to identify the face she had worn then as the same species of fake as her ex-husband's. It was only in the wake of the divorce that she had discovered her own talents and ambitions as a businesswoman, the equal of Marguerite's.

Jane snagged her handbag, an enormous handquilted fringed carryall, from under her desk and pawed at it. She produced an enameled tin box and, from that, a joint, which she offered silently to Liv.

Liv shook her head, as always.

Jane winked and lit up. Sitting loosely cross-legged, she closed her eyes and toked deeply.

"Oh, wow," she said in a dry, gravelly voice, and opened her eyes wide in mock ecstasy. Both sisters laughed.

"So," she said, "how's your tooth-that-isn't-there?"

"Happy in fairyland, I guess," Liv said. "I'm okay."

Jane shook her head in desperation, and tried the joint again.

"That's what you kept telling me all summer, when I called," she said. "I don't know what you were proving. But I'm not going to believe you anymore when you tell me you're okay. It's like the boy who cried wolf."

"No," Liv said, "the boy who *didn't* cry wolf."

Jane giggled. "The *girl* who didn't."

"Hmmm," Liv agreed and sloshed her little cup of wine idly.

"When's Pat home again?" Jane asked.

"Weekend. I talked to him last night."

"And when is it finished? The movie." Jane finished her wine and tossed the cup at the wastebasket. "Two points," she said, as it dropped neatly into it.

"Halloween."

"That's a long time," Jane said.

"Ayuh," Liv agreed.

Jane took another toke. "Think you can stand it?"

"Guess I have to," Liv said.

Jane snickered. She pinched the coal of the joint, to kill it, and replaced it in the tin box.

"To quote Marguerite," Jane said. " 'You made your bed, so you have to lie in it.' "

Liv scooched over to the plastic-lined wastebasket to place her cup, all but untasted, carefully into it. "Only some people make the bed," she said, "and some people just lie, right?"

"Right," said Jane. "Here speaks the voice of experience, slightly stoned."

"You want me to drive you home?" Liv asked.

Jane shook her head. *"I'm okay."* Jane gathered up her handbag and dropped the tin box into its depths. "Are you?"

Liv smiled. "Yes. So stop fussing."

Jane got up and patted Liv's cheek. "You don't take care of yourself, baby sister. Your husband's never home. Someone has to look out for you."

Liv leaned on the desk and stretched her legs in front of her. She examined the toes of her sneakers, which were splitting.

"Look," said Jane, "if it was me, I'd leave him. What difference will it make? You're not together. But," she raised her hands to show her palms, "what do I know? I've got my prejudices. All I know is a woman has to look out for herself, baby."

"We talked a long time last night," Liv said, "we talk a lot. We're going to be fine. All we need is time."

Jane smiled and hugged her. "Just remember I'm around if you need me, don't tell me you're okay when you're not."

Liv nodded.

Jane picked up her sweater and headed for the door. She stopped to look back at Liv, and winked.

Liv listened to her footsteps rattling down the iron stairway. She found her own bag and turned off the lights. Only a few tokes, a few ounces of wine, she should be okay. College for Jane had been a sorority; a cardigan worn backward with a string of pearls; a bouffant hairdo; being pinned to good old rotten Curt, who had eventually left her with four kids; and the gradual realization that what being a good girl had earned her was undeserved and very early termination, while everyone else was out there having fun, including Curt. The man Jane had lived with for three years was a mellowed-out ex-cowboy, who transparently didn't give a shit about conventions and legalities of any kind. Unlike Curt the banker, who paid lip service to such things, but who did what he could get away with, Web was straight in his dealings with Jane. He loved her and was faithful to her, and with his example, he set her free. It was Web's homegrown she carried in her handbag, and indulged in as if it were a Happy Hour martini. She and Web observed Liv's strictures against the illegal weed in Liv's home, and that was as far as Liv cared to impose her own concerns on Jane.

Her own concerns, it came to her, were immediate. The market, home to the kids.

CHAPTER 6

T HAT'S ENOUGH. End it," Liv shouted over the sound of
the bickering.

Silence was observed for a couple of seconds before they
both burst out in simultaneous complaint against the other.

"She changed the channel!" Travis said.

"He's watched that tape a hundred times!" Sarah countered.

Liv put the bag of groceries down in a chair and switched off the
TV.

"I have not," Travis said.

"You have too," said Sarah.

"Stop it," Liv said. "Sarah, there's a television upstairs. Go
watch that. Travis was running his tape before you came in. He's
entitled to finish it. You want to watch MTV, right?"

"The color's better on this one," Sarah said.

"The other one doesn't have a tape player on it," Liv said. "If
you watch MTV on this one, then Travis gets zero. You can watch
upstairs, he can't."

"It's not fair," Sarah said. "You always take his side."

"That's not true and you know it. And aside from that, life's not
fair. You'd better get used to it, kid."

Sarah picked up the books she had strewn over the couch. She
could have carried them on her lower lip. She took a vicious swipe at
the top of Travis' head as she stomped out, but he ducked routinely.

He did not react at all. "Would you start my tape again, Liv?"
he asked.

"Come here," she said.

He climbed off the couch and stood next to her.

"This is Play," she said.

He nodded.

"Push it," she said.

He placed one fingertip on the button and pushed down on it.

"Just remember it's the one with the green stripe."

He trudged back to the couch.

"Stop has the red stripe on it."

He nodded.

This was not the first time she had tried to teach him these simple operations. She knew he was going to ask her to do it, just the same, when he wanted it off. He didn't seem to want to master the controls, simple as they were, the way he didn't seem to want to learn to read, though he knew his alphabet backward and forward. He wanted her to go on running the tape machine for him, and reading to him. It was a way to cling to her, and she didn't know what to do but be patient.

There was a list of phone messages and a note pinned to the refrigerator. Liv scanned the messages, found Pat had called about the time she was standing in line at the supermarket, but when she rang him back, there was no answer. She dropped the receiver back into its cradle with an impatient thunk: They kept missing each other. There was a note from Mrs. Fuller, her housekeeper, saying she would have to go as soon as Sarah was home to look after Travis, to have her gum treatment. Which was where Liv had come in.

Liv drew a glass of cold water and drank it down, hoping it would open up her throat. She rolled her head and tried to relax her shoulders. There was still too much to do today to give in to the tiredness she felt. Her hands, wrists, arms, and back ached with unaccustomed use—about what was to be expected for a week or two, after months of idleness. The mental tiredness, though, was just coming home to a pair of screaming kids. She had to shake that off.

Her parents were due for dinner. If she started it now, she might be able to have a brief soak in the tub before they came in.

Forty-five minutes later the scalloped potatoes were in the oven, and the Caesar salad only wanted dressing. The fish—mako shark steaks she had lucked upon at the market—she meant to sauté at the last minute, and then douse in light cream. There were two bottles of

California wine chilling in the fridge. She was just taking off her apron when she heard the Cadillac in the driveway.

"Shit," she muttered. "There goes my bath."

Another thing she should have expected. Marguerite and Doe had spent the summer in Canada and hadn't seen the kids since June.

Travis shot off the couch and opened the door for Marguerite, who came in bearing a pie-shape wrapped in aluminum foil.

"Darling," Marguerite said and scooched down to kiss Travis.

Travis submitted, and then shot around her, asking, "Where's papa?"

Marguerite Dauphine straightened up with an expression of heroic resignation on her face. Liv's children always managed to remind her that being a grandmother was as unglamorous and thankless a task as being a mother. Doe drew Travis like a magnet, as once he had drawn Liv herself. Watching Travis hustle his short legs out the door after Doe, she could certainly see the resemblance between grandfather and grandson, and of course like called to like, but she couldn't help feeling like a rock in white water, something to go around. Between Travis' blissful ignorance of her and Sarah's barely restrained insolence, she felt quite battered, when she allowed herself the luxury of useless railing against reality.

Liv, looking tired and strained, met her in the hallway between the living room and the kitchen. There was a new touch of gray in her hair that had not been there last June, making Liv look older than her years. Somehow Marguerite would have to manage a gentle hint that it was time for a little discreet coloring. It was bad enough Jane was as gray as a rat and insisted on staying that way.

"Mom," she said, and kissed Marguerite on the cheek.

Marguerite kissed her back, and gave her the pie. "Doe made it," she said.

"Thanks." Liv resolutely stopped herself asking where he was. Her mother would only take it as another proof that Doe was more beloved. She thought she knew, anyway. No doubt he had headed directly for the garden to see how her roses were faring.

"Doe's in the garden," her mother confirmed. "I think Travis followed him."

"Oh. Well, would you like a glass of wine?"

"God, yes."

She looked around the kitchen while Liv poured her a glass of Chablis, and asked where Sarah was.

Clearly she wasn't here, where she belonged, greeting her grandmother. It was obvious that if Liv had answered "in jail," or "a Sarah Crittendon Home for Unwed Mothers," or "a drug rehabilitation center," Marguerite would merely grunt with satisfied expectation.

"Upstairs," Liv answered.

Marguerite took the glass and sipped it. "Mmmm, that tastes good," she said. "In a snit?"

Liv poured herself a glass. "She usually is, isn't she?"

"It's her age," Marguerite offered. It was as much consolation as she thought Liv had coming.

Liv sat down on a stool. "I know. How did the summer go?"

"Fine." Marguerite looked Liv up and down. "You've lost some weight," she said.

"Yes."

"You needed to."

"Yes. I can't take any credit for it, though. It was the trouble I had with my teeth."

Marguerite nodded. "All taken care of now?"

"Yes."

"How's Pat?" Marguerite's voice was neutral.

"I talked to him this morning. He seems fine. They expect to wrap by Halloween."

Marguerite sipped her wine. "You ought to have gone with him."

Liv shrugged. "I've a business to run. And I wanted my summer on the lake. It's my time for original work."

"Well, it's none of my business, I'm sure," said Marguerite, who was good at having her say while disclaiming any right to it.

Liv looked out the window over the sink into the garden. Her father and Travis were examining the rosebushes together. Papa Bear and Baby Bear. They were physically dense people, with enormous strength that they carried diffidently, as if they feared accidentally damaging other people.

Doe had a way with green things, notably with roses. A pharmacist by trade who had made a modest fortune with a chain of drugstores called Medicine Man, he had retired to pursue his hobby. The trip to Canada had been a tour of Canadian rose gardens.

The first of the chain had been an old-fashioned drugstore and ice cream parlor, Pinkham's, then. When he acquired it from Wilfred Pinkham, Jr. after World War Two, he had been an energetic young fellow with a driving, ambitious, and fertile wife. The business had grown with their family. He couldn't have kept her at home if he had wanted. People got used to Marguerite's perennially big belly, and the baby on her hip, or in a crib in the office, the knee-babies clinging to her skirt. After her mother, Nana Martin, retired from nursing, she came to live with them, freeing Marguerite from most of the housework and childcare. Doe never doubted it was Marguerite who made them wealthy.

It amused him still to hear the name of his store, his own whimsical revenge on an officious physician, ticked off at Doe for some imagined encroachment on his prerogatives, who began to refer to Doe nastily as the Medicine Man. He was only half-Penobscot, born off reservation and thoroughly detribalized. But the face in the mirror was unadulterated cigarstore Indian, the spit of his distant cousin Louie Sockalexis, who for a brief shining time at the end of the last century wowed the country as a big league baseball player, the second greatest American Indian athlete, after Jim Thorpe. Louie had not been the first nonwhite big league baseball player, for once upon a time big league baseball had not been segregated, and then it was, until Jackie Robinson, but he had given pride to his people and had not been forgotten.

Doe liked to go into the main store occasionally to help out still, and it pleased him that people asked after him. His customers trusted Doe more than they did their own doctors. Indeed, he had saved lives on occasion by asking the right question: Did Dr. So-and-So know when he wrote this prescription, Mrs. Gout, that you were still taking X for your arthritis? Did you tell Dr. Blatty-blah, Mr. Coffinchoke, about that bout of pneumonia you had five years ago? And your mother was a diabetic, wasn't she, Miss Drymouth? Have you told the doctor? Are you sleeping, Mr. Bags? Have you told the doctor?

Has the doctor asked you, he often meant. Has the doctor told you?

It was not to be expected that Marguerite, who collected the bills, would be as popular with the customers as Doe, who often jollied her into letting someone's overdue account go on being overdue. Knowing how she would have gloried in such a popularity, how she envied it, he felt for her, and tried to make up for her disappointment. Now they had younger managers running the shops, and were both officially retired, but nothing much had really changed. When there was nothing to do in the greenhouse, Doe wandered into the old store that had been Pinkham's to make up prescriptions, and Marguerite still saw to it, as chairwoman of the board, that accounts were collected, the business run as tightly as ever, the name and goodwill not devalued by cheapjack practices.

All very satisfying, or it ought to be. Marguerite had achieved a comfortable, even elegant old age. It was not surprising she looked after herself with the same will she had brought to the acquiring of a fortune. She exerted her will even over Doe. It had taken Liv a very long time indeed to overcome the disgust she felt for a grown man who wore whatever his wife laid out in the morning. Now she understood it was something that was not important to Doe. And it made her mother happy as much as anything did, so he did it. In the end, Liv finally understood, he permitted exactly as much domination as suited him, so it wasn't really domination at all. Marguerite had gotten herself a husband who did what she said to do about all the things she thought were important; the dissatisfaction that had settled into closed-purse lines around her mouth stemmed in part from the suspicion he didn't give a shit about any of the details over which she hemorrhaged. Liv could see in her father's face that it saddened him not to be able to make her mother happy, but Marguerite could not change her nature, even to save herself unnecessary grief.

When she had married the big, quiet man with his totemic face, Marguerite must have thought she was marrying someone like herself, someone who understood the damage that uncontrolled emotion could do. What a shock it must have been to realize Doe was an enormous reservoir of emotion, like a trench in the deep sea, whose surface nothing seemed to disturb, yet who was, in fact, all roiling depth. The roses, the love he drew from people, were only the visible signs of his grace.

So deep were the roots of what he felt, that he seemed not to need to share those powerful feelings with other people. Or perhaps he sensed that like his physical bulk and strength, his emotional muscle might overwhelm other people—Marguerite for one, who had locked up her own heart to keep it safe and felt it weaken and atrophy until it was as fragile as she had always been afraid it was. *Take what you want, and pay for it,* Liv often thought, when she thought of her parents.

She looked over her shoulder to catch her mother, staring at her with her red-lipsticked mouth (why did old women wear such red lipstick?) uncharacteristically softened, and eyes full of worry. Marguerite blushed. Her rouge showed hectic against the natural pinking of her pale skin.

Liv felt suddenly unsteady, and must have looked it.

"Oushh," Marguerite said in alarm, and hurried to put her arms around her daughter.

"Oh, God," muttered Liv, blinking back tears. She wasn't about to cry in front of her mother.

Marguerite patted her back awkwardly. The two women looked at each other anxiously. Unable to think what to do or say next, Marguerite fell back on tried and true methods.

"Why don't you have a nice hot soak?" she murmured. "You'll feel ever so much better. What's left to do for dinner?"

Liv looked around helplessly. "The table. We're having fish."

Marguerite released her.

"Sarah and I will set the table," she said. "Shall I do the fish?"

"No, it won't take long."

"Send Sarah down, then," Marguerite ordered briskly, "and take your time. We'll take care of everything."

You will, oh yes you will, Liv thought and immediately felt ungrateful. Marguerite was doing what she could do. And that was what she wanted, wasn't it? A soothing bath, a few moments of quiet in which to compose herself.

She was almost drowsy when there was a discreet knock at her bathroom door.

"Just a minute," she said, and floundered out of the water, reaching for her terry cloth robe.

When she opened the door a crack, it was Doe, carrying a glass of wine like a child's tea cup in one great paw.

"Here you go, Livvie," he said, and winked at her.

"Thank you, daddy." The glass was cool in her bath-warmed hands.

He used to bring her a glass of wine when she was a teenager having menstrual cramps. She slid back into the tub. Perhaps Jane had been talking to them, to make them start babying her. She wondered if they were being kind because she had had an abscessed tooth, lost too much weight and too much sleep and showed it, or because her husband never seemed to be home anymore. The only one to talk to about it was Pat. The habit of turning to him brought her face to face with the blank wall of his absence.

Thanksgiving brought Pat home for a whole week.

The Friday after, Pat sat hunched over a cup of coffee, with all the mindless intensity of a caveman guarding a bone, at the kitchen table, scratched his beard stubble, and tried to come to. The holiday, with its surfeit of relatives and food, had left him feeling bloated, useless, and out of it.

Travis shuffled in and climbed into his chair. His hair was cowlicked to the point of punk. He looked sweaty, as if he had not had a very good night. He slumped in the chair as blankly as an old wino on a city curb.

Pat cleared his throat. "Long day's night?"

Travis rolled a bleary eye and fumbled in his kimono pockets for his army guys.

"Turkey hangover," Pat said.

Travis nodded solemnly.

"Yeah," said Pat. "Much as I hate to bring up the subject, how about breakfast?"

Travis groaned.

"My feeling exactly." Pat stared at his coffee cup.

Sarah bounced in, looked the two of them over, and snorted. She made for the coffee machine, poured herself a cup, and carried it to the table. Her braces had been removed during Pat's last absence. Every time she smiled he thought how spectacular her teeth looked, like a movie star's. She had taken to wearing her hair braided or ponytailed to one side. Her latest pair of earrings were a barbarous tangle of beads, feathers, and leather that she clearly saw as exotic and sophisticated. Marguerite had taken one look at them yesterday and snorted in disgust, which was probably the most satisfying reaction Sarah got to the earrings, outside of the squealings of her friends. Liv had managed to keep a straight face, and with her elbow in his ribs, so had he.

Pat watched her slop milk into the coffee and then stir in three teaspoons of sugar. He began to feel uneasy in his stomach.

Sarah tasted it and wrinkled her nose. "Jesus," she said, "who made this shit?"

"I did," Pat growled. "Watch your mouth, Miss Teen Queen."

Sarah gave him a snotty, "Oh, wow, sorry."

He considered bellowing at her and decided it would hurt him more than it would her. And it would take too much energy.

Pat and Travis stared at each other. Travis silently pointed a finger at Sarah, then at his right ear, and described a circle in the air.

"I saw that, twerp," Sarah said.

Travis stuck his tongue out.

Sarah sneered back.

"Oh, God," said Pat.

Sarah looked out the kitchen window. It was clear and cold outside. "What a great day," she said. "Let's go the Mall."

"It'll be hell out there," Pat said.

Sarah flung wide her arms in an extravagant pose. "It's hell here," she said.

Travis had entered battle around the redoubt of the sugar bowl. "Pttuiee," he sputtered. "Pow!"

Pat squinted at Sarah and scratched his beard.

She tried another tack. "Hey, twerp, you could go see Santa Claus."

Travis stopped in mid-attack. He looked at Pat. He studied the soldiers poised to kill and be killed. "Okay," he said.

Pat sighed and scratched behind one ear. "You really want to?"

Travis hunched over his men and peered at Pat. "I guess so."

"I really need to, daddy," Sarah said. "I'm way behind in my Christmas shopping."

"Well, that carries it," Pat said sarcastically, and then, to make up, "All right, all right. It'll be a madhouse, but you're nuts, so it's appropriate."

Sarah squealed. "Can Heidi come, too?"

"Ask your mother," Pat said, and pushed himself away from

the table. It hurt his head to stand up. Too much beer with Web and Doe and the rest of the tribe.

"When are we going?" Sarah asked. "If we go early, it won't be so bad."

On the day after Thanksgiving, Pat thought, three A.M. just might be early enough to avoid a crowd at the Mall. Oh, well, in for a penny, in for a pound. He groped his way toward the stairs. An hour in the shower, and if he didn't die, he could probably handle the Mall.

Liv met him on the stairs.

"Takin' Travis to see Santa Claus," he mumbled.

She looked fine, as if yesterday had never happened. Hair down and soft around her shoulders, a blushing sweater with shiny ribbons woven into it, like the magic words of a spell, loose trousers gathered at the ankles, in a silvery wool.

She brushed a flopping lock of hair out of his eyes, picked a mysterious thread from his chin. "Are you sure? It's going to be a madhouse."

It had been unwise to hesitate. Now he had to shift gears out of idle again, and it was all up, up, up another eight steps that felt as far away as Ste. Anne de Beaupre by knee.

"It's a madhouse here," he said.

"I'd better go with you," Liv said after him. "You're going to need me."

"Wouldn't consider doing it any other way," Pat said, and reached the top. By the time he had gotten into the shower, without either scalding himself with hot water or shocking himself into a heart attack with cold, he was so pleased with himself for agreeing to the madness of going to the Mall on the day after Thanksgiving, taking Travis to see Santa Claus, not yelling or swearing or in any way giving in to what he thought of as his weakened state, making it upstairs and into the bathroom, and choking down two extrastrength Excedrins, that all sensible impulses were entirely suppressed.

The line was at least forty-five minutes long when they joined it. Santa was a red blob inside a tiny gingerbread house about the size of a phone booth. The walls of the house were about as thick as cardboard and brown-flocked, so at a distance they were vaguely cake-like. Up close, they were merely tacky. Plastic candy canes framed the doorway, which had no door, and the three large windows, so that Santa was visible on all sides. The windows had candy-striped muntings, but no panes, as if vandals had smashed out all the glass. Plastic gumdrop lights the size of oranges blinked and burbled along the eaves of the frosted white roof. A photographer in a Tyrolean hat stood by to record the encounters of Santa Claus and children if not exactly for posterity, then for their grandparents.

Sarah took one look at it, exchanged superior and amused glances with her friend Heidi, who had come with them, and split. She was supposed to meet them in an hour and a half.

Pat squeezed Travis' hand, which was already damp.

"Hungry yet?" he asked.

"Yeah," Travis said.

"Why don't you bring Trav a hot dog, and see if you can find the new G.I. Joe comic?" Pat asked Liv.

"Sure," she said. "Hot dog and orange soda?"

Travis grinned nervously.

When she came back, the line had lengthened dishearteningly. Travis and Pat had made scant progress.

"Slow?" she asked.

Pat nodded.

There were Mall security people drifting around, cheerful but also watchful, on the lookout for pickpockets, the inevitable argument about line-jumping, the inevitable fainting.

While Travis ate his hot dog, Pat read him the comic book. Kids just ahead and just behind them listened in because it was a dramatic rendering. Pat liked to do the voices and the sound effects. The large elderly woman directly behind them also fell under his spell. She had three children with her, the oldest looking about Travis' age, the youngest just walking. They called her Nana. They all had runny noses, and the colorless skin of children who spend the entire winter in a daze of untreated ear infections, chest-rattling croup, and rampant colds. She was herself plump as a turkey, pink and scented with talcum powder. Her teeth were very white and even.

Liv fell to watching her, discreetly, for something to do. The woman at first ignored the story, then began to listen to it, and was rapidly caught up in it. At the end, her fists clenched with the triumph of the Joes against the enemy Cobras. The kids huddled around her, open-mouthed, wiping their running noses with the backs of their fists.

While the story went on, the line had moved. Santa was now only a few mendicants away. He was large and jolly as required, though to Liv his face was very young under the glossy curls of the white beard. His stomach in the red velveteen suit appeared to be genuine. The suit itself was at least not cheap, but it was a little theatrical, not the sort of thing to wear on a long cold and probably rough ride, and impossible for the shimmy up and down chimneys. The dry cleaning bills would be horrendous.

Pat leaned close to Liv and whispered, "Remember last year at that mall in Lewiston? The Santa Claus that was molesting the kids? I hope they checked this guy out."

She looked quickly at Travis. He was pale and nervous, too distracted to have heard. She put her fingers to lips to shush Pat.

The woman behind them, having eavesdropped on the story, was still all ears. Her eyes narrowed, and she stared suspiciously at Santa Claus.

It was Travis' turn. He rooted himself for a second, then Liv nudged him forward. Staring back at her anxiously, he moved like a zombie up the path and through the doorway.

"Who's this?" boomed Santa Claus, and reached down to lift him up.

Travis' eyes sought Liv and Pat, and then fearfully, looked up at Santa.

"What's your name, honey?" Santa asked.

Travis' chin sank onto his chest and he muttered into his jacket zipper.

"What?" asked Santa, cocking his ear.

"Travis," whispered Travis.

Santa frowned. "Travis?"

Travis shook his head in quick confirmation.

"Well, Travis," Santa said, "have you been a good boy?"

Again Travis nodded.

"Ho Ho Ho," boomed Santa. "Ho Ho Ho."

Travis' twitching hands went to his stomach.

"Well, Travis," Santa asked, "what do you want for Christmas?"

Travis swallowed hard. "Wil' Bill," he muttered.

Santa looked puzzled.

"G.I. Joes," Travis said. "Wil' Bill's a new guy."

"Oh," said Santa. "Sure. I've heard of G.I. Joes. Anything else?"

Santa reached into the box of candy canes at his side.

"Ah," said Travis, and vomited explosively over Santa's beard and lap. The vomitus was bright orange and contained identifiable bits of hot dog.

"Jesus Christ!" Santa Claus screamed, jumping up and dumping Travis onto the floor. "He puked on me, the little fucker puked all over me!"

Behind them, there was a sharp click of glass teeth from the elderly woman, a horrified intake of breath. Pat's reaction time was better than Liv's: He reached Travis first. Travis screamed and bawled in equal volume with Santa Claus.

The Mall security force converged on Santa's house.

The grown-ups in the line hissed and glared at Santa, who was frantically scraping vomit off his suit and picking it out of his beard. His bellowing faded to muttered oaths and whimpers. The children giggled and covered their mouths and clung to their parents and grandparents.

Travis, sobbing more with humiliation and fright than any pain, for in fact his stomachache was nicely cured, buried his head in his father's chest. "Are you all right, honey?" Liv asked, her hands on Pat's arm, around Travis.

"He needs air," Pat said, and began to push their way out of the crowd. A small woman in the uniform of the Mall security force worked her way to them.

"Is the kid okay?" she asked.

Pat nodded.

Outside, where they could hear themselves, Pat stopped and shifted Travis in his arms.

"You'd better go back and find Sarah," he said.

Liv patted Travis' head. "Okay," she said.

"We'll be in the car."

Sarah and Heidi were waiting near the Santa Claus house, clutching an assortment of small paper bags. A sign over the doorway said SANTA ON BREAK. Underneath the letters was a cardboard

clockface numbered for sixty minutes, with the hands set at ten minutes.

"What happened?" Sarah asked. "We heard some kid got sick."

"Travis did," Liv said shortly, and hustled them out to the car.

"Oh, gross," Sarah said several times.

Heidi did, too.

They both said it again getting into the station wagon. Pat had
taken the front passenger seat, still holding Travis. He was patiently
mopping the front of Travis' snowsuit with tissues. Travis glared red-
faced and red-eyed over his shoulder at the two girls.

Liv slipped behind the wheel.

"I'm so embarrassed," said Sarah. "God this car stinks. I think
I'm going to throw up."

Giggling, the two girls rolled down the window in the back.

Liv started the car.

"Sarah," she said, "shut up."

"I'll second that," Pat said.

There was injured silence in the backseat.

"I have indelible olfactory memories," Pat said, "of taking you
to visit my mother when you were eight months old. It was August.
We were a mile from ma's house, and your mother was saying what a
great traveler you were, when you were spectacularly carsick. That
car still stank of sour milk puke when we sold it in October. That's
why we sold it. Your mother's Saab that she'd had since she was
seventeen."

"Jeezus," Sarah said.

Pat looked around sharply and caught her eye. She flinched.

"I was just a baby," she muttered.

"Travis isn't quite old enough to vote yet," Liv said. "Maybe we
could allow him a little leeway."

"I wasn't done shopping either," Sarah said.

"You never are," Pat said.

That was something Sarah and Heidi could giggle over. They
fell to examining each other's purchases.

Pat felt a wash of cold air. Liv had surreptitiously opened her
own window a little.

She shot a hasty glance at Travis and seemed relieved. She
leaned forward over the wheel and blinked rapidly. She bit her lower

lip. Her chest heaved once or twice suspiciously. She peeked at Pat out of the corner of her eye, and he knew she was trying not to laugh.

"Gross," he mouthed at her.

And her mouth worked, but she fixed her eyes firmly on the road ahead. "Plug in a tape," she suggested.

So he rummaged in the glove box among the assorted tapes and found Travis' "Born to Add," a Sesame Street parody of Springsteen's "Born to Run."

"Oh God," Sarah said at the first sound of Bruce Stringbean's quavering nasal voice, but Travis cheered up immeasurably.

The stink *was* gross, and Pat had to open his window, too, and lean against the cold glass with his nose as close to the crack as he could get without being obvious, and his diaphragm tightened and his throat closed, and as soon as they were home, he rushed into the downstairs bathroom and vomited a sour, acidic aspirin-tasting vomit, until he shivered with the chills.

He stripped to his undershorts and crawled back into bed and fell asleep and when he woke up, late in the afternoon, Travis, in his undershorts, too, was snuggled up against him.

CHAPTER 7

MIDWEEK there was snow, and flurries on Christmas Eve. Doe and Marguerite held open house then, as always, and everyone was there to exchange presents, except Pat, who arrived from the West Coast in time to hang his stocking under the mantel and tuck Travis into bed.

Christmas was gray and bone-gnawing cold, and it was Pat and Liv's turn to receive the relatives. The parade—four sisters: Jane, the oldest at forty, Natalie, Josephine, and Emily; three brothers: Arthur, Noel, and Charles, the baby at twenty; their spouses or shack-ups; their get; and Marguerite's mother, Nana Martin, a rawboned country woman near ninety who had seemed for two decades to be fading away, like an old general or the Cheshire Cat, rather than failing, until she was mostly a creaking skeleton poorly clothed in a tissue of flesh—began at eight o'clock with Marguerite scolding Doe at the back door not to drop the cardboard carton of pies. Like visiting kings, they all brought something, some token part of the feast, until the refrigerator was crammed and there was no place to put anything down on the kitchen counters. The meal was necessarily buffet, the offspring of Liv's visiting sibs alone numbering fifteen, plus a couple of steps acquired in marital rearrangements.

As if everyone were rising consciously to the occasion, the holiday passed more quickly and more smoothly than it usually did. There was always a sister—usually Josephine, wise-cracking and grabbing a cigarette from an ashtray for a quick restoring puff with soapy fingers that wet the cigarette paper and made it transparent, because she was a nervy, fast-talking woman who had to be doing

something with her hands—at the kitchen sink, washing up and re-
loading the dishwasher, Marguerite making more coffee, a sister-in-
law collecting ashtrays and used and abandoned dishes, a brother
emptying the trash or opening the refrigerator to put in or take out
beer or ice. Sudden swells of male guffawing or outrage erupted from
in front of the televised football game. Women bent heads together
and whispered, sank wearily into kitchen chairs with yet another cup
of coffee, and told and retold family stories that often ended in gentle
explosions of lascivious giggling. The teenagers had Sarah's stereo
pumping on the second floor. A flock of toddlers twisted around
ankles and table legs chasing The Poor until Liv put the cat in the
cellar as a mercy. It was noisy, frequently raucous, overcrowded,
chaotic, stuffy with too many people's body heat and cigarette
smoke, and in the middle of it all, Nana Martin managed to fall
asleep in the rocking chair in the kitchen.

Taking the serving dishes from Pat in the kitchen, Liv suddenly
saw his mother in his face. A quiet misery, a tension shadowed in his
eyes and collapsed his upper lip like the roofline of a decaying barn.
She wished fiercely that Ellen Russell was still alive. It must be hard
on him to be immersed in her overwhelming family for the second
time since Thanksgiving and to be received with suspicion, unspoken
accusation, wariness.

The back door became a bottleneck as sisters and brothers collected their families to leave. There was more noise, more talk, a
ritual tithing of leftover food in tin foil and plastic wrap and Tupperware carried away. By four, she and Jane and Marguerite and
Nana Martin, refreshed from her nap, remained in the kitchen to
finish the washing up.

When she peeked into the living room, only Web still stared at
the tube with unseeing eyes, logey with drink and food and more
drink. Doe had fallen asleep on the couch. Pat and Travis had fallen
asleep together in the blue leather recliner. The lights of the Christmas tree in the corner blinked on and off like warning lights. Nana
Martin shuffled up behind her, took her by the elbow, and snorted a
dismissive old woman snort.

Liv returned to the kitchen to continue making cream of turkey
soup. After extracting the bones from the broth, she strained and
clarified it, then threw in the gravy; the mashed potatoes and the
pureed squash for thickening; the boiled, creamed onions; stewed

tomatoes; chunked turnip; and sautéed mushrooms. Leftover peas and carrots she held back until near serving time when she would also add the cream. About the only things that didn't go into the soup were the condiments—of which the cranberry jelly could have —the jello salad and the desserts: the apple, mince and lemon pies, coffee jello, and the Indian pudding and whipped cream—Doe's jokey little contribution. What was left of those had been dispensed to the exiting relatives, less small portions for the Russells. Even so, the refrigerator still seemed hopelessly crammed. By then, streetlights were on in the thickening twilight outside the kitchen window.

Marguerite and Jane and Nana Martin closed the family albums that had been spread out on the kitchen table and rousted Doe and Web from in front of the tube. There was an awkward, heavy silence when everyone was gone and the Russells occupied the living room together. The house felt suddenly small and stuffy and dusty, as if its walls were closing in on them. Liv bent over and flicked off the TV set.

"Let's go for a walk," she said.

The rush of harsh cold air shook them all out of their postbinge dullness. The sky was unstarred and unmooned. Dense, impenetrable snow cloud weakly reflected the lights of the city and the jetport lights that arced like the hands of a watch across it, hinting at the dimpled underside, the enormous empty blimp of air and crystallized water riding over them, like a huge soft roof, that implied a cozy fire and piny smells indoors, the very opposite of the humbling, open blackness of a clear winter night. Outside, they were all alone. Everyone else in the world was walled up inside the old houses lining the streets. The blue light of TVs shone in one or more windows of each house like some magic campfire. They passed down a tunnel of wide old trunks of century-old elms, most of them stricken and dying, a skeletal arch of branches overhead, through which the streetlights shone to make their shadows grotesque on the brick-paved sidewalks.

Liv wondered what different words they would each use to describe the mood the moment evoked. Sarah had a dreamy look on her face; she must be finding the night romantic. Travis was wide-eyed; he was not often out after dark so it was exotic, of course, and exciting, perhaps even a little frightening. Pat squeezed her hand; she sensed he was comforted by the tradition and continuity of family life the old Victorian structures housed, the blue-lit windows signaled, the holiday itself marked. She felt some of that herself. But she also felt the change in the air, the cold in the night, winter seizing hold, like an ice chip in the heart. And that none of this was really safe at all. There was no comfort, no continuity. Not even the seasons were reliable. Only the winter could be counted on, and that was always coming, even as it grudged spring, and summer stood still in green fields, it was always waiting to reclaim its hegemony.

The clean cold air was energy to Travis; hands in his pockets for warmth, he skipped and danced and sang tunelessly to himself a little ahead of them. Sarah, lagging behind Pat and Liv, jogged passed them, and caught up with Travis. His formless song ground down, and he looked up at her.

"Race you to the corner," she said.

Travis shot away from her at full speed. She only had to jog to catch up with him just before he reached the corner.

"Tie," she said.

"You didn't even try," Travis said.

Sarah shrugged.

He stumped away in the lead again. Just around the corner, he stopped and shook one foot, then scraped it over the pavement.

"Is this a game?" Liv asked, and Travis grinned at her over his shoulder.

"Follow the leader," Travis said.

He hopped forward, then backward.

Liv did the same, then locked her wrists behind her head like a prisoner and began to twist from side to side while hopping. Pat followed her, then Sarah, then Travis, watching them carefully, giggling, then imitating them with extravagant precision. Sarah made up her own bizarre goosestep, which they all followed down the block. Then Pat turned around and skipped backward, which is how they all arrived home, hilarious and out of breath.

The house was warm and welcoming now, just the right size again, home again.

"That was a very good idea," Liv told Travis as she helped him out of his jacket.

"What was?" Travis asked.

"Follow the leader," Liv said.

"Oh," he said. He sat down and unlaced his boots. "I had dog-shit on my boot, Liv."

Pat made a strangled noise. Liv met his eyes over Travis' bent head. Pat hooked her around the waist and dragged her into the kitchen. They laughed until they were teary. Then she felt him tight-ening with tension and the joy went out of her.

"I have to go back tomorrow."

She turned in his arms, twisting away from him, but he held her wrists tightly to stop her escape. "I'm sorry, babe. I have to."

She would not look at him. "How long this time?" She bit the words off as if she were tearing raw red meat.

"A week. No more."

That meant ten days.

"And after that?"

"I'm home free. I promise."

She kept her face turned away. "All right."

He let go of her hands and traced the line of her jaw with his knuckle. She turned her face reluctantly to him. His face was pale. Hangdog, whipped, guilty, desperate. *"Don't kick me anymore,"* it said. *"I won't snatch any more steaks off the table."*

"I want to show you something. Come on. I want the kids in on this." He was pleading.

She followed him stiff-necked into the living room, stopping at the bottom of the stairs to summon Travis and Sarah back from their bedrooms.

He had a new cassette.

She flopped onto the couch. "More movie," she guessed, expect-ing another segment, another one of the pieces of the movie he had been giving them like a jigsaw puzzle as it was cut.

"Nope," he said, and pushed Play and sat down next to her and put his arm around her without looking her straight in the eye. He was nearly trembling.

Sarah collapsed onto the floor. Travis climbed back into the blue recliner. He spilled little men out of his pockets and began to arrange them on the arms of the chair.

The cassette turned blankly on the spindles of the VCR and then they were looking at a striking woman in expensive West Coast mid-dle age. At once Liv felt like a drab.

The woman introduced herself. "I'm Vera Danzig," she said, in the professionally confidant way that separates ordinary unfilmmed and untelevised mortals from TV newscasters, "and I'd like to show you a Vera Danzig exclusive listing."

"Wow," said Sarah.

It was something to see. Vera Danzig led the camera through too many rooms to count or remember (except Liv counted and remembered them all) of a stunning contemporary house hung on a northern California coastal cliff. The tour went on for half an hour and included an inspection of a separate studio on the property. The tape came to an end without Vera Danzig ever mentioning a price, but Liv guessed what that house, had it ever been built, would cost on the East Coast. Double plus half again, she estimated, for California.

Pat jumped to punch the Rewind button. "What do you think?"

"I love it," Sarah said. "Are we going to buy it?"

Pat didn't answer. He flopped down next to Liv and dropped one arm around her shoulders. "Well?"

Liv examined her hands. Then she looked at him. "It's gorgeous. Surely it's too expensive."

"Not anymore," Pat said. "We've got a distribution deal from Warners. And Warners has offered me a separate contract to rewrite two other properties they're holding."

"That's great," Liv said, and meant it. "That's wonderful. I know that's what you wanted."

Pat squeezed her shoulders.

"Are you sure we have to be on the West Coast?" she asked.

Pat was sober, earnest. "It's absolutely time, babe. I need to be there. And I can't take another year split up like we've been. Can you?"

"No," she said. "But I don't want to live in California, Pat. I've got a business here. I can't run it long distance."

"You can relocate," Pat said. "Expand your market."

Liv shook her head. "You make it sound easy."

"I know it wouldn't be," he said, all reason. "But we can't go on like this, Liv."

"No," she said. "I know."

"Well, I want to move to California," Sarah said. She bounced to her feet. "You've got my vote, daddy."

"Thanks," said Pat.

"This isn't a voting matter," Liv said.

"It ought to be," Sarah said.

"We'll consider your opinion."

"I don't want to move," said Travis. "I want to stay right here."
He had been so quiet, they had all forgotten he was there.

"You'll like it there," Pat said. "Wait and see."

"Let me think about it," Liv said.

Pat shifted uneasily. "I can't keep these people hanging forever,
babe."

"The weekend," she said. "The world won't end over the weekend."

The phone on the end table rang. Liv stretched over and picked
it up. "Hello."

"Merry Loot Day," said Bayard Rohrer. "How are you, good-
looking? Guess we've got enough to celebrate, huh?"

"I'm fine," said Liv, automatically. "We do, don't we?"

"Do you like the house?" he asked. "The minute I saw it, I said
to Pat, it looks just like Liv. And that studio!"

"It's impressive," Liv agreed.

"You'll love it," Bayard promised. "Don't sweat the furniture.
Vera said she'd take you to the best places."

"That's kind of her," Liv said. "I'll have to see it first."

"Come back with Pat tomorrow. You could be moved in for
New Year's."

"That quick?" Liv said.

"The place is empty and they've got Pat's money," said Bayard.
"What's the problem?"

Her throat closed up.

She didn't answer Bayard. "Do you want to speak to Pat?" she
asked.

"Thanks, babe," Bayard said.

Liv handed the phone to Pat and left the room. She put the soup
back on and threw in the carrots and peas and cream.

Sarah came in and began to set the small table in the kitchen for
supper without being asked.

"I really like that place, mom," she said, putting out the soup
spoons. "It would be just fantastic to live in California. Do you think
I could have the bedroom with the octagonal window?"

"I don't know," Liv answered.

Pat came in and took the soup bowls out of Sarah's hands and began to finish laying the places.

"I was thinking you'd love that room, kid," he said. "The kids would love that place, Liv."

"I know I would," Sarah said.

"So you've told me," Liv said. "Several times now."

"Well, I should have a say."

"You mean," Liv said, "if you want it, it should happen."

Sarah crossed her arms and pouted. Liv bit her lip and reminded herself Sarah was still only thirteen, even if she looked seventeen.

"Why should we have to stay here just because you don't want to go?" Sarah demanded.

"That's enough, Sarah," Pat said.

Sarah slunk into a chair at the table and smoldered.

"Good question," Liv said, and stirred the soup.

Pat came up behind her and put his hands lightly around her waist. He seemed to need to keep touching her. Hoping she'd stick, she thought, like the Goose Girl.

"I wish you were more open to this, babe."

She turned around in his arms to face him. "It doesn't matter if I am or not, does it?"

He protested. "No, no, it matters everything."

"Bayard told me you've bought the house already," Liv said. "Are you sure it matters whether I want or don't want."

Pat paled. There was panic in his voice. "Listen, babe, I had to put something down, or lose it."

She twisted under the circle of his arms and leaned against the refrigerator. "But the weekend's too much time for me to take to make a decision, and Vera can't wait to help me buy furniture."

"That goddamn big mouth Bayard," Pat said.

"Really," Liv said. "You ought to speak to him about that. While you're at it, ask him not to call me babe, either."

Pat stared at her. His mouth twisted in wordless anger. He clenched his fists.

Sarah jumped up. Her chair clattered and fell over. She ignored it. "You just want to spoil everything," she said shrilly. Her face was blotched with red and her fists clenched white-knuckled. "You just want to spoil *everything.* Well, I don't care what you want. I want to go live in California with daddy."

"Fine," said Liv. "You can finish out the semester here and go live in California with daddy."

There was a stricken instant. Then Sarah gasped as what Liv was saying sank in, and she burst into tears.

Liv walked mechanically across the room and put her arms around Sarah. One hand smoothed Sarah's hair just as it had so often since her birth, soothing and comforting and caressing after childhood bumps and bruises and disasters. Then Liv drew a deep breath and let her go. Sobbing, Sarah collapsed into another chair and buried her head in her arms on the table.

Pat stood stunned at the stove. The smell of the cream of turkey soup suddenly overwhelmed him, and he thought he was going to be sick.

"Pat," Liv said from the bottom of the stairs, "I'm going to take Travis and go to Nodd's Ridge for a while."

He closed his eyes.

"I'm sure Marguerite and Doe will be happy to stay with Sarah," she went on. And then she stopped.

She met Travis, sitting at the bottom of the stairs, slumped over his soldiers wrapped in his old blanket. He wore a toy machine gun slung over his shoulder.

"I'm hungry," he said. "Is supper ready?"

Liv stooped over him and kissed the top of his head. "Get daddy to give you some soup. Then come knock on my door and kiss me goodnight, okay?"

Then she hurried up the stairs, not wanting to give him time to notice she was upset.

Travis watched her go. He went into the kitchen and climbed into his chair.

"Liv said for you to give me some soup, Pat," he said.

Pat blinked. "Oh," he said. "Sure." He turned around and stirred the wooden spoon through the soup. Then he realized the bowls were on the table.

Travis took little men out of his pockets and circled them around his empty bowl. He looked up at Sarah. She still had her head in her arms on the table. Her back heaved now and then with great sighing sobs.

Pat reached over Travis' right hand for the bowl.

"What's she sniveling about?" Travis asked.

Sarah's head snapped up. "I'm *not* sniveling," she hissed at Travis.

"Yes, you are," Travis said.

Sarah's fists crashed onto the table, rattling the dishes and cutlery. "Oooo, shut up, you little creep!" she shouted. Slamming her chair to one side, she stamped out of the room.

"Sarah," Pat said, after her. "Sarah!"

All the response he received was her pounding up the stairs to her room. He sighed and carried the bowl to the stove to fill it. Then he made himself a cup of instant coffee and sank into a chair at the table where he blew on the hot coffee and sipped at it while Travis blew and sipped at his soup.

"Why is everybody mad at each other?" Travis asked, between swallows.

"I guess we're all tired," Pat said.

"That's what Liv always says, too," Travis said. "I wish you didn't get tired so much. Maybe you should take a nap."

Travis knocked on her door, was kissed and tucked in. She knocked at Sarah's door, and asked her to turn off her music for the night or use the Walkman. Sarah responded by turning up the music. Liv tried the knob; it wouldn't give.

"Open the door, Sarah." She had to shout to be heard over the music.

Pat, coming up the stairs, heard. He turned on his heel, went to the cellar, and threw the circuit to Sarah's bedroom. The music died with a squeal. Sarah scrambled to unlock her door. Her face when she opened the door was wild with both anger and panic. She flew at Liv. Liv caught her by her wrists and pushed her back against the wall.

Then Pat was there again, breathless from pounding up and down two flights of stairs, and Sarah realized who had killed the power to her room.

"Sarah," he gasped, "you just lost the use of that stereo for the next month."

With that, he walked into her bedroom, and began to unplug and unhook the unit.

"You can't!" Sarah said.

"Yes, I can," he said. He wound wires around the components. "And if you lock us out again, I'll take the lock right off the door. From now on, when someone speaks to you, you open that door and answer."

Sarah threw herself onto her bed facedown.

"Goodnight," he said.

There was a pause. "Goodnight," Sarah said sulkily.

He carried the components to the hall closet. When he passed Sarah's room again, there was the sound of sobbing. Liv had disappeared into their bedroom. He knocked softly and let himself in to Sarah's room.

"Go away," Sarah said into her pillow. "Just go away."

"You don't get rid of me that easy," Pat said, and sat down on the edge of her bed.

She rolled over, holding one arm over her eyes.

"Baby," he said. "We need your help right now."

She sniffed.

"If you really want to live in that house in California, you have to help me sell it to your mother. It's a lot harder for her to leave here than it is for you and me."

Sarah lowered her arm enough to peek at him.

"Catch more flies with honey than with vinegar," he said, "right?"

She was quiet. "I'll try," she said.

"Good." He kissed her forehead. "Go to sleep now."

He peeked into Travis' room. Travis was already asleep, had been half asleep when Pat sent him up the stairs. Pat knocked at the door of the bedroom he and Liv shared. Liv opened it. She was in her nightdress, her face scrubbed and her hair down.

"Did you hear what I told Sarah?" Pat asked.

"Yes," said Liv. "Thank you."

"May I come in?" Pat asked. "I'd like to talk."

Liv shook her head. "I'm too tired, Pat. I think you'd better sleep in the guestroom tonight."

Pat reached out for her, but she backed away.

He gave up. "All right," he said. "If that's the way you want it."

She closed the bedroom door gently on him.

Liv crawled into her bed and stared at the sky through the window. There were little sequins of light on it, reflected from the streetlights, where small flakes of snow, blown against the glass, were melting. Condensate fogged corners and edges of the multiple panes of the window. She shivered. The house was very quiet, the children at last in the truce of sleep. She could hear an occasional cough, the squeak of the bedsprings from the guestroom. Pat was still awake. Outside, the snow stilled the restless night of the town. The cloud from which it sifted settled over the town like a roof. The air was filled with snow, so the few people still awake and abroad would hardly be able to breathe without drawing in tiny cold sharp flakes that stung inside the nose and melted at once. She wished there was a magic way to make her bed out of doors, and have the snow falling on her like cold kisses, and still be warm in the cocoon of her quilts. It was not a night on which she expected to sleep, but she did.

Part Two

An empty house is like a stray dog,
or a body from which life has departed.

—SAMUEL BUTLER

Part Two

CHAPTER 8

THE HOUSE seemed just the same. Nothing had changed. It still looked empty.

Liv nudged Travis and said, "We're here."

He yawned and looked around blankly. "I want to go home."

"We're here," she insisted.

He rubbed his eyes and blinked.

It was not like coming home at all. It was not the green place they had left behind in September. Snow had worked its transcendental magic. The leafless, skeletal branches of the trees were decently clad in rime. The decayed remains of summer were sheeted by the pure homespun snow. But it was all deathly still and quiet, a lying out in the parlor of the wilderness. The house, despite the plume of woodsmoke drooling from the chimney over the roofbeam, was empty. Its windows, with their drawn shades, were like the glazed eyes of the dead.

Liv stretched and drew the cold unbreathed air into her lungs. She crunched around the car to open Travis' door for him. He barreled out with his fists bristling with G.I. Joes, like bizarre brass knuckles, only the knuckles were miniature plastic body parts, some clad in camouflage and some in various uniforms that signaled a particular antiterrorist specialty.

She opened the hatch and unhooked the pet carrier door. The Poor glided out and bounded to the ground. Like a lady lifting her skirts, the cat picked her way over the surface of the snow into the snow-frosted bushes.

Liv and Travis crossed the crusted driveway to the back porch, which had been shoveled clear of the accumulation of snow. The plowed snow was piled in a dune at the bottom of the looping driveway. Kindling and logs cut to fit the stove were stacked under a sheet of heavy plastic near the door.

"Walter's been here," Liv said.

As they stepped over the threshold, The Poor streaked through their feet into the house. Inside it was warm; the perfume of woodsmoke prickled their noses. There was a note pinned to the refrigerator, under a magnet chocolate real enough to provoke saliva: "Welcome Home! Grub all put away. Need anything, call. Walter."

Liv opened the fridge. Inside it was a stale cold, a negative of the house, a little bit of the winter outside boxed up and brought indoors. Milk, eggs, butter, a wedge of cheddar, homemade jam with Walter's own label on it—FROM THE KITCHEN OF WALTER MCKEN-ZIE/WILD STRAWBERRY JAM 1983—did not fill up the shelves but made them seem emptier, just as the snow made a funeral parlor of the out of doors.

Dear old Walter.

The Poor twisted around Liv's ankles, mewling over the cold-faded smells of Walter's stock of food, evoking déjà vu: last summer, when Sarah was at camp and Pat was on location, the cat and Travis and herself, by their lonesomes. The house breathed a subtle and particular silence that was more than just the weeks of emptiness. It was like a secret passage known only to herself and Travis. Secrecy rendered it shared and special; within its walls they were safe, the two of them, and it was too easy to hide here. It was too easy to pretend the passage led back to a tranquil, quiet summer—summer had been a pain-fogged lie—when really it was a kind of den in which to hole up for the winter.

She went into the living room and fed the fire, which was nicely banked. Walter must have been in the house very recently. She had called to alert him as soon as it was decent that morning. He must have hurried to clear the driveway and warm the house.

Travis slumped into a chair at the kitchen table, still clutching his army men, staring at her.

She blew her nose. "Want to help me bring in the bags, or would you prefer to have a pee first?" she asked.

"I don't have to pee, Liv," Travis answered her, a little sharply. He had begun to resent outside interest in his eliminations.

"Fine," she said. After two hours in the Pacer, she was certain he did have to go, but it was up to him if he wanted to punish his bladder. "Leave those guys on the table, and let's get to it."

Once the bags were inside, she made for the bathroom herself and heard behind her the sound of Travis' snowsuit zipper. When she came out, she went to the door of the children's bathroom and found it firmly closed. The snowsuit was a heap on the hall floor. A strong, healthy stream could be heard splashing into the bowl. She smiled and went on to Travis' bedroom, and heaved his suitcase onto his bed. The water sounds trickled off as she unpacked, and there was more sound track: Travis pulling up his pants, which always seemed to slip to his ankles while he peed because he had not yet figured out how to work his penis through the Y-front of his underpants and then the zipper of his jeans, then the ripping sound of the zipper, water in the basin and his hands sloshing and slapping, and the bathroom door unlocking as he turned the knob.

"Liv!" he called.

She stuck her head out his door.

"Right here, chief."

His face untwisted in relief. "Oh," he said.

He wandered into his bedroom. At first he watched her unpacking, then he climbed onto his bed next to the open suitcase and rolled onto his belly. His head hung over one side of the bed, his legs, from the knees, over the opposite edge.

"I'm hungry," he said.

"I'll make supper when I'm finished unpacking," Liv said.

That held him for a few seconds. Then he turned onto his back, crossed his hands on his chest, and stared at the ceiling.

"Are we all alone here, Liv?" he asked.

She flipped his small suitcase shut. "Yes. It's very quiet here. I think that's kind of nice, don't you?"

"No," he said. "It's creepy. Can I watch a tape?"

"No," she said. "Go play with your guys."

He slid off the bed onto his knees, staggered to his feet, and swaggered to the door.

"I can tell," he said, addressing the ceiling, "this is going to be more fun than humans should be allowed to have." It was a flawless imitation of Pat. He grinned over his shoulder at Liv.

"Right," she said, and made a grab at him.

He squealed and evaded her and danced out the door. She felt a little better.

They ate by firelight, in the premature night of December's tag end. The dark was another house around them. The firelight, like the flickering of an angelic sword, showed them glimpses of the trees, the shore, the frozen lake, and all the wild out of doors that surrounded the house, separating them from their own kind not just by miles, but by other dimensions, not the least of which were time and human silence. The cat slept on the hearth, coiled upon herself like a braided rug, her nose stuffed into her belly. Her sides rose and fell gently, fur catching the light of the flames now and again so for once she was picturesque and therefore comforting, if not handsome. Travis spread cards on the carpet and they played the simple games he had learned from Pat and Doe, and then she read him stories until he fell asleep against her.

When the pricking of pins and needles in her feet told her his weight was cutting her circulation, she gathered him up, noting as she did it was beginning to be an effort, and carried him to his bed. She did not undress him but tucked him in and kissed him, plugged in his nightlight, and returned to the living room to bank the fire.

A great weight of tiredness settled on her. She went to her own bed, let down her hair, and laid down, still dressed. When she was Travis' age, it had seemed such a victory, such an act of freedom-taking, to sleep in her clothes. She remembered her father winking even as her mother asked her if she thought she was a little wild animal. It was impossible to recapture that feeling; she only felt defeated, lying on her bed in the clothes she had put on that morning in the house in Portland, miles away, after a sleepless night. They were wrinkled and sweaty and soiled and so was she, but just then, she felt no amount of washing was ever going to make her feel clean again. At last she got up and washed her face and brushed her teeth and her hair. Then she went back to bed, still dressed, still keeping to the outside of the bedclothes. She lay on her back and waited for the telephone to ring, waited for Pat to call, but he didn't, or if he did, she had already fallen asleep.

Early the next morning, Walter McKenzie huffed up the steps and across the back porch. Mrs. Russell peeked out the kitchen window at him and then disappeared. He knocked shave-and-a-haircut on the door, and she opened it right away.

She was just out of bed, running her fingers through her hair for a comb, her face still damp from a wake-up splash. She hadn't had time for more, he knew, because when he had come down the hill in his Scout, he had seen her dark hair fanned over her pillow through the top third of the window in the master bedroom, which was uncurtained because it was so high, nobody at a normal height could see in, but in a vehicle, halfway up the hill, he could. Not time enough even to dress, but she *was* dressed, in jeans and a plaid shirt that looked like maybe she slept in 'em. So he guessed probably she had. She was still a little underweight, not filling her jeans or her shirt as much as he appreciated, but she didn't look yellow sick anymore, which was a relief. But it wasn't a good sign for a woman as fastidious as she was to be sleeping in her clothes. Leastways her eyes weren't swole up and red, so she didn't pass out drunk anyways. He misdoubted she was any kind of drinker. There had never been any evidence of it, and he would know that kind of thing if he saw it. Her scrawny, wild-looking excuse for a cat was twining around her ankles, wanting her breakfast.

" 'Mornin', missus," he said, taking off his ancient porkpie hat and grinning at her. "Somebody musta left a door open. Heck of a draft out here."

Most of his teeth were gone, which only emphasized the remaining dozen, small and yellow and sharp, as well as the veined and plummy ridges of his gums from which the teeth poked in all directions. He needed a shave and a haircut and very likely a bath, but he would always smell of the cats who bred unchecked in his woodshed, and the menagerie of wild animals which included birds, coons, and foxes that he kept, as well as the milk cows, an ancient nag, goats, rabbits, and his ugly, mis-bred dogs. Though considered a great catch because he was a reformed alcoholic, did not cuss in the presence of women, and held a lien-free title to his farm and woodlot, and despite the machinations of several local women who had worn out one or two husbands already, he refused obstinately to remarry, or to go to church. He wore a red plaid mackinaw and black rubber galoshes that flapped open where the metal catches were broken or missing.

Liv clutched the edge of the door and smiled at him. "Brrr," she mock-shivered. "Come on in out of the cold. Cup a tea, Walter?"

He grinned again. Something about Mrs. Russell made him grin a lot. She had a dewy look when she was well. Didn't often see that. Russell was a born fool if he was treating her bad. "Don't mind if I do."

He took off the two layers of holey, home-knitted gloves he wore and held them in the same hand with his hat, waiting politely for her to tell him what to do with them.

"Take off your jacket, Walter," she said. "There's an extra hanger in the hall closet."

He ducked down the hall, heard the can opener in the kitchen and the cat yowling to encourage it, and was glad she had remembered to bring vittles for the animal, as that was one thing he had forgotten on his shopping list. Didn't even hear the boy over the jangle of the coat hangers and when he turned around, he jumped a mile.

"Hey, old hoss," he said to the boy.

The boy looked up at him without blinking, and said, "Hello, Mr. McKenzie," like they met at the closet every morning. The kid looked just the same as he had at the end of the summer, big for his age, both feet firm on the ground, steady. Not one of those pants-afire little kids that made old folks like himself nervous, skittering around underfoot so a body didn't know where to put a foot down. Can't expect 'em to know old bones is easy broke, but you'd think the parents would know. Someways one of the things he liked best about Mrs. Russell was how calm that boy was. Like Travis always knowed inside and out he was safe, his ma was right there looking out for him. Nothing but good mother-love could make a yowen sure of that.

Travis led him back to the kitchen, moving slow like a horse that knows his own size and wasn't about to be hurried. He had those little army men clutched in both fists. Once he boosted himself onto a chair, he put 'em down on the table, and started to arrange them in ranks.

Mrs. Russell gave him a peck on the cheek in passing. Travis ignored her, which Walter remembered clearly, even at eighty-three, doing to his own ma. It made him want to chuckle. Instead, he cleared his throat and settled onto a chair. He patted his three or four strands of crinkled, colorless hair over his mottled scalp. He smoothed the legs of his green wool trousers, held up by red suspenders that had lost most of their elastic and gotten crinkles like an old woman's stretch marks in them, and were secured on one side by a big rusty safety pin, under cover of a faded plaid wool shirt that showed his yellowed long underwear shirt at the throat and cuffs and in the gaps where his shirt buttons strained over his belly. He reflected he was not exactly dressed for a tea party. He did have a good black suit, purchased at Sears & Roebuck during Harry S. Truman's first few months in office, but it was rare now he had occasion to wear it except for funerals. Mrs. Russell wouldn't pay no nevermind anyway, which was another one of the things he liked about her. She brought the tea, with milk and sugar, for all three of them. The cat had climbed into the fourth chair at the table and was licking herself just as vainly as if she had something to be vain about.

Walter rubbed a hand over his jaw, where his beard stubbled through skin the color of a crust of dirty snow like blades of old grass, still and lifeless and near enough to colorless so they were mostly dry shadow. He cleared his throat again. "Have a good trip?"

She sipped her tea and said, "It felt awful good to come home to a warm house and find food in it, too. Thanks."

Walter nodded. "No trouble."

The boy stirred in his chair. He tugged his cup toward him and stared at its contents, then sipped tentatively.

The cat leapt into Walter's lap. Starting, Walter nearly upset his own cup. He laughed, and rubbed the cat behind her ears. She sank onto his lap and made herself at home. Walter winked at Liv.

She smiled at him, and he reflected that was another one of the things he liked about her. She had a nice smile. Still a mite crooked, even after all the work on her teeth, but that gave it a charm perfection wouldna had.

"Ought to warm up later," he said.

She nodded.

"Talked to Mr. Russell last night," he said to her as genially as if they were discussing the weather.

She sipped her tea. He waited for her sympathetically.

"Oh," she said. "What did he say?"

"Wanted me to see if you got in all right. Said he tried the number here but it didn't go through."

She looked up quickly, catching him looking concerned before he could blink it away.

"Damn telephone company," she said.

"Ayuh," Walter agreed.

As long as it wasn't she'd taken it off the hook, as long as it wasn't she wasn't here last night, though where she'd be he couldn't guess. Just sometimes she was here and she wasn't, like when she was here, here wasn't here anymore, it was someplace nobody could reach or know about but her. The way it had been this season past, when she seemed to be fading right away to wherever it was she went when she wasn't quite here. Russell was afraid he was losing her; there'd been a terrible panic in the man's voice, underneath the cheerfulness he had been putting on for Walter's benefit, and to save himself embarrassment.

"Look Walter," he had said straight out, in a rush, "she's not herself, and I'm worried about her, but she won't, she's pissed at me, Walter, and I can't talk to her. I guess she's right, I did something I shouldn't have. I wanted it so much I conned myself into believing I could talk her into it. I'll come out there as soon as she cools down. I'll come in a minute if you think she's not okay. You'll check on her, won't you?"

Walter woulda checked on her without the asking. A woman alone with a little kid out in the woods, it wasn't what he'd call safe. Oh, ordinarily it was, prob'ly safer than in the city, amongst all those desperate strangers, all crowded together like a garden choked with weeds. But trouble in the woods was twice trouble. Whatever the trouble between Russell and herself was, she could be in a bushel more if the boy hurt himself or sickened in the middle of a bad storm. Or if the power was out or her vehicle broke down.

He wouldn't have allowed it of Mellie, rest her soul, but then, Mellie wouldn't have run off even if she had had a place to run to, which she didn't. Whatever he might have done, not that he ever give Mellie any reason. Mrs. Russell had always seemed a sensible girl, a lot more sensible than her husband, for sure, but it didn't surprise him, her turning up out of season. It seemed like he'd been waiting since September for her to call and ask him to open the house, and for Pat Russell to call up and ask him to look after her. Whatever was wrong, it had been wrong since last summer.

He squinted at her slyly. "Needed a rest from the city?" One hand resting on the cat's head, thick fingers of the other hand gripping the back of his chair, he twisted in his chair to follow Mrs. Russell as she rose to plug in the toaster, open the bread. The skin of the back of the hand, drawn taut and transparent, was mottled with liver spots like the skin of an exotic snake.

She looked over her shoulder at him and smiled, forgiving him his nosiness. "There's no place like here, Walter," she said. "I've been thinking about it all fall."

Walter studied the residue in his teacup. As always, it didn't look like anything but flecks of tea leaves to him. No doubt she really didn't know her own intentions. Best to let her idle a few days, and perhaps boredom and loneliness would drive her back to her husband.

Gently he lowered the cat to the floor. She stretched and wandered away. He pushed away from the table, gathered up his cup and saucer one-handed, and put them in the sink. "Thanks for the tea," he said. "I can do anythin' for you, you holler."

Liv gripped the edge of the sink and from the kitchen window watched him stump down the back steps.

Travis came up behind her and wrapped his arms around her waist. He yawned a jaw-cracking yawn.

"Liv," he asked, "is Walter going to die?"

"Someday," she said. She ruffled his hair, then smoothed it. "Everybody has to die someday. Walter's getting on, but he's a tough old bird. I'll bet he's got a few years left in him yet."

She didn't say to Travis: He's beginning to look eighty-three. Sometime between last spring and today he started to stoop and shuffle. There's a rheumy yellow cast to his eyes, which in May had still been clear white, the irises translucent gray as the water of the lake in the morning mist of August. And his skin had acquired that sheen of transparency, as if it were beginning to melt.

Her own vision of him, treasured and immutable, as she had seen him when once she had stopped in on him, came to mind:

Walter, shirtless in his long johns and wool pants, for it was summertime, and he adapted, as did all his race, who had invented the
layered look donkeys' years before the outastaters had discovered
L.L. Bean, Walter, swabbing bean juice from a plate with a slice of
bread, jaws working steadily under their beard stubble that was always just the same length, never longer, never shorter, always three
days old, as if he lived in a fairy tale. Or was a low-rent bachelor
Santa Claus. No, a nursery rhyme, he was Old King Cole, a fat,
smelly, entirely jolly old soul. There was just the one corner cleared,
about a foot square, where Walter could fit his plate and fork and
mug. The painted table was invisible under a mountain range of
books and papers and magazines: his bills and receipts; canceled
checks; tax forms and records; letters from the granddaughter who
lived in Alaska; yellowing snapshots, like dry leaves scattered among
the papers, of great-grandchildren he had never seen in the flesh; a
year or more's accumulation of *Field and Stream* and *Yankee;* and
paperback westerns, often coverless, bought for a dime from bins in
Dewey Linscott's junkstore in Greenspark. His favorites were by J.C.
Devereaux, who was really a woman named Bobbie Anderson who
lived only a hundred miles northeast in Haven, a wide place in the
road on the way to Derry and Bangor, a fact that amused the hell
out of Walter when Liv told him. In summertime, the litter spilled
over onto the cold cast-iron Atlantic range, under which Walter's
smelly old beagle bitch, Fritzie, slept. That time of year, Walter did
his bit of cooking on a grubby two-burner gas stove acquired in a
swap with Dewey for one of Fritzie's pups when Fritzie was still
capable of whelping, a long time ago now.

   His one son, who went for a soldier in 1941, had been dead even
longer than Mellie, his wife. Walt, Jr., had not died without issue; his
marriage, made in 1943 and broken in 1950, seven years before Walt,
Jr., finally died of pneumonia in the VA hospital in Togus, had produced two daughters. One of Walter's granddaughters, Lucinda, was
too far away and had a disabled husband and two daughters, both
divorced and with growing children and inadequate incomes, to look
after. The other, Jean, had married a foolish lad with more looks, of
the weak kind that are swiftly coarsened by hard living, than sense, a
no-account, and everyone told her so too, who had gotten one child
on her and then, while stuporously drunk, driven his old Ford
pickup into another pickup truck, killing himself and the unlucky

Indian family of five crammed into its cab. After struggling several years on her own, Jean had remarried, to the first man that asked her.

Her second husband was older than she and had two sons from a previous marriage. Arden Nighswander had a local reputation as a brutal, dangerous, vainglorious man, as well as a deadbeat. He quickly reduced Jean to a quivering drab. Her son, moonfaced and spineless, considered by the locals to be little more than simple, fared better than expected; while the Nighswander boys tortured him a little more than they did their dogs, with less success in creating a vicious temperament, they also adopted him as a kind of mascot. Nighswander had quarreled with Walter, as he quarreled with everyone, and Jean no longer dared to have anything to do with her own grandfather. So Walter, in his dotage, was as good as childless. Liv wondered if anyone hereabouts kept an eye on him, if there would be anyone to take care of him if he needed it.

CHAPTER 9

FIREFIGHT
Rough Cut #4

On a scenic turnout overlooking an arc of
beach, two young policemen in crisp, short-
sleeved summer khakis sit on a large, flat-
topped boulder, eating sandwiches and drinking
pop. Their compact and very clean black patrol
car is parked at this end of the turnout. At the
end is a large trash barrel and a public phone
booth of the head-and-shoulders variety. From
this vantage the policemen can see not only the
length of the beach but also the entrance, a
kiosk in the middle of a lower curve of the same
road. The sky overhead is robin's egg blue in
which a few tenuous tatters of cloud are so
overwhelmed they seem wistful. The sun is white-
hot, the color of the beach sand that by this
time of day had absorbed enough of its heat to
tingle naked feet. Several hundred bodies, some
of them quite as white as the sun and the beach
sand, many of them as bronzed as an Air Mexico
billboard girl, heroically interpose
themselves between sun and sand, recklessly
courting skin cancer and alligator wrinkles.
They are mostly teenagers, in as little as the

law allows, a great leveler, making them all
nearly naked, rather than idle rich or
unemployed. Their bikinis and French pouches
also create another mechanism of
classification, between the naturally endowed
and fit and the unlucky and weak. But there is a
minimum of the latter and a maximum of the former
class. Whether because the fat and ill-favored
are shy of the beach or because they are also
poor and so have to work while the sun shines one
can only speculate. The kids have ceded one end
of the beach, where the water is shallow and
there is a tidal pool as well, to young mothers,
some of whom are last summer's bikinied beach
sprites, and their babies and toddlers. There
are only a few old people braving the sun, those
really dedicated to turning their skin into
handbag leather. Those few are petulant and
nervous; they are intimidated by the youth, and
the youth, on turf or at least sand they regard
as their own, delightedly flex their bully
muscles as well as their well-basted and browned
biceps and quadriceps.

One of the policemen, Patrolman William
Kerry by the name tag on his breast pocket, is
young enough to have been one of the teenage
beach lords in the recent past. He would have
been perpetually sunburnt, as he is now, for his
skin is naturally whiter than the beach sand,
whiter than the sun. He is losing his crisp,
curly hair, exposing more white scalp to the
merciless rays, and is thickening in face and
body, working on a policeman's belly. But he
seems content to be so close to his own careless
youth.

The other is older, slimmer, indeed a man who
will never grow fat, inheritor of the leanness
of people who have never been fat and sated. And
he is a middling shade of brown, born a color the
teenagers, obsessed with the depth of their own
tans, will never achieve and in fact universally
scorn as evidence of inferiority. He has a

military bearing the other cop can only fake.
His badge identifies him as Sergeant Emery
Ratcliffe.

He and Bill Kerry share a laugh as they finish
their lunches. Bill Kerry's laugh is high,
almost a giggle, and he blushes like a maiden
aunt whose drawers have let go in the middle of
Woolworth's. The hectic red on his cheeks stand
out like round spots of rouge against the
translucent sheen he has built up out of sunburn
after sunburn. Ratcliffe's eyes crinkle when he
laughs from his belly. He shows a mouthful of
minstrel-white teeth, capped at government
expense during military service, when he grins.

Ratcliffe wraps up sandwich baggies and
paper napkins in a brown paper bag and disposes
of them in the trash barrel at the side of the
scenic turnout. His empty soda pop bottle goes
into a small wastebasket fixed to the dash of the
patrol car. Bill Kerry chews up the last of his
salami sandwich, belches resonantly, and goes
through the same ritual of housekeeping.

"I'm going to report in," Ratcliffe tells
Kerry.

"Okay if I take a leak?" Kerry asks.

Ratcliffe grins. "In the bushes, man, where
the tourists can't see you. The chief wouldn't
like that."

Kerry laughs again and wanders away toward a
footpath that leads into the woods.

Ratcliffe slips into the front seat of the
cruiser and takes the radio mike. He identifies
the car to the dispatcher. "We're still at
Pillsbury Beach," he reports. "The natives are
quiet."

He listens to static and then a clearly
audible message. "Hold your position." Then,
"Message from home, Rat. Give Myrna a call, will
ya?"

"Ten-four," Ratcliffe answers and clips the
mike to the dash.

Kerry is wandering back to the car, checking his zipper.

Ratcliffe sticks his head out of the car. "I got to call home, Bill."

A cloud of concern passes over Kerry's features. He is a single man, contemplating marriage. Its responsibilities seem awesome to him.

Ratcliffe walks to the open phone kiosk at the edge of the turnout, feeds a dime to the machine, dials home, and talks to his wife.

"Hi, babe," he says. "What's up?"

"Oh, tiger, it's you," his wife greets him. "I don't know, it's a message."

Ratcliffe becomes very still. "Tell me about it, Myrna."

"It's from Denny. Except it wasn't Denny who called, tiger. It was that girlfriend of his, the one he had with him in Florida last winter."

"The trash," Ratcliffe says.

"That's the one. Barbie Sue, took off her top when we was out on the boat. She said he told her to call you and tell you Court was coming your way. He said to tell you Court took out Jackson and Taurus done it for him, which doesn't make any sense to me. Anyway, he said to tell you right away pronto, it was urgent."

Ratcliffe closes his eyes.

"What's that mean, tiger? All that Barbie Sue knew was Denny said it was real important and then he took off and she don't know where he's gone to."

"Yeah," Ratcliffe says. "It's real important. Look, I'll be home in fifteen minutes. Start packing for me, babe. I'll explain when I get there."

He hangs up quickly without giving her a chance to respond or ask any more questions, and trots back to the cruiser.

"Take me home, Bill," he says, slipping into the passenger seat. "I'm feeling poorly."

Bill Kerry inserts himself quickly behind

the wheel and starts the car before peeking at
Ratcliffe curiously.

"Sure. Rat, you okay?"

"Sick to my stomach," Ratcliffe says
shortly, laying his head back against the head
rest. "That chicken sanwich musta gone over.
Feel like I'm going to lose it."

Kerry sneaks another glance at his partner.
There is a sheen of perspiration on Ratcliffe's
face, and he is ashen. Either he has really
gotten a bad sandwich or he has gotten some kind
of news from his wife that is bad enough to make
him as sick as if he had food poisoning. If one of
his kids is hurt or sick, he'd say so, wouldn't
he? Or if Myrna had had some kind of accident.
But that wasn't likely, he'd been talking to
her, so she must be able to talk to him. Kerry
hides his troubled imaginings behind his
customarily cheerful expression.

One arm held against his stomach as if it
pains him, Ratcliffe reaches for the mike and
raises the dispatcher.

"Rat here," he says. "Sicker than a dawg, I
think I got a bad sanwich." His voice is faint
and shaky.

"Read you," the dispatcher says. There is a
staticky pause while the dispatcher reports to
the day officer. "Chief says for Kerry to take
you home and report back to the station to pick
him up. He'll sub for you today. He says take
care of yourself Rat and you owe him one."

"Much oblige," Rat says. "Ten-four."

Kerry pulls the cruiser into the driveway of
a well-kept suburban ranch house. Parked neatly
next to the garage is a small G.I. Joe bicycle. A
little girl in a ruffled romper, straddling a
pink Strawberry Shortcake HotWheel cycle, cries
"Daddy!"

The front door is open, the screen door
closed. A young woman, darker than Ratcliffe,
frowning with worry, opens the screen.

"Tiger?" she says. Then she sees Ratcliffe,

who has heaved himself out of the cruiser and is
supporting himself against the open car door.
The little girl hops off the cycle and heads for
Ratcliffe. Ratcliffe bends hastily over a
rhododendron bush to vomit.

His wife hurries to him, crying "Tiger?"

The little girl stops in her tracks, confused
and suddenly frightened. Bill Kerry reaches her
in two giant steps and picks her up. "Sylvia!" he
exclaims. "How'd you get so big? I ain't seen you
in a week and you went and grew three inches at
least!"

The distraction works. Sylvia giggles.

Ratcliffe leans on his wife briefly, then
pushes her gently away. "I'm awright, Myrna."

He stumbles toward the door. She follows him,
smoothing her skirt nervously.

Hoisting Sylvia to his shoulders, Bill Kerry
carries her inside.

There are gargling sounds from a nearby
bathroom. Myrna stations herself in the hallway
outside it, wringing her hands. Bill Kerry
deposits Sylvia on the sofa and takes a seat. On
the mantel is a gold-framed photograph of the
Ratcliffes' eight-year-old son, Joey, in a Boy
Scout uniform. On a day like this, Joey is
probably splashing with his buddies at the
nearest public swimming pool. Kerry looks
around at what is a women's-magazine-perfect
living room, except for Sylvia's crayons and
coloring books on the coffee table. It is
tasteful to an extreme. Ratcliffe calls Myrna
houseproud and says she is overcompensating,
which Bill Kerry takes to mean Myrna is worried
the neighbors will think she is a nigger slut if
she doesn't keep a fastidiously clean and
tasteful house. Bill Kerry's own housekeeping
is haphazard, though he tries. He wishes his
fiancee Doreen's place gave some evidence that
she would be as good a housewife as Myrna. His
mother said with more accuracy than bitchiness
that Doreen's place could qualify for federal

disaster relief funds. Myrna's neighbors would
definitely class Doreen as a slut. But they
wouldn't be saying "Uh uh, what do you expect,
they're all like that, bunch a animals," not
about Doreen because he and Doreen wouldn't be
the only wrong-colored folks on the block.

Ratcliffe comes out. "Thanks," he says. "I'm
a lot better now."

He looks better.

"Good," Kerry says. "I'll be going then. You
take care."

Kerry climbs into the cruiser. He can hear
Myrna through the open bedroom windows.

"Tiger?"

"You'll be okay, hon. You got the checkbook.
I'm just taking this one check."

"But why? Why are you running off? Where you
going, Tiger?"

"He coming for me, babe. He coming for all of
us. I'll let you know where I am when it's safe.
It's better you don't know for now."

"Tiger, damn you, you can't just run off and
leave me. Who's coming for you?"

"Court," Ratcliffe says. "He's coming for
me."

Myrna was crying now. "What about Sylvia and
Joey? What do I tell them?"

"I'll call you when it's safe." Ratcliffe's
voice was gentle, reassuring, guilty as hell.
"Court won't hurt you," he says. "He only wants
me."

Kerry turned the key in the ignition. He
didn't want to hear anymore. He didn't want to
know what kind of trouble Ratcliffe was in. It
was enough to make Rat sick. Whoever Court was,
Rat was scared of him, and somebody Rat was
scared of was too goddamn scary for Bill Kerry,
that was for sure. He just hoped Rat could take
care of himself. He hoped nobody else got hurt.

SARAH folded the dish towel and hung it over the chrome bar on the oven door. She looked around at her grandmother.

Marguerite finished polishing the last glass and closed the cupboard door gently on the shining ranks. She cast a critical glance around the kitchen. With her glossy white hair tied up in a black-and-red houndstooth-checked scarf, Marguerite wore a no-nonsense unbleached cotton baker's apron over tailored gray wool trousers and a black cotton knit turtleneck shirt. She sported short red boots with flat heels. She moved with something less than her normal crisp assurance, as if she were tired but was not about to show it.

"Good enough," she said. She squirted hand lotion into her left palm and massaged it into her hands. "We'll have to get the windows tomorrow."

Sarah grimaced. Except for her jeans and T-shirt, and her long hair hanging loose around her face, wisps of it glued with sweat to her brow, her temples, the back of her neck, she looked a fifty-years-younger version of her grandmother. "Let Mrs. Fuller do them."

Marguerite smiled. "Mrs. Fuller won't be in, Sarah. With your mother and Travis away, and your father leaving today, I told her to take the week off. You and I can do all that needs doing."

"Jesus," Sarah muttered. She backed up against the counter and crossed her arms.

"What did you say, dear?"

"Nothing," Sarah answered. "Nothing."

"Well, I'm ready for a cup of coffee," Marguerite said. She reached into a cupboard and took out a cup and saucer. "What about you?"

"Yuck," said Sarah. "You make it too strong. I'd rather have a Coke."

"That's not good for your teeth or your complexion," Marguerite said, examining the cup for dust by delicately swabbing its interior with one finger.

"Jesus!" Sarah bounced off the counter into the center of the kitchen. Unconsciously, she touched a red bump on her chin where a pimple was forming under the surface. One always seemed to come up right there a few days before her period started. She examined her nails, which were painted luminescent celery green. The housework had chipped and scarred the polish.

"Sarah!"

"Well, doesn't coffee stunt your growth?" Sarah said.

Marguerite pursed her lips but calmly went about filling the glass carafe and pouring the water into the reservoir of the coffee maker before answering, "I hardly have to concern myself with stunting my growth, young lady, but you had better concern yourself with your language. And your attitude."

Pat put down his suitcase in the door from the hall and cleared his throat. He was freshly shaved and dressed for the long plane journey, wearing comfortable shoes and a suede jacket that wouldn't wrinkle even if he rolled it up into a pillow to sleep on. Just lately, what he wore seemed to be the only thing over which he had any control. He hoped to be able to sleep on the plane; last night had been endless, restless. He had been alternately too cold and too hot, as if he were feverish. Liv had not called and he had been afraid to call her, though he did finally call Walter McKenzie to whom he had lied about not being able to reach Liv, but at least now Walter would check on her.

Marguerite turned her back on Sarah and opened a cupboard. She took out a two-pound can of Maxwell House, and examined it critically. She preferred Folger's.

Sarah rushed at Pat and threw her arms around him.

He hugged her tightly.

"Coffee, Pat?" Marguerite inquired brightly.

He patted Sarah's back and released her. "Sure," he said. "Sure."

Marguerite closed the can opener on the lid of the Maxwell House. The can opener bit into it and chewed it open with a buzz saw whirring. The instant the vacuum was broken, the kitchen was full of the rough, granular spice smell of the coffee.

"Please can I go with you, daddy?" Sarah said to Pat in a low voice.

He slumped into a chair. "I'm sorry, hon."

"I *hate* her," Sarah said through her teeth.

Pat stared at the floor, chewing his lower lip.

Sarah clenched her fists. "Nobody cares what I want. Nobody."

"That's not true," Pat said.

"That's enough, Sarah," Marguerite said.

Sarah burst into tears. Pat reached out and took her in his lap. She buried her head in the shoulder of his suede jacket, spotting it with hot tears, the thought of which irritated him and then made him feel guilty for being unduly concerned with appearances. He wished for the kind of soft, worn old diaper Liv had always handed him, when Sarah and Travis were infants, to throw over his shoulder for a burp cloth. He patted her back awkwardly. He had not realized she was getting so tall, as well as filling out at the bosom and bottom. It was uncomfortably like holding a grown woman on his knees.

Marguerite ignored them. She finished measuring coffee into the coffee maker and replaced the plastic lid on the Maxwell House. She plugged in the machine and turned it on. It began at once to bubble. Then she sat down opposite Pat and Sarah at the table.

"Sarah," she said, "go check the dryer, will you?"

Sarah bounced out of Pat's lap and slammed out of the room.

When the sound of her stomping down the hall faded, Marguerite bent across the table and squeezed Pat's hand tightly.

"Pat," she said, "stop this foolishness now before it becomes a habit. Do you want to live like this?"

Pat looked up at her. "She's under a lot of stress," he said. "She's got a right to be upset."

Marguerite sighed. "If you mean Sarah, Sarah's going to go on playing you against Liv forever if you let her. If you go live in California in your new house without Liv and with Sarah, you're going to be raising a thirteen-year-old who wants the freedom of an adult with the responsibilities of a ten-year-old. You'll be living with a world-class blackmailer. Working your guilt, taking advantage of your obsession with your work and your anger and guilty feelings for Liv. It'll be very expensive, Pat. Not just a housekeeper for that fancy house and a cook, but there'll be Sarah's private school, her clothes. Her allowance, commensurate with what her friends have, for which she does nothing. Not so long from now she'll have to have a car because all her friends have one. There'll be the dope, the marijuana and the coke, that she'll buy with her ridiculous allowance. Then she'll steal yours, Pat."

"Wait a minute," Pat said. "Just a goddamn minute."

Marguerite held up her hands. "Let me finish, please. And spare me the goddamns. Don't think Liv told me. I'm not stupid. You think I don't know what the baby laxative is for, you keep in your desk? I'm married to a pharmacist forty-one years, Pat. And I wasn't snooping. I couldn't find the telephone book and there it was. You don't even bother to lock it up, Pat. Are you foolish from it, already, or do you want Liv to find it so you two can have something more to fight about? You think Sarah doesn't know about it?"

"About what?" Sarah said, coming down the hallway.

"Don't be smart with me," Marguerite said. She stood up and went to the coffee maker.

"It's a stupid law," Sarah said from the doorway. "The government doesn't want anyone to have any fun."

Pat stared at Sarah. "Sarah," he said.

"Is that so?" Marguerite said. "Well, Pat, what are you going to tell her?"

"Look, Sarah," he said, "I tried the stuff, yes. But I don't do it anymore. It can really mess a person up. I may not think the government is handling the issue just right, but that doesn't mean I think you or anyone else should be doing that stuff."

Sarah shrugged and slumped against the door frame. "You're a grown-up. Grown-ups are always saying 'Do as I say, not as I do.' If you can handle it, so can I."

Pat closed his eyes and gritted his teeth. "You are not an adult, Sarah, not yet, whether you think so or not." *Even if you look and feel like one.*

"Your coffee," Marguerite said gently, putting a cup in front of him.

"Thanks," he muttered.

"You're welcome," Marguerite said. "There's another saying, Sarah."

"What's that?" Sarah said, examining her nails to underline her utter boredom.

"Children should be seen and not heard," Marguerite said. "It means you don't know shit from Shinola."

Sarah's mouth dropped open. She had never heard her grandmother use a rude word. Marguerite had been known to wash out the mouths of excessively daring children for that offense, until Liv found out about it and stopped it.

Pat shot a worried glance at Sarah. "I've got to go soon if I'm going to make my plane, Sarah, but we're going to talk about this a lot more. I'll call you from L.A. tomorrow. After school tomorrow. Three o'clock, all right?"

Sarah sulked. "I have basketball practice."

"When are you home, then?"

"Four-thirty."

"Good. I'll call at four-thirty."

Sarah nodded.

He looked at the cup of coffee. Drinking it would probably interfere with sleeping on the plane. He knocked back most of it anyway. "I have to go," he said.

"Have a good flight," Marguerite said.

Pat kissed Sarah's cheek. "Be good, sweetheart," he said. There was a note of pleading in his voice.

"Sure," she said sullenly.

"She'll be good," Marguerite said confidently.

Pat backed into the hall, grabbed his suitcase, an overcoat and muffler, and hurried out.

Sarah and Marguerite sat alone in the kitchen, on opposite sides of the table, staring at each other. Pat's car started in the driveway, and then was gone. It was very quiet, the only sound in the house the metronome of the grandmother clock in the front hall. Marguerite sipped her coffee. At last Sarah's eyelashes fluttered slowly, and then Sarah stared at the top of the table. Marguerite grunted.

"Sarah," she said.

Sarah did not look up. Silent tears wet her cheeks.

"Sarah," Marguerite repeated. "Your parents are going to divorce over my dead body. There's no chance in hell you're ever going to live in that glass house in California. You're going to spend the next five years right here, so get used to it. Cheer up. It won't be so bad. So you'll have to postpone making a horse's ass of yourself until you're eighteen and you go off to college. That's not too late. Believe me."

Sarah wiped her eyes with the back of her hand. "Why are you so mean?" Sarah whispered.

"I'm not mean," Marguerite said. "I'm just telling the truth. You know what you don't like about me?"

Sarah looked up and snuffled.

"We're two of a kind."

"Hah," Sarah said, fishing a tissue out of the box on the table. She blew her nose. "You and my mother, you're two of a kind."

Marguerite blinked. "Your mother? Hah to you, Miss Smarty-pants." She leaned across the table and thumped her knuckles on it. "Your mother is all Doe. You'll never win against her."

"Why not?" Sarah challenged her.

"I never won anything from him, that's why." Marguerite got up and poured herself another cup of coffee. "You ought to tell your father that when you talk to him. Tell him changing one of those two is like trying to hold onto a handful of snow. They just melt away on you. And you think you've lost them. Then you realize you're hip-deep in them, and they're down the back of your neck and inside your boots and they're going to bury you. They're going to bury you." She stared out the window at the cold sky. "Did you know, Sarah, that every snowflake is supposed to be unique?"

"That's what my mother says," Sarah said.

"Remember when she did all the snowflake Christmas ornaments? She showed me a library book she had once, the first photographs of snowflakes ever taken, by some fellow in Vermont. They made me shiver just to look at them," Marguerite hugged herself.

She turned around at the sound of Sarah sobbing. Great heaving, sucking sobs, her face in her hands, with their wildly colored nails. Marguerite went to her and put her hands on Sarah's shoulders. "Poor baby," she said, and kissed the top of Sarah's head.

The ride to the jetport wasn't long enough to be soothing. Pat kept punching the radio buttons, switching stations, looking for the right song, the one piece of rock 'n' roll that would speak to him and take him out of himself. It was one of those periods when he was almost certain rock 'n' roll had finally and truly died. He suffered through Metal Health's "Lick It Up" on BLM out of Lewiston, and then the astrological forecast from the Cosmic Muffin, who hadn't been funny since he went into syndication. Jay Jay followed, on the Weatherdeck, reporting that the weather was lookin' bad, folks, heavy snow, possibly a blizzard in the mountains tonight. Pat punched the button, and found David Bowie singing "White Christmas" with Bing Crosby. At the next stoplight, he fumbled frantically in the glove box for a tape, and shoved one into the slot without even looking to see what it was. It was "Born to Add," the Sesame Street rock parody they had listened to last coming home from the Mall the day after Thanksgiving. He couldn't help laughing. The sound of Bruce Stringbean evoked the image of the Mall Santa Claus, with his glossy white beard stained orange with the dye from Travis' regurgitated orange pop, swearing and screaming. And as always, it brought to mind Sarah's adoration of the real Bruce. He arrived at the jetport with his children on his mind.

I'll call Liv from L.A., Pat told himself, hurrying past the telephones, though there was time. Too much time, really.

He had fled his wife's kitchen, where things were subtly wrong, cupboards rearranged, and surfaces too bare, as if she had died and Marguerite had come in to exorcise Liv's presence, to demonstrate to Liv's soul that her kitchen was no longer hers, or to cleanse the kitchen from the contamination of the dead. He had fled Marguerite, across the table, with her cup of coffee, and her mother-in-law's bright and knowing eyes that said *I know you're fucking my little girl, sonny, and don't think just because you made an honest woman of her I'm ever going to unload this shotgun, because you're still fucking her,* the shotgun not a real one, of course, although both Marguerite and Doe, the amiable bearlike Doe, were perfectly capable of taking up a real one and blowing him away. Sorrowfully and solemnly and soberly and with proper gravity, on grounds of personal honor. And he had fled Sarah with her woman's tits and ass and her petulant blind stubborn adolescent stupidity.

Between the tiny orange cushions of her Walkman headset, there seemed to be nothing going on in her head but rock 'n' roll lyrics. He didn't know how to tell her that for him they were a sweet, nostalgic, romantic dream of a youth that never had been and wasn't now. It had never occurred to him she would really believe in them, all those lies about love and rebellion and dying young and leaving a beautiful corpse. Was there anybody so young and stupid they didn't know there is no such thing as a beautiful corpse? He had fled the baby laxative he had left in his desk drawer with the sieve and the razor and the polished slice of stone that he could not explain to Sarah, even if she would unstop her ears and hear him.

How did he say Look kid you had to have been there. The government does lie, like the gang of mad bastards it is, it lies about everything on principle but it's not because it doesn't want anyone to have any fun, it's because it wants to keep the prices UP, and when fun's illegal, someone's got to make money off it, cheap fun is un-American, and the government likes it that way, sweetheart, you're absolutely right about that. But the thing is, that doesn't make it A-okay for thirteen-year-olds, or lots of people. Just okay for me. And I know how that sounds, kid, but see, I've smoked dope since nineteen sixty-eight, not every day, or even every week, of course, but now and then, and I know goddamn well it does less damage to me than booze, which I drink every day, every single goddamn day, two martinis before dinner, wine or beer with dinner, a few beers or six after dinner, once in a while a snifter of brandy or a little cognac, and I don't miss the brain cells at all, because there's billions of the little bastards, most of them just layabouts collecting welfare any-way, and I love getting mellow, and I love getting kited on coke, it feels like it's bringing those deceased brain cells right the fuck back to life and making new ones, and all it costs me is money, Kleenex, a little sleep, and a mild case of diarrhea now and then from the baby laxative or whatever else the stuff's being cut with, but you have to understand, Sarah, I'm a grown man, thirty-five years old, I work eighteen hours a day, I fly to L.A. and it takes three days to get over the jet lag and then I fly east and there's another three days of jet lag; I do that over and over again, and I can't afford to be slow, I have to produce wherever I am, and besides, I know what I'm doing, Sarah. A man has a lot to cope with, Sarah. Earning a living, raising a family, keeping a wife. And I'm losing my wife, your mother.

The thought of Liv so desolated him that he forgot about Sarah and sank miserably into a molded plastic seat in the new terminal. Everything around him was white or brightly colored—purple, like his chair, or red, or yellow—and new and modern, with expanses of glass that a man seemed always to be cleaning, and the people wait-ing with him—for arriving passengers, or to leave, to flee, like Pat himself—were cheerful in anticipation of whatever the next few min-utes would bring. The carpet underfoot was tough, low pile stuff in a muddy tweed that had looked worn and dirty since the day it was laid and always would. The ashtrays were shiny chrome cans with lids that opened inward and clacked shut like hostile mouths. There was a row of coin-operated TVs that adults fed quarters to distract bored and restless children. The children watched long enough to see they had been cheated, and then abandoned, leaving the TVs to show their few minutes of grainy, ghosted, rolling images to no one. He had seen carpets and ashtrays and TVs like them in dozens of airports. His dreams were full of them.

He wished he had called Liv last night or this morning, or from the convenient bank of telephones he had cruised past on the way in. Even as he looked at his wristwatch, there was an unintelligible announcement that he knew was his boarding call: People around him were gathering their belongings and queuing up at the security gate. Now it really was too late to call.

Standing in line, with the strap of his carryon biting into his shoulder, he looked out the windows and at the sky. It was white and low with more snow. The forecast said anytime now, and through the night. The runways were broad charcoaled roads stenciled on the ivory snow. Light wind off Casco Bay, the thin warmth of the short winter days, the exposed site of the airport, had all combined to diminish the accumulation to sheer, gleaming crust, broken by long brown grass. At LAX, the grass would be brown, too. Not just now, most of the year, it seemed. And the sky would be brown, too, with smog. It would be humid and muggy there, and he would not need his overcoat.

He wished Liv was with him, standing in this line, holding hands, watching her tote bag trundle down the conveyor belt through the X-ray machine. Joking about whether carryon shoulder was a permanent deformity. There wouldn't be time to call her when he changed planes in New York, but he would call her as soon as he was on the ground in L.A. He would tell her he missed her and ask her right out if she missed him. Maybe she did. Maybe all they needed was to say that and everything would be all right.

He found his seat on the plane and strapped himself in. A few flakes drifted by outside the little window that always looked to him just like the one in the cat's carrier cage. A flight attendant was smiling and welcoming people onto the plane. Pat released his belt buckle and stood up.

"Excuse me," he said to the lift-tagged coed coming down the aisle. She smiled uncertainly and let him pass. He excused his way back to the flight attendant, who awaited him with raised eyebrows and helpful professional smile.

"I'm getting off," he said.

The professional smile crumpled. "Oh," she said. "Oh."

He rummaged into the closet and retrieved his carryon.

"Is there something wrong?" the attendant asked anxiously.

"Yes," he said. "But I'm going to fix it."

She covered her mouth with one hand and took a step backward. "Oh," she said. She couldn't tell him she was glad he had flown Delta when he hadn't. Professional training took over. She recovered her poise and called after him. "Have a nice day."

Marguerite had her feet up, watching TV, when he came in.

He was surprised how much the look of astonishment on her face pleased him.

"Where's Sarah?" he asked.

Marguerite gestured toward the stairway. "In her room, lying down."

He went up the stairs two at a time.

There was no answer to his light knock on her door. She probably thought he was Marguerite, so she was playing possum. He tried the door and found it unlocked.

The curtains were drawn as if in a sick room. Sarah was curled up on her bed, a damp cloth folded over her eyes.

"Sarah," he said.

She sat bolt upright, catching the cloth one-handed as it fell from her eyes. Her mouth fell open.

"Daddy!"

One hand around her waist, he set her to her feet.

"Come on," he said, "we're going to Nodd's Ridge."

"What?" she said.

"Come on," he repeated. "I'm going to put this family back together."

Moving so fast she had no time to react, he grabbed her hand and shoulder and hustled her downstairs.

Marguerite stood at the bottom of the stairs, her eyes bright and curious and a little frightened.

"We're going to Nodd's Ridge," he said.

Marguerite clapped her hands. "About time," she said.

He threw open the closet door, hooked out Sarah's jacket and tossed it at her.

"Wait a minute," Marguerite said. "You can't go out like that."

He and Sarah, the one thing on their minds interrupted, stopped and stared at her.

Marguerite flicked a hand impatiently in the direction of the door. "It's snowing," she said. "Dress for it. Snowsuits. Boots. Mittens. Cover your heads."

"Right," Pat said.

Dragging a pair of old wooden sleds behind them, Liv and Travis stomped a path to the studio. The Poor bounded along behind them, light enough to be able to walk on the surface of the snow.

Travis grabbed the leg of her ski pants.

"Look, Liv," he commanded, and sank to his haunches, pointing out a new track in the snow.

They had seen the paw prints of squirrels and coons already. This new print was much larger, and familiar.

"Dog," said Liv, touching it. "A big dog." *Maybe a coyote.*

"I thought there was nobody here but us," Travis said.

"Well, it could be somebody's dog off their leash," Liv said. "Or a stray or a runaway."

"Oh," said Travis.

That seemed to be enough for him. But Liv looked around as they straightened up, noting that the dog tracks, if that was what they were, seemed to skirt their house and head into the woods. That was fine by her. Any dog could be dangerous, unleashed, or stray, or gone wild. At least there was only one. Sometimes the wild dogs gathered into packs to hunt. And then there were the coyotes, which the farmers and hunters hated so much. Liv made a mental note to keep The Poor indoors more, and especially at night, to keep her out of harm's way.

They went on toward the studio, Liv watching for any more signs of the large dog, but they found only more squirrel tracks and some bird prints that Liv thought might be one of the ground-dwelling game birds, pheasant or woodcock or whatever.

The studio was forlorn and cold. Liv turned on the heat and swept up the usual die-off of flies near the windows.

"Give it a day," she told Travis, "and we can work out here."

Travis climbed off the stool he had been sitting on. "Don't forget the water, Liv."

"Right," she said. "The water."

It had been shut off and the pipes drained months ago by Walter.

Travis tried the faucets. "Dry," he said.

"Yup," Liv agreed. "I'll have to call Walter to fix them. Maybe he'll come out today and do it. Then we can still work tomorrow. And if he can't come today, we'll just carry a pail over from the house."

"Now we can go sliding?" Travis asked.

"Ayuh," Liv said. "Right now. Over the hill to Miss Alden's house."

They set off through the woods. First it was uphill, and then the land fell naturally toward the boundaries of Miss Alden's property. Stopping to take a breather, Liv leaned against a tree trunk, and then slipped behind it.

"I've got you now," she growled at Travis, and jumping out from behind the tree, fired her forefinger at him. "Ptu-ptu-ptu-ee. Die, Commie dog!"

Travis flopped onto the snow clutching his chest. "Aargh," he screamed. He rolled over and fired back. "Ka-pow. Ka-pow."

Liv flopped into the snow, too, rolled onto her back, and stared at the sky. Snowflakes fell onto her lashes and she blinked. She opened her mouth and let them fall on her tongue. She moved her arms and legs in arcs to make an angel.

Travis crept up next to her. "Good angel, Liv," he said. "We playing commando or what?"

She laughed and sat up. "I'll give you a head start, okay? Just don't go too far."

"Gotcha," Travis said, and disappeared into the brush.

Liv gathered up the sleds' dragropes and set off along the path, moving as quietly as she could, looking and listening for him. Once she saw a flash of boot heel under a bush, and several times heard a distinct giggle. She arrived at the orange-flagged pine that was one of the markers along the property line. There she looked around rather anxiously.

"Travis!" she shouted. "I give up. Show yourself."

But there was only the soughing of the wind among the trees.

The snow was falling steadily now. Liv shivered and stomped around the tree.

"Goddamn it, Travis," she muttered. "This isn't funny."

She clambered to the top of an outcropping of rock and stared into the woods in every direction.

"Travis!" she shouted.

His name echoed back at her from the woods. She slid down the rock and paced, her throat tightening.

And then there was a low growl, and he leapt at her from behind, knocking her facedown.

His arms around her knees told her instantly it was Travis, but it was not enough to stop her screaming, or the flare of terror in her gut. She rolled over in the snow and grabbed him under the armpits.

"You little bastard!" she shouted in anger, and then hugged him, and laughed.

He wrapped his arms tightly around her neck, and kissed her, and said, voice atremble, "I'm sorry, Liv."

She kissed him back, and sat up. "Goddamn, you scared me."

He grinned. "Did I?"

She snatched off his cap and ruffled his hair. "You know it."

His face lit in delight.

She pushed him off and stood up. "Let's go sliding, kid, before this snow buries us."

"Woooo-eeee!" Travis shouted and tossed his cap into the air.

The hill sloping down to the old Dexter house was nigh on to perfect for sliding. Liv was sure Miss Alden wouldn't mind. It might be technically trespassing, but it was just sliding, as harmless a thing as a trespasser could do. The old stone house, windows blanked by its shutters, stood forbidding as a tombstone between the shore and the orchard. The snow had risen over the raw-looking bricked-up cellar windows and had erased the driveway. Clearly, no one had been around for weeks, perhaps months.

Liv decided to drop Miss Alden a note to tell her the place was undisturbed. It might make her feel better to know the vandals hadn't struck, at least not yet.

An hour or so of this, she thought, pushing Travis off on his first trip down the hill, then they would have to go to the village for more milk and orange juice and a newspaper. He screamed ecstatically all the way to the bottom.

"Here I come, Commie dog!" she shouted to him, and threw herself belly down onto her sled.

Travis jumped up and down. "Come and get me!" he screamed.

CHAPTER 10

S CREAMING ENGINES shattered the midday quiet. Roaring over the frozen lake, they threw extravagant plumes of snow into the balmy air as they chased one another in playful circles and figure eights, like skaters. The men astride them hollered and whooped. From the Narrows, the three machines raced all out toward North Bay.

On the shore behind them remained the trailer on which they had transported the snow machines, the truck that had drawn it, and Arden Nighswander, sitting in the cab, watching them go. He cupped his hand around a cigarette to light it, though there was no breeze entering at the open window to threaten the flame of his match. Nighswander bent his head to the Camel, drew it, then looked up and around, as if he thought someone was going to try to take the cigarette away from him. The snow machines had grown small and indistinguishable in the white distance. Nighswander grunted, then started the truck and drove away, leaving the trailer on the shore. The sound of engines, truck and snow machines, faded away, and that place was quiet again.

The snow machines sped straight up the lake for several miles, until the shore flattened and became continuous with the surface of the lake at Merrill Beach, the northerly of the town's two public beaches. Rand Nighswander led his brother and stepbrother on their machines onto a path through the woods. Except that Rand wore an army surplus camouflage jacket, it was hard to tell them one from the other in their identical black ski masks and dark snowmobile suits, moving as fast as they were. In the depth of woods that speed also rendered anonymous, trees and brush and rock blurred into something like walls on either side of the path. The machines, too, were nearly identical, though the Nighswander brothers' were a little heavier and more powerful than Gordy Teed's. The trees grew younger and closer together, the brush scrubbier, the rocks bigger, so the machines were forced to slow.

One by one they left the cover of the woods and entered the clearing that was the Winslows' backyard. The lawn furniture and picnic table were stored away, the Winslows' motorboat tucked underneath the porch of the cottage. The shades were drawn. The driveway had not been plowed since the first snow, as the Winslows belonged to the school of summer residents who took it as a tenant that a plowed driveway only made things easier for the thieves, and the fire department would never get there before the place was cinders anyway. The most recent snow had been tracked only by squirrels and coons and foxes passing through, though under that was buried the shuffling, heavy snowshoe tread of Walter McKenzie who had checked the Winslows' cottage the day before yesterday.

Rand Nighswander stilled his engine and dismounted his machine. He looked over the property as if he had just come into proud ownership.

"Ricky," he said, "look under the house for the motor to that boat."

"Asshole can do that," Ricky said.

Rand poked his brother's elbow almost gently. "He's liable to drop it and break it."

Gordy slouched and whined.

Ricky Nighswander shrugged and made for the porch.

Rand and Gordy strolled up the steps and onto the porch. Rand paused and looked around, then kicked the door in with one savage thrust. The door splintered and sagged inward. Gordy giggled.

Irritation flashed in Rand's eyes and Gordy swallowed hard.

Rand stepped through the broken frame into the shaft of daylight it admitted into the gloomy interior of the cottage living room. He unzipped his snowmobile suit and fished a pack of Pall Malls from an inside chest pocket. He shook out a cigarette, inserted it between his lips, and held it there.

The sheeted furniture on the machine-made braided rug crowded the room like boulders in shallow water. Rand strolled into the kitchen, a narrow galley across a bar at one end. A rooster with an electric clock for a body was over the range. Its greasy black cord hung unplugged from its tail like a broken and bedraggled feather. A trio of calico cozies cut in the shape of curled up cats covered a blender, a toaster, and a coffee maker. Rand opened drawers and poked around in them, until he located a box of wooden kitchen matches. Holding the box in one hand, he extracted a single match, scraped it over the abrasive strip on the side, and hunched over it to light the cigarette. He dropped the matches back into the drawer and slammed it shut, then stood, looking at it thoughtfully.

Behind him, on the bar, a sectional candy dish formed a glass dachshund. From the other side, Gordy Teed checked each part of the candy dish carefully and found only one elderly Hershey's Kiss that had melted in its foil wrapping, and a quantity of dead flies.

"Check the cupboards," Rand Nighswander told him.

"Ayuh," Gordy said in his high voice.

Rand's mouth twisted in disgust. He disappeared down a narrow hall toward the cottage bedrooms.

Gordy cheerfully banged the cupboard doors open and closed until he found the one where the Winslows stored their liquor. Even Gordy could tell it was the liquor cabinet by the bottle rings on the plastic shelf liner. It was otherwise bare.

"Shitagoddamn," said Gordy mournfully.

Rand, with his lips pinched shut on the cigarette, came out of the bedrooms dangling a gun. It was a rust-speckled, nickel-plated Smith & Wesson thirty-two. In his other hand, he cupped a faded, feather-cornered box of thirty-two slugs as delicately as if it were a woman's breast.

"They didn't leave a drop," Gordy announced. Then he noticed Rand's find. "Hoo-eee."

Rand studied the thirty-two. He took the cigarette out of his mouth. "They didn't leave anything worth shit," he said. He shoved the gun and the box of ammo into an interior pocket of his snowmobile suit. He put the cigarette back between his lips.

A shadow caught his eye. He dropped to his knees and reached into the back of the cupboard. "Hot damn," he muttered, around the butt, and showed Gordy an unopened bottle of Jim Beam. "The old farts missed one."

Gordy's face brightened and he reached for the bottle.

Rand held it away from him. With two fingers, he removed the cigarette from between his lips, dropped it to the floor, and ground it out with his heel. "Wait a frigging minute. I found it."

Gordy's face fell. "Ayuh," he said. "That's true. I guess it's yours."

Rand opened the bottle. Gordy watched him, open-mouthed, as he raised the bottle to his mouth and knocked back a mouthful.

"Ah," said Rand.

"Good, huh?" Gordy said.

"Ass-kickin'," said Rand.

Gordy grinned. "Ass-kickin'," he said.

"Piss-cuttin'," Rand elaborated.

Gordy nodded and grinned wider. "Piss-cuttin'," he said delightedly.

"Blow me for it," Rand said.

The excitement went out of Gordy's face again. He slouched and dug one heavily booted toe into the rug. "Jeez," he muttered. "What you wanna tease me for, Randy?"

" 'Cause you're such an asshole," said Rand. He slugged a little more of the liquor.

There was muffled cursing and crashing from under the house, then the stomp of boots on the steps and across the porch. Ricky Nighswander thrust his head in at the broken door.

"That motor's a piece of shit, Rand," he said. "I give it the heave-ho."

Rand grunted.

"What's that you got?" Ricky asked.

Rand extended the bottle. Ricky had a turn at it.

"I found it," Rand said. "Asshole here missed it."

Gordy glowered.

"It was way in the back," he said.

Ricky snickered. "So's your asshole, and you couldn't find that in broad daylight without a search party."

"Jeez," muttered Gordy.

"This place is a bust," said Rand. He drew out the Smith & Wesson and showed it to his brother. "Looks like they sent away for it with them cereal box tops, don't it? Just the kind of nigger blaster you'd expect that dried-up old cunt to have under her pillow."

Ricky laughed.

Rand returned the gun to his pocket. "Not very kindly of the good ol' Winslows to leave the cupboard so frigging bare," Rand said.

"Nope," said Ricky.

"No sirree," agreed Gordy.

"Shut up, asshole," Ricky said.

"Okay, okay," Gordy said.

"Go to it, boys," Rand said.

Ricky picked up a barstool and hurtled it through the nearest window. Gordy ducked and came up giggling.

"Hoo-ee," he said, and began pitching the sections of the candy dish dog against the walls.

Rand Nighswander laughed. He lit another cigarette. Once it was pinched between his lips, he took out a hunting knife and began systematically slashing through the sheets that covered the old-fashioned overstuffed furniture and into the upholstery. Wads and tangles of stuffing flew through the air.

Ricky went into the bedrooms. He could be heard breaking glass and wood. There was a satisfying crash as he landed with both feet on the Winslows' double bed and it collapsed. Then there was silence.

Gordy whooped and hurried down the hall to the second bedroom, inspired to break the twin beds that furnished the Winslows' guestroom.

Ricky strolled out of the Winslows' bedroom, pulling up his ski pants. He leaned in at the guestroom door and watched Gordy bound onto the first twin bed. His weight drove the mattress and spring to the floor. The ends of the bed collapsed toward the middle. Gordy clambered out of the broken frame.

"Left Mizz Winslow something to go with her dog turd collection," Ricky said.

Gordy covered his mouth and giggled.

"Jesus," Ricky said, rolling his eyes at the ceiling.

"Let's get outta here," Rand shouted at them from the living room.

They hurried back and found him chugging from the bottle. Motes of chair stuffing still hung in the still air, in the light of the broken door.

Ricky repeated his remark about leaving something for Claire Winslow's dog turd collection.

Rand laughed and handed the bottle to his brother. "You're a dirty little bastard, Ricky," he said.

Ricky grinned happily.

Rand dropped his cigarette to the floor. He studied it a few seconds before putting his heel to it. "I'd love to leave it lay and torch this hole. Don't need the frigging fireboys around here this afternoon, though. Not yet." He stepped through the doorway. "It's getting colder," he said. "Give Gordy some of that firewater so he don't freeze his teensy little pecker off."

Gordy reached eagerly for the bottle.

Ricky held it away from him. "Blow me," he said.

Gordy pouted. "Rand says to give me some."

"Blow me," Ricky insisted.

"Rand," Gordy said loudly. "Ricky won't give—"

Ricky stomped hard on Gordy's foot.

Gordy blubbered.

"Shut up, asshole," said Ricky.

"Rand says to give me some," Gordy insisted. "He says I don't have to blow you no more."

"When'd he say that?" Ricky said. "I didn't hear him say that."

"Rand says—" Gordy began, and Ricky stomped down on his foot again.

Gordy squealed and danced away from Ricky.

Rand stood in the doorway. "You jerk-offs," he said. "Ricky, I said give 'm some firewater."

Ricky passed the bottle reluctantly to Gordy.

"Don't get any spit in it," Ricky said.

Gordy chugged eagerly.

"Come on," Rand said. "It's starting to snow. I told daddy we'd be back at the landing at four. We got a lot to do before then."

"Right," said Ricky.

The doorway was empty again, Rand's boots crunching down the steps.

Ricky grabbed the bottle away from Gordy and stepped through the doorway. "Blow me," he said to Gordy conversationally, and was gone.

"Meany," Gordy complained, shuffling after him. "Meany,

meany Ricky," he called after him. "Jerk-off," he muttered. "He's a
dirty little bastard." Gordy stood on the top step. "I don't have to
blow you," he shouted. "Rand says so."

The Breens' cottage was much tougher to crack. It was only a
few years old and constructed of first-class materials. The two doors,
one on the driveway side of the house, and sliding doors on the deck,
were both glass, and had bars of iron wedged in the channels to
prevent them being opened. Without the police locks, of course, they
would have been easy to bust, as the locks in the aluminum frames
were soft as the snow.

The windows were set high, a stretch for a grown man from the
ground. On Ricky's shoulders, Rand was able to break one with a
wrench from his snowmobile toolbox and, after clearing the glass
shards, boost himself through it and into the house. It felt like hard
work by the time he had the police locks out of the channels of the
deck doors.

He let Ricky and Gordy in.

"This should be rich," he said. "Be thorough, for once."

The living room was a big boxy two-story room with a loft
where the bedrooms were. Snow diffused the light admitted by two
large skylights in the cathedral ceiling. One end of the room was set
up for dining with a round glass table and bamboo-legged chairs. In
the near wall was a pass-through into the kitchen. Like the Winslows', the furniture was sheeted, but it was otherwise very different,
all sleek and modern, glass where glass could be used, well-oiled
hardwood, shiny chrome, and bright cushions in rough-textured
cloth. The living room rug had been rolled and covered in plastic.
Ricky slashed the plastic and unrolled it.

"Nice rug," he said.

"Too big to move," Rand said. "If it were springtime, and we
had a truck, yeah."

Ricky lifted his knife over the rug and thrust down, screaming
"Huh!"

Gordy, hunkered next to the liquor cabinet, jumped. He hooted
softly. Turning back to his work, he rummaged with both hands. He

hooted again, loudly, and held up a partial bottle of vermouth and another almost full of Triple Sec.

Rand examined them. He grunted. "They got alcohol in 'em. That's all you can say for 'em."

Ricky gave off stabbing and slashing the rug and pounded up the spiral stairs toward the loft bedrooms.

Gordy unscrewed the cap of the vermouth and tasted it. He rolled it around in his mouth, and swallowed it noisily.

"It's okay," he assured Rand seriously.

"Sure," Rand agreed, "if you like that kind of dogpiss."

Gordy's face fell.

Rand followed Ricky up the spiral stairs.

He found Ricky in the master bedroom. The bed was round, and there was a mirror on the ceiling. Ricky was alternately patting the mattress and looking at the mirror.

Rand whistled.

Ricky sat down on the bed. "Geez," he said. "I don't know what to do."

"Nothing new," Rand said. "You find anything?"

Ricky flicked a glance at the mirror. "This," he said. "Geez, Rand, you ever see yourself screwing in a mirror?"

Rand swaggered into the room. "Sure." He stared at the mirror and licked his lips. "Not this one," he admitted. "I wouldn't mind it. Too bad the pilot didn't leave his wife here, too. It wasn't too neighborly, when you think about it. Get me all hotted up looking at the mirror and nothing handy to screw except you two polecats."

Ricky chortled and then frowned. "There's too many good places to take a dump, in this place. That glass table," and Ricky held up one finger, "that fancy rug," and he showed two, "and this bed."

Rand laughed. "So you don't know whether to shit or go blind."

Ricky grinned. "Nope."

"I have to do all your thinking," Rand said. "No contest, see."

"How's that?" Ricky asked.

Rand swatted him lightly across the crown of his head. "How many chances you gonna have to watch yourself shit on a round bed?"

Ricky's face lit up. He pounded the bed with both fists ecstatically.

"Just wait 'til I'm done here," Rand said.

There was a built-in dresser and vanity that took up one whole wall. Rand pulled out drawers, looked into them, and then threw them on the floor. He found nothing.

He turned to the closet that took up the opposite wall. A few old clothes hung inside plastic bags. He rattled the bags, unzipped them, groped the clothes. A stack of shelves stood at one end. Straw hats, an old hairdryer, a retired electric shaver, an old airline shaving kit occupied a tier of shelves at one end. Rand shuffled quickly through the oddments, until he reached the shaving kit. Fly the Friendly Skies was printed on the sides. He opened it, patted the interior, and was rewarded.

"Hot damn," he said.

He fingered the lining until he felt the loose edge he was sure would be there, then tore it open.

"What you got?" Ricky asked.

Rand thrust his fingers into the lining and pulled out a foil-wrapped package the size of a package of soup mix.

"It might be a rubber for the Jolly Green Giant," Rand said, "but I don't think so."

Ricky skittered across the room to get a closer look.

Rand peeled back the foil. He threw back his head and howled with delight.

The rising wind whipped stinging snow into their eyes as the Nighswander brothers and Gordy Teed paralleled the shoreline a few dozen yards out on the lake, forcing them to proceed at a slower rate. The brothers had customized the snowmobiles for brute speed, so the machines racketed and coughed, unhappy at less than all out. The traveling surface at least was still good. A few hours of this kind of snow and the machines would bog down in the soft drifts.

The short day was being shortened further by the onset of the snowstorm. The sky seemed to be closing in on them, sucking up all the light so that the shoreline was increasingly blurred, and they had to put on headlights. With the light went the elusive warmth, and they felt the chill even through the thick snowmobile suits and their long underwear. The sight of the Russells' house was an unspoken relief, a shelter from the storm. They brought the machines ashore and dismounted. All hunched over against the wind, they hurried toward the lake-facing deck of the house. It wasn't until they had mounted the steps and were crunching across the deck that they realized there was a light on inside.

Rand raised one hand and stopped them in their tracks.

"It's just one of them timed lights," Ricky whispered. "Make you think somebody's ta home."

Rand shook his head. He sniffed the air. "You've been jerking off so much, you've gone foolish," he said. "Don't you smell the woodsmoke?"

Ricky sniffed the air. So did Gordy. They looked at each other.

"That's woodsmoke awright," Gordy observed.

"Go round the other side," Rand said to Ricky. "See if there's anything parked in the driveway."

Ricky stood where he was. "This ain't safe," he said. "Daddy'd have your ass for trying a place where somebody was ta home."

Rand peered in the sliding glass doors. He smiled at what he saw. "Daddy ain't here," he said. "He's sitting on his fat ass by the fire, bending his elbow with Jeannie."

Staring at the deck, sneaking nervous peeks at Rand and Ricky, Gordy began to mutter under his breath about the implied slur on his mother. He shuffled his feet and rubbed his gloved hands together.

The Nighswander brothers ignored him. Ricky hesitated another moment, then went to do as he was bid. He was back in a hurry, patently relieved.

"Driveway's been plowed, and there's old tracks, snow's filling 'em up now. No car there."

Rand nodded.

"Somebody's been here and gone," Ricky said.

"But they'll be back," Rand said. "They've gone out on an errand."

"No," Ricky said. "I think they're really gone."

Rand looked at him. He unzipped his suit, and reached inside for his cigarettes. "They left the fuckin' cat," he said.

That shut Ricky up a minute. Gordy giggled. Ricky shuffled his feet on the deck.

"Then let's get the fuck outta here," Ricky said. " 'Fore they get back."

Rand grinned at him. "I want to have a look around first. Don't you know whose place this is?"

Ricky grinned back. "Russell, ain't it?"

"Yeah," Rand said. "I'd like to have a pair of her drawers, see?"

Ricky and Gordy looked at each other. Ricky snickered.

Rand tried the sliding glass door. It resisted, then slid open.

"Hot damn," he said. "She knowed I was coming, and left the door open for me."

The other two followed him inside. They left the door open behind them. Snow blew in and sprinkled the aged Oriental rug that covered the living room floor. Instantly it melted into the tight wool. On one side of the room, floor-to-ceiling shelves housed books and tapes. Some of the shelves had been made into cupboards with the addition of small sliding doors. There was a comfortable, brightly patterned couch, an elderly platform rocker, a bulky old chair with a standing lamp next to it. An old rolltop oak desk filled one corner. A low table with a pack of cards scattered over its glass top squatted on brass casters in front of the fire. The fieldstone fireplace had several niches in it. There were handmade pots displayed in all but one, which was tall and narrow as if for a vase, but it housed instead a Peach kaleidoscope.

The Poor, curled up on the hearth, where the fire was banked but still glowed, opened one eye. She uncoiled herself, stretched, and yowled plaintively.

"Nice kitty," said Gordy. He held out his hand toward her. She licked his palm with her rough pink tongue. He giggled.

Ricky slid open one of the sliding doors in the bookcase, revealing a VCR. "Lookee, lookee," he said. He flicked open the door just below it. "And here's the tube."

Rand grunted, and disappeared down the hallway toward the children's bedrooms. It took only a moment for him to check them out before he was back again and went into the short hallway that led to the master bedroom. He noted the single suitcase tucked behind the bedroom door, peeked in at the bathroom, and saw but one toothbrush and a neatly arranged clear plastic sack of makeup, a bottle of perfume, a frilly shower cap. He flipped the lid of the wicker hamper in the bathroom and rummaged quickly through it, hooking out a pair of panties. They were some navy blue silky material, and very bare. Smiling, he tucked them into his snowmobile suit. He rummaged quickly through every drawer in the two dressers, and the nighttables on either side of the bed, and found no more treasures. Then he tried the bed, sitting on its edge, bouncing the mattress gently with one hand.

"Bet she fucks like a mink," he said softly.

He wished he had time to whack off on it, leave her a calling card. Next time, baby, he promised himself.

When he came back into the living room, Ricky was putting a tape into the machine.

"Looka this," Ricky said. "They got some wicked good tapes."

Tapes had been removed from their shelves next to the TV and scattered over the couch and floor.

Rand moved so swiftly Ricky had no time even to flinch before his brother's hand on the back of his head drove his forehead into one of the shelves.

"You stupid fuck," Rand said. "Get those fucking tapes off the floor."

Ricky rubbed his forehead and stumbled around the room, scrabbling frantically for the tapes and whining.

Gordy came out of the kitchen, carrying a dusty gallon jug of Gallo Hearty Burgundy and wearing a huge grin, which disappeared instantly at the sight of Rand's face, and Ricky's fumbling.

"She's liable to be back any minute. We might not have time to unhook this shit and get it outta the house before she does. I figure to hit this place when they ain't nobody here," Rand said. "So don't you jerk-offs touch nothing, or when we come back, there won't be nothing here to take. They'll clean it out."

Gordy looked uncertainly at the jug of wine.

"Put it back, asshole," Ricky growled.

Gordy shrugged and wandered back into the kitchen.

"What about them panties?" Ricky said sullenly. "I know you got 'em. You was in there long enough."

"Last thing she'll think is somebody came in and took 'em. She'll think they dropped behind somethin' or the washing machine ate 'em," Rand said.

"Wisht I was the washing machine," Ricky said and snickered.

Going out hadn't been too difficult in the Pacer. Its studded tires and wide-based stability increased Liv's confidence in it. Coming back, there was a lot more new snow, and more falling, to grease the way. She found herself babying the Pacer down the slopes and around the curves. She had a strangle grip on the wheel, and was hunched over it, peering at the road ahead.

Travis as always sensed her tightening up before she did. He leaned over the backseat, watching the road with her.

"Tough, huh, Liv?" he asked.

She pushed her shoulders back and down to ease the tension. "It's no piece of cake," she admitted.

He patted her shoulder. "Don't worry. We can walk home if we have to and Walter will get the car out if you crash it up."

"Thanks," she said. "I'm going to try not to."

It seemed to take forever, and she felt like she had rolled a boulder up a steep hill by the time they arrived at their own driveway. She decided on the spur of the moment she had pushed her luck all she wanted; they would walk down the hill to the house. She and Travis were both dressed for the weather; she had never forgotten her father's dictum that in the Maine winter, it took a professional fool to go out bootless and half-dressed, trusting to the shelter of an automobile. There was always the chance a body would be forced to motivate on its own two feet through snow and ice.

"End of the line," she said to Travis, and pulled the car to a stop in the widening of the road at the top of the driveway.

Travis sighed and began to collect scattered G.I. Joes and stuff them in his pocket. Liv collected the small bag of groceries and helped Travis out of the car. He let go of her hand as soon as his feet were on the ground. It was better that way. If one of them slipped and fell, there was no need for the other to do it, too, which would surely happen if they linked hands. As it was, they had to pick their way cautiously, in the growing dark, not talking to each other, concentrating on staying upright, homing on the house.

Snow always made Liv cheerful. Partly, she thought, it was because it made the world clean and beautiful and spanking new. The air was charged with its cold, crystalline sweetness and it roused her. She wanted to roll around in it. As soon as she had deposited the milk and orange juice in the refrigerator, she decided, she would turn on the floodlights in the yard and take Travis back outside so they could slide down the driveway. She was glad she had left the car at the top of the hill. It would be a treat for Travis, playing out of doors in the almost-dark. He would go to bed tired, and with roses in his cheeks.

She did take his hand again when they reached the steps of the back porch, and he smiled up at her. She had gotten them home safe, and it made her happier to know she had fulfilled his trust in her. That weird moment in the woods when she thought she might have lost him and he had sprung at her, and then the difficult drive home, had the compensatory effect of reinforcing her happiness.

She opened the door and stepped into the hall ahead of him. By the light of the lamp she had left on in the living room, she saw the three men moving toward the deck doors. In weird chorus, their heads turned to look at her, surprise flickering there and then something else, a predatory gleam, and she knew who they were, and understood she had surprised them, and she was afraid. Without thinking about it, she stepped between them and the sight of Travis, and shoved him backward toward the door with her bottom.

"Liv!" he exclaimed in exasperation.

She had lost the edge of surprise. The three men started to move toward her.

She whirled and grabbed Travis and barreled through the open back door and across the porch.

There were hands snatching at her, heavy bodies close behind her breathing hard, and fingers snatching her cap, then tangled in her hair, jerking her head backward, hurting her, and throwing her off balance. She stumbled and fell down the stairs, still carrying Travis, who was screaming, and there was someone on top of both of them, falling with them. Pain flashed in her elbows rapping hard on the snow-slippery steps. She hit a shoulder, scraped her chin, and Travis was torn away from her.

"No!" she screamed, and a hand cupped her chin and drove her head backward into the snow. She stared up at Rand Nighswander. Then he punched her in the stomach, and she curled up, the breath knocked out of her, and retched into the snow.

"What you want to run for?" she heard him asking softly, and behind him, Travis screaming and struggling and being cursed by one of the others.

He helped her to her feet. She was dizzy and staggered and he caught her and picked her up. He carried her up the steps again and into the house and settled her gently onto the couch. She tried to sit up, and he put one big hand flat on her sternum and pushed her back down.

"Relax," he said.

He turned around and addressed the one who had Travis, the one who looked like him. His brother.

"Put the kid down," he said.

Travis was loose and across the room and clinging to her at once. He was sobbing, and shaking with fright. She gathered him close to her, her own pain and fear put aside in the need to soothe and comfort him.

Rand took the chair from the desk, turned it around, and sat in it, resting his arms on the back. "We had some trouble with our machines," Rand said. "Saw your woodsmoke and thought we could use your phone, but you weren't here. We tried the door in case you were and didn't hear us. It was open. We got warmed up and was just leaving."

"You punched me," Liv said.

Rand smiled. "I am sorry about that. Truth is, you scared the bejesus outta me. I figured you was going to start screaming and getting us in trouble. You didn't give me a chance to explain, see?"

Liv closed her eyes. If she pretended to believe the lie, would they go away? She was outnumbered and outmuscled. It wouldn't do her any good not to play this game.

"All right," she said, avoiding his eye. "No lasting harm done. But you'd better go along now. You've scared my boy," she said, trying to sound more rueful than accusatory.

Rand got up and put the chair back. Gordy was sitting on the hearth, stroking the cat. Ricky leaned against the mantel, chewing on his nails. Rand reached into his snowsuit for his cigarettes. The panties came with them. He grabbed them as they floated toward the floor, trying to palm them but Liv was faster.

She felt Travis lift his face from between her breasts. She stared at the panties, and blushed furiously. "How dare you?" she blurted.

Rand's hand fell over hers, holding the blue panties. He covered her hand entirely and crushed it in his so she instinctively pulled away, but still he held on.

"It was easy," he said.

Travis' head dropped forward onto Rand's hand over hers and he sank his teeth into it.

Rand bellowed and struck Travis with the back of his hand. She rolled Travis behind her onto the sofa, and came up after Rand, with a wail of rage.

"You bastard," she screamed, and went for his face, slapping his ears and using her nails.

He backhanded her, driving her back onto the couch.

Travis had come up from under her, and he hurtled himself past his mother at Rand. Ricky Nighswander seized him from behind, and tossed him casually onto his back on the rug, knocking the wind out of him. There was a gleam at the corner of Travis' eye and then he felt the razor edge of Ricky's knife at his throat, as Ricky crouched over him. When Travis rolled his eyes to see where Ricky was, he could see the third man, the one who looked stupid, crouched on the hearth. The stupid man was watching them with wide-open blank eyes, his mouth open, too, so he was drooling a little. The cat, squeezed in his hands, squeaked, and he looked at her, surprised.

The sounds of scuffling stopped at once. Travis could hear his mother sobbing, and the heavy breathing of the man with the crooked lip.

"Don't hurt him," she said.

"Settle down," the man said. "We ain't going to hurt the kid. Let 'm up."

The sharp edge was gone, though his throat felt suddenly very stiff and sore, and he realized he had been holding his breath. Rough hands jerked him to his feet and he was thrust toward his mother. He hid his face in her belly.

Liv sank back onto the couch, holding Travis. "Please go away," she said.

"Sure," said Rand. "Just you remember this."

She looked up at him. "What?"

"Nothing happened here," he said.

She stared at him, then lowered her eyes. "Nothing happened here."

Rand nudged Ricky. "Move it," he said.

Gordy put down the cat. "Nice kitty," he said. "Nice kitty."

Ricky came up behind him and slapped the back of his head. "Move it, Rand says."

Gordy rubbed the back of his head. "Okay, okay."

He went through the door first, followed by Ricky, who booted him in the rear as he went out. Gordy stumbled across the deck. Ricky roared with delight.

"Shut up," Rand said, and Ricky shut up and hustled away across the deck into the snow-filled darkness.

Snow swirled out of the dark and into the living room through the open door.

Rand stopped in the door to look back. "Don't forget," he said.

Liv nodded.

Then he was gone.

"Stay there," she said to Travis. She jumped up and slammed the door closed and locked it. She drew the curtains across the glass. Then she ran to the back door and locked that. She ran from room to room, checking the window locks. When she was sure everything that would lock was locked, she hurried back to the living room, and hugged Travis.

"We're safe now. Okay?"

Travis buried his head between her breasts and clung to her.

She reached over him for the phone on the end table. "I'm calling Walter now," she said. "He'll come and stay with us. Tomorrow, we'll go home."

Travis raised his face. "Good," he said.

Liv put the phone to her ear. The line was dead.

CHAPTER 11

FIREFIGHT

Rough Cut #5

Night again, flurrying snow melts on the
pavement and the blind windows of the darkened
bar and then refreezes to a fragile glaze,
floating on a skin of water, so the glaze
crackles and moves with the water, a study in
plate tectonics in microcosm. The streetlights
glimmer on the slick wetness. The street is as
empty as the bar. The neon sign is crusted with
the unstable snow like something brought up from
the ocean bottom rimed with the salt and
minerals that in the sea seem to grow as easily
as organisms. A man's weak night shadow,
courtesy of the streetlights, falls like a ghost
on a hand-lettered sign taped to the inside of
the glass door: CLOSED BECAUSE OF DEATH.
The shadow-man darkens a narrow alley
between the bar and the parking garage next to it
that leads through a parade of garbage cans and
smashed cardboard boxes to a thick, scarred back
door. The shadow-man passes by it, and corners
the building. In the thick cement wall there is
but one window, like a cellar window, but much
higher. It is not barred, but the glass in it is

thick and rippled. The cement sill is deep and
slanted downward. The shadow-man feels of the
sill, and then withdraws. He is back in seconds,
with a wooden crate from the trash around the
corner. It is a precarious perch; the crate
cracks audibly under his weight and he freezes.
There is a long moment while he holds his breath.
At last he moves again, so delicately and
carefully that his movements seem stylized. In
his hand there is a glass cutter. He removes the
glass in one piece. As he steps carefully off,
the box collapses, he staggers, and nearly drops
the glass. But he recovers, and stands
motionless until he is satisfied he is yet
undiscovered. Dispensing with the broken crate,
he leaps for the sill, catches it, and hauls
himself through the opening. On the other side
of the frame, he drops into impenetrable
darkness.

Again he waits, breathing a little harshly at
first but almost immediately dampening it down,
forcing himself to inhale and exhale evenly and
quietly. In due course he permits himself a few
seconds' light from the narrow beam of a tiny
flashlight. In those few seconds of light he
sees the entire room: a high-ceilinged shallow
rectangle containing three urinals and two
doorless stalls. The floor is tiled, the walls
grimy and graffitoed but in such scant light the
scrawls are unreadable abstractions. Nor can
the color of the walls or the tile be discerned.
The flashlight renders the room in chiaroscuro,
like a moody black-and-white snapshot of the
grim-and-gross-is-real school of artistic
photography.

The shadow-man crosses the room. He slips his
hand into his jacket in the vicinity of his
heart, and when he withdraws there is something
black and dense in it. He sidles out the door.
Now he depends on night vision and sense of touch
as uncanny as a blind man's to guide him through
a no-man's-land mined with liquor cases. A

swinging door, opened very slowly, a fraction of
an inch at a time, opens to the barroom. Here the
streetlights leak in and outline the room: the
horseshoe shape of the bar from the inside, the
big rectangular windows with neon advertising,
black scrawls of names written backward in them,
the round edges of tables, the shoulders of
chairs, the sharp corners of the walls of
booths, and the blackness within them.

The shadow-man slips, crouching, through the
swinging door, and into the U of the bar. He sits
there on his haunches for long moments. He
cannot see, but he can listen, and the bar
protects him on three sides. A glimmer of light
from the streetlights bounces off the object in
his hand.

In preternatural silence, he hears his own
heartbeat, his own breathing. And then,
another's.

There is a rustle across the room, from the
booths, and he flattens himself to the floor and
edges around the bar.

Straining now to hear anything that might
reveal the location of the other, he is a snake
waiting to strike.

And then there is cold iron at the back of his
neck.

"Don't move, you son of a bitch," the other
growls.

The shadow-man tenses, and as suddenly
relaxes, goes limp. He slowly extends his left
hand, which holds his own gun loosely. "You win,
you bastard," he says out loud, and laughs and
rolls over on his back and grabs the muzzle of
the gun and thrusts it upward with all his
strength.

The explosion of the bullet from the chamber
is deafening. But the bullet is directed toward
the ceiling; it will do no harm. The shadow-man
twists the gun from the other's hand, and flips
it around so it is now pointed at his assailant.
The shadow-man produces his little flashlight

and turns it on, to reveal the face of Ratcliffe,
the black policeman.

"Ah, Ratty," the shadow-man says, and his
voice and accent identify him as Denny.

"Motherfucker," Ratcliffe says.

Denny laughs. "I knew you'd be here, Ratty."

Ratcliffe is silent for a second, then says,
"I wish I'd blown your motherfuckin' head off."

Denny clucks reproachfully. "Where's your
sense of brotherhood, Ratty. We're in this
together, you know."

"The fuck we are," Ratcliffe says. "You done
it, you got The Man on our backs. You the one
oughta have his balls stomped."

The safety clicks on the gun Denny has taken
away from him. "There," says Denny. He turns the
gun toward himself and extends it to Ratcliffe.
"Your weapon, my man. I ain't your enemy,
Ratty."

Ratcliffe leans forward to take the gun back.
"How'd you know I'd be here?"

Denny grins. "You was the one taught me the
safest place was at the bottom of a pile of
corpses. Best jungle fighter I ever met."

Ratcliffe's hand snakes out of the dark and
has Denny by the throat before Denny can do more
than get up the side of his hand in protection.

"Tell you somethin' else, you piece of white
trash," Ratcliffe growls. "Best thing I could do
is cut your miserable lyin' throat wide enough
so you got two stupid grins instead of one. The
Man, Court, he be satisfied then, and leave me
alone. That's something I never taught you, boy,
on account of you can't be trusted. Sometimes
the only way to survive, boy, is to give the
enemy what he wants."

Denny is motionless under Rat's hand. But his
eyes are bright. He shows all his teeth in a
carnivorous grin.

"Hey, Ratty," he protests. "I don't believe
it. See the day Ratty was scared of old Court."

"I'm smarter than you," Ratcliffe says, "is why."

"Yeah, maybe you are," Denny says. "You're right about one thing."

"What's that?" Ratcliffe asks.

"Ain't your fight, Ratty," Denny says. "Between me and Court. So whyn't you let me settle it?"

Ratcliffe releases Denny's throat and hunkers back. "Court don't know yet it's between you and him."

"Yeah," says Denny, and his hand tightens around his own gun reflexively, and it rises in a slow-motion arc as Ratcliffe reacts and dives under it, and Denny reaches with the other hand for Ratcliffe's gun, and Ratcliffe loses it, as Denny's gun comes down and catches him on the temple, with a sound like an apple hitting a wood floor, and Ratcliffe collapses.

Denny rises over him. "An' you ain't going to ever tell Court it's between him and me, Mr. Almighty Smart Nigger, who ain't smart enough."

And he bends close to Ratcliffe's head and pulls the trigger.

IN the dark out of doors, the three machines snarled through twisting veils of snow. The beams of their headlights did not really illuminate the darkness but rather the myriad snowflakes, so many that they made a gauzy fabric to the eye, though they were more like cobwebs that melted in stings of cold against exposed flesh. Mere transparent fragments made substantial by their uncountable numbers, they reflected the light and absorbed it at the same instant. They drew all the light into their crystalline structure, until they seemed less mirrors than sources, galaxies spewed through space in black-and-white photographs taken outside the distorting atmosphere of the planet. The dark of night was only the emptiness, like outer space, the snow filled up. A frenzied wind drove the snow in every direction at once.

The machines stopped and huddled together. The three men

met in the pooled light of the headlamps. Their ski masks were drawn down against the lacerating windchill. They dropped instinctively to their haunches and bent their heads together.

"I can't see a frigging goddamn thing!" Ricky bawled at Rand.

Rand squatted easily on his haunches and forced a glove-thickened hand inside his snowmobile suit. He drew out his pack of cigarettes and his lighter. He had to shove his face nearly into the flame, holding the lighter in the windbreak of his own body, to light the cigarette.

"Sure is a bitch," he said calmly.

"How we gonna find daddy in this shit?" Ricky demanded.

Gordy Teed's eyeballs showed white as he cast a fearful skittish glance around them. "We ain't never gonna find your daddy in this shit," he said.

Rand looked at him. "That's right, Gordy. We best lay up someplace until this dies down."

"But daddy'll be looking for us," Ricky protested.

Rand flicked cigarette ash directly in front of him. Ricky flinched. "Daddy's warming his fat ass by the fire, don't you worry," he said.

Ricky shifted on his haunches and looked around. The visibility was no more than a few feet, and that shifting with every whim of the wind. "Where to, Randy? We can't see if we're coming or going."

Rand drew thoughtfully at his cigarette before answering. "Best go back the way we came. We ain't come too far."

Gordy Teed's mouth dropped open. A string of saliva glistened against the malodorous stumps of his teeth in the artificial light of the headlamps.

Ricky giggled. "Jesus Christ, Rand. By now that bitch'll have called the cops. Or her hubby or maybe old Walter. Somebuddy, anyway."

"No she won't," Rand said. "I pulled the telephone line while you two were frigging around starting your machines."

Ricky hooted and dug an elbow into Gordy Teed. Gordy Teed flinched.

"I don't wanna go back there, Rand," he whined.

"It's warm back there," Rand said.

"She ain't gonna welcome us with open arms," Ricky said.

"You know it. We'll have to break in. We'll get in a heap of trouble doing that. If we ain't already."

"Ain't you the cynical little bastard," Rand said. "Missus Russell is a decent Christian woman. She ain't gonna let us freeze on a night like this."

"Sure," Ricky said. "She's gonna open the door and say, 'Come on in, fellas. How 'bout a drink?' "

"She might," Rand said.

Ricky hooted again. "Then she's gonna offer to keep us all warm, that right, Rand? Cuddle right up?"

Rand examined the butt of his cigarette. "She might."

"Me first," Ricky said.

Rand stared at him.

Ricky stood up and kicked the snow. "Second then."

"We'll get in a heap of trouble," Gordy Teed said. "Won't we?"

Rand stood up and shook snow off his shoulders. "You two fuckin' animals behave yourself, we won't."

Gordy struggled to his feet.

"First thing is, you ain't gonna act like a coupla barbarians. Act like you're civilized. Shake out your please and thank-yous. Just get it through your thick skulls, what we got here is a woman alone out here with a kid. Now why ain't her hubby with her? 'Cause they ain't getting along, is why."

"How do you know that?" Ricky demanded.

Rand smiled. "I can smell it on her," he said.

Ricky hooted derisively. "On them panties, huh?"

"I'm saying we play our cards right, she might be real nice to us. One of us, or maybe all of us. Just remember, it was my idea is all. I found her. I say who gets her."

"Sounds like you mean to keep her for yourself," Ricky said sulkily.

"What if I do?" Rand said. "I'm entitled, ain't I?"

"Act like it," Ricky said. "Talk like it, don't you?"

"Goddamn right," Rand said.

"What you gonna do, Mister Big, if she yells rape?" Ricky said.

"She's gotta prove it, stupid. It's her against us."

"Like with Loretta Buck?"

"Like with old Loretta," Rand agreed.

"She sure did squeal a lot, didn't she?" Ricky asked, overtaken by sudden reminiscence.

"Come on," Rand said. "I'm freezing my balls off."

Slowly they groped their way back toward the shore, toward the Russells' summer house. Leaving the machines pulled up on the snow-layered beach, they moved as soundlessly as they could toward the house. The curtains had been drawn; they could not see in.

"What do we do?" Ricky whispered to Rand. "Bust a window?"

"You really are a fuckin' barbarian," Rand said contemptuously. "We're gonna knock on the friggin' door."

"Sure," Ricky said. "I gotta see this."

The three men tramped around to the back porch. Rand opened the storm door and rapped casually at the inside door. He shot a quick bright smile at Ricky over his shoulder.

Liv heard the tail end of the knock from the bathroom where she was checking on Travis in his bath. Tightening his grip on the bar of soap to a stranglehold, he looked up at her nervously at the sound.

"Maybe it's Walter, checking on us," Liv said.

Relief showed in Travis' eyes. "Maybe it's daddy," he said.

Liv stooped to brush his hair across his clear wide brow.

"I'll find out," she said. "Don't worry, okay?"

Travis nodded, and dug his nails into the bar of soap.

Liv wiped her hands on the legs of her jeans and forced herself to leave the warm well-lit bathroom. She hesitated, then flicked off the hall light and walked in darkness toward the back door. She could not help glancing nervously from side to side, or edging around the corners. At the same time she was glad she had drawn the shades so no one could look at them; she was dismayed to realize she could not see out. There was no way for her to know if someone was creeping around the house outside. Nothing could be heard above the howl of the wind and the resisting creak of the house. She passed the back door and went into the kitchen without turning on the lights and sidled up next to the window that looked out on the back porch. Of course, she had left the light on, when she and Travis had gone to the village and she knew the daylight would be going when they returned, and it was still on. For an instant she thought she was going to faint, she felt her heart jolt at the sight of them, and then Rand was looking right at her by the light of the porch. She shuddered and backed away.

She had wanted to believe it was the wind that had taken out her telephone line, but here they were again. Taking another step backward, and one to the side, she snapped off the porch light. She froze, unable to breath or think what to do next. She wished desperately for a gun, then remembered the kitchen knives. Creeping noiselessly back into the kitchen, she groped by memory in the proper drawer and took out the carving knife. She crept back to the kitchen door and then she waited.

When the light went out on the porch, Rand cursed under his breath.

Ricky started to swear out loud. Rand stomped on his foot and he shut up.

Gordy Teed whimpered. "She ain't gonna let us in," he whispered hopefully to Rand. "Let's go som'eres else to lay up. The old dyke's, maybe."

Rand ignored him and rapped at the door again, more urgently. When there was no answer, he rapped again and called out, "Missus Russell, we don't mean you no harm. We're freezing, Missus Russell. Won't you let us use your telephone to call my daddy to come and get us?"

Ricky poked him, giggling.

Rand stomped on his foot, harder, and Ricky backed off, limping and muttering.

On the other side of the door, Liv tried to breathe. If he did not know the telephone line was out, perhaps he had not cut it. Or perhaps he was trying to fool her. However the service had been interrupted, he wasn't going to be able to call Arden Nighswander if she did open the door, so why should she? She couldn't tell him that the telephone was dead, though, because of what he might do if he knew she had no contact with the outside world. Then again, if he knew, if he had done it, he might do the very same things anyway. Break in, force his way in. Then what? It was more than she could bear thinking about.

Rand rapped again. "Please, Missus Russell. We'll get lost in this storm. We might freeze to death out here."

She closed her eyes but saw nothing anymore clearly. Did a woman with a small child, afraid and alone, have the right to refuse shelter to strangers, to more-than-strangers, to enemies? What if they did freeze to death? Would that be murder? Manslaughter, she decided. It would be manslaughter and people went to jail for it, even if they were the mothers of small children. Even if the people they killed were thieves and vandals or worse.

She did not hear sloshing water, or the small footsteps slapping on the bathroom tile, or the bathroom door opening. Suddenly there was a short naked ghost, slick and dripping water and soap foam on the carpet, materializing out of the dark hallway.

"Mum?" Travis said, his voice quavering.

She put down the knife on the counter behind her and stooped down and held out her arms. Holding his slippery body in her arms, feeling the slick round torso, the solidity of him, she thought, *I'm Mum again, for the first time since he was three, and it only took half-scaring him to death.*

Fists crashed angrily against the door and they jumped.

"Missus Russell," Rand bawled. "We're freezing!"

Travis clutched her frantically. "It's them," he said, and the terror in his voice made up her mind for her.

She hugged him tight, then nudged him toward the hall. "Go back in the bathroom," she whispered. "Lock the door. Don't open it or come out until I tell you."

He nodded. "You won't let them hurt you, will you?" he whispered back.

"No," she said. "Now go on."

He skittered away in the dark of the hall.

She picked up the knife and waited.

"She ain't buying it," Ricky said. He grinned happily.

Tight-lipped, Rand slammed his right fist into his left palm. He wouldn't look at Ricky. He backed off to the edge of the porch and stared at the door. Lowering his head moodily, he padded toward the door and leaned heavily against it on his palms. He stared at his own boots, at the floor of the porch. His hands curled into fists. Suddenly his head snapped up and he pounded his fists on the door in rage.

"Let me in, bitch!" he bellowed. "Let me in!"

He punished the door steadily for a minute or so. It shuddered and bucked under the force of his blows. Then he stopped and cocked his head against it, listening.

There was no answer from within.

He pushed himself off the door and whirled around. "Come on," he muttered, and bounded savagely down the steps into the blowing snow. Ricky shrugged and followed. Gordy Teed slunk out of the shadows after them like a cur dog with his tail between his legs. Behind them, the storm door swung in the wind.

Liv crouched behind the door, flinching with every blow. She heard Rand with a faint smile that was mostly bravado. She could not move for some time after the heavy thud of boots on the porch told her they were gone. Then she crept to the window to peer out. The porch was empty, save of shadow and the snow blowing onto it.

She hurried to the living room and tweaked the curtains aside. There was blurred light on the beach, the headlights of the snowmobiles, and an erratic engine cough under the sound of the wind. Liv let the curtain drop and sagged against it. Her stomach hurt where she had been punched, and from holding her breath. The roots of her teeth hurt, too, from clenching her jaw. Her fingers were stiff from clenching the knife. She released the knife gently into the nearest niche in the fireplace. She rubbed the edge of her jaw, swallowed hard, and hurried to the bathroom.

Knocking softly at the door, she said, "Travis, it's me."

The lock clicked, and Travis, wrapped in a towel, opened the door, and threw himself into her arms. She hugged him and ruffled his hair.

"Hey," she said, putting on a good cheer she did not feel at all, "it's okay."

Travis snuggled closer. "Are they gone?" he asked.

"Yes," Liv said. "They're gone."

She pulled up his towel, which was disarranged. "You must be cold. Let's get you dressed again," she said.

She thought an immediate return to routine would be reassuring and she was right. He let her finish drying him without protest, and

consented to be wrapped up again in the towel and carried down the
hallway to his bedroom.

Behind the bedroom door it was not quite pitch dark; E.T.'s
heartlight still glowed, small and opaquely rosy, next to Travis' bed.

Cold, Liv thought the instant she felt it. *It's cold in here.* She
hesitated on the threshold.

Travis tightened against her.

Out of the dark, Rand sprang upon him.

There was an instant when she howled, a wordless, wholly animal and at the same time emotional sound that was like a terrible
rending and ripping, as he bowled her over.

Travis shrieked with her. She tried to turn, to put herself between Travis and Rand, as Rand's weight propelled them backward
into the hall, against the opposite wall, and onto the floor, and succeeded enough for Travis to roll himself away. He scrambled to his
feet and skittered a few feet away.

"Run!" she screamed. She struggled against Rand, trying to
wriggle out from under him, pounding at him with her fists. One of
his hands caught in her hair and yanked her head back, while the
other cupped her chin and thrust upward. The back of her head
struck the floor in a burst of darkness. Dimly, she heard Travis,
shrieking, and felt his weight as he leapt unexpectedly on Rand and
Rand lost his balance, Rand's whole deadweight dropping onto her
along with Travis', with an ooof and curses, and Rand's elbow
clipped her chin, and she passed out entirely.

Arden Nighswander leaned against the sagging post of his back
porch and pissed unsteadily into the snowstorm. He grinned painfully, exposing his partial front plate to the very gums, in a grimace
that would have suited a Halloween skeleton mask. Afterward, there
was a terrible dull ache in his groin, but it was nothing to the misery
he knew with a full bladder, or the agonizing burning of passing
water. His urine was the color of weak coffee that had sat a while and
then been moved, clouding it with sediment. Had been for some

months. But he kept it to himself, telling himself the VA doctors at Togus were all quacks, and the doctors he had to pay out of his own pocket (though, in fact, he never did unless so forced by a Small Claims Court judge) were worse.

Only Jeannie knew, because she heard him cursing, in the night, from the toilet on the other side of the wallboard that separated their bedroom from the bathroom. They knew the habits of everyone in the house, knew the boys by the time and length and frequency of their movements, knew them by the characteristic sounds of their straining and grunting, knew also the sounds of slick magazine pages being turned and then faintly rattled as Ricky or Gordy masturbated.

At least the boys' bedrooms, the large one that was Rand's and the smaller, slovenly zoo shared by Ricky and Gordy, were at the other end of the house, so Jeannie and Nighswander did not have to hear what went on there at night. Rand had women in; had since he was fifteen or sixteen.

Jeannie protested just the once, when she had taken the bloody sheets off his bed and displayed them to Rand's father.

Nighswander glanced at them, guffawed, and punched Rand's shoulder playfully.

"She old enough?" he demanded.

Rand grinned. "Old enough to pee, old enough for me."

Nighswander hooted and scratched his chest. "I'm getting old," he announced. "Used to be me breakin' 'em in."

The boys laughed dutifully, exchanging yeah-sure looks.

Nighswander turned on Jeannie suddenly. "Well, what are you standin' around holdin' them cunt-filthy sheets under my nose for? You'd think they was yours, provin' you saved it for wedlock. 'Course you'd a had to fake 'em, wouldn't ya?"

He laughed, and this time his boys laughed with him without reservation. Gordy blushed and looked confused.

Jeannie blushed, too, and bundled up the sheets. "It ain't right," she muttered.

It seemed to her that there was a lot of blood, more than she remembered from her first time, which in truth had happened in the bed of her Harry Teed's 1951 Ford pickup truck, before he was her husband. Other explanations, that Rand had been unnecessarily rough, or the girl more of a bleeder than usual, or that it was not actually first blood but menstrual blood, did not occur to Jeannie. Jeannie was as modest as any countrywoman about her menses. She had no occasion to mention them at all to her first husband, except before they were married, in the cab of the '51 Ford truck, when, blushing fiercely, she told him that she had missed two monthlies. After Gordy's father choked on his beer, he glared at her and demanded to know if she was sure. And then, when she meekly answered yes, he had wanted to know if she was sure he was the father, which he knew very well he was. Again she meekly answered yes, hurt but expecting to be hurt, assuming it was his right and privilege to hurt her with the implication of promiscuity. His pride as a man required it. But Nighswander had a fastidious horror of and contempt for menstrual blood.

She had come to look forward to that day of the month when she could say in a low voice, "Time of the month coming, need to go to Greenspark for my female notions," and have Nighswander, lip curling with disgust, dig into his pocket and hand her the money, the only cash money she ever saw, as he did all their other cash dealings with the world. And then he would drive her into Greenspark and sit in the car outside the drugstore while she went inside and bought what she needed. It was a chance to look at the makeup and the scents displayed on the cosmetics' counter, and the garishly colored magazines on the magazine rack, the mysterious superfluity of products, shampoos and toothpastes and aspirins and baby oil that they never had because Nighswander bought a harsh tar-smelling shampoo by the gallon from government commissaries and baking soda for their teeth and nothing else, because he said they did not need such fripperies. Just a chance, and she dared not linger but made her purchases and cast nervous covetous glances over the luxuries she was not allowed during the transaction. The ride home, like the ride into Greenspark, would be wordless.

Then, of course, as soon as it started, Nighswander would leave her alone until she said it was done, which she sometimes lied about to gain an extra day of grace. He never came to her anyway except when he was drunk, and then was most often impotent, though neither of them ever made any connection between the two conditions. All Jeannie knew was that at a certain stage of drunkenness he would begin to paw at her and more often than not nothing would come of it except a beating for failing to rouse him sufficiently.

He made it clear it was her fault, for being old and ugly, and she knew it was true. She had lost what looks she had when she was young and fresh, and the large breasts that had once attracted Gordy's father, and Nighswander in his turn, were sagging and wrinkled, like all the rest of her. That Nighswander had aged no less ungracefully did not matter to either of them.

She knew he had other women when he could get them. The women he picked up in bars and on street corners when he went to Portland or Boston on business, which was invariably the pressing of some claim against the Veterans Administration, were at best sluts and at worst prostitutes, the cheapest kind, as hard-used or harder than she herself, and lacking even her personal cleanliness. But she did not complain of them, not even when she had to be treated for the clap he picked up from them and passed to her. Giving a social disease to his wife did not embarrass him; he used it as an excuse to accuse her of being unfaithful to him and to give her a beating. Jeannie knew, had known all her life though she could not name the source of that information, which might have been something as insubstantial as the way the married women crossed their arms and set their mouths whenever two or more came together at the store, or the post office, the church, or at the side of the road, that men were different; they needed more sex and different women, could never be satisfied with merely marital relations. It made her less guilty about her failures as a sexual object and partner and about the relief she felt to be left alone a little while. Whatever he said to her or about her, she was a decent woman, even if her first marriage had been shotgun. Not the least of her proof was that she did not and never had enjoyed the sex act. So far as she knew, the only women who did, or admitted they did, were sluts. Even Nighswander's contempt for her when she was fouled with her menstrual blood was bearable, not just because it was natural and right, for she was dirty then, wasn't she, but because she did not deserve his contempt for being glad of it.

Nighswander zipped his fly with shaking hands and went back indoors. The clock on the wall said five-thirty. It was blacker and colder than a witch's crotch outside. He was supposed to be meeting the boys at the landing near the Narrows, but he couldn't see beyond the hood of the truck, the snow was that thick, and the wind that vicious.

Jeannie looked up from the table. She was peeling potatoes into a pail at her feet. She stole a look at him. He was poorly looking again, she thought. His waterworks giving him trouble still. She regretted his discomfort only because it made him uglier and meaner, but knew if she pushed him to see a doctor, she would most likely earn a black eye for her trouble.

"You going after the boys?" she asked.

"Christ-a-mighty," he exploded. "I ain't Rudolph the Red-Nosed Reindeer." He spat onto the stove. "It's a goddamn fuckin' roaring jeezer out there, woman."

Jeannie wiped her hands in her apron. "Boys'll take shelter, won't they?"

"Rand and Ricky will," Nighswander said. "Gordy ain't got sense enough to come in out of a piss-storm."

"Oh, now," Jeanne said. "The boys'll look after each other."

Nighswander grunted.

"I wish they weren't out, though," she said. She got up and drew back the curtain to look out the window. She shivered. "Can't think why they wanted to go out today with the weather report so bad."

"This wasn't supposed to hit until tonight," Nighswander said. "They shoulda had plenty of time."

Jeannie let the curtain drop and looked at him. "For what?" she asked. "Plenty a time for what?"

"A little run in the woods," Nighswander snapped. "What the fuck business is it of yours?"

Walter McKenzie swabbed up the last of the bean juice on his plate with a fragment of bread and popped it in his mouth. He washed it down with cold tea and pushed his plate a few inches away from him. The accumulated litter on the table did not permit pushing it very far, but it was only habit, the signal he had finished his meal that he had given his wife for decades and still did, though she had not been alive to read it for too many lonely years. He settled back comfortably in the straight-back chair and farted softly.

On the floor in front of the stove, Fritzie opened one eye. Her nose tilted up from her paws a second and then dropped down again. She moaned.

"Go on," Walter said. "I've smelled enough of yours, and they're worse."

Fritzie closed her eye and rumbled in her throat.

Walter carried his dishes to the sink and rinsed them off. The window over the sink was fogged with freezing condensation. The wind moaned in the chimney and the house shuddered.

"Bitch out there," Walter said.

Fritzie snored.

The pendulum clock on the wall over the gas range tocked. It was six o'clock.

Walter dried his hands on a stained, old-fashioned roll towel, and wandered down the hall to the deal table where a thirty-five-year-old black telephone sat on a yellowed lace doily. There was no chair convenient to the table; Walter McKenzie conducted his telephone calls on his feet. He used his telephone for taking and sending messages, not chatting. Chatting was free at the post office or the diner or almost anywhere except on one end of a telephone set.

He picked up the receiver and fished the little brown leatherbound notebook in which he kept his telephone list from his back pocket. Muttering the necessary five numbers to himself as an aid to memory, he slipped the notebook back into his pocket and dialed the Russells' summer house. He waited patiently with the receiver to one ear. The dial tone was staticky with the storm outside. There were clickings and ticks. Then a long dead silence, even the dial tone gone. Walter frowned. He dialed the operator and asked him to ring the Russells' number for him. In a minute the operator came back on and told him the number was out of order.

Walter shuffled back to the kitchen and pulled the tea kettle forward on the woodstove, giving it a shake to measure the quantity of water in it.

"Missus Russell's phone's out," he said to Fritzie.

Fritzie rolled over in her sleep and lay on her back. The hair on her belly was sparse and white. Her jaw dropped open a little. Walter could smell her breath. It was awful.

He showed his hands the stove and rubbed them together over the rising heat. "Don't like that much, old girl," he muttered.

Hauling a crumpled handkerchief out of one pocket, he went to the window over the sink and wiped a patch clear of condensation. Fat flakes whipped against the glass on the other side, melted, and

dribbled downward. It seemed very dark out there, as if walls had
come down all around his house.

Walter scratched the back of his neck. She had plenty of wood,
he had seen to that. She should be all right. He hoped she and the
boy weren't scared, out there all by their lonesomes.

The kettle whistled at him. He stooped over Fritzie and rubbed
her belly gently. "First light, old girl," he said. "We'll have a look-
see."

The first public telephone Pat found in Greenspark was a booth
in a down-at-the-heels shopping center, outside an abandoned
K-Mart. It smelled of old cold pee. It was also out of order, which he
discovered after it had eaten his last two dimes.

He slammed the receiver down violently, and stalked back to his
car, swearing. Sarah huddled in the car.

"Goddamn phone's out," he muttered.

"Oh," she said. "Great."

Greenspark was shut up for the night. There was nothing open
on Main Street, not even the police station under the courthouse,
where Pat rattled the doorknob and shouted to no avail, while Sarah
waited in the car.

The town was under the spell of sleep. The houses were all
darkened, showing only porchlights or the lights of bathrooms or
children's nightlights, dimmed by curtains or frost, veiled by the
falling snow, so it was almost as if he were seeing the lights at a great
distance. The people inside were tucked into their beds, warm and
safe. They would not like being wakened, or opening their doors to
let in a stranger and let out the precious warmth. But he didn't know
what else to do, except knock on someone's door and ask to use their
phone until he noticed a rusted old public telephone sign on the side
of a take-out pizza joint. Like everything else, the pizza joint was
closed. But the phone was outside, hung on the cement wall under
the protection of a hard plastic hood. If he leaned his elbows on the
meagre shelf under the phone, and hunched over it, his head was
almost covered by the hood, but the snow fell into the gap between
his shirt collar and his wool cap, directly down the back of his neck.

He examined the change from his pockets and fed a quarter into the slot. Though he did not expect he would get his nickel's change, he opened his palm under the change chute. He had never gotten a nickel's change back from New England Telephone in his life, and he didn't this time. Not only did he have to pay twenty cents for a call that in many other places in the country cost ten cents, if the only change he had in hand was a quarter, New England Telephone took a nickel premium, which Liv called the Wrong Change Again, Sucker, Tax.

He shivered when the cold trickle of melted snow reached the small of his back. There was snow melting on the end of his nose, and on his eyelashes. He stamped his feet and waited and listened to telephone noise, mechanical clicks and thunks, buzzing, dead air, a flurry of frantic clicking and spectral voices from other lines bleeding in, before an operator cut in to ask what number he was calling, in a brisk, impatient tone that implied he certainly was fucking it up, wasn't he? In due course he was told the line was out of order.

He found another quarter, paid his Wrong Change Again, Sucker, Tax, again, and dialed Walter McKenzie's number. While he waited for the call to go through, he hauled out a big handkerchief, and shook it open.

Walter picked it up in the middle of the second ring. "Ho," he said.

"Sorry to wake you up," Pat said, and blew his nose into the handkerchief.

"Huh?" Walter asked. "What say?"

Pat shouted. "Sorry to wake you up."

There was a pause and a brief clatter. "Shit," said Walter. Another pause. "Knocked my bifocals on the floor," he explained. "That you, Russell?"

"Ayuh," said Pat. "Sorry to wake you up, Walter."

"Yes, yes," Walter said. "I'm sorry you woke me up, too. Wanna tell me what you woke me up for?"

"I can't reach Liv," Pat said. "Phone's out."

Walter grunted. "I know. Road ain't plowed either. Won't be a crew down there to fix the lines until tomorrow."

"Oh." Pat wiped the end of his nose and stuffed his handkerchief in his pocket.

"Look," Walter said. "She's got wood to keep her warm, and

candles and lanterns. She'll be okay. No need to fret. I'll be down there first thing in the morning by snowshoe if I have to."

Pat nodded as if Walter could see him. He wanted to hear Walter say she'd be okay.

"Hope they're not too scared," he said.

"Oh, she don't scare too easy, and she'll take care of the boy," Walter said. "Now whyn't you go to bed? Get some sleep. Like me."

"Thanks, Walter," Pat said.

Walter hung up with a clatter.

Pat hooked the receiver and shrugged so his collar rose a little over the back of his neck. Walter hadn't asked where he was, let alone whether he was on his own. The motels in and around Greenspark were full of skiers during the winter holidays. Nodd's Ridge, if they could reach it tonight, had only two small inns that closed between October and April. If they couldn't get home to Liv and Travis tonight, they would have to turn back or sleep in his car. He was dead on his feet; he couldn't go back. So their choices were really to go on and walk in, or sleep in the car. At least they had good boots and multiple layers of thick clothing. He rejoined Sarah in the car.

"Walter says our phone is out, but he's sure mom and Travis are okay. They've got wood and candles and plenty of food."

"Are we going to be able to get there tonight?" Sarah asked.

Pat hesitated. "I want to try. Worst case is we might have to sleep in the car."

"Oh," said Sarah. Then she shrugged. "Last summer I spent a night in a tent in a thunderstorm. I didn't melt."

Pat leaned over to take her hand and squeeze. "Good girl," he said. Of course the danger wasn't melting, it was freezing.

So they started off, slowly, toward the Pondicherry Causeway, and Nodd's Ridge. They were on the Pondicherry Causeway when he realized, sleepily, that he couldn't see the boulders that marked the edge of the road. He couldn't see a goddamn thing except the snow, white and white and white.

CHAPTER 12

LIV came to on the living room couch. Travis was curled up against her, still stark naked and shivering. He was staring at her, wild-eyed. His nails bit into her arms. When she touched his white face, to wipe away tear streaks, a tremor passed through him as if he had taken an electric shock.

Liv looked around her. The Poor was on the hearth, disposed on her side, watching Liv with bright unreadable eyes. Rand sat next to the cat, with the fire at his back. The sleeves of his heavy sweater were pushed up to the elbows, so his thermal underwear showed. His brother Ricky sprawled on the rug near him. Gordy Teed sat awkwardly in a straight chair. He wiped his nose on the back of his hand, looked at it, and wiped it on his overalls. The three men had taken off their snowmobile suits and thrown them over the backs of chairs. Their boots sat on the hearth in puddles of melting snow. They were all wearing jeans and commando sweaters over thermal long underwear and woolen socks. The fire's warmth brought out the smell of sweat from the boots and the long underwear, with a faint note of old pee underneath.

Liv pushed herself up onto one elbow. "My boy's cold," she said.

"Get a blanket off a bed," Rand said to Ricky. Ricky scrambled up and disappeared.

Rand turned to Gordy. "Get that jug," he said. Gordy jumped and scuttled for the kitchen.

"And some glasses," Rand called after him.

Ricky reappeared with the quilt from Travis' bed. He offered it awkwardly to Liv. She snatched it one-handed, holding Travis with the other, and bundled him into it. She glared at Rand.

Her feistiness excited him.

Gordy came back with the jug of Gallo and a stack of juice glasses.

Rand examined the glasses critically before taking two of them. Gordy scuttled back to his chair.

Rand crossed the room and crouched next to Liv to offer her a small glass of red wine.

"Come on," he said. "You'll feel better."

She took it. Rand passed the jug to Ricky, who raised it at once to his mouth. Rand poked him in the kidneys.

"Ow," he said, "that hurt, Rand." But he lowered the jug. "Gimme a glass, asshole," he demanded of Gordy.

Gordy started, looked at the glasses he was holding, and passed one hastily to Ricky. Ricky sat down on the floor again, using the hearth for a backrest. When Gordy held out the remaining empty glass, Ricky slopped wine into it and then cradled the jug in his crotch.

"Good," Rand said. He spoke softly and earnestly. He settled himself more comfortably on his haunches and tucked his hands together between his thighs. "Sorry we scared you. But you shoulda let us in. A man could freeze to death out there tonight." He rebuked her with a smile. "It wasn't very neighborly of you, O-liv-i-a."

Liv took another swallow of the wine. It was harsh, but it warmed her, loosened her throat. "You're not my neighbor," she said. "You're a barbarian."

Rand threw back his head and laughed. "Ain't I trying to be nice to you?"

Liv drew Travis a little closer. "You've frightened my little boy seriously, twice now. You've assaulted me twice. You've broken into my home twice."

"Yeah," Rand said. "You got shitty locks on your windows, you know," he confided, as if he held an especially created town office, Public Locktester.

Ricky Nighswander sniggered and filled his glass again.

Liv closed her eyes wearily. Travis squeezed her hand and she squeezed back. There was a nagging ache in her jaw. She felt bruised all over. She had to try for the best deal she could make. She took a deep breath and opened her eyes.

"Look," she said to Rand. "You're inside now. I don't want you here but there's nothing I can do to make you go away. All I can do is ask you to act like civilized human beings while you're here. I don't want my boy scared anymore. So you let us be, let us go about our normal routine, and I won't make a fuss when this is over. I won't make any complaints about breaking and entering or assault."

Rand rubbed his hands on his thighs. "Can't ask for a better deal than that, O-liv-i-a." He looked around at Ricky and Gordy. "Right, boys?"

"Right," Gordy echoed.

"Yeah," said Ricky. Ricky rolled over on his back. "I'm hungry," he said to the ceiling.

Rand looked expectantly at Liv. "Spare us some grub, O-liv-i-a?"

Liv sat up. Travis clung to her. She kept one arm around his waist. "First things first. I want to get Travis into his pajamas. Then I'll feed you."

"Good enough," said Rand.

Liv rearranged the blanket around Travis. She stood up slowly and carefully, still holding him close, fighting dizziness. Rand Nighswander reached out to help her. She pulled instinctively away from him.

"I'm all right," she said.

"Suit yourself," he said, and smiled at Travis, as if sharing a joke with him.

Liv wanted very badly to smash some gaps in his even white teeth. Instead she stiffened her spine and led Travis down the hallway toward his room.

Behind her, Rand said, "Ricky, check the place out."

She swung around angrily. Ricky and Gordy were on their feet, poised to be about Rand's business.

"Don't go breaking anything," Rand instructed them. "Don't worry about it, O-liv-i-a. I just don't want no surprises, is all."

"If I had a gun here," Liv said, "believe me, I'd have used it already."

Rand smiled indulgently and waved Ricky and Gordy on. They headed toward her bedroom.

She took Travis' hand and headed toward his room. Rand followed them, as if they needed his protection. The hallway seemed suddenly longer and darker. With each step forward, they grew colder. Travis' towels were a tangled heap outside his bedroom door. Even while forcing herself forward, Liv had to herd Travis along. He dragged his feet and kept a deathgrip on the leg of her jeans. When she reached his bedroom, she let him fall back. She nudged open the door, telling herself there was no one in there, the monsters had already shown themselves, and they were behind her. E.T.'s heartlight glowed next to the dark catafalque shape of Travis' bed. The cold made her shiver. She thrust her arm into the near-dark, found the switchplate, and turned on the light.

The room revealed seemed naked and small. The one window was wide open, the sill crusted with slush from the boots that had passed over it. Snow blew in on the carpet and melted there. The wind shook out the curtains and turned the pages of comic books that Travis had left on the floor. The electrical baseboard heaters crackled and clanked, trying to compete with the cold.

Liv crossed the room quickly and shut the window. The lock was distorted where it had been forced, the wood of the window's frame splintered.

Travis watched her, peeking around the door frame. She gave him a quick smile, braver than she really felt.

She took footed Dr. Dentons out of a dresser drawer, Travis' plaid blanket kimono from its hook inside the closet door, plucked his slippers from next to his bed and his old baby blanket from under his pillow. Rand Nighswander watched her every move from the doorway. The smile on his face was like a cat waiting by a mousehole. She stepped past him quickly, switching off the light, closing the door behind her. Travis grabbed her leg. She took his hand and led him into the bathroom, picking up the abandoned towels on the way.

"It's warmer in here," she said.

It was, but not by much. Rand stood in the open door again. Travis even consented to her helping with the snaps on his pajamas. She took every excuse she could find to touch him, cuddle him, hug him, trying to comfort and reassure him wordlessly. While he shuffled into his slippers and put on his kimono, she picked his G.I. Joes out of the tub and bundled them into the damp bathmat. She helped him put them into the pockets of his kimono, then quickly straightened the bathroom, putting the bathmat, the towels and washcloth, and Travis' discarded clothing into the hamper.

The kitchen was too narrow to allow both Rand Nighswander and Travis to shadow her every move. She loosened Travis' grip on her leg and boosted him into his usual chair at the kitchen table. Rand stopped at the threshold, produced smoking materials from the rolled sleeves of his sweater, lit a cigarette, and propped himself against the door frame.

Liv dumped Chicken Soup With Noodles into a pot and put it on the stove. She slapped tuna sandwiches together. Whenever she looked up, Travis was watching her with woebegone eyes. She didn't need to look at Rand; she could feel him watching her. Needing to do something, anything, to keep busy, she took down the Nestlé's Walter had thoughtfully, perhaps sentimentally, provided, and made cocoa from scratch. It took a lot of stirring.

Ricky and Gordy shuffled in to report they had found nothing. Rand dismissed them.

"There's not room enough to feed everyone at this table," she said to Rand, when everything was ready. "Why don't I feed Travis here and bring you trays in the living room?"

Rand frowned at his cigarette and flicked it into the sink. It sizzled and went out. He wasn't so soft-headed he was going to allow either of them out of his sight. Maybe she didn't want the kid around Ricky and Gordy, in case they did a number on his head or something, but that was just tough. "Sure, O-liv-i-a. I'll help you. But don't make the little guy eat by himself. Let's bring his grub in with ours."

Liv bit her lip and stirred the cocoa. The thought of breaking bread with these creeps revolted her. She didn't want Travis to have to be in the same room with them. But it looked like she couldn't get them out of it.

In the living room, Ricky had opened the cabinets again and scattered tape cartridges over the rug. He jumped when he saw Rand and dropped the tape he was holding.

"Lemme help," he said and scrambled up, putting distance between himself and the incriminating evidence.

Rand growled at him. "You stupid—"

Ricky showed Liv all his teeth. "Sure got a lot of movies here, Olivia," he said.

"He's gonna pick 'em up," Rand said to Liv.

Liv ignored them. She nudged Travis back onto the couch, and set up a TV tray in front of him.

"Can we watch a movie?" Ricky asked.

"Sure," Liv said. "Why not?" She was almost grateful to him for the idea. No one would be watching her for a little while, and she wouldn't have to watch them. They could all get lost for an hour and a half or so.

"Good," said Gordy Teed, with his mouth full.

Revolted, Liv picked at her own food and then pushed it away.

Ricky worked his way through the entire collection of tapes, sandwich in one hand, mechanically chopping out huge bites. Frequently he stopped and studied the title, then mouthed it silently.

At least he cleared his mouth first.

Rand wolfed two sandwiches, drank the cocoa, and put his chicken soup down on the hearth. The Poor approached it cautiously and began to lap at it. Rand watched her a minute, then pushed her away. He picked up the soup and offered it to Gordy. "More here than I can put away. Want this, Gordy?"

Gordy took the bowl, settled it into his empty one, and slurped it up.

Rand picked up The Poor and began to stroke her.

Ricky fanned half a dozen tapes in front of Rand. "What about one of these, Rand?"

Rand shrugged and looked at Liv. "Ask O-liv-i-a."

Ricky scuttled to Liv's side and showed her. "You like any of these, O-liv-i-a."

Assault on Precinct 13, Dirty Harry, I the Jury. She thought of more appropriate titles she could add. *Silent Rage. Straw Dogs.*

"I don't think any of them is suitable for Travis," she said. "If you're going to watch these, I could take him in my bedroom and read to him."

Ricky sulked.

"Got any cartoons?" Gordy Teed asked and was ignored.

"No," said Rand. "We'll all stay right here. Play that *Dirty Harry* one. I've seen it. It ain't sexy. Just a cop movie. Drive-in was full of little kids that night."

Travis nudged Liv and whispered, "I've seen that one, too. It's okay, Liv."

Liv gave in. Travis needed to be distracted, too.

"What's this?" Ricky asked, and showed her a tape marked *Firefight, Partial Rough Cut.*

Impulsively, Liv reached out and took it. Pat.

"Piece of the movie my husband's making," she said.

"All right!" Ricky exclaimed. "What's it about?"

"Gross bloody killings," Travis said. "It's about army guys. My father made it up. He's in it, too. He gets killed. But it's just pretend."

Liv squeezed Travis' knee. He looked up at her and smiled wanly.

"No shit, man," Ricky said. "I gotta check this shit out." He looked at Rand hopefully. "Maybe we could have some of that nose candy while the show's on?"

"I'll think about it," Rand said. "You got the wine already."

Ricky shrugged. Rand always kept the best stuff for himself. He didn't expect Rand would be sharing the woman, either. Unless she wasn't much good anyway. What Rand called a fuckaroody. He'd only shared Loretta Buck because she was so drunk and scared it was like fucking a sofa cushion.

"Check it out," Gordy Teed said. "I like war stuff. Sometimes war stuff is as good as cartoons," he added thoughtfully.

"Shut up, asshole," Ricky said.

"Watch your mouth, Ricky," Rand snapped.

Ricky peeked at Liv from under his chorus girl lashes. "Sorry," he muttered, then looked at Rand.

He examined the tape player. "How's this thing go?" he asked.

"I can do it," Travis said, and slid off the couch. "Like this." He punched On, then the Eject button. Ricky handed him the first tape. Travis inserted it and pushed the tape platform down.

"Now you have to have the TV on," he said. "Then press the button with the green stripe."

Ricky nodded. "This one?" he asked, and pointed it out.

"Yeah." Travis scooted back to Liv and snuggled up against her. For the moment, he had forgotten to be afraid. It was Pat's doing, his movie, the mention of him, that had done it. Somehow that seemed important.

CHAPTER 13

FIREFIGHT

Rough Cut #6

Jungle track. Dogfaces in camouflage glide
through jungle swamp to the edge of a clearing.
The point man is the sergeant, Court. The faces
under the mud and beard stubble are unmistakably
American, though the spectrum is from the
peeling, blue-white skin and spit-colored eyes
of the red-neck-hillbilly Jackson to the
sunburnt fair skin and blue eyes of Taurus the
Michigan Irishman to the admirable tan and
liquid brown eyes of Denny Corriveau, the Cajun,
to the blue-black skin and flashing black eyes
of Ratcliffe. The only somehow un-American face
is Court's. He is a broad-chested, short-legged
tartar, too substantial to be Charlie, yet in
his features there is a kind of bridge between
the races at war.
The Cajun sucks on a huge bomber joint and
passes it, with a nudge, to Jackson. The
hillbilly grins, showing numerous gaps among
his small, brown teeth. His teeth are as bad as
the antique hags, the Charlie-mamas, who wash
clothes for the G.I.s because they are too old,

in their thirties and forties, to be whores
anymore.

Beyond Taurus, two other members of the
patrol become visible in the shadows. One of
them is a big, balding black private with a gold
earring. He is sweating profusely, and his eyes
roll nervously as he tries to see in every
direction at once. The other is a white man, his
six feet of height diminished by the stature of
the black, so his slimness seems slightness.
Horn-rimmed glasses pinch a rather Judicial
Establishment nose, with an authoritative hook,
but thin enough to breathe the rarified air of
saintly, overbred Boston. The eyes behind his
lenses are hazel. Nervously, he brushes a lock
of fine blond hair off his high intellectual
brow. He wears insignia that identify him as a
lieutenant.

The lieutenant passes to the front and squats
briefly with Sergeant Court. The two examine a
map and hand signals are exchanged, first with
each other, then with the other men. The
sergeant and the lieutenant assume the point and
step into the clearing. The other men wait
nervously. The lieutenant stops and looks
around, then turns and signals to come ahead.

At that instant a fusillade explodes,
cutting him down, knocking the sergeant
backward into the swamp. The G.I.s fall to the
ground or into the water, take cover anywhere
they can, and return fire. Ratcliffe crawls into
the swamp, and drags the sergeant to a more-
protected position. Court is badly, perhaps
fatally wounded. The gunfire is deafening, and
it quickly becomes apparent that the Americans
are badly outnumbered.

Court grasps Ratcliffe's wrist. "Call in the
choppers," he gasps.

Ratcliffe, sweating, ashen, signals the
others. The radioman, the other black, does as
he is ordered. But the shooting goes on. It is a
long, terrifying time before the sound of the

choppers overwhelms the ripping, rending sound
of the machine guns. The choppers pour on the
lead while the G.I.s hug the mud. There is an
enormous, blinding explosion that shakes the
ground as one chopper takes a direct hit and
plunges into the jungle only yards away. Now a
sheet of fire flares behind the trees, rendering
black, twisted abstractions like Chinese
ideograms. Beneath the roar of the fire a great
ripping and tearing and rending as of some
enormous monster feeding, and huge black
shadows, the giant armored bulldozers, are soon
silhouetted against the fire's light.

When the enemy gunfire finally fades away,
and the battle moves forward, the dozers
following, and only the hungry hiss of the fire
remains, Ratcliffe takes command, because the
sergeant is either dead or unconscious, and
signals to call off the choppers. Taurus finds
the radioman nearly cut in two by the chopper
fire. Taurus takes the radio from the dead man
and calls them off, requesting medical
evacuation.

Ratcliffe crawls back into the swamp,
keeping his head low in case of less-than-dead
or otherwise ambitious Charlies, and drags the
lieutenant's body out. As he lies next to the
sergeant, the lieutenant is nearly
unrecognizable. One side of his face appears to
have been shot away; mercifully, it is so
covered with mud and blood that the gory details
are only hinted at. But on the side of his face
that remains, one half of his glasses, the lense
cracked and dirty, still hangs from his ear.

T HAT'S MY DAD," said Travis. "It took four hours to put
all that gunk on his face so it looks gross and bloody like
that."

Yeah, thought Liv, *and it makes me want to puke.* She had worried about Travis seeing it. But it had upset her, and still upset her, a lot more than it did him.

"Kids are pretty good at sorting out fantasy and the real world," Pat had assured her, and it seemed he had been right, at least about this.

She nudged Travis. "Bedtime."

His fingernails dug into the palm of her hand.

"Better sleep in my room," she said. "I think your room is a little too cold tonight."

Travis looked relieved. He stopped digging into her palm.

Rand stood up and tossed a cigarette butt into the fireplace. "Put the kid in his room," he said.

Liv was suddenly frightened. "He'll never go to sleep in there tonight." She pulled Travis close. "How about Sarah's room instead?" she asked.

"Why can't I sleep with you?" Travis asked.

Ricky Nighswander guffawed. A look from Rand shut him up.

"Not tonight," Liv said. "Tomorrow, okay?"

Travis gave up. There were blue shadows under his eyes.

Rand followed them to the bathroom, and then to Travis' bedroom, where Liv unplugged the E.T. nightlight. It looked out of place in Sarah's bedroom down the hall, but Travis seemed comforted by its presence. He hung his bathrobe with its pockets full of G.I. Joes on the bedpost, and climbed in willingly. Liv sat down on the edge of the bed and tried to pretend Rand Nighswander was not standing in the doorway, watching and listening.

"I wish you could stay right here," Travis said.

"So do I," Liv said. "I'll be right handy, though. Okay?"

Travis nodded, but Liv, her hand on his chest, felt the tension in him. He was frightened again, too. And she didn't know how to reassure him. She couldn't imagine that he would be able to go to sleep in such a wound-up state.

She kissed him. "I'll be right back."

In the hallway, she stopped Rand. "He's not going to go to sleep very easily. He's too keyed up."

Rand shrugged. "So what."

"I've got some Valium," Liv said. "I'd like to give him some in a cup of cocoa. He'll sleep deeply that way."

Rand looked at her. "Maybe that's a good idea." His eyes glittered. He put one hand on her hip.

Liv stepped backward so his touch barely grazed her. If he touched her again, she might scream, or go for his face. She didn't know what she might do, and she was almost as afraid to lose control of herself as she was of him.

"Go do it," he said.

She hurried to her own bathroom. She hooked the small bottle that contained a few 2-mg. tablets of Valium from the top shelf of the medicine cabinet. Just as she started to shut the door of the cabinet, the rest of what was on that shelf registered. Ricky and Gordy hadn't made such an efficient search after all. Or perhaps the medicine cabinet was the last place they looked for drugs. Or maybe reading the labels was too much trouble. That didn't matter. What counted was they had missed it. Container after container of narcotics—a half dozen white tablets that looked like generic aspirin but were really 50-mg. Talwins, seven or eight fat red lozenges of 100-mg. Darvocet-N, nearly two dozen little pink capsules of 65-mg. Darvon, a baker's dozen of red-and-white capsules of Darvon Compound-65, nine 400-mg. Motrins that looked like orange Reese's Pieces, five yellow tablets of Percodan—forgotten, left behind at the end of the summer, legacy of the summer's bad tooth. She looked quickly back over her shoulder.

Rand was in the bedroom, lighting another cigarette, looking out the windows at the snow.

"Excuse me," she said in a rushed voice. "Call of nature." She shut the bathroom door and locked it.

"Wait a minute," Rand said, and realized he was too late, even as he rattled the doorknob.

She listened to him, breathing heavily, on the other side of the door.

"I'll take this fucking door right off if you're in there too long," he said.

"Okay," she said, pretending testiness, which she thought sounded more innocent than apology or showing fear. "I'll be right out."

Unzipping her jeans with one hand, she snatched a hand towel from the towel bar. She plucked the pill bottles from the top shelf carefully into it, trying not to rattle the contents. Then she put the rolled towel on the floor in front of the toilet. She pushed her jeans and underpants down over her hips, sat on the toilet and made water. As she did, she bent between her knees and opened each bottle, dumping the capsules and pills into a little pile on the floor. As soon as she was done, and had her pants up again, she flushed the toilet. Under cover of the water, she inserted capsules and pills into the tops of her ankle socks, and pushed them down, so they collected under the high arches of her feet and in the niches between her toes. She tucked the empty containers behind the toilet and inside the toilet brush holder. She turned on the faucet and washed her hands. When she unlocked the door and opened it, she had the towel in her free hand. She continued to dry her hands with it.

Rand was right there, sucking on his cigarette impatiently, thoroughly vexed. "Don't you shut no more doors in my face, O-liv-i-a," he said.

"You like to watch women pee?" Liv asked him. "Are you some kind of freak?"

He backhanded her so swiftly she didn't see it coming.

She staggered backward. The bathroom doorknob smashed her right kidney. She dropped to her knees, in agony.

"You bin askin' for that," Rand said softly.

She looked up at him. "You wanted to," she gasped.

Rand reached down and grabbed her elbow. He hauled her roughly to her feet and shoved her toward the bathroom. "Get the goddamn sleepin' pills for the kid."

The Valium was where she left it on the counter. She picked it up and put it in her shirt pocket. She caught a glimpse of herself in the mirror, and hastily turned away.

In the kitchen, she reheated the leftover cocoa from supper and dropped one of the 2-mg. tablets of Valium into it, stirred it until it dissolved, and carried it back to Travis. She ignored Rand as he watched her. He thought he had taught her a lesson.

As she expected, Travis was still wide-awake, and sat up when he saw her standing in the doorway. She hesitated, but apparently he had not heard the brief commotion in her bedroom.

"I brought you some cocoa," she said. "Thought it might help you sleep better."

"Good idea, Liv," he said solemnly.

She sat down next to him while he drank the cocoa. Travis took his time, and watched her over the edge of the cup every time he took a sip. At last he handed her the empty cup. He sighed hugely.

"That was good cocoa, Liv," he said.

"Thanks," she said, and ruffled his hair. "Mind if I sit with you a little while longer?"

He shook his head. He reached up and touched her face where Rand had struck her. "Your face is red," he said.

"I walked into the bathroom door," Liv said quickly.

"Does your tooth hurt?" Travis asked.

"No," she said.

He closed his eyes.

She glanced at Rand, then turned her back to him and snuggled up to Travis. After a few moments, she sensed he had gone away, and when she peeked, the doorway was empty. From the living room she heard the sounds of movie gunfire, and Ricky's voice cheering it on. Next to her Travis had relaxed, his breathing evened out.

She remembered when she had come home from having her tooth out, she had gone directly to the bathroom to take some aspirin and wash her face. Travis had followed her.

"Can I see?" he asked.

"It's pretty gross," she warned him. "And it stinks, from the blood."

He shrugged, so she opened her mouth and showed him the bloody socket. He admired it a few seconds, and then patted her shoulder to comfort her.

"If you put the tooth under your pillow," he confided, "the fairy'll leave you some money."

She hadn't expected to be laughing so soon afterward, and her jaw was stiff and sore when she did, but she had to. And then she had hugged him. A tooth wasn't so much to lose.

"Don't go away," he said with his eyes still closed.

"No," she said.

Her face throbbed where Rand had struck her. The kidney that had been rammed into the doorknob ached. She felt stiff and tired as if she had worked hard at something physical, chopping wood, or washing windows, or gardening, all day. But she wasn't sleepy. She envied Travis the swift working of the Valium. She wondered if she had enough to put herself to sleep, hard enough so nothing would wake her in the night. Then whatever Rand Nighswander did to her, at least she wouldn't be aware of it. She shivered, thinking about how he looked at her. And there was always Ricky and simple Gordy to consider. What if he couldn't or wouldn't continue to restrain them? Everything old Joe Nevers had said about them came back to her, and seemed more threatening. But she couldn't go to sleep. She had to take care of Travis. All she had was her socks full of pills.

Liv stopped to look back at Travis. Posters of Bruce Springsteen and Clarence Clemons and Miami Steve Van Zandt and Roy Bittan looked down at him from the walls, like the four angels in *Now I Lay Me Down to Sleep.* Maybe the creeps would be gone before he woke up in the morning. She drew the bedroom door closed behind her.

CHAPTER 14

RAND NIGHSWANDER'S HAND dropped onto her shoulder.

"You bastard," she hissed.

He smiled and wrapped an arm around her waist. "Relax, mother."

She tried to pull loose and he clamped his hands around her wrists and nudged her back toward the living room, murmuring, "Good girl, now."

Gordy and Ricky were sprawled on the floor, watching the TV. They were both intensely involved with the action on the screen. Ricky's left hand rested possessively on the half-empty jug of wine. When Rand bent over and hooked his fingers around the jug's throat, Ricky reacted instinctively and lunged for it, missed it, and settled for Rand's ankle.

"Son of a bitch," he cried. He was at that stage of inebriation when the fight in a man is sorrowfully tempered by an undeniable failure of coordination. He was beaten by his own drunkenness before he could begin.

Rand shook him off casually.

"Son of a bitch," Gordy cried in imitation. Gordy clenched his fists and pounded his own thighs. "I found it! It was mine!"

Rand patted Gordy's shoulder. "You've had more'n you can hold, old hoss, now ain't you?"

Gordy settled back down onto the rug with a mournful "Sheee," like air hissing out of a tire.

"You'll be puking on the rug next." He nudged Liv toward her bedroom. "Come on, now. Let's you and me have another glass a wine and relax."

Ricky and Gordy stared at them open-mouthed. Rand winked. Ricky and Gordy broke up in sniggers.

Liv took a deep breath. "I don't really want any wine," she said. "Why don't I make more cocoa for everybody?"

Gordy sat up on his elbows. "I'd like some."

Ricky knocked Gordy's right elbow out from under him. "Nobody gives a fuck what you'd like."

Rand took Liv's elbow firmly. "Nobody wants any cocoa, O-liv-i-a."

"Oh." Liv went blank and let him lead her away. She had tried and they hadn't bought it. She could dope the wine and maybe make Rand pass out and then what? Offer what remained to Ricky and Gordy and hope it was enough to knock them out, too, before they had any dangerous ideas of their own? What if she doped the wine and Rand forced her to drink it, too? Everything she could think to do was too unpredictable.

Rand shoved her at the bed. She caught herself on the bedpost and faced him angrily.

Rand put the jug on the dresser. "Goddamn," he said. "I forgot the glasses. Well, we'll just have to swap spit on the bottle."

"No," said Liv.

"You rather toot a little, O-liv-i-a?" Rand asked, patting the sleeve in which he stored his cigarettes.

She shook her head.

He sighed. "I hear your old man likes his coke. No wonder, living with a tight-ass like yours."

"Fuck you, Mr. Nighswander," Liv said.

Rand stared at her. He fumbled in the sleeve of his sweater, as if for his cigarettes.

It was the wrong sleeve, Liv thought, then he showed her the gun.

"Cute, ain't it? Cheap little half-assed nigger-blaster is what it is. Your dumb neighbor, the silly bitch with the stupid little dogs— what are they? Shits-zoos?—she left this for me. Thoughtful of her, wasn't it? Of course, next summer, she won't have anything to stop a moose from raping her, will she?"

Suddenly he reached out and caught Liv by the hair and shoved the gun in her face. "I could make you eat this, bitch."

Liv spat at it. Rand seized the back of her head and slammed her mouth into the gun. Then he jerked her head back. Blood gouted from splits in her lips. She gagged, and spat broken teeth and shards of caps over the gun and Rand's hand. He shoved her onto the bed.

"Stupid cunt," he muttered, and shoved the gun back up his sleeve.

Liv hid her face in her hands. *My teeth,* she thought, *Jesus God, my teeth.* The initial burst of pain seemed to come from the outside and explode inward. She probed the jags and gaps with her lacerated tongue, noting the taste of blood, shredded edges of gum and lip. Her front teeth had taken the brunt of the damage. At her core, she was numb with shock.

"Sit up," Rand ordered.

He had to haul her into a sitting position. He held a wet hand towel against her mouth. The cold water stung, but it also numbed a little.

He let her go again. She curled up into a ball on the bed. He shook her by the shoulder. "You got any painkillers?"

She gagged laughing. She couldn't very well tell him they were all in her socks.

He muttered a curse and went into the bathroom. She heard him rummaging in the medicine cabinet and drawers. She peeked over the edge of the towel and saw him in the mirror. He was staring at the top shelf of the medicine cabinet. Studying the pattern of rings left in the dust by all the little bottles that weren't there anymore.

She groped frantically in one sock, and hooked out the first thing she felt, a biggish tablet—a Percodan, she thought—and got it into her mouth and swallowed it, along with tiny shards of broken teeth, real and ceramic. She buried her mouth in the hand towel.

He came back, tugging a foil-wrapped package from his sleeve. When he ripped the foil away, she saw it was a baggie two-thirds full of white powder. The coke he had been talking about.

"Open your mouth," he ordered.

She shrank away from him. He snatched the towel from her, flung it away, and made a grab for her chin. She rolled away from him. He took the baggie between his teeth to free both his hands and tackled her. The bed rocked with his weight as he threw himself across it and pinned her, first with his body, and then with one hand by the neck. He simply choked her until her vision darkened and she stopped struggling. Then he straddled her on his knees and took the baggie out of his mouth. He tipped a small quantity of coke into the palm of one hand and thrust the fingers of the other hand into her mouth over her split lips to spread the powder roughly over her torn gums and broken teeth. The immediate sensation of numbness from the cocaine stilled in her any desire to resist, had she the strength to do so.

"Ouch," he said, and pulled his fingers out. "Fuck, cut my finger on something." His fingers were smeared with blood from her lips, and pink-tinged spittle. "Open up," he ordered. He stared into her mouth. "Nasty. Jagged ends."

Rand dipped his fingertips in his palm and powdered her lips.

"There," he said. He snorted the rest of the powder. He rolled off her and lay next to her. "Ahh, that's good shit."

Liv was a little dizzy. The pain in her mouth was still there, glazed with the numbness of the coke. The strange sensation of the coke combined with the Percodan, perhaps, just now going to work, was loosening her focus on the here and now. *This is an interesting thing that is happening to me,* she thought. On the outside, she was just the same: Liv, naked inside her clothes, clay-stained fingers, sore jaw and aching mouth, bleeding slowly onto the handmade quilt that covered her bed, but she could feel the ends of each and every hair on her head, and see the insides of her eyelids and feel her tongue swollen and numb in her mouth. There was a bitter, chalky taste at the back of her throat. When she opened her eyes, they would not focus. She closed them again.

"Sorry about that," he said. It was not an apology; he felt not the slightest remorse for the damage he had done her. His only regret was the damage he had done to the completion of his own fantasies about the woman's mouth. "You know, you're your own worst enemy."

"Huh," Liv responded. She knew who her worst enemy was all right. It was just too much trouble to make her bruised throat and jaw say so.

"You oughta have a toot," Rand said. The bed shifted as he sat up. She heard him opening the baggie again and inhaling. Then he hovered over her again, getting an arm under her head, lifting her up. She opened her eyes and glared at him and tried to make herself heavy. He shoved his palm into her face and yanked her head back. Some of the coke simply wafted over her face, and she felt it as numbing little prickles on her skin. But most of it was drawn into her nasal passages by her own instinctive inhalation. The bitter chalky taste was in the back of her throat again. She gagged a little, and then sneezed.

Rand laughed and released her.

"Feel better?" he asked.

She did. She felt distinctly weird, but she also felt quite a lot better. She was suddenly very conscious of the snow pattering against the windows and the house creaking against a raging wind. *I'm all alone,* she thought. *There's no escape.* Panic flared hotly under her breastbone, and died away quickly. Everything was all perfectly clear and real.

She watched Rand get up and go into the bathroom again. He came out with paper cups from the bathroom dispenser and tipped wine from the jug into them.

"No," she said, and raised a weak hand to fend off the cup he offered her.

"Suit yourself," he said.

He climbed back onto the bed and sat cross-legged. "Now where's the stuff that was in the medicine cabinet?"

Liv laughed. "What stuff?" she said.

Rand emptied the tiny cup and reached for the jug again. "You know. The stuff you hid."

Liv opened her eyes wide. She shook her head. "Didn't hide an'thin'," she said slowly. Talking hurt. Her lips were swollen. She pretended to think about it. "Maybe he," with a wave toward the living room to indicate Ricky, "kep' it."

Rand glared. "The dirty little bastard," he muttered. "He might have." He looked at her. "He won't for long. What the fuck was it?"

Liv furrowed her brow. "Don' know," she said. "Din' know about it."

"Yeah," said Rand, "but I'll bet you did."

Liv tried to smile but it hurt too much. "No."

Rand scratched behind his ear. She hoped he would decide to confront Ricky right away. She might have a chance to get the pills out of her socks and hide them again before he was sure Ricky didn't have them. It would be okay with her if they killed each other over it. Just so long as they didn't wake Travis up.

But Rand had other things on his mind. He reached over and fingered the collar of her shirt.

"I can take care of my punk brother anytime," Rand said. "Right now I feel like a little loving."

She wriggled away from him.

He laughed and emptied his paper cup again. "That's right. Skitter away. Only one thing I like better than chasing. Just remember when I decide I'm done chasing, you're done skittering."

She drew a deep breath and propped herself up on her elbows. "No," she protested furiously. She made a further effort, though it hurt like hell. "Can't get no through your dope-stewed head?"

Rand laughed again. "I ain't the only dope-stewed head around here." He took out the baggie and waved it under her nose. " 'Nother toot, O-liv-i-a?"

She turned her face away. "No."

"More for me," Rand said, and put a pinch in one nostril, as if he were taking snuff. He resealed the baggie and tucked it up his sleeve again. Then he leaned over and took her by the throat and slammed her flat on the mattress.

The force of his hand cut her off in mid-scream. She thrashed upward, and was driven down again, with one brutal thrust of Rand's arm.

"Now listen, O-liv-i-a," he said, as she lay there gasping, "you're gonna move your ass. This is gonna be the best I ever had, or I'll put that kid of yours out into the storm tonight. He'll go real well out there in his cute little Doctor Dentons, with a skinful of tranks, won't he?"

With that he let her go and rolled off the bed.

She needed to breathe deeply, but every breath she took shook and sobbed, revealing how badly he had succeeded in frightening her. Fear and humiliation provoked hate, and a violent rush of adrenaline that only made the trembling worse. She hated him for threatening Travis, for using her child against her, with the bitter recognition that it was always and ever so. Women could always be trapped simply by trapping their children. He had defeated her. And in defeat, in fear and hate and anger, Liv found, or so she thought, the strength of the loser. She would teach Rand Nighswander the power of the slave. He wanted her to move her ass, give him the best he ever had. She didn't think it would be hard to be the best this backwoods barbarian, coupling with drunken teenage girls and bar bags, had ever had. He wanted fucking. She would fuck him silly, if she couldn't fuck him to death.

Rand removed the baggie of coke and his cigarettes and matches from one sleeve of his sweater, and put them on the nightstand. He took the gun and the box of ammunition from the other sleeve and considered them. He put them in his jeans pocket. He hauled the sweater over his head, and tossed it onto the floor. Then he went into the bathroom.

Liv heard him unzip his pants, and the sound of his making water. He flushed the toilet and came back, with his jeans still unzipped.

"My little brother," Rand said, "ain't house-broke, you know. You oughta be glad it ain't him. He'd be pissing on you."

Liv turned her face away, pretending to be disgusted. She didn't want Rand to see that the Percodan or the coke or both were getting to her. She felt like she was falling, like a dead leaf from a tree, floating randomly on currents of air. She felt a flutter of panic; she didn't want to lose control.

He went back into the bathroom, rummaged in a drawer again.

"Turn over," he said, when he came back. He had a roll of white adhesive in one hand, the gun in the other.

Liv was too paralyzed by drug-induced confusion to respond. While she struggled to anchor her senses, Rand misread her hesitation as fear.

He grinned. "Christ, you got a dirty mind, O-liv-i-a. Your old man must be a real freak. Well, I ain't. That back door stuff makes a man feeble-minded."

Finally, it sank in. He was telling her he wasn't going to sodomize her. She was immediately light-headed again, partly from the dope, but also from real relief, and unexpected amusement that he was reassuring her of his righteousness on the subject of anal rape. Not that she wasn't thankful. She was, she'd be an idiot not to be. Rape was rape, but its variations hardly more bearable. Carefully, she rolled over.

"Turn your face away and put your head down," Rand said.

She did as she was told.

She heard the thunk of the gun against wood. The frame of the bed, she thought. Rand ripped tape from the roll. He grunted over his task.

"Okay," he said.

When she looked up, he no longer had the gun or ammo. He dropped the tape on the nightstand. He had taped the weapon to the bed frame, beyond her immediate reach or sight.

"Not that I don't trust you, O-liv-i-a," he said. "I don't."

Rand began to strip. She turned her face away again and listened to the rattle of his jeans, the soft wump as they met the carpet.

She felt rather than saw his nakedness as he climbed onto the bed and touched her arm.

"Look at me," he said.

Seeing him naked she realized what had always seemed familiar about him. The narcissistic quality of the male model. One of those stunning square-jawed, muscled young men in the glossy ads for Strohs, or Pall Malls, or Paco Rabanne. In the world of ads, the muscle had something to do with hard hats, cowboy hats, or a toga of tangled sheets in an arty-looking loft in some big city. It was an implicitly and sometimes explicitly heterosexual world, though she always felt, looking at them, that the models were more than likely in love with their gym instructors or themselves. Real construction workers had beer guts, real cowboys had skin like leather and lungs to match and cowshit or horseshit on the heels of their boots, and the missing tagline of the cozy sexy conversation between the handsome Mr. Goodbar in the fucked-over bed and last night's pickup on the phone was Hot Shot telling Hot Pants that she might have his Paco Rabanne, but she had also his herpes.

It was easy to imagine Rand Nighswander lifting weights in front of a mirror. He was hairy for a blond man, his chest matted with curly reddish hair, and his armpits and groin heavily tufted. His penis, already half-erect, was large and uncircumcised. Idly, unconsciously, his hand drifted to it and tugged it.

She noted all of that, and felt sick to her stomach. It was not that he smelled of old sweat, or that there was that disturbing narcissism, though she was repelled by those factors. It came down to an utter absence of desire for him, and that made the thought of sex with him nauseating. Pat had been her sole lover for all the years of their marriage. Intimacy with this man, forced or not, devalued her intimacy with Pat in a way that she felt physically. It was an invasion that made her understand for the first time what that word meant.

He fumbled at the buttons on her shirt. She pushed his hand away.

"Undress myself," she said. "Bathroom, firs'."

He settled back. "Yeah." He reached for his cigarettes. "Leave the door open."

She pushed herself past him and stumbled off the bed. He clenched his teeth around the butt in his mouth and laughed. She caught herself and groped her way into the bathroom.

Not fighting the combination of drugs permitted her to be clumsy in untangling herself from her clothes. Making a certain amount of noise and staggering around the bathroom at convenient points, she was able to keep the pills inside her socks as she slipped them off, and rolled them together. It seemed like a good idea to pop another pill while she had the opportunity, and she was too befuddled and in too much haste to be bothered figuring out just what it was she swallowed. She tucked the socks into the pocket of the terry cloth bathrobe she had left hanging on the hook on the back of the door.

Once naked she was immediately cold. Shivering, she hugged herself once, held her head up and her spine straight, and left the shelter of the bathroom.

Rand looked her over calmly and grunted. He patted the bed on the other side of him.

She approached the bed with all the dignity she could muster and managed not to stumble or weave once. Then she realized she was going to be forced to crawl over him, that he had deliberately not moved over to make room for her. She blushed violently and started around the bed, to get onto it from the other side. Rand grabbed her by the elbow and jerked her back.

"Just climb over me," he said.

She glared at him, but, of course, she didn't have any choice anymore. She put a knee to the edge of the mattress and bent over Rand, reaching for the bed beyond him.

He waited until her butt was over him and slapped it. "Hooraw!"

Liv yelped and jumped, tumbling over him.

He lay back, grinning, and took a last draw on his cigarette. He dropped it in the paper cup of wine that Liv had refused. It sizzled, and the air was briefly perfumed with the smell of hot cheap wine. He passed a hand over the arc of his penis and rolled over her, grinding himself into her belly. His breath in her face stank of the cigarette.

She turned her face away and gritted her back teeth. Placing her hands on the small of his back, she traced the swell of his butt. Her touch seemed to electrify him. He stopped grinding against her.

"Relax," she said into his left ear. It was dirty.

He pulled back and stared at her.

She passed the ball of one thumb over his left nipple, then rolled the nipple between thumb and forefinger.

He gasped. "Yeah," he said. "Do that again."

She wondered sardonically what he thought male nipples were for—symmetry? She pinched both nipples very hard. He loved it. His penis against her thigh went prodigiously hard and he moaned. He shoved his hand between her thighs and separated them, and immediately drove his penis into her. It hurt.

She cried out and tried to lift herself away from him, pushing down on his shoulders, and twisting her body, trying to get out from under him. He pinned her by the shoulders and continued to force himself into her, though he was abrading his own organ against her resisting flesh. He would not really feel the damage he was doing himself until after, when his nerve ends were no longer deadened by his own tumescence. Liv's flailing hands found the hair of his head; she yanked a handful of it hard enough to make him yelp. He hauled back and slapped her once, hard enough to nearly knock her out. Then he heaved back and drove into her again, releasing her shoulders long enough to seize her wrists and pin them to the pillows.

"Move your ass, cunt," Rand shouted at her.

For an instant, Liv could do nothing. He was hurting her, he was inside her, fucking her, tearing her. He was raping her. Nothing she had ever read or heard or imagined had prepared her in any way for the reality of rape. Beyond the physical sensations, she felt nothing, she was paralyzed. Terror, anger, and the strength of her own muscles drained out of her. The nothing that was left was despair. At that instant, the idea of fucking him to death was an unbearable joke on her. He was shouting at her, shouting filthy degrading things about what he was going to do to her, what a terrible fuck she was.

She felt the trickle of hot tears dripping over her cheeks before she knew she was crying.

Then she was terribly dizzy again, and she thought she was fainting, but she did not. Her perceptions suddenly cleared and became sharper. She could see the skylight over his shoulder. When the house was heated, the glass stayed warm enough so snow falling on it melted and trickled away. Even when the house was unheated or it stormed hard enough to allow the snow to accumulate, as soon as the sun shone again, the heat of the sun, intensified by passing through the crystals of snow, warmed the glass, so the melting plaque of snow slipped off it and onto the roof, sometimes suddenly, and all at once, sometimes in large pieces. But tonight, the window glass was like the glass in a framed picture of snow, not falling snow, but snow packed and solid as if in a wall, a slice into a snowbank. The lights in the bedroom twinkled off the crystals of snow on the other side of the glass, gleaming like the satin lining in a coffin. But there was blackness beyond it. It was the negative of the sunny day. The cold of the night multiplied through the layered crystal snow and chilled the glass. She felt cold and naked then, and curiously calm, as if she had already died.

Rand's weight was on her. She was intensely aware of his body, the fresh sweat over old sweat over old tobacco smell of it, the texture of hair and skin, his panting. She concentrated on feeling him inside her.

You asked for it, she thought. You bastard.

And then she tightened her vaginal muscles.

He hesitated. She squeezed again. He stopped.

"You doing that on purpose?" he asked.

She kept her face turned away from him, and squeezed again, setting up a rhythm. "Movin'," she said. "You wan'ed it."

He resisted for a few seconds, then let her take it over.

"I don't know if I like it," he said.

But he didn't tell her to stop and she didn't. She kept on drawing him in, releasing him, drawing him in again. When she stole a look at him, he had closed his eyes and wore an agonized expression. She had to suppress a laugh. None of the drunken, doped-up little teenagers he had terrorized or seduced in the past had ever given him a hint of what it was really all about. Her own terror receded. She didn't need to fuck him to death. It was enough to humiliate him.

Now she felt her power and calmly and deliberately brought him, first with a quicker rhythm, a second of respite, and then an irresistible pressure, to sudden orgasm. Like squeezing the last toothpaste out, she thought.

He groaned and twisted against her, then pushed himself up on his elbows and glared at her. "You bitch," he said. "I wasn't finished."

She turned her face away to hide her smile.

He cupped her chin and jerked her head to face him. "You made me come," he accused her.

She fought to keep a straight face. "Sorry," she said.

He drew his fist back as if he were going to slam it into her. She grinned at him, and showed him the ruins of her front teeth. He dropped his fist and pulled out of her, with as little care as he had slammed into her. Sitting on the side of the bed, he slugged back the contents of his cup of wine, and reached for the coke.

"We ain't done yet," he said sullenly. "You'll see."

The pleasure went out of her victory. She felt enormously stupid, ashamed of her own foolish pride. The power of the slave had been nothing more than coke talking. There wasn't any winning with this man. He would only become more dangerous to Travis and herself. All she had done by showing him resistance was provoke him.

She slid by him, intending to go to the bathroom. He caught her arm and jerked her back.

"Where you think you're going?"

She pointed mutely at the bathroom door.

He shoved her hard again. "You bin enough. Just let it dribble."

She pulled herself backward onto the bed and waited.

"Sit up," he said.

She propped herself on her elbows. She was cold, and tired, and felt dirty.

He held his palm with a pinch of coke in it under her nose. "Suck it in, O-liv-i-a. It's good for you."

She turned her head. He grabbed her chin and jerked her back. "Do it before I break some more of your teeth making you. Do it."

She bent over his palm, closed one nostril, and inhaled the powder through the other. It tingled and burned a little. Then she felt better.

Rand lit a cigarette. "Feel your ass loosening up?"

She ignored him. It was all the resistance she dared.

He sucked at the cigarette a little, then set it on the edge of the nightstand.

She thought about telling him when it burned down it would char the wood, and the ash would certainly fall onto the rug and dirty it, and if the butt became unbalanced between ash and burning end, it might fall onto the rug and burn a hole in it. Or burn them up. But he was fondling his penis with one hand, and feeling her breasts with the other, and he pinched one nipple hard enough to break the skin and make her cry out and knock his hand away.

"Ooops," he said, and reached for the coke baggie. "Fix that right up." He dipped a fingertip in the powder.

She covered the irritated nipple with one palm.

"Suit yourself," he said. "I got a better idea." He pinched a generous amount of coke into one palm and rolled his fingertips in it. Then he began to spread the powder over her labia.

"How's that?" he asked.

"Stings," she said. "Numb."

He seemed pleased. He continued his application until his palm was empty. He pinched her labia experimentally and she felt nothing. He snorted a little coke himself and then ordered her to open her legs wider. He placed one hand firmly on her pubis, and began to insert small quantities of the powder into her vagina.

She twitched and tried to close her legs. "Hold still," he said, "less you want me to twist your tits some more."

It was like the biopsy seven years ago, after a falsely suspicious Pap smear. The gynecologist had taken the tissue sample in his office, after injecting her with a local anesthetic that had felt much like Novocain or one of the other anesthetics dentists used. It felt like that. Except for being injected. She was absorbing the coke directly through mucous membrane. She wondered what damage he might be doing her, how much could her body absorb of the stuff, and whatever it was cut with.

Rand propped himself up next to her and snorted a little more. He took her hands and put them on his penis. "Get me up," he said. "Wish your mouth wasn't full of them jagged edges."

"Me, too," she said, stroking him.

He laughed. "I could always break 'em off for you."

"Thanks," she said, "you've done enough."

"You blow your hubby?" he asked.

She didn't answer him. He had grown thick and hard again in her hands. She squeezed the base of his penis gently and then stroked the tip. That distracted him sufficiently.

He pushed her down and climbed onto her, entering her as crudely and violently as before. "I always wanted to fuck a couple grams of coke," he said.

She felt him within her but very little else. Her muscles did not respond to her. She was beginning to feel very strange and distant. She could hear her heart hammering hard a long ways away. Her body slicked with a cold sweat.

He rode her viciously for what seemed like a very long time. She lost track of it. It was like being in a canoe on the river. The river was drawing her with it. The thrust of the oar only made the rhythm, pushed her into the river's flow. The water thickened as if she were in a net of weeds, and she arched, reaching out to escape it. As the tangled web of weeds let go, she realized what was happening, but it was too late. She screamed, but not, as Rand Nighswander thought, with pleasure. With despair.

The lights went out.

Rand swore. Liv caught him by surprise and pushed him off. She twisted over the side of the bed, feeling frantically for the gun he had taped there. He hooked an arm around her throat and hauled her backward. They lay tangled together on the bed, panting.

They could hear Ricky and Gordy stumbling around the living room and cursing.

All at once, perhaps because the dark of the night had invaded the house, Liv felt very cold. Now it seemed quite extraordinary that they had not lost the power earlier. Triumphant, the wind howled around the house.

Rand shook her by the shoulder. "Where do ya keep your candles?"

"Nightstand," Liv said. She untangled herself from him and undid the tucked in blankets and linen. She slid under them and turned her back to him, curling up on herself for the warmth.

He groped for his matches. By the light of a match he opened the drawer. A stub end of candle rolled out of the back. Rand grunted and picked it up.

Liv's eyes, shielded from the flare of the match and then the meagre candlelight, adjusted quickly to the almost total dark. But she was paralyzed by confusion and pain and the drugs she had taken. She couldn't think of anything very clearly.

Ricky pounded at the bedroom door. "Rand!" he yelled. "We lost the fucking power."

Rand got up and opened the door. "I noticed," he said.

Ricky stumbled through the door. "You got a candle," he said.

"Ayuh," Rand answered. Rand turned to Liv. "Anymore a these around, O-liv-i-a?" he asked.

"Kitchen," Liv said. " 'Bove the fridge."

Gordy Teed's face showed like a faint moon at the bedroom door. "Power went out," he said.

"There's candles in the kitchen," Rand said. "Look in the cupboard over the refrigerator."

"Think you can do that?" Ricky asked Gordy sarcastically.

Gordy nodded eagerly and scurried away. He could be heard bumping into things and muttering swear words.

Ricky cast a knowing glance at the bed. "How was it?" he asked.

Liv cringed under the blankets.

"Find out for yourself," Rand said.

Ricky hooted. "Do I get some of the coke?"

Rand draped an arm over Ricky's shoulders. "Listen up," he said, and whispered in Ricky's ear. Ricky's eyes brightened and he covered his mouth and giggled. He poked Rand in the chest.

"Fucking A," he said. "You watching?"

Rand picked up his long johns and started climbing into them. "You need a cheering section?" he asked.

Ricky shrugged and rubbed his hands together. "Your idea, that's all."

Rand walked over to the bed and picked up his cigarettes. He pulled the rocking chair closer to the bed and sat down. "What you waiting for?" he asked.

Ricky hauled his sweater over his head and unzipped his jeans. He scuttled closer to the bed and bent over Liv.

"Hey, Olivia," he said, snatching up the baggie of coke. "I got something here for your tight ass."

Liv shuddered and curled herself a little tighter.

A light wavered in the hallway. "Hey," Gordy said. "I found them candles."

He stood in the doorway grinning. Nobody seemed very interested in his accomplishment. Rand just sat there smoking, and Ricky was shucking his pants with one hand and waving the baggie in the other. Gordy thought about it a minute. It looked like Rand was giving Ricky some of the nose candy. It looked like Rand was going to let Ricky whack off a piece of the woman, too. Gordy shuffled into the bedroom for a closer look.

"Hey," he said. "Watcha doin'?"

Ricky kicked his jeans away and struggled out of his long johns. "What do you think, asshole?"

"Can I have some?" Gordy asked. He crept a little closer to the bed. The candle dripped hot wax over his fingers but he seemed not to notice.

Rand laughed.

Ricky tore back the blankets and climbed onto the bed. "It's my turn now, O-liv-i-a," he said gleefully.

Liv shrank away from him. "Leave me alone," she said. "Get away from me, you creep."

"It's my turn," Ricky explained.

"Don't you touch me," Liv said. "Don't you touch me."

Ricky slid his hand under the blankets to Liv's belly. "Come on, Olivia."

Liv slapped his hand away. To her surprise he backed off and looked at Rand.

"Come on," he whined. "It's my turn."

Rand sighed and stood up. He leaned over the bed. "You just don't have no technique," he said. "You have to say the right words to her."

Ricky turned sullen. "I don't have to say nothing to her."

Rand sank to his haunches and pushed his face close to Liv's. "You better let him, O-liv-i-a, or he'll be corn-holing your kid instead."

Liv exploded from the bed, tearing up the linen as she came up in one motion and heaving them over Ricky and Gordy. She struck

Rand in the chest in passing and he staggered back and fell on his behind. She was out of the room and down the hall before they could react. Behind her, Ricky and Gordy struggled, cursing, to free themselves from the bed linen. There was a violent whoosh and hysterical screaming. Liv saw light reflected on the walls like shadow. One or both of the candles had ignited the bed linen. The shadows of the three men danced on the wall in the tormented postures of demons in hell.

Ricky freed himself from the burning sheets and stumbled into Rand's arms, shrieking. Rand thrust him aside. Gordy, the sheets still tangled around him, struggled frantically to escape the flames licking his ankles and knees as if he were being burned at the stake. He kept up a ceaseless screaming like a teakettle on the boil. The fire was the only light left in the room. He was between Rand and the door Liv had fled through. Rand hesitated, then leapt on Gordy, knocking him to the floor.

"Towels!" Rand shouted at Ricky, cowering by the bathroom door.

The habit of obeying Rand took over. Ricky could always do something, anything, if someone just told him what. He dove into the bathroom and ripped towels from the bars and shelves and threw them through the open doorway toward Rand.

Rand snatched towels from mid-air and buried the flames with them. Gordy sat up and pounded at them, beating out the fire, first hysterically, then angrily. The room was suddenly dark again. Rand leapt over Gordy and tore out into the hallway after Liv.

In the blacked-out living room she stumbled against furniture, knocked over trays that still had dishes on them, and tripped over The Poor, who seemed to come from nowhere, as if she had coalesced out of the dark itself. It was cold there; they had let the fire go out. Liv scrambled for the fireplace and found by memory and feel the niche where she left the kitchen carving knife hours before. Then she dashed back across the room toward the hallway to Sarah's bedroom and Travis.

Rand hurtled out of the dark, intersecting her at the entrance to the hall.

There was no time even to scream. Liv struck at him with the knife. She felt the resistance of flesh as the knife caught and slashed the side of his face. Rand's hand closed like a manacle around her wrist and twisted. She felt her ulna twist with it. Her whole body was lifted up, her bare feet left the floor. She cried out in pain and hopelessness. Trying to tighten her grip on the knife, she realized she had lost control of her fingers. They felt boneless. They seemed, of their own accord, to loosen. Rand shook her wrist lightly as a dog might shake a dead duck by the neck, and her fingers let go. Rand put out his other hand and caught the knife as it fell.

Casually, he shoved her into the living room. She sank onto the couch and curled up, shivering. He was breathing hard. He felt his face, and then looked at his fingers.

"Bitch," he said. "You cut me."

Ricky padded into the living room, and peered at them.

"You got her, Rand?" he asked.

Rand grunted. He studied the knife. "Get some more candles."

Ricky ducked into the kitchen.

Gordy shuffled into the living room. He was weeping. He stank of burnt cloth and urine.

Ricky came back clutching a fistful of candles. "Gordy pissed himself," he said. "Too late to put the fire out, but he tried." Ricky giggled.

"You're mean," Gordy snuffled. "You're always mean to me." He crept to the hearth and slumped onto the floor, hugging his knees.

Rand tucked the carving knife under his arm, and took a candle from Ricky. "Matches?"

Ricky shrugged.

Rand looked around impatiently, then went to the fireplace. He picked up the poker and turned over ashes until he found glowing coals. He rolled a cone of newspaper and lit it from the coals, then lit the candle from the newspaper taper.

"Rand," Gordy whimpered, "I got burnt, Rand. It hurts, Rand."

Rand crouched and examined Gordy's burns. Gordy showed him blistered hands, feet, ankles.

"Ain't pretty," Rand said. "But you'll live." He looked at Ricky. "Go look in the bathrooms and see if you can find some first-aid cream or some burn spray or something like that."

"Kid's bathroom," Liv said. "Burn spray there."

Rand nodded. "Thank you, O-liv-i-a."

Ricky lit a candle from Rand's and scurried off.

Rand took the knife out from under his arm, and sat down on the sofa, next to Liv. "I oughta cut your throat," he said conversationally. "I oughta cut the kid's throat."

Liv rocked herself gently. She was very cold, shaking with it, cold all the way through, as if she were all surface, and all exposed.

Ricky came back with the burn spray. He glanced at Rand, and took the spray to Gordy.

"Don't say I never did nothing for you," he said to Gordy.

Gordy took the can of spray gratefully. "Oh, no, Ricky. I won't never say you never did nothing for me. Not ever."

"Ricky," Rand said. "Where's the coke?"

Ricky started. "Fuck me," he said. "I think I dropped it. I'll go see."

"You cold?" Rand asked Liv.

Liv nodded.

"Good," Rand said. "I oughta put you right the fuck outta doors."

Ricky slunk back behind the wavering light of his candle. He showed Rand a charred towel with the remains of the baggie in it. The fire had melted both plastic and crystals into a stinking, unappetizing lump.

"Great," said Rand. "Great."

"Yeah," said Ricky.

Rand poked the carving knife at Liv's bare breasts. "Come on, O-liv-i-a," he said, and stood up.

Liv pushed herself off the couch and into a standing position.

Rand took her elbow and shoved her toward the bedroom.

The air was thick with the smoke from the fire. Rand unlocked a window and opened it. The smoke fled to the out of doors, along with the heat in the room, and snow blew in, in bone-chilling gusts. Liv took a spare blanket from the closet, and wrapped herself in it. Rand looked over her shoulder, and took out a blanket for himself and one for Ricky, who was still buck naked. Ricky giggled and wrapped it around his waist.

"Find your clothes," Rand said. "And mine."

He shut the window. "You make up this bed, O-liv-i-a."

"Be easier if I had real clothes on," Liv said.

Rand nodded.

Liv slipped a nightdress over her head.

"My feet are cold," she said.

"So put something on 'em," Rand said.

"My socks are in the bathroom."

"Go on."

She pulled on the socks quickly, wiggling her toes and flexing her foot to redistribute the contraband narcotics into crevices between toes and under her arch. When she came out, Rand was kneeling by the bed, removing the gun and ammo he had taped under the frame.

While Ricky kicked burnt toweling and linen out of the way, and sorted his clothing from his brother's, and the brothers dressed, Liv stripped the bottom sheet from the bed and remade it with fresh linen.

"You take some pills outta that bathroom?" Rand asked Ricky.

"Did not," Ricky said. "Never did. Who said I did?"

"O-liv-i-a thought maybe you got 'em and kep 'em."

"She's a goddamn liar," Ricky said. "Kep 'em herself, I bet."

"You heard him, O-liv-i-a," Rand said.

Liv shook the fresh sheets over the bed. "Maybe there was never anythin' there."

"Maybe," Rand said. "Maybe I oughta let Ricky worm it outta you."

Liv bent over the bed, tucking it in.

"There was something there, Mr. Nighswander," she said. "A whole lot of narcotics. Your basic collection of heavy-duty painkillers. Now do you want your nasty little brother and that pathetic thing out there overdosing themselves? If you do, I'll show where it is this minute. I don't give a goddamn if they kill themselves with it."

"Hey," Ricky said. "You hear what she called me."

"Shut up," Rand said. "I can't think with you running your fat mouth."

Ricky sulked and Liv finished making the bed before Rand spoke again.

"Ricky," he said, "take a couple a these blankets and you and Gordy go bunk on the living room floor. Get that fire going again. It's all we got for heat tonight."

"What about them pills?" Ricky asked.

"You don't need 'em," Rand said. "Here, take this jug. That'll kill some pain."

"All right!" said Ricky and hustled off with the jug.

"Sure you don't want to put some of them pills in that jug?" Rand asked Liv.

"Love to," Liv said, "but you'll have to get it back."

Rand laughed. "Ain't you got no compassionate feelings for poor old Gordy's blisters?"

"A little," Liv said. "I could spare him a pill or two."

"I'd appreciate it," Rand said. "Ricky devils him too much. He ain't responsible, you know."

"I need to go to the bathroom," Liv said.

Rand nodded. He sat down in the rocking chair and shook loose a cigarette. It was the last one in the pack. His face in the flare of the match was very tired. If she had done nothing else, she had worn him down.

Liv slipped into the bathroom and locked the door behind her. She extracted a couple of Darvocettes and a pair of Darvon 65s from her socks. She swallowed the Darvon capsules herself, and then brushed her teeth, washed her face, and then her thighs, where Rand's semen had dried. She urinated in the sudden luxury of privacy. Her water burned in passing, making her conscious of having been used and used hard. There was blood in it, like threads of red ink. Debits. Someone owed someone something.

When she came out, she handed Rand the two tablets. He ducked his head by way of thanks and left her alone in her bedroom.

She slipped into the bed. It was warmer. The electric heaters weren't giving off anything anymore. It was going to be very cold in the bedrooms before morning.

Rand came back. "I checked the kid," he said. "He's still sleeping."

"Amazing," Liv said. The Darvon was beginning to work. Pulling her under. It was like being good and drunk. Cement overshoes. Taking her right to the bottom of the deep, the deep something. The currents bore her upright, and lifted her hair from her scalp. It drifted into her eyes. She swayed with the current until it was rooted inside her, and she no longer even knew she swayed.

Part
Three

. . . whatever the mute winter of your teeth or
the hate of your eyes, whatever the warfare
of perishing beasts who guard our oblivion,
in some dominion of the summer, we are one . . .

. . . hurl yourself into your grief like a dove,
like snow on the dead . . .

—PABLO NERUDA,
"The Woes and the Furies"

CHAPTER 15

FIREFIGHT
Rough Cut #7

Myrna Ratcliffe is picking up her living
room. It is not the room it was late last summer.
Dust on the mantelpiece, a litter of playthings,
a laundry basket spilling over with unfolded
towels and clothing, a subtle degree of
disarray, reflected in Myrna herself, who wears
a wrapper with a ripped pocket, and fuzzy
slippers.

"Damn kids," she mutters as she stoops to
pick up crayons strewn across the rug, and
scraps of paper covered with childish scrawls.

She drops the crayons into a tin box on the
magazine-heaped coffee table, and balls up the
paper to stuff into the other pocket of her
wrapper, the one that isn't ripped. She stacks a
pile of coloring books and shoves it onto the
shelf of the coffee table. Straightening up, she
presses her lower back with her hands. She
surveys the room and closes her eyes and shakes
her head. She picks up a hi-ball glass from the
coffee table, sips it, and then sinks cross-
legged onto the rug in front of the hearth.
Staring into the fire, she plucks from her

pocket the little balls of paper she has
accumulated, and begins to throw them into it.
When they are all gone, she sighs, and takes
another sip of her drink, and clasps her hands in
her lap.

"You know what," she says to the fire, "you
know what, Emery Ratcliffe. I hate you."

"Hot damn," says the man behind her. "That
mean there's a chance for me?"

Myrna, turning, is cut off in mid-scream by a
hand clapped over her mouth. The man's other
hand is under her chin, jerking her backward.
Her struggling opens her wrapper and the top
button of her pajama top. He flips her onto her
back on the rug easily, and shows her a knife. He
lifts the hand from over her mouth slowly.

"Court," she breathes. "Thirteen years, and
you come back, like a fairy godmother's curse."

Court settles back on his haunches and tugs a
forelock of his coarse hair. "Yassum, Miss
Myrna," he says.

Myrna sits up calmly and tugs her wrapper and
the pajama top closed.

"I ain't scared of you, Court," she declares.
"You already did all the bad you can do to me."

Court strokes his mustache. "I ain't got no
quarrel with you, Miss Myrna," he says. "I want a
word with Rat, is all."

"You and me both," Myrna said. "Can I have my
drink?"

Court looks around, stretches for it, hands
it to her.

She takes it without thanks and drinks. The
first swallow is painful; she touches her
throat.

"My apologies, Miss Myrna," Court says.

Myrna looks at him contemptuously. "You can
stuff your apologies up your skinny white ass,"
she says.

Court taps the tip of the knife on his teeth
and sighs. "S'pose I've got that comin', Miss
Myrna. Well, never mind. Just you tell me where

Rat is, and I'll be going. I'll be happy to tell
him you're pissed at him."

Myrna stares past Court at the fire. "I don't
know where Rat is, and don't ask me no more."

Court squats silently for a long moment. Then
he moves close to Myrna and puts an arm about
her.

"You wouldn't lie to me, would you, Miss
Myrna?" he asks.

She jerks away from him. He grabs her wrist
and twists her arm behind her. Myrna cries out in
pain. The front of her pajamas gapes open again.
Her left breast is almost entirely exposed.

"Where is he?" Court demands.

"I don't know," she wails. "I don't know."
She breaks into sobs.

Holding the knife against the side of her
face, tightening the pressure on her wrist, he
says, "Let's be reasonable, Miss Myrna. I'm
gonna cut those cute little kids of yours into
stew meat if you don't tell me, right this
goddamn minute, where the fuck Rat is."

"You touch my kids," Myrna says, "and you're
a dead man."

Court smiles and hauls on her arm. She
winces.

"What do you want Rat for so bad?" Myrna asks.
"I know what I want the son of a bitch for, but
what you want him for?"

"We got old business to settle," Court says.

"That the business you settled with
Jackson?" Myrna asks.

"What do you care, Miss Myrna. You hate Rat
yourself. I heard you say so."

"I got a good reason to kill Rat," she says.
"What's yours?"

Court strokes her bared breast. "He's a
murderer," he says.

"Get your hand off my tit," Myrna says.

Court laughs.

"Rat's a son of bitch for running out on me,
but he ain't no murderer," Myrna says.

"This was a while ago. Probably he's forgot
all about it. Someone he murdered in the war."

"Anybody Rat killed in the war, he killed in
self-defense. He never murdered anybody," Myrna
insists. "You the murderer. You done Jackson,
Denny said so."

Suddenly she has Court's full attention.
"Corriveau? When'd you see him?"

"I didn't," Myrna says. "He called the day
Rat left."

"They're together then."

"I don't know."

Court releases her arm. She rubs her wrist
and grimaces. Casually, Court drapes an arm over
her shoulders. She casts a distasteful glance at
his hand hanging loose over her collarbone. She
tries to pull the front of her pajamas together.
Court smiles, and hooks his arm around her
throat and jerks her backward, unbalancing her.
In one smooth motion, he pushes her flat on the
floor and straddles her. She stiffens under him
and tries to wriggle free. He drops over her, the
back of one arm across her throat, and places the
point of the knife under her right eye.

"I'll tell you who they murdered, Miss Myrna.
They murdered a little girl named May. About
your size, actually."

Myrna trembles. If she was not afraid of
Court before, she is now.

"I know how to bring Rat home, Miss Myrna,"
Court said conversationally. "I know how to bait
a little trap for Ratty."

"I ain't interested," Myrna says, with
bravado that Court reads as bluff.

Court lifts himself onto his elbows. "I'm
going to do to you what they did to her," he says.

"Who?" Myrna asks. "Who done what to who?"

His free hand tugs at the sash of the wrapper,
the waist band of her pajamas.

She tries to push his hands away.

He slaps her viciously, so hard she hardly
makes a sound, and afterward lies stunned.

He is ripping her pants off. She starts to draw up her knees protectively.

"There's just one of me," Court gasps, "so you ain't gonna be raped the way they raped her, but I am going to crucify you, Miss Myrna, like they did May, and I won't have to look for Rat no more, 'cause he'll come to me."

Myrna rolls her head from side to side on the carpet and stares at the ceiling. "You gonna do what they done," she says. "That your idea of justice? You be a murderin' rapist, too?" She laughs bitterly, and lifting her head with great effort, spits at Court.

Court freezes. Spittle trickles down his face. "Why not?" he asks her. "Why shouldn't I?" and begins to weep.

W HEN Pat woke up, curled up on the front seat, the windows of the car were curtained with snow. Except for the evidence of the dashboard clock's advance from eight to five, it might still have been night. Snow had blown in through the tiny crack he had left at the top of the window on the front passenger side and dusted the dashboard, the top of the seats, the steering wheel. It had gathered more thickly in corners and crevices on the dash, and in the bend of the seats.

And on Sarah, stirring in the backseat.

Fearful of the exhaust, they had done without heat. Their breath blew white in the cold. Pat tried the nearest door, the driver's side, where his feet pointed. It was frozen. He kicked it open and climbed out. He struggled through the snow to the nearest bush, turned his back to the car, and urinated into the falling snow. At least he was able to see where his urine yellowed the snow. The visibility had improved enough for him to see he was, as he had feared, only feet from the Pondicherry Causeway over the narrows. He could distinguish the causeway from the lake by the lines of its guardrails, welting the white surface of the snow. The causeway was only a few feet higher than the lake. Big boulders every few yards broke and rose above the guardrails. High caps of snow teetered on their crests and occasionally collapsed before a shift in the wind.

On the passenger side, which had been in lee of the wind, the snow had risen to the hubcaps. Snowdrifts sealed the doors, veiled the windows, and crept long fingers over the hood, on the driver's side. Getting back into the car, accumulated snow fell into it through the open door, littering the seat. Pat stopped to brush the seat and clear the hinges and door frame.

Sarah rested her elbows on the back of the front seat.

"I really have to go, daddy," she said.

"Sorry, kid," he said. "You'll have to use Mother Nature's restroom like I did."

Sarah sighed. She slid over the back of the seat. "My doors are frozen, too."

Pat held the door open for her. She staggered in the deep snow. "This is so gross," she said.

Pat laughed. "Don't let the frost bite."

Sarah laughed.

Pat went around to the back of the car, and shoveled snow with his hands to free the exhaust. Fortunately, his gloves were thick, foam-lined skiing gloves. Sarah skittered back through the snow. Pat slid back into the front seat, next to her, and they huddled together in the front seat, sharing their body warmth. After warming the ignition key with his breath, he inserted it. The starter ground a few seconds, caught, and died. He forced himself to wait, counting off two full minutes by the clock. Then he tried again, and this time, the engine caught and roared. He felt like roaring, too.

"It started!" Sarah shouted.

Pat allowed the motor to idle for several minutes before turning on the heater. As soon as the warmth began, they both thrust their hands over the heating vents. Sarah giggled and sang snatches of "Light My Fire." The hot air hurt. Pat flinched and rubbed his hands together to stimulate the circulation. Even then, he reveled in the heat, long enough to feel almost normal again. Then he put the car in gear. He didn't really expect it would go anywhere, not in three feet of snow, and it didn't. It shuddered and lunged and growled and whined and rocked when he really gassed it, but it didn't actually move.

He idled it back and sat in the warmth a while longer. The road crews should be out again soon, with the improved visibility. But when would they reach the causeway? Should they wait for them, or walk? He tried to remember what there was for human habitation within walking distance. There was the marina, a yardful of boat sheds and a fuel pump. That was locked up and closed for the winter. The landing was public, but the snowmobilers and ice fishermen who used it wouldn't be out today. The ice couldn't be reached, and snowmobiles would founder and sink in this depth of soft snow. There were farms behind them, back toward Greenspark, the last one two or three miles ago. There were farms and houses on the other side of the causeway, beyond Little Partridge Hill. And closest of all, there were summer houses on the lake, some of them only a few hundred yards away, empty and unheated but a form of shelter, like a chain, leading toward Liv and Travis. The lake reached seven miles on one side of the causeway toward North Bay, where home was. There was shelter nearer, if they broke into the marina sheds, or made Little Partridge, but they could get to Liv and Travis directly just by hiking up the lake. It would be easier on snowshoes, but that was one need Marguerite had not foreseen.

"This vehicle isn't moving until the road crew gets here," he told her. "You want to stay here, or try walking up the lake? It's maybe five miles as the crow flies. What you might call the direct route."

Sarah shivered. "If we just stay here, the car will keep us warm."

"For a little while, yes," Pat agreed. "Then the gas will be gone and the battery will run out."

Sarah ducked to peek at the gas gauge. "It's almost empty."

"Right."

She sighed. "I guess this is when we have to do everything the hard way."

Pat laughed. "I'm going to turn off the ignition, baby, and leave the keys in it. The road crew might need to move it."

He turned the key and the engine died. The silence was huge.

"Come on," he said to her and opened the door.

She slid out. Arm in arm, they picked their way to the overhanging branches, pruned to a man's height, of an old spruce. It was miserable going, the first sample of what it would be in any direction. They were cold and hungry and stiff from sleeping in the car all night. But the world around them was ecstatically beautiful. It could kill them, Pat thought, would kill them, if it had the chance. In any event, it was and would still be beautiful. Nothing they did or didn't do really mattered, not in the context of this place. Mostly, he decided, he really wanted to see Liv again and make sure she and Travis were okay. Resolutely, they left the shelter of the spruce tree and set off over the embankment toward the lake.

It was like climbing stairs built for a giant. One foot up, balanced on the other, shift the weight back until they felt the hard edge of the snow against the back of the knee, reach forward awkwardly with the raised foot, and bring it down, weight coming forward after it to drive it into the snow, and sinking, sinking so far that they had to fight falling face flat, and often did, until it seemed they were crawling, or swimming, up the lake, not through water, but through a malevolent powder. The causeway and the car disappeared in blowing snow before they had gone very far. Very very quickly, they were lost, though Pat did not say so to Sarah, and she did no more than cast anxious glances at him now and again. And as quickly, they were too numb to do anything but go on.

Walter McKenzie scratched his chest and yawned. His exhalation fogged the bedroom window. He rubbed the glass with the heel of his hand and squinted at the world outside. There was precious little to be seen except snow, fallen or falling, drifted, drifting, blown and blowing, hither and yon, so the only way a body could tell up from down and one thing from another was from safe inside, where the fix of things could be extrapolated into the out of doors. Walter shook his head. He pulled his wool trousers on over the long johns he slept in, and went down the back stairs, hand on the rail to steady himself, and taking care with his footing. The rubber treads on the stairs had loosened dangerously over the years, but Walter never thought to tighten them, or replace them, or just take them off, but compensated unconsciously by slowing his step and using the railing.

The fire in the woodstove was at its nadir, having kept the kitchen pipes from freezing during the night. Walter could feel the cold linoleum right through his doubled socks, which served him as slippers. Fritzie had crept under the stove as the warmth diminished. She dragged herself out and rolled over for a good morning scratch.

When Walter opened the back door to let her out, he found the snow had drifted against the door waist-high, so he had to lift Fritzie up and push her out. She yelped and disappeared in a cloud of snow. Walter closed the door and went in to pull on another pair of socks and his packs, a wool shirt and an ancient cardigan out at the elbows, and his heavy coat. Fritzie barked at the door to be let in. Bringing snow in a cascade, she fell into the house when he opened the door for her. This time it took some effort to close the door again against the weight of the snow.

After he fed Fritzie, he turned on the radio and listened to the weather report from Mount Washington in New Hampshire, which overlooked the whole region. Standing up next to the stove, he ate a piece of toast, and washed it down with a cup of strong tea. According to the report, the storm was abating, having deposited three to four feet throughout the region, on top of an eight-inch crust. The winds had peaked at fifty miles an hour and were diminishing. Clearing was expected by nightfall. Electrical outages were common, as wind and snow had felled trees and torn down lines. Roads were being cleared slowly because of the considerable accumulation, and extreme caution was advised. Unnecessary driving was discouraged. The schools were on vacation, of course, which meant on the one hand the lumbering buses would be off the roads, but on the other, that there would be kids out playing. Then he put on two pairs of gloves, equally holey, but with the holes mostly in different places, so together they made almost one whole pair, jammed a wool cap with thick earflaps down over his head, and wrapped a muffler around his throat and the lower half of his face.

"Off to the wars," he said to Fritzie, and got his shovel from the shed.

It took him an hour to shovel his way to his Jeep. His snow-shoes were in the back end. The plowblade was already on, which was a saving of time and effort. In fact, he was inclined to leave it on despite the extra gas to cart it around, and the way it made the Jeep sludgy to handle. The fact was, he didn't like taking it off or putting it on without help anymore. He needed some excuse to go into Reuben Styles' garage, which wasn't easy, as he changed his own oil and did most of the other maintenance on the Jeep, but when he could think of something, some adjustment, sometimes making something up, which was always plausible because it was well known that machines sometimes had mysterious complaints that went away on their own, just as people did, or were accidentally fixed in frigging around with them, but without the mechanic knowing exactly what he had done, well then, Walter would say, "Reuben, whyn't you give me a hand with this frigging blade." And Reuben, genially, would, since it was only courtesy to help a neighbor of whatever age, to move such a heavy object. Then Walter would allow the blade ought to be left on or off, depending on how the weather looked.

Walter plowed his yard, and then his own long dirt driveway to the road. The road had been plowed, and the road crew had sealed the driveway with a huge bank in passing, but he didn't hold it against 'em. They couldn't stop to clear everybody's driveway, and besides, they knew he had his own rig.

Once on the road, he headed for the causeway. The most direct routes from his farm to North Bay were one-lane town roads that he knew from long experience would be slower than crossing Pondicherry Causeway and taking Route 5 north through the village of Nodd's Ridge, then turning lakeward again on the Dexter Road. It meant a long, sweaty slide down Little Partridge Hill, the Jeep lunging against the brake, and slipping all over the road, to get to the bottom, but that was the worst of the roundabout route.

He saw the first blinking red light at the bottom of the hill, from the other side of the causeway. Soon he could make out the town's yellow plow. It was sitting empty next to an abandoned car on the other side. He pulled up and got out.

Frankie Styles and Bo Linscott stood in the lee of the wind behind the plow, hunched up inside their macs and smoking cigarettes, held awkwardly in thick insulated gloves.

Frankie waved laconically at the sight of Walter.

"Son of a whore," Bo said.

Walter nodded. "The radio said it's lettin' up."

Bo and Frankie laughed.

"Christ a mighty, better," Bo said.

Walter hemmed and hawed and hawked a glob of phlegm into the snow. "What you got here?"

Bo shrugged. "Some asshole left it here in the night. Christ knows where he is."

"Like this when we come up on it," Frankie said. "Right smack in the middle of the road. Musta stopped dead in the middle of a white out."

Walter nodded. "Pretty bad last night."

"Son of a whore," Frankie said.

Bo nodded and flicked his cigarette into the snow. "Come on, Frankie," he said. "We gotta move this shit heap outta the way and call it into the sheriff."

Walter stumped over to the abandoned station wagon. He squinted at it. Then he turned around and waved at Bo, who was climbing back into the cab of the plow.

"Bo!" he bellowed, hoarse with excitement. "Pat Russell! This is Pat Russell's wagon!"

Bo hung on the door of the cab. "What the hell is he doing out here this time a year?" Bo yelled back, and took off his cap to slick his hair straight back in puzzled disgust.

Frankie Styles hurried up to Walter. "Jesus, Walter," he said, "you think he's wandering around out here someplace?"

Walter shrugged. "Hope to Christ not," he said.

Frankie looked at the butt of his cigarette mournfully and then pitched it out into the storm. He peeked at Walter from under long, boyish lashes. Frankie was all of nineteen, as blond and open-faced as his father had been at that age.

"Don't tell dad I bin smoking, okay?" he asked Walter.

Walter grinned, showing all his bad teeth. "I ain't no tattletale, Frankie. You know them coffin nails ain't no good for you."

Frankie squirmed. "Yeah." He peeked at Walter again. "Don't tell dad I bin swearing, okay?"

Walter patted him on the shoulder. "Frankie, don't you tell your dad I told you, but he used to swear some when he was your age, too. Most young fellas do, on account of they think it makes 'em sound like one of the men. Now your dad knows you was raised right and you got good sense. I wouldn't worry about your dad so much, if I was you."

Frankie nodded. "Yeah."

"You want to worry about somebody," Walter said, staring out at the lake, "you oughta worry about Pat Russell. If he's out there in this Christer, he's in trouble."

Frankie followed Walter's line of sight. "He must not have no sense at all," he said.

Walter sighed. "He oughta have better sense than to walk away from a vehicle he coulda sheltered in and out into nine square miles of shit, that's for sure. But I guess I don't blame him. He prob'ly just wanted to get home."

Jeannie poked wood into the stove and watched it kindle. She sank down in a chair in front of it, and hunched into the warmth. Behind her, Arden Nighswander shuffled into the kitchen and hawked and spat into the sink.

Nighswander peered out the window.

Jeannie poked the fire again, and loaded in another stick of wood. "Boys back?" she asked, flattening her voice to hide her nervousness.

Nighswander dragged a chair from the table and sat down next to her before he answered. "No, they ain't."

She sighed and closed the stove door and stood up. After she had filled a kettle and put it on she sat down again. "They ain't never been out all night in weather like this," she said.

Nighswander shook a cigarette from a crumpled pack impatiently. "Shit, Jeannie, they're growed up. They're probably tomcattin'."

She stared at him incredulously. "In this storm?"

Nighswander shifted from one cheek to another and farted. He glared at Jeannie. "Goddamn it, they can take care a themselves."

"You oughta call the sheriff," Jeannie said. "What if they had an accident?"

Nighswander opened the stove door and threw the empty pack into the fire. He stared at the fire moodily. "I ain't callin' the goddamn sheriff," he said. "Now shut up, and leave me alone."

Jeannie turned away from him and looked out the window over the sink. She grasped the lip of the sink desperately. "There's something wrong," she said. "I can feel it."

Nighswander looked at her. "You shut your trap, I said."

Tears spilled from Jeannie's glazed eyes as she stared out the window. "It's all wrong," she said.

Nighswander shoved his chair back from the stove. "Shut the fuck up!" he shouted at her.

She cringed.

Nighswander saw the tears on her cheeks and clenched his fists. If it didn't hurt so much to move he would have punched her out for her trouble. Instead he slumped back onto his chair. "Them boys can take care a themselves," he muttered. "They'll take shelter in one of them summer places." He looked up at her. "Call the goddamn sheriff and he'll say they broke in. Can you get it through your thick head they're a sight better off takin' care of themselves than doing a stretch at Shawshank Prison?"

Jeannie covered her mouth and turned back to the window. The snow outside was like a blank wall. She could not see around it or over it.

The sheriff had been around before, with warrants. Arden and the boys had stood sullen, muttering swear words, while deputies had searched the house and barn and outbuildings. Each time the sheriff and his deputies had gone away empty-handed, but not before saying bluntly that sooner or later he would have the lot of them. She had believed they were victims of prejudice, because otherwise they were thieves and vandals and worse. There were all the girls Rand had had trouble with, that they all joked about. She had never been able to say to herself, Rand is a rapist. All the trouble Ricky had had in school, until he was old enough to quit, had been more than just growing pains, she had known that, but had not ever accepted he was what the school people said—immature, disturbed, paranoid, violent. Nighswander was so certain the boys were being persecuted. She had thought if she admitted that her Gordy was simple, that was enough truth to have to face. It was all true, all the bad things, she knew that now, and was afraid. And not because the boys might go to prison. Facing the truth, unavoidable now, she thought they ought to go to prison, even Gordy, who was not competent in any legal sense, not able to understand the consequences of his own acts, but because they were wild and dangerous, and wild and dangerous things ought to be locked up. She was not afraid they were dead of exposure; she believed Nighswander, knew as well as he did, they could take care of themselves. Besides, she had no sense they were dead, and was sure she would, if they were. But she was afraid of what she didn't know. Where were they? What had they done to save themselves?

What did the snow; that the wind blew in twisting veils and piled up into walls, hide? She did not think, when it was all over, that either she or Nighswander would want to know the truth.

The cold woke Travis. He rolled out of Sarah's bed and wandered bleary-eyed to the bathroom to pee. The tiled floor was cold underfoot. The whole house was much too cold. He went back to Sarah's room. Sitting on her bed, putting on his slippers over the feet of his pajamas, he noticed that E.T.'s heartlight was extinguished. Experimentally, he flicked the switch on Sarah's bedside lamp. Nothing happened. Sarah's clock-radio, which was old and had a dial face, was stopped at 12:13. That must be what time it was when the electricity went out, either twelve noon or twelve midnight. But it wasn't midnight any longer. It wasn't dark enough. It was sometime pretty early in the morning. Travis pulled on his kimono and stuck his hands in the pockets for the warmth. Silently he counted his G.I. Joes. Then he set off for his mother's bedroom.

Because the lights were out, and the snow was still falling steadily outside, the house was creepily quiet, as well as a little dark, as if it were sleeping with a blanket pulled over its head. In the living room, two men slept on the floor, rolled up in old spare quilts. Travis squinted at them long enough to establish that they were Ricky and Gordy. The Poor was curled up on Gordy's stomach. She did not wake when Travis passed by. The TV trays had been knocked over. Broken dishes and dishes turned turtle were scattered over the rug, and spilled food stained it. On the hearth, two of the dirty dishes held the guttered stubs of candles. Live coals blinked red-eyed from the heap of ash in the hearth. Travis would have put some wood on it, but the stack of wood Walter McKenzie had piled neatly next to the fireplace was gone, its place marked only by scabs of bark and splinters.

Travis went on down the hall into his mother and father's bedroom. In the half-light he could see two forms sleeping in the bed. Creeping a little closer, he could make out his mother's hand, lax on the counterpane. He slipped around to her side of the bed, and bent over her. Her swollen lips were parted. Her breath smelled like it had after she had her tooth out. Like something died in there, she had joked. Saliva tinged with dark that he knew must be blood crusted from the corner of her mouth across her cheek. Her hair was a dark tangle on the pillow. Travis placed his hand against her cheek.

She opened her eyes. They were blank, unseeing, blind. Then they focused. She came into them, she recognized him. Her body tensed. She reached for him, touched his face and hair.

The man on the other side was still, breathing evenly. It made Travis uneasy to see him there where before only his father had ever been. But it was not something he wanted to know about. He knew perfectly well this man and the other two had forced their way into the house. They were *enemies, robbers, bad guys.* He knew his mother had done nothing since the three men had come that was not meant to protect him. He hated them and feared them, not least because they reminded him he was a defenseless little kid, who could not stop them from hurting his mother while she desperately tried to stop them from hurting him. That was enough to know.

Quickly and quietly she took him under the blankets and hugged him, just as she would have if his father had been sleeping next to her instead of the man the others called Rand. It was comforting to feel the warm thick wool of her nightdress, the one she kept in this house for wintertime, when they came to snowshoe or ski cross-country or just to be out in the country for a weekend. He knew she was wearing socks; it was just something his mother always did when she went to bed in the winter. At the other house in town, she even had a pair of pajamas with feet on them, like his, except hers had red and white stripes all over, that Sarah had given her one Christmas. Sarah and his father went barefoot to bed; it was only Travis and his mother whose feet got cold at night.

Liv wiped her mouth with the back of her hand and grimaced. It was very quiet in the house. The wind outside sounded as if it were lessening, though it would still be cutting. The house was dark, but it was not the dark of midnight anymore. Without looking at a watch or a battery-powered clock, she could only guess, but she thought if it was not day, it was nearly so. She held a finger against her lips.

"Shhh."

Hand in hand, she and Travis slid out of bed and crept around it. They had reached the bedroom door when there was stirring in the bed behind them. She froze and Travis bumped against her.

"Where you going?" Rand demanded, his voice slurred with sleep.

She had trouble talking. "Bat'room," she said. Nothing seemed to work.

He sat up and yawned. The quilt fell away from his body. His chest was all furry, like Travis' father's, and there was dark fur in his armpits, too. His eyes were red-rimmed, as if he had stayed up all night.

"Hi, boy," Rand said. "What are you doin' up?"

"It's cold," Travis answered. "The fire's almost out."

Rand sniffed and cleared his throat and nodded. "It is cold. Colder than a witch's tit. You got a cigarette tucked away somewheres?"

Liv shook her head.

He threw aside the covers and pulled his right hand out from under the pillow long enough for them both to see the gun, then used the gun to hook his long johns from the floor. "Go to the bathroom. I'll see about the fire."

Liv nudged Travis toward her bathroom. Rand dropped his long johns around his ankles and grabbed Travis one-handed. Travis stared at the gun hanging casually from Rand's fingers.

"The boy'll come with me." Rand looked down at Travis. "I bet you already peed, didn't you?"

Travis nodded yes. Liv let go of him.

"Boy can help me with the wood," Rand said.

Rand hauled on his clothes and led Travis from the room. Liv snatched her clothing from the floor and hurried into the bathroom. Her jaw hurt when she moved it; the inside of her mouth, her tongue, her lips, were all enormous with swelling, as if they had been packed with sand. She grabbed a couple of pills from her socks and swallowed them dry. She did not intend to leave Travis in Rand's company for any longer than it took her to get dressed.

She was too hurried to more than glimpse herself from the corner of her eye. She did not want to know how she looked, because she would then remember it. She promised herself she was going to forget everything about the last twenty-four hours, utterly and completely, as soon as she could.

She found Travis at the open back door, receiving the wood that Rand passed him from the stack on the back porch. He was piling it neatly in the hallway. Sawdust and scraps of bark clung to the pile of his pajamas. His hands were already red from the cold. But he smiled at her, and that bucked her up. Something could be done about the cold. She picked up some kindling and hurried into the living room. Ricky stirred and opened his eyes. Gordy still lay open-mouthed on his back, breath whistling past a web of saliva in his mouth. She knelt at the hearth and arranged newspaper and kindling over the coals. The back door closed, and Rand stomped in, Travis at his heels, both carrying wood by the armful.

Ricky propped himself on his elbows. "Jesus Christ, it's cold," he said.

Rand sank to his haunches by the hearth, holding a stick of wood in his hands, waiting for the kindling to burn down a little. "That's your fault. You got a cigarette on ya?"

Ricky laughed. "Everybody's always blaming me for somethin'." He jumped up and displayed his nakedness. "Where you think I got a cigarette hidden, Rand?"

Rand ignored him. "What time do you think it is?" he asked Liv.

Liv stood up and dusted off the knees of her jeans. "Clock in the kitchen is on batteries. I'll check." She hooked Travis by the hand as she went by him and hustled him into the kitchen.

The clock over the table read 6:27.

"Stay here," she ordered Travis, and boosted him onto his chair.

In the living room, she told Rand, "Six twenty-seven."

Ricky stood stark-naked, yawning and scratching himself. He kicked Gordy casually. "Wake up, asshole," he said.

The Poor leapt off Gordy, landed next to Liv, and stretched slowly and deliberately before climbing onto the hearth and planting her rear end comfortably close to the fire.

Gordy snorted and coughed and rolled over. He looked up at Liv with pain-glazed eyes.

Liv felt sick to her stomach.

Rand tossed a couple of pieces of wood onto the fire. "How's your war wounds?" he asked Gordy.

Gordy sniffled. "Hurts a lot, Rand."

Rand looked at Liv.

"Excuse me," she said and hurried toward her bedroom. She heard Rand rise and follow her but did not slow for him. He caught up with her at the bedroom door. "Getting some pills for him."

"Fine." Rand reached into the sleeve of his sweater and showed her the gun. He shoved her up against the door. "Now you show me where they are, before I get itchy with this gun."

"Glad to," Liv said. "Want to know when you're leaving."

"I ain't proposing a trade," Rand said. "Not unless you got some cigarettes somewhere's. Even an old stale butt would taste good right now."

"Maybe," Liv said. She went to the closet and began to rummage through the pockets of the clothes Pat had left behind at the end of the summer. Old, baggy, or threadbare at the elbows or collars, some of them hangovers from his days of teaching English lit and drama at the university, consigned to the summer house rather than discarded out of hand, they had always seemed like good omens to Liv, if only because they were proof Pat wasn't ready to throw out his own history. And they delivered. In the breast pocket of an old gray suede sports coat, she found a pack of Pall Malls, stale but nearly intact.

"Jesus Christ in a handcar," Rand said when she tossed them to him. He shook out a cigarette and lit it reverently.

Liv pried off one sneaker with the other, by the heel, then applied her toes to the remaining sneaker. She hooked off her socks and held them out to him. "Every last goddamn one 'n' the butts, too," she said. "Welcome to 'em. Use 'em in bad health, hope it's terminal lung cancer."

Rand took the socks and shook them. He laughed around the butt in his mouth. "O-liv-i-a, you're a ticket."

"Light out," Liv said. "Storm's slackening: Hear the wind? Whyn't you pill up poor dummy 'n' haul on outta here before Walter McKenzie or the power crews show up? I'll forget you were ever here."

Rand tucked the socks up one sleeve, then the gun up the other. "Right," he said. "Wouldn't feed me and the boys somethin' first, would you?"

"Can't cook anything," Liv said. "There's cereal and milk."

Rand nodded. "Good enough."

She snatched a pair of socks from her dresser and hurried back to the kitchen. Travis sat where she had left him. He had taken out his G.I. Joes and arranged them around his placemat. She went directly to him and hugged him. He hugged her back.

"How 'bout some grub?" she asked him.

Rand crouched next to Gordy and examined a handful of pills. They didn't look like the amphetamines with which he was familiar. Finally, he picked out four of the biggest kind, figuring the bigger they were the more painkiller they packed. Gordy choked them back gratefully, washing them down with the dregs of last night's sour wine, fetched from the bedroom by Ricky under Rand's orders.

"Olivia is putting out some cereal," Rand told them.

"That's kid shit," Ricky protested. "I hate that shit."

"Maybe it's got marshmallows in it," Gordy said.

Rand ignored them. "We're going to eat it and then you two are going over to Miss Alden's place."

Ricky stared at him and then hooted.

Rand put a finger to his lips to silent him.

"Olivia don't need to know about it. I'll meet you over there."

Gordy shifted, and winced. "Jeez, Rand."

"You'll be okay," Rand said. "Give them pills time to work. You'll feel like goin' dancing."

Gordy nodded. If Rand said so.

Ricky peered at Rand slyly. "Why can't you come with us?" he asked. "You got somethin' better to do?"

Rand grinned. "Maybe I do."

Gordy sniggered. "Jeez, Rand," he said.

Ricky turned sullen. "How come I don't get any?"

Rand looked at him. "You won't want this when I'm done with it," he said.

Ricky stared at him.

Rand took out the gun and studied it. "You want to go to Shawshank for a spell? Get your ass reamed?"

"They gotta catch us, first," Ricky said. "Ain't daddy always said so?"

"Yeah," Rand said. "Daddy's right, too. Now O-liv-i-a is full a promises about how if we just leave, she'll forget we was ever here. But I don't trust her. I ain't gonna trust her. So now you know."

"What?" Gordy asked.

"I'm gonna keep your ass out of Shawshank," Rand said.

Ricky giggled. "How come I can't have a piece first?"

"Because you're a nasty little bastard," Rand said, and "I don't want to catch nothing from you."

"Hey," Ricky said. "That ain't called for."

Rand put the gun away and stood up. "Go get your cereal from the Missus and get your asses in gear. I expect you to have Miss Alden's place busted open and waiting for me."

That cheered Ricky up. He poked and prodded Gordy into the kitchen.

Liv and Travis left the kitchen almost as soon as Ricky and Gordy sat down at the table and found Rand sitting by the fire, contentedly smoking another of the stale cigarettes.

"Go get some clothes," Liv told Travis. "Bring them back here to dress."

Travis scooted down the hall toward his room. Liv saw him skid to a halt at his bedroom door, and cautiously push it open and peek in before he disappeared into it.

She began picking up the living room, mopping the trays with a damp rag, breaking them down to stack in their holder, picking up the dishes. The Poor had surreptitiously cleaned the dishes and snapped up the crusts of sandwiches and bits of chicken and vegetables from spilled soup. Even the places where broth stained the carpet had been licked until the wool was flattened and shiny. Now the cat sat on the hearth near Rand, washing her paws and face.

Travis shot back into the room. Liv stopped righting the furniture to help him, but he frowned at her and she backed off.

"I can dress myself, Liv," he said, and grinned so she wouldn't think it was personal. He went as close to the fire as he could while keeping his distance from Rand, and proceeded to unzip his pajamas and dress himself.

Liv went back to work, wondering at the adaptability of children. She had been afraid he might never want to go into his bedroom alone again. Now he was exhibiting his independence again.

Ricky and Gordy returned to the living room to retrieve their out-of-doors gear. Gordy was limping but the painkillers had clearly helped.

Ricky finished dressing first. He handled some of the video tapes idly then suddenly reached out and grabbed Liv.

"Hey," Rand protested.

Liv stomped on Ricky's boots and tried to pull away from him. Travis hurled himself from the hearth against the back of Ricky's legs. Rand jumped up and hauled Travis off.

"That's enough," he warned Ricky.

Ricky was giggling with excitement. "Just funnin'," he cried. Then he grabbed Liv by the back of the neck and forced his mouth onto hers.

She nearly fainted with the sudden fierce blossom of pain at the pressure on her swollen lips. He forced his tongue into her mouth. She bit down hard, though it hurt the exposed stumps of her teeth as much as it did him.

Ricky's head snapped back, and he let her go, in order to cover his mouth with both his hands. Tears started in his eyes.

"Jesuth," he gasped. "She bith me!"

Rand laughed. "Good."

Liv put the couch between her and Ricky. Travis scrambled away from Rand and wrapped his arms around her legs. She scooched down and hugged him.

"Got what you deserved," Rand said. He prodded Ricky toward the back door. "Get the fuck outta here, now."

Gordy shuffled after them, sneaking amazed and frightened looks back at Liv.

Rand came back and sat down. He took out the found cigarettes again. "Bet that hurt," he said.

Liv nodded.

"You want somethin' for it?" Rand asked, and fished one of the socks full of narcotics from his sweater sleeve.

"No," Liv said, and then a flair of pain changed her mind for her. She nudged Travis behind her. "Yes," she said. "Please."

Rand handed her the sock. She shook out a handful and rummaged through them, selecting a couple of Darvon.

Rand reached into his sleeve and showed her the gun. "Whyn't you just take a few more? Enough to go to sleep on."

She stared at him.

"Give us a few hours before you start running your mouth," Rand said.

She pushed the sock away and shook her head.

"You want me to hurt the boy?" Rand asked.

She dry-swallowed the Darvon. "You do and you'll go to jail."

"Only if you live to tell about it," Rand said.

Travis hugged her tighter.

"Fuck you, Mr. Nighswander," she said.

He tensed, then forced himself to relax. "Look," he said, in a reasoning tone, "be sensible, O-liv-i-a. I want you and the boy to sleep a while, is all."

Liv twisted around and picked up Travis. "We'll go in the bedroom and stay there until Walter or someone shows up. That's the most I'll do."

Rand sighed. "All right. I ain't forgot you found me them butts." He looked her up and down. "You was okay last night."

Liv's lip curled, but she held her tongue about that. "It'll be cold in there. I want to put on our snowsuits so we can stay warm."

Rand studied her. The scene he meant to leave behind would be a tragic but unincriminating one: a woman and a kid overdosed, murder, suicide, with a fire, like last night's but bigger, to blur the evidence. Snowsuits didn't fit in. On the other hand, he couldn't shoot either of them because bullets would be recovered from the bodies.

"Take 'em with you," he said. Once they were in the bedroom, he would work out a way to make her eat the goddamn pills. The boy he could force-feed once she was on her way.

They trooped to the bedroom, stopping at the closet for the snowsuits. Liv insisted on gloves and mittens and wool socks for their extremities. Rand shrugged and let her take them.

The bedroom was still cold and stank of the burnt linen, the scorched rug. The Poor appeared at the door, twisted past Liv's ankles, and bounded onto the bed. She began to circle, making herself a nest. Liv went down on one knee to help Travis into his snowsuit.

"Hold it," Rand said. He gestured toward the bathroom. "Put the boy in the bathroom for a while. Tell him to stay there."

Liv stared at him. He had caught her off-guard, and she couldn't think how to respond.

"Do it," Rand said. "You don't want to give him a complex, do you?"

Travis clung to her. Rand had succeeded in frightening him half out of his wits again.

She shooed him gently into the bathroom, hugged him, and asked him to wait. Rigid with fear, he sat down on the closed seat of the toilet and clasped his hands together. As she closed the door on him, shutting him in darkness, she could see his white face and wide eyes like a mask.

She shot a look of fierce hatred at Rand. He laughed softly.

"How's your mouth feeling?" he said.

"Have you forgotten what I did to your creepy brother?" she asked.

Rand reached for her and drew her close. He stroked her hair. "I ain't Ricky. You liked it well enough last night."

She pushed away from him. "I hate you."

"You keep saying 'fuck you,' " he said. "Gives me ideas."

His hands fell on her shoulders and he put his weight on her. She resisted him, twisting away from him, but he held her deliberately, digging his fingernails into her shoulders, until she gave way with a gasp, and fell to her knees. Rand unzipped his jeans and reached into them.

Ricky and Gordy struggled through knee-high snow to the machines under the trees by the beach. The tree line along the shore was all that distinguished the barren lake from the land anymore. The wind was sculpting fantastic dunes on it, so it looked as it might have if it were suddenly frozen in violent motion. Gordy hunkered down in the shelter of the trees. His face was ashen and shiny, his eyes a little glazed. Ricky bent over him and grimaced.

"You don't look too fuckin' chipper," he shouted over the wind.

Tears provoked by the cold, rather than pain, which the narcotics were successfully killing, trickled down Gordy's face. The wind burnt them into his skin until it was red. If he stayed out long enough, the first place the frost would bite would be his tear-dampened cheeks.

Ricky started Gordy's machine for him, and helped him onto it, then mounted his own and led Gordy out onto the lake. Head down against the wind, they ground slowly along the shoreline toward Miss Alden's house. It should have taken them five minutes. It took them fifteen. The machines left the lake and crossed the beach directly to the empty house. Ricky led Gordy into the lee of the house.

Gordy pulled his machine close to Ricky's.

"This is gonna be fun," Ricky said. He dismounted and poked Gordy in the chest. "At least we'll be outta the cold."

Gordy tried to grin. "Okay with me, Ricky."

Ricky bounded up the steps to the porch. He bounced impatiently from foot to foot, but Gordy moved very slowly through the deep snow.

"Come on!" Ricky shouted. He opened the storm door and fixed the spring to hold it open.

Gordy stopped. "I can't," he said. "It hurts."

"Fuck," said Ricky, and grabbed the old hand-wrought iron door handle. He rattled it furiously. He stepped back and raised his leg.

Gordy arrived at the bottom of the steps.

Ricky kicked the door. It shuddered but did not give.

Gordy struggled upward to the second step.

Ricky stepped back again, and threw all his strength into the second kick. The frame that held the antique hinges splintered.

Gordy panted his way to the top step.

Ricky hooted and kicked the door a third time. It fell slowly, heavily inward. He hooted again and jumped through the door frame. He felt the slight constriction of the wire as his chest hit it but there was no time to even wonder what it was before the shotgun went off. It caught him square in the chest and blew him out onto the porch. He was dead so quickly he didn't even scream.

But Gordy did. He stumbled backward against the railing of the steps, screaming, first with surprise, and then with fear, and then with horror. He fell to his knees and climbed back up the steps, staring at Ricky. He ran out of breath for screaming. Sobbing, he crawled to where Ricky sprawled. Ricky's chest looked like hamburger. Gordy crept close enough to look into Ricky's eyes. They were open. Snow spritzed over the porch railing and dusted Ricky's eyelashes.

"Dead," said Gordy, spraying spit on Ricky's face.

He had seen enough dead deer and moose and varmints, legal and poached. He had seen numerous dogs and cats die at the hands of the Nighswanders. He knew dead when he saw it. It was as good as a doctor's declaration of death.

CHAPTER 16

DISTANTLY, there was an explosion. Rand froze, startled. Liv grabbed The Poor and hurtled the cat into Rand's face.

Cat and man screamed simultaneously. He stumbled backward, clawing it, as it clawed reflexively at his face.

The bathroom door flew open, and Travis stood on the threshold, agog.

Liv grabbed the pottery-based lamp from the nightstand and backhanded it onto Rand's head. A huge chunk of the ceramic flew off the base of the lamp and shattered against the floor. The lamp rolled off Rand's head and onto the rug. He went limp with an oofing sound. The cat scrambled away, and disappeared out the door at top speed.

"Get into your suit," Liv ordered Travis, snatching his snowsuit from the floor and throwing it at him.

She looked around frantically, then tore a handful of old ties from the rack in the closet. She straddled Rand's limp body and tied his hands together, then his feet. He was already semiconscious, rolling his eyes, starting to move, making sounds.

With shaking hands, she helped Travis zip his suit.

"What was that noise, Liv?" Travis asked her anxiously. He kept his eyes on Rand, and pulled on a cap.

"Gunshot," Liv answered. She was climbing into her own snowsuit, zipping it, grabbing the socks and mittens and caps from the floor.

She kicked off her sneakers. Travis quickly began to take his off.

They pulled on the socks, the mittens. She grabbed his hand and dragged him from the bedroom to the hall closet, where they quickly pulled on their boots. There was no time to buckle Travis' boots or tie hers. She threw open the door and dragged him out into the storm.

Rand rolled against the wall and pushed himself into a sitting position. He shook his head to clear it, but it still hurt fiercely where the lamp had broken. He applied his teeth to the knots in the ties. The woman had been too hasty; he was out of his bonds in half a minute. He scrambled to his feet and loped to the living room to snatch up his snowsuit and boots. Carrying his boots, by their strings, in his teeth, he kept moving as he dressed, so he had his legs in his snow pants and camouflage jacket and was half-zipped up by the time he hopped to the back door. She had not closed it. The snow was blowing into the house in cold little puffs. He stopped on the porch to pull on his boots. Looking quickly at the sky, Rand could see it was not that it was still snowing all that much, but the wind was blowing erratically, spraying the light dry granules in all directions. The tracks she and the boy had made were still discernible, but they wouldn't be for long. Bare-headed, Rand plunged into the woods after them.

Behind him, The Poor stepped delicately through the open door, onto the path beaten through the snow on the porch. She watched the man hurrying into the woods. He kept his eyes on the ground, following tracks. Curious, she began to stalk him, bounding lightly in his bootprints.

Gordy crouched next to Ricky's body, sniveling. In a few minutes, he began to feel the cold. It came to him he ought to get help. He peered around, staring at the lake, at the woods, at the fringe of orchard he could see, mounting the hill behind Miss Alden's house.

Her driveway that snaked down the hill from the cottage road was buried beneath the snow. Rand was closest, back at the Russells' house. Probably fucking that woman again. Rand would be very angry if Gordy interrupted him, and he was going to be even angrier when he found out Ricky was dead. But there was no getting around it. He would have to know about it, and so would daddy and mum. Maybe no one would blame him. He was already hurt. Maybe they would all say "Poor Gordy."

Gordy hauled himself up on the porch railing. He did not think at all about Ricky. It had not occurred to him yet that Ricky's petty torture and molestation was at an end. He didn't think about covering Ricky's body, or moving it out of the weather. Dead was dead. The body was gruesome, yes, but otherwise of no interest. He understood only vaguely that Ricky had tripped some kind of trap, without wondering who had set the trap or why. It was no more than he and Ricky and Rand and daddy had done to hundreds of animals over the years, and he no more wondered about who and why than did those animals in their death throes. He wiped his mouth with the back of his mitten. The wind blustered down the lake in a long shriek. Gordy suddenly felt wet and realized he had peed himself. Again. His face went hot with shame. Now he was really in for it. He started to cry. The hot tears stung his cheeks and reminded him he was very cold. He shivered and turned instinctively toward the shelter of the house. But Ricky's body lay between him and the threshold. He stared into the interior twilight of Miss Alden's house. At first there were just shapes and shadows, but suddenly he saw, with instant recognition of its significance, the gleam of light in the lucite circle of the telephone dial. He could call Rand. Eagerly, he stepped over Ricky's body. Then he remembered Rand had torn out the telephone line at the Russells' house. This was disheartening, and Gordy started to turn away. Something in the slow-workings of his brain turned, too, and reminded him that he could call daddy. Clumsily, he trod on Ricky's hand, turning himself around. But he was grinning as he stepped over the threshold. It came to him he had stepped on Ricky's hand, and he felt a fresh rush of embarrassment, mostly at his clumsiness. It was not very different from what he would have felt if Ricky were still alive and had sworn at him for the transgression. It was better inside, where the wind didn't cut right through him or throw gritty snow in his eyes, but it was gloomy and he had to wait a few seconds for his sight to adjust to the semidark. The light from the open doorway helped a little. He stepped forward, and felt something brush his arm. Someone quicker might have stepped back reflexively. But Gordy wasn't that quick. What he was, was hurting from the burns on his legs. He staggered, and the second shotgun blast shattered his right arm. He drew in his breath instinctively, and passed out from shock before he could let it out in a scream.

Liv heard the second shotgun blast from inside the gingerbread house–studio. She had opened the kiln door; it was large enough for both herself and Travis to hide in the firemouth, but first she had to remove the racks and saggers, the forms that held the greenware while it was being fired.

The sound of the shotgun froze her. All at once she realized their tracks led directly to the studio and stopped there. She didn't need to look around to realize the studio was a trap, one door in, no place inside that wasn't visible through the windows, and no way out. All Rand would have to do is torch the place. If he didn't just break in and start throwing open cupboards and doors.

She grabbed Travis by the hand and hauled him toward the door. No time even to tell him what she was doing. They plunged out the door and into the snow.

Rand erupted out of the woods. He shouted in triumph. They both saw the glint of the gun in his hand.

She and Travis sprinted into the woods. She heard Rand laugh, and yell, but the wind took his words away.

They did not hear the shot until it pinged into a tree trunk just ahead of them. The wind shrieked distantly, and snow whirled around them. Travis' short legs could not keep up with her. His weight strained her arm from its sockets as she dragged him. She zigged and zagged, using the trees and brush for cover. In the brief silences when the wind caught its breath, she could hear Rand behind them, panting and gasping, in counterpoint to her own desperate breathing, and Travis'. Like them, he was forced to slog through the deep snow, not running so much as climbing it. It slowed and tired them, yielding niggling returns for their effort. She prayed for a great wind, a whirlwind to blind him, and to cover their path.

Who was firing the shotgun, and at what or whom? Friend or Foe? Was it someone who would help them?

They went downhill, because that was the lie of the land. It was not a direction they chose so much as they were driven to it. She knew Ricky and Gordy had gone to Miss Alden's. That was also the direction the shots had come from, she was sure of it, hearing the second one. It was closer, and so were she and Travis, since the studio lay on the path to Miss Alden's. Was it too much to hope that fate had brought Miss Alden to her house, that she had stood off Ricky and Gordy, perhaps even wounded or killed them, and that there might be shelter there for Travis and Liv, shelter from Rand? Otherwise, she and Travis were being driven into a trap, right into Ricky and Gordy's collective arms. She decided she and Travis would go, if they could make it that far, close enough to Miss Alden's to look. If they crept through the woods and the orchard, cautiously, they might be able to tell what had happened. In any case, they couldn't go home again.

Travis staggered and fell. His hand slipped free of Liv's. She cried out in exasperation and fear.

Looking back the way they had come, she saw Rand's dark shape among the trees. At the same instant he saw her and dropping to one knee, took aim.

Seizing Travis by the armpits, Liv picked him up. His weight nearly unbalanced her. She staggered backward.

The bullet Rand fired passed downward along its already distorted trajectory and clipped her right knee. The thick snowsuit further slowed and deflected it, and then kept the bone splinters tight against the bone, and began to absorb blood. She fell, letting Travis go. At once, she picked herself up, grabbed Travis by the hand, and dragged him onward. Blood spattered evergreen needles and juniper bushes, and the snow. *Even if we get out of his sight,* she thought, *he'll be able to track us now. Just looking for blood.*

She and Travis reached Miss Alden's boundary line before she stopped. Rand was somewhere behind them, but they had somehow, miraculously, gained ground. They knew these woods a little better than he did, maybe. She pushed Travis under bushes, whipped off her scarf, and tied it around her knee. A glance around, then she dove back through the snow to a huge old hemlock that overhung their passage through the woods. She could hear Rand now. Liv grabbed a low-hanging branch of the hemlock and hauled it back, wrapping it backward, so both she and it were hidden by the trunk. She held her breath and hugged the rough bark. Rand plunged into view, along the pathway she and Travis had made. He held the gun in his hand. She let him almost reach the hemlock before she let go. It whooshed out of her hand. Snow exploded from the whipping branch. Rand yelped when it caught him in the face and knocked him backward. The gun flew from his hand into the snow. He lay flat on his back, the wind knocked out of him, blinded by the needles that had slammed into his face.

Travis literally flew through the air as Liv hauled him out from under the bushes. His first step in the snow was a running one.

Rand lay stunned for precious minutes. Gradually his vision cleared, and as he stared up into the branches of the hemlock overhead, the cat suddenly materialized there, squatting in the tree like a malevolent bird, staring down at him. The cold and the snow spitting in his face spurred him to move. But when he did, his head ached fiercely. He hunkered in the snow, holding his head and shivering. Snow whispered down the back of his neck. He wiped his running nose on the back of his hands. His ears burned with the cold, and so did his fingers. His own body heat was melting the snow in his hair so his head was damp. Melted snow trickled along his temples and in front of his ears into his collar. He blinked away droplets from his eyebrows. The world around him was abruptly silent, as the woman and the boy slipped beyond his hearing. He poked desultorily in the snow for the gun, but it was gone.

He tried to think over the roar of anger that possessed him. The woman had knocked him on his ass twice. She had escaped. Behind him he had left clear, convicting evidence for Walter McKenzie to find any time now: his snow machine. Somewhere out there the woman and the boy were living witnesses. She would have him charged with rape, assault, breaking and entering, enough felonies to put him in Shawshank until he was a fat cockless old man like his father. The best he could hope was that she would run right into the open arms of his brother Ricky. Ricky was out there, with Gordy. But so was someone with a shotgun, and they had used it twice. The gunfire had come from the direction of Miss Alden's. He would be kidding himself not to assume that Ricky and Gordy had had the ill-luck to surprise the old dyke herself, and that she had succeeded in defending herself and her property. If Miss Alden had taken Ricky and Gordy out, that meant the woman and the boy had a chance of reaching safety with the formidable old bitch. And if he could figure that out, so would the woman. She was undoubtedly headed toward Miss Alden's. At least he knew where she was going. No need to track her. He could go back and get his machine and ride over there. Give her time to get nervous about where he was or maybe make the mistake of thinking he had given up.

It was enough to make him smile. He hauled himself to his feet and set off, a little unsteadily at first, the way he had come. Behind him, the cat dropped out of the tree, landing neatly on all fours according to folk wisdom, and leapt away, over the snow, in the same direction, but not following him, merely using his tracks, in the time-honored, practical way of cats.

At some point, Liv stopped thinking. She just kept moving. Once in a while she came down on her wounded knee just right and staggered as it punished her. It only took happening once for her to learn to favor it. That was not enough, in their rough passage, to forestall all discomfort, but she had painkillers in her system, and a degree of shock to help her onward. There was an instant of relief when she realized she and Travis were now struggling steeply down-hill, the way the land tilted abruptly toward Miss Alden's house. Seconds later, they broke out of the woods onto the slope they had been sliding on yesterday. Just below them, Miss Alden's house, the old Dexter place, still stood, thick-walled as a fortress. The shutters were closed and there was no smoke from the chimney. It looked as empty and lifeless as it had the day before. The driveway remained unplowed; there was no car, or four-wheel-drive vehicle visible. That small hope that Miss Alden was there, defending her property, faded and Liv felt more than a little heartsick. She wondered if the wind had played a trick on her, distorted the sound of the gunshots so they had only sounded as if they had come from this direction.

She held her fingers to her lips, signaling Travis to keep quiet. He could not have said anything if he wanted; he was out of breath, all but done in.

It didn't matter, Liv decided, if Miss Alden was there with a protective gun or not. If the two of them could get into the house, they could hide there. They would be safe, until Walter found their own house empty and in disarray and came looking for them. That could not be long now. She did not think about her knee. There was nothing she could do about it. She had to think about where Ricky and Gordy might be, how close Rand was to them.

"Travis," she whispered. "We're going to be commandos."

He nodded. The old familiar game.

They crept from tree to tree in the orchard, until they were close to the house. Liv kept glancing back at the woods, but Rand did not appear, nor did she hear anything to suggest he was at hand. Ahead, in the house, there were no sounds of habitation or battle—only the wind, which seemed to want to pick them up and blow them against the side of the house. They put their backs to the stone walls and began to sidle toward the corner. Liv peeked cautiously around it.

She could see the length of the back porch. She could see someone lying there, in front of the door. The snow was feathering long fingers over him. She could see the straw-colored hair, and the pink hue of the snow on his unmoving, disturbingly ragged chest. Ricky, she knew at once, was dead. She felt suddenly faint. She drew back and sank to her unwounded left knee. The right she held straight but let slip to one side a little, so it was for a moment bearing none of her weight.

Travis crouched beside her. "Mom?" he whispered.

She covered his mouth gently with her hand. She drew a deep breath. "Stay here," she whispered.

She dragged herself on the one good knee to the corner of the porch. From there she could see the yard. There were snowmobile tracks coming up from the beach, fast disappearing under blowing snow. She crept around the corner and came to a stop, hunkered down below sight of anyone in the house.

Gordy sat on the top step. His arm hung in tatters at his side.

His snowsuit was soaked with blood from his collar to his boots. His eyes were closed.

Liv scuttled back, and gestured to Travis. He scooted around the corner. She stopped him and hugged him.

"There's a body," she whispered, "and one of them's badly wounded. Don't look if you don't want to."

Travis squeezed her hands.

She leaned on him a little as they approached the steps together and was surprised at the degree of support he seemed willing and able to give her.

But he moaned involuntarily at the sight of Gordy.

Liv held on to him tightly.

Gordy opened his eyes.

She gasped and Travis grabbed her leg tightly, making her wince.

Gordy's eyes rolled. He tried to focus them. He pushed himself forward, and slipped down to the next step, with a thump. He grinned at her. He found the porch railing with his good hand and hauled himself, face a rictus of effort, to a standing position. He staggered to the next step, and then to the last. He let go of the railing and stood, weaving before them.

Liv and Travis stepped backward.

Gordy held out his good hand, and then pitched forward onto his face into the snow.

Liv dropped down next to him and turned him over, as gently as she could. He grinned at her. He moved his good arm in the snow, up and down, making a one-winged angel. He looked up at her.

"Ol' bitch," he said. "Trap."

He seemed to giggle and then Liv realized he was choking. She lifted his head, so his mouth dropped open. Using her teeth to snatch off her glove, she thrust her fingers into his throat. The tongue was slippery; it was like trying to get a grip on a piece of raw liver. But she did, and pulled it out. He lay gasping and heaving like a dying fish. She felt a wave of revulsion and wiped her fingers compulsively in the snow. She sighed, and let his head down again gently on the cold pillowing snow. She placed her bare fingertips on his carotid artery. The pulse was slackening and distant. Looking at the state of his arm, she thought he was bleeding to death, might already have bled too much to be saved, even if rescue were at hand.

Travis stood next to her, staring at Gordy.

"He said trap, didn't he?" she said. It was the first time they had spoken above a whisper since they had left the house. She hoped to distract Travis, but she wanted more than that to alert whoever was in the house that friends and no foes had come on the scene.

Travis nodded.

"Maybe there's more," she said. "We'll have to be careful." She looked up at Travis and took his hand. "We can't do anything for him, Travis," she said.

Travis blinked away snowflakes. "Maybe Walter will check here soon. In time to help."

Liv nodded. She knew Walter didn't check this house. But, of course, he could arrive at their house anytime now. He might be in time to help them. She didn't think there was a chance in hell he would be able to help Gordy.

She led Travis up the porch steps, keeping her body between him and the house. Showing herself. They stopped to look at Ricky.

Liv shuddered, and Travis twined his mittened hands through hers. Through the broken door, they could see very little of the dark interior of the house. They paused and there was no sound or signal from within.

Liv looked around. "On the floor," she said to Travis, and he obediently dropped to his belly, only inches away from Ricky's corpse.

Liv crept along the inside wall of the porch to the big window that looked out on it from the living room. It had a storm window on the outside, the bolted Indian shutters on the inside. She looked around the porch. All the old-fashioned wicker furniture had been put away. But on the other side of Ricky's body, tucked into the corner, there were two red clay plant pots the size of bowling balls, full of sand. They had had mixed clusters of cacti in them last summer, she remembered. Miss Alden must have transplanted the cacti and taken them back to Wellesley with her. Perhaps she had left the pots handy to sand the steps if she came in winter.

Liv limped cautiously around Ricky's body, and picked up one of the pots. As she bent, she whispered to Travis, "Turn your face away, okay. The glass is going to fly."

Travis nodded.

She propped herself at an angle to the window against the arching pilasters of the porch, pulled up her collar, and heaved the pot. The instant it left her hands, she covered her face and ducked. There was a satisfying explosion of glass and the thump of the pot against the wood of the shutters, followed by the shattering of the red clay on the porch floor. Liv felt shards raining on her snowsuit and the woolen cap she had pulled down over her ears.

Travis jumped and stifled a cry.

"It's okay," she reassured him. She brushed broken glass off herself. Travis tentatively brushed at the bits that had reached him.

Liv crunched across pot shards and glass and examined the window. There were big jagged pieces still in the frame. She wiggled them back and forth in the old putty until they came out, and then stacked them carefully in the corner of the porch. She threw her whole weight against the shutters and they bowed in, straining against the bolt, but the test discouraged her. They seemed very solid. She wondered how in the hell the Nighswanders had broken into this fortress in years past. Breaking in doors seemed to be the height of their finesse. Then she remembered Ricky Nighswander, like his brother, carried a knife—and if once it had seemed wicked, she now thought eagerly of its sharpness and strength.

She limped to Ricky's body. Travis pulled himself up a little to watch her.

Some of the flying glass had embedded itself in Ricky's face and hands, and lay twinkling on the snow on his chest, but had drawn no blood. Liv glanced at Travis. He had looked at Ricky and then turned his face quickly away, to stare at Gordy. It being its nature, the snow was building a dune over Gordy.

Liv gingerly patted the gory remnants of Ricky's snowsuit until she felt the hard blade of the knife in its sheath, tucked up the left sleeve. She had to pick his arm up to draw out the knife. It was limp and heavy. She dropped it quickly. She scrambled back to the shutter, drew out the blade, which now did not seem so much barbaric as substantial. It was easy to insert it between the shutters, which had not been fitted with any concern for tightness. The blade nicked against the iron bolt. She drew it out and began to splinter the wood on each side of the shutter, digging to expose the entire bolt. Her hand rose and fell frantically. More than once she looked over her shoulder.

"I've got my eyes peeled," Travis reassured her, and she forced a smile for him.

The old pin disintegrated rapidly under the tough steel. At last she broke through into the homemade mortise, a simple tunnel in the wood, revealing the bolt. Crouching as low as she could and still retain her purchase, she inserted the tip of the knife between the end of the bolt and the wall of the mortise and pushed the bolt backward, out of the hole. Ducking even lower, she pushed the left hand shutter back into the wall. Then she sat down with her back against the wall.

"Whoosh," she said, and mopped her brow elaborately.

Travis grinned at her.

Liv propped herself up again and peered into the house, through the single layer of dusty glass of the interior windowpane. The new source of light spilled over the old familiar shapes of Miss Alden's furniture. And winked on a web of wires that criss-crossed the room in every direction, and at heights from under two feet to five feet high. In the shadows, Liv could make out the muzzles of a dozen shotguns and the occasional gleam of a glass eye in the heads of Miss Alden's trophies.

She sank back to the floor, breathless with shock.

Travis scuttled around Ricky's body and cuddled next to her. "Mom?" he said.

"It's a trap," she said dully.

Travis peeked over the window ledge. He sucked in his breath.

Liv hooked an arm around his waist and drew him down next to her. "Scary, huh?"

"I think Miss Alden musta been crazy," he said.

A brief smile twitched at Liv's lips.

They heard the distant foundering whine of a single snowmobile from the lake at the same instant. Travis tensed against Liv. She pushed herself upward, craning to see over the ledge again.

"Remember the secret passage," she said.

Travis nodded eagerly and squeezed her hand.

"We could crawl," she said. "Do you think we can get the secret door open without touching one of the wires?"

Travis popped up and down. "If we don't open it all the way."

Liv took a deep breath. "We have to try. There's no place else to go." She couldn't have gotten anywhere else, but she wasn't going to tell Travis.

She tucked the knife into her own sleeve. There was no telling when she might need it again. She decided there was no point in closing the shutter. Rand would not miss the shattered glass, not with Ricky lying there like a pincushion, nor the exposed bolt on the shutter. More important, she and Travis needed the extra light the open shutter provided if they were to have a chance of reaching the secret passage alive.

"Fill up our caps with snow," Liv told Travis, passing him her own. "We'll need to try and cover our tracks."

Obediently, he scrambled to the steps and packed the caps.

She unzipped her snowsuit and tucked in the capful of snow, and Travis did the same.

When she started to pull herself toward the door, she was surprised to find Travis hard by her right side, trying to give her support. It was mysteriously cheering and made her want to laugh out loud. And then, just as unexpectedly, she was weak and dizzy, and he was there for her, like a little fireplug, panting and red-faced, but hearteningly substantial. Reassuringly dense, like his grandfather.

Over the threshold, it was suddenly quieter, as the wind was outside the thick walls. She rested against the frame of the door, on her left haunch, the knee slightly bent, and eased her right leg straight out in front of her. Travis hunkered down next to her. The wind had blown snow into the room, dusting the floor, bared of its animal skin rugs, in a great fan halfway across the room. Before her and above her, the web of wires criss-crossed like a cat's cradle. The broken ends of two wires coiled in and out of the layer of snow on the floor, within their reach. With the light from the open shutter, here and there in the gloomy corners of the room, she could make out parts of many shotguns—a glinting long bone of a barrel, the dilated pupil of a bore, with its steely rim of an iris, the gleam of polished wood in a stock, the checkering of the small of the stock—close to a dozen of them. The trip wires must be repetitive, many of them leading to the same trigger.

The lion's head roared silently at them out of the shadows. Its tongue lolled blood-red over its cold, white teeth.

The piano was gone. Miss Alden must have taken it away with her. Hadn't wanted it damaged by a stray blast, Liv thought.

Across the room, a birchwood fire had been laid in the enormous hearth, presumably for Miss Alden's next visit. A box of Blue

Diamond wooden matches in a brass dispenser hung on the wall near the secret door. There seemed enough wood for bonfire, but it was a colonial fireplace that a small man or a woman could stand in and no doubt the draw of the huge chimney was wickedly inefficient. It would eat a lot of wood, heating the stone of the chimney, and not much else.

The lowest wires in the trap looked to be about eighteen inches from the floor. Travis ought to be able to make it, if he didn't panic. If no one came bursting in on them.

She hugged him. "You first. Commando style, on your belly. Keep your head down and your butt down and you'll be fine. When you get to the other side, roll into the fireplace. You can stand up inside it. I'll come after you. If something happens, you throw the snow in your cap over the floor so your tracks won't be obvious and then get inside that secret passage and stay there. Don't make a sound. Wait for Walter, okay?"

Travis sighed. Then he popped up and kissed her cheek. "Okay." He scuttled away from her.

She took the cap of snow out of her snowsuit and put in the crook of her knee, just to have something to do with her hands, so she wouldn't reach out after him. And all at once he was beyond her reach. As she watched him, she marveled at the ease of his passage, at how natural it all seemed. Just another game of commando.

The wind outside continued to rise and fall according to its whim, spitting snow into the room over her extended leg. In its calmer passages, she could hear the closing roar of the snowmobile. Then the wind would blot out the sound. She was increasingly afraid Rand would be upon them without warning. When she looked nervously over her shoulder, there was no one there except Ricky, whose open eyes were filling up with snow. Beyond him, at the bottom of the steps, the wind continued burying Gordy. There was no telling if he was dead yet.

Travis rolled smoothly out from under the wires over the hearth and up against the kindling and logs. He sat up and brushed his hair out of his eyes and grinned triumphantly at her. Her throat closed and she fought tears. He was safe.

"Can you reach the secret door?" she asked.

He sidled toward it, reached out, and fumbled along the molding. The panel suddenly slackened in its frame.

"Got it," he exclaimed, and grabbed the edge.

"Careful," she warned, leaning forward and at once regretting it. "How far can you open it?"

He pried it gently, and inserted himself in the space he had opened. It was startling how quickly he disappeared into the crack and how dark it was in there. The door cleared the nearest wires only by an inch or two. He slipped out again.

"Da da," he sang.

She laughed, suppressing her own dismay. It was going to be tough for her to enter it without setting off one of the guns to signal their presence. But first she had to get there. Of course, if she didn't, Travis' capful of snow wouldn't make any difference. There would be all the evidence Rand could want that they had entered the house.

She pulled up her right leg and got it behind her, then dropped herself gently onto her left side. She lifted the right leg and rested it on the left. Then she rolled onto her belly. She felt like a mermaid. It was uncomfortable and clumsy, but she couldn't afford to leave an uncoverable trail of blood smears. Face to the floor, she reached out to place both hands flat on the floor, and said, "Travis, I love you."

"I love you, too, mom," he piped. "Don't worry, you can make it." But his voice was trembling. She was glad she couldn't look up and see his face. She pushed forward from her left foot, and dragged herself forward by her hands, and was under the wires.

"Great," he said, coaching her.

Inside her snowsuit she was a slick of sweat. *It's a game, just a game. No shotguns. Ricky's not really dead. Gordy's not really dying.*

Suddenly, there was a break in the susurration of the wind. And now, there was no sound of a snowmobile to be heard, distant or near.

Liv hesitated. She could hardly breathe.

"Mom!" Travis whispered urgently.

She pushed on. Dragging and wriggling and twisting. She stopped and looked around as much as she dared without lifting her head, to see where she was.

"Okay, mom," Travis said. "You're okay."

She dropped her head wearily again and inched onward. It seemed as if she had been doing it forever. She could not afford to feel her own panic or fear or terror, but Travis' worry and impatience reached out to her. She imagined her love for him as a strong wire that she could draw herself along to him. Then her shoulder brushed something, and she collapsed flat on her belly, letting her right leg flop where it would. The pain nearly made her pass out.

"Mom!" Travis cried out.

"Stay," she croaked. "Stay where you are."

She could sense him, tensed at the edge of the hearth, ready to dive under the wires. She could hear his breathing, fast and frightened. She turned her head to try and see him. Above her the wires glinted in their deadly net. She could see the one she had touched from the corner of her eye, but she couldn't see Travis.

The wind took a breath. Snow crunched under boots at the edge of her hearing.

"Mom!" Travis said again and there was agony in his voice. He had heard it, too. His boot heels scuttled on the hearth.

She reached out again, dragging herself forward as hard as she could. His hands touched the crown of her hair. Sobbing, she pulled herself toward them. His fingers tangled in her hair as they had casually twisted in it as an infant while he nursed. Then they were face to face, and he was dragging on her hair, as if he intended to pull her by it to safety. Together they rolled onto the hearth, and fetched up against the wood.

"Inside," she whispered. "Give me your cap."

He thrust it into her hands, and disappeared into the secret passage. She hauled herself up onto her one good leg against the side of the fireplace, and thence to the waiting firewood. Propping herself against it, she tossed the snow in handfuls from the caps, trying not so much to cover their passage, for there was not enough snow to do that, but to confuse it. She sprinkled the last of it on the hearth and over the wood in the fireplace, and tucked the caps inside her snowsuit. Painfully, she pulled off her right boot, then her left. Holding them under one arm, she crouched on her good knee and printed first one and then the other, this one with deliberate clumsiness, in the snow. It wasn't until she had finished, she realized the right boot was bloody at the neck. Sudden inspiration moved her to tip the boot upside down on the logs. A few drops of blood spattered over the white birch. Then she tucked the boots under her arm again, hauled herself up, and sidled along the wall to the secret door. Travis pushed it open a little for her and reached out to take her boots. She grabbed the edge of it eagerly as another crutch, with the wall, and very carefully inserted herself through the opening. As soon as she was through, she pulled the door tightly to, and nudged Travis to go up the stone steps. She sank down on them, and lifted herself up as a child learning to go up and down the stairs does, on her bottom. They went up about mid-way and she reached out and touched Travis. He slipped down next to her and they hugged each other. She placed her fingers over his lips. He reached up and sealed her lips with his own pudgy fingers. They smelled like very old wood ash, from the hearth.

Rand put his back to the broad trunk of a hemlock and lit a cigarette with shaky fingers. From there, he could see the yard and house, but anyone inside was unlikely to be able to make him out through the veils of blowing snow and in tree shadow.

As Liv had, he noted at once the absence of vehicles and wood smoke, signs of habitation. It must be the old bitch had hiked or snowshoed in, and was sitting inside that house all bundled up, playing a waiting game. It looked that way.

He could see the shape of the body on the porch, looked long enough and hard enough to be sure it was Ricky, and that he was dead. Before he had died, he had broken in the front door, and it was still broken open, letting in the weather. One of the shutters of the window on the porch was open, most likely as a lookout. It had taken a little longer to discern Gordy, within a shroud of snow, at the bottom of the steps. That's when he had decided there was enough snow being blown about to cover a little cigarette smoke in the trees near the beach.

He didn't give a goddamn about Gordy; he was no loss. Gordy had never been anything except a drooling burden since the day his father had fetched home Jeannie McKenzie Teed and Gordy in his ten-year-old Cadillac and announced Jeannie was his new wife. Arden Nighswander hadn't mentioned Gordy, but there he was, already fat as a piglet, and twice as stupid. Gordy had never changed except to grow larger. His body was still somewhere in mid-adolescence, unfinished, sprouting sparse red hair in his pits and groin, but still with a boy's penis, and boy's scrotum, as his balls had not descended, even in his early twenties. Well, now they never would, and the world was less one idiot.

But he was angry over Ricky. Not because he cared much more for his younger brother than he had for Gordy; Ricky had been even more trouble. The world might have been better off if Ricky's balls had stayed where it was safe and warm. Ricky had more bad habits than he could count, and no talent at all for getting away with any of 'em. Rand had known that Ricky sometimes sodomized Gordy, and more often forced Gordy to fellate him, and at first been both mildly amused and mildly disgusted. Later it seemed to him that Ricky grew to like the arrangement too much. Like Ricky's promiscuous pissing, what had once seemed mostly exuberant acting up showed signs of hardening into permanent and embarrassing tastes. Still, Ricky was his brother, for all they had fought and schemed against each other. When the old bitch murdered Ricky, she was spelling out a message for Rand, and he read it perfectly well: You next.

Rand finished his butt, feeling calmer and more purposeful. Crouching low, keeping his head down, he began to zigzag across the yard, from tree to bush wherever there was sufficient cover. A few yards from the house, he hunkered down again. He could almost reach Gordy. At this distance, he could see how the snow was disturbed along the foot of the porch. The snow had gentled it, but clearly, someone had been there. The steps had been used, and by more than one, more than just Ricky in his last moments, but he couldn't tell now how many.

He circled around the house toward the orchard, and satisfied himself the woman and the boy had been there. The track was being buried fast, but it was there, two of them, the woman dragging. It actually cheered him to think they had reached the house and gained entrance. Now they were inside with the old bitch, and he could settle all of them at once.

He had returned to the Russells' house, collected his cap and gloves, and tipped a burning log and coals onto the old carpet in front of the fireplace. He had thrown the pills Olivia had given him into the fire. Just in case he had the bad luck to be picked up. He didn't need a possession of scheduled drugs charge. At best, he thought, the house would be fully engaged before old Walter arrived, and then it would take a while for the fireboys to come to the rescue. They would all be very busy for a long time, trying to rescue the

woman and the boy, who weren't inside to be rescued. Then they
would stand around and talk about it, and feel bad about having to
dig out the bodies they thought were inside. At worst, the fire would
merely confuse the evidence he and Ricky and Gordy had left behind
—the charred linen from Gordy's accident, the splintered lock on
the boy's bedroom window. In the meantime, Rand would settle
accounts with the old bitch, and the woman and her boy. And set
another fire, a sure thing, that would consume not only his enemies,
but Ricky and Gordy, too. Only Rand would ever know what really
happened, Rand and maybe his father, if he felt like telling the old
man. He would have to explain what had become of Ricky and
Gordy, and between them, he and his father would put it about that
Ricky had gone to Massachusetts or New Hampshire for work, or
into the service, perhaps with some pregnant girl to inspire him, and
that Gordy had been put into a home. No one would be much surprised. No, that would be his father's job. This might all be God's
way of telling Rand it was time to head for someplace warm. California. Texas. Maybe Mexico.

Rand crept completely around the foundation of the house. The
cellar windows had been bricked up. The foundation walls were
Christless big stones set in homemade mortar since the Year One. He
listened a long time at various places, and heard no sounds within.
The old bitch was playing a waiting game. How could she be so sure
he would come, that there were three of them? The woman, of
course, had warned her, if she didn't already know. Another thing to
thank O-liv-i-a for.

He squatted by the porch steps, thinking. It was only to be
expected that a woman with a talented cunt, instead of making a
fortune using it, was also a raging bitch. Probably a dyke, just like
Miss Alden. But she wouldn't be much use; he had done her sufficient damage to sideline her. There was nothing to fear from the boy,
of course. It was still him against the old bitch, who had at least one
shotgun on her side. The only gun he had had, the tin-plated Saturday night special he had liberated from the dog-lady, was in the
woods, rusting. Some more.

Rand dropped back to the corner of the porch, seized the porch
railing with both hands and swung himself over it, landing on the
tips of his boots and rolling at once into a crouch in the far corner.
He was surprised by the crunch of glass, and then by a dozen little

firepoints in his palms and fingers where shards of glass had penetrated his gloves, when he came down on all fours.

"Jesus!" he shouted, tearing them off. Most of the glass came
out as he pulled off the gloves, but his hands were running blood. He
willed himself to freeze. There were no sounds inside the house, not
so much as excited breath, or a footstep or a creak of a shutter being
cracked. He felt safe to examine his hands. One by one, he picked out
a half dozen bits. He was sure there were more, but he couldn't get
them without tweezers. When he thought of the coke that got cooked
and the pills he had nonchalantly tossed into the fire he had set, he
felt like kicking himself. What he really needed was a local anesthetic, some of that burn spray she had found for Gordy. Only it was
burning up back at her house. It was almost funny, but it also pissed
him off even more.

Only then did he wonder where the glass had come from. It was
a question easily answered. The glass of the storm window was gone
from the one large window in the porch wall. There were pieces of
plant pot among the glass to show how it had been done. The Indian
shutter was more than open; the bolt had been gouged open. In their
past adventures here, they had always just broken in the door. Why
had Ricky bothered to frig with the lock on the window, open it, and
then break down the door? It didn't make sense. It might be the
woman had done this, but why? Why hadn't the old bitch just admitted her and the boy to the house? All they had to do was give a
holler.

Rand crept under the window, expecting any moment to see a
shotgun come poking out it. He planned to grab it from underneath
and yank it out of the old bitch's hands. So he waited several minutes, but still there was no sound, and no gun over the sill. He stuck
an empty glove, half inch by inch over, over the sill. Still nothing
happened. He dared to peek, lifting his head even more slowly than
his glove, ready at any sound to duck. *Sweating like a pig,* he thought
he would tell his father. *'Bout ready to shit.*

He was stunned. At first it didn't make sense, he couldn't make
head nor tails of it, and then he understood, all at once. The old bitch
wasn't there. But she had left him a message all the same, and it was
still the same: You next.

He moved cautiously toward the doorway. The snow on Ricky's
chest was like a thick pad of gauze, soaked red-brown at the center,

pinking toward the edges. It made a thin tattered veil over the rest of him, covering his eyes entirely as if in observation of some natural rule of decency. But his jaw had slackened so his mouth hung open and his tongue protruded from his lips. Here the snow dusted and gathered in the corners and did not hide an increasing purplish coloration. When the wind flicked at the snow and exposed a few centimeters of Ricky's cheek, the skin had no more color, less, to it, than the snow had. A wave of revulsion turned Rand's stomach. *Daddy,* he thought, first in supplication, and then in righteous anger, *Daddy, I like to puke.*

He worked his way past Ricky and peered into the house. Snow had drifted in. People had disturbed it, passing through, and dragged it farther in. Someone had hunkered only inches away, just inside the door, and done some bleeding there, all in one place. Not Ricky. His gore was spattered on the door frame, and the broken door, and the floor, but it was evenly distributed, and there was both blood and tissue, in a readable pattern. The shotgun blast had blown Ricky right out and killed him at once. Someone had scattered snow from the other side of the room, from the hearth, back over the room, obscuring but not obliterating the evidence, like a snail's glistening trail, of a belly march under the wire. More than one someone, less than many. The woman and the boy. They had entered the old bitch's trap and reached the hearth and disappeared.

He studied the wires, sure now that what triggered the trap was tripping the wire, that there was no danger from anywhere or anything else, unless the woman had gotten hold of a freelance shotgun from the old bitch's armory. He could see how easy it would have been for the boy, and how possible, if not easy, for the woman. The lowest wire looked about eighteen inches from the floor. It would not be impossible for him, for though he thought he ran about twenty-six inches shoulder to shoulder, he ought be able to do it flat on his belly, the way the woman must have. His margin, his odds would be a lot worse than hers. A sneeze might get his head blown off. He wouldn't be able to lift his head so much as an inch to see where he was, let alone who might be creeping up on him, shotgun in hand. Wounded or not, O-liv-i-a, Our Lady of the Talented Cunt, was a jungle fighter. She had gotten away from him, hadn't she? He had to assume she had one of the old bitch's shotguns and would be waiting to take him unawares.

Where was she? There were stairs to the dormer bedroom, but to reach them, the woman and the boy would have had to crawl in another direction. The bedraggled snow led directly inside the hearth, where the fire was laid. No, there was faintest dusting of snow on the wood. And dark spots—a scattering of polka dots—on the birchbark that were all wrong to be knots, or scabs, or natural markings, and just right to be blood. He nearly grunted with satisfaction. She had tried to cover her tracks, but not hard enough. She and the boy were hiding inside the chimney. He had looked up the throat of the particular chimney once or twice, on previous visits, and knew it had a ledge wide enough to accommodate a narrow, steady foot. He had looked right up and seen a patch of sky as big as a TV screen. That particular chimney was big enough to house half of Nodd's Ridge. So she would have to give up her hidey hole to take a shot at him. But she couldn't do that without him hearing her. Still, he couldn't see how he could afford to pin himself down under those fucking wires, where even if he heard her he wouldn't be able to move fast enough to save himself. It was just a frigging shame he hadn't gotten her in the small of the back or somewheres a little more useful in slowing her down. And it was a frigging shame he couldn't put it to the old bitch today, but he would, sooner or later, settle that account, too.

Rand cleared his throat.

"O-liv-i-a," he said. "Little mother. How's your leg, O-liv-i-a? Hurt some? Bleedin' some? How's your cunt, O-liv-i-a? Getting lonely for me, O-liv-i-a?"

He waited. He fingered the crumpled pack of cigarettes. There was just one stale butt left. He was saving it for when this was over. Maybe he'd light it with O-liv-i-a's little finger. There was no response.

He sighed loudly. "I'm hurt, O-liv-i-a. Don't you love me anymore?" He laughed. "Shit." He coughed. "I know where you are," he said. "I'm coming for you."

Then he withdrew.

CHAPTER 17

ONCE they were beyond the causeway, it had become immediately apparent that they would have to choose one side of the lake and follow the shoreline, for as the lake widened, the poor visibility would blind them to where they were. They might wind up traveling in circles in the middle of the lake. So they had gone to the north side, and were almost as lost anyway. Cottages on the shore offered shelter, but they had ignored them, because however near, reaching them meant taking steps out of their way.

Pat had stopped trying to keep his nose dry. From the growing numbness in his extremities, he knew he was being frostbitten. But it didn't hurt too much. What worried him most was the fear that Sarah's hand might slip from his without his realizing it, and so they would be separated, and lose each other in the swirling snow. But she clung tight, struggling alongside him, as if she knew. It was hard to think beyond holding onto Sarah's hand and putting one foot in front of the other. He was chilled and weary to the bone. He cursed himself for not having stayed in the car back at the narrows, or at least for not leaving her. But there wasn't any turning back. They had come too far.

Then Sarah tugged at him. Just ahead, a small peninsula surged into the lake. At its tip was a dilapidated boathouse. She led him, stumbling, into the shelter of its lee side. There they crouched and rested.

Sarah studied him anxiously. She raised fingers to his face.

"Feel anything?" she asked him.

He shook his head.

"Shit," she said. "You're frostbit. I was touching you."

He seized her wrist and raised it to his lips.

She hugged him quickly. Then she hunkered back and looked around. "It's not so far now. Do you know where we are?"

The blowing snow stung his eyes. "No. No idea."

"This is Spellmans' boathouse."

"Great," Pat said. "Let's get going."

Sarah's hand on his elbow tugged him back. "You need a rest."

"I need to shelter. I need to get home, baby."

Her smile was understanding, motherly.

"Right. Miss Alden's place is between here and home. How about we go there, and you get out of the weather? Then I can go the rest of the way and bring back mom."

"Thanks," he said, "but I can make it home."

"All right." Sarah gave way. "But we'll rest a little longer, okay, and then we'll stick close to the shoreline, just in case."

"Okay."

Resting, Pat tried to think about what a tale he would have to tell. His revenge on the elements. This wouldn't go to waste. He'd make something back on it, one way or the other. The only thing was, he couldn't come up with a story. Just here he was, an American hero, freezing his balls off, wandering around on a frozen lake with his teenage daughter, who seemed to be better equipped to survive it than he was. It was very tempting just to squat where he was, working on the problem.

But after a while, Sarah tugged gently at his arm, and led him back onto the ice.

Shortly thereafter, he grabbed her wrist and halted. "I smell smoke," he said.

She sniffed the air. "So do I."

"Woodsmoke?" he asked.

Sarah shook her head. "I don't think so."

And as they stood peering into the blowing snow, they realized some of what was blowing over the increasingly familiar tree line on the shore was not snow. Leaning on each other, they watched it thicken and begin to billow, and flicker with sparks.

"Lady bird, lady bird," Sarah recited. "Fly away home."

"It's a house," Pat said. "It's too big."

"Mom!" Sarah screamed, and tore free from Pat's grasp. She ran a few steps, remembered him, and stopped.

He was running after her, in his fashion, like a baby who was just learning how to walk.

Light seeped in from around the doors so that at the top and bottom of the secret passage it was possible to see a little. But in the middle, where the passage bent around the chimney, it was so dark that even after their eyes adjusted, they could see next to nothing. They hugged each other for a while and then Liv whispered, "Trav, we need to know about the bedroom."

He squeezed her hand.

"Take off your boots," she advised and while he did that, she began to push herself up the steps on her bottom. The stone steps were rough and cold, but the method evoked her childhood and cheered her, or perhaps it was only relief at having achieved a sanctuary. Travis, in his stocking feet, caught up with her and eased open the panel at the top. Liv got a good look at him and her courage faltered. His face in the light the crack admitted was like melted candle wax, translucent and too pale. It occurred to her she probably looked worse, and she shrank back a little into cover of the darkness, for his sake. She forced herself to concentrate on the slice of room visible in the opening of the secret door.

There was only one shotgun, on a tripod, aimed at the bedroom's one window, but the room was thickly webbed with trigger wires, except for a small space directly behind the gun, between the gun and the door to the secret passage. Looking at it was a revelation.

"Miss Alden did this first," she whispered to Travis. "Set up the gun, and went down the secret passage."

Travis bobbed his head in agreement. The thought seemed to excite him.

She tugged at his sleeve, and he pulled the door shut. They crept back to the turn of the passage.

"I could get that gun for us," Liv whispered. "But then he could come in through the bedroom."

Travis cuddled up next to her. "Let's stay here."

Liv put her fingers over his lips.

In the still thick quiet, they could hear the wind sucking at the chimney, but it seemed far away because of the thick stone walls that entombed them, sheltering them from the weather. The cold in the passage was the cold of the stone itself, unheated by sun or fire. With one great shiver, Liv realized she was chilled as much from loss of blood as from the absence of warmth in the passage. Sitting still in the narrow passage, with Travis tucked against her, she could tell without touching the leg that the bleeding had slowed. She could feel blood-soaked cloth drying against her skin. She was suddenly sleepy, yet she was also too cold to go to sleep. But Travis had dozed off, leaning against her.

Rand cursing on the porch woke him up.

She clapped her hand over Travis' mouth and held him tightly. He burrowed into her tensely.

She thought how lovely it would be if the next sound was one of the shotguns blowing Rand to hell. But though she listened very hard, little sound penetrated into the passage. He was creeping around out there, and that was all she could be sure of. He might already be halfway across the floor, taking their route under the wires, though his iron pumping had made him so bull-heavy in the torso that it would be slower and riskier for him than it was for her. The waiting made the time go slower and seem longer, so when he finally spoke to her, she actually felt relief.

He called her name mockingly. She smoothed Travis' hair over his brow. Through the stone, the words were not always intelligible, but the anger and the threat were. The last part was very clear.

"I know where you are," he said. "I'm coming for you."

Soon she would know if her false trail had succeeded. She wondered where Walter was, where Pat was. Then she heard the growl of a snowmobile, close to the house, and sat up straight, transfixed with unbelieving joy. The threats had been all bluster. He was leaving.

Rand crouched over his brother's body, drawing off Ricky's polyvinyl snowmobile gloves. The exposed flesh of finger and hand was candle-white and ghastly except at the tips, which were turning blue-black under the nails. His brother's fingers in Rand's were slack, as the rigor had not yet set in, but like a spaceman's, the thick, foamlined gloves were stiff. Rand discarded his own rent and bloody gloves and pulled on Ricky's. Their thickness cushioned his glass-perforated palms.

From the porch, he slunk down the steps and around to the snowmobiles Ricky and Gordy had left on the lee side of the house, started Ricky's and rode it well into the orchard. The ancient apple trees spread a low sprawling roof over him that baffled the wind, and camouflaged him among its dappled bark and shadows. He let the machine idle, gradually choking it off, trying to imitate the fading sound of an engine departing. A gap in the roof of branches framed the single window of the bedroom. He thought he could make out the black gleam of a muzzle. Craving his single remaining cigarette in its pack, he felt the length of his sleeve to locate it, like a finger bone loose in its crumpled package. But it was for later. He sighed heavily and dismounted.

Hunching into the wind, he abandoned the snowmobile and made his way back to the house as quickly as he could and still be quiet. Again he went to the blind corner of the porch. This time he hoisted himself right onto the railing and, from there, reached for the roof. With the gutter in his grasp he swung himself over and up onto the porch roof. The thin sheeting of snow covered a glaze of ice on the old shingles. He scuffed wildly for footing, at the same time scrabbling for purchase with his hands. Here the thick, slick-skinned gloves worked against him, binding his fingers and desensitizing them. The wind whipped over the ridgepole and spit hard granules of icy snow into his face. It gusted and shrieked and all at once his footing gave way with one of the treacherous old shingles, and he lost his tenuous hold. He felt himself going as in a dream, the roof slipped away from him, and he reached frantically for the gutter.

He caught it with a shock, jerking his arms in their sockets, and hung from it. As he dangled in the wind, the gutter creaked in its moorings. He felt the metal channel twisting, widening with the downpull of his weight. He tried to still the swaying of his body to lessen the stress on the gutter. Gritting his teeth against the pain in his hands and his shoulders, and against the curses that roared in his head, he concentrated on lifting himself evenly and steadily as he would on a chinning bar. The gutter shook and shivered under his weight. He could feel it tearing away from the roof, nail, and bracket.

Sweat dripped from his eyebrows onto his lashes and he blinked it rapidly away. As he lifted himself above the roof line, the wind attacked him again, whipping snow into his eyes. When he grimaced with effort, he felt the freezing sweat on his face crackle. The gutter shuddered and dropped a few inches, and he dropped with it, expelling all his breath in sudden shock. But the gutter held there in its distorted brackets, a few inches below the eaves. Rand gasped, and grabbed with both hands for the eaves. The gutter shrieked at the sudden lifting of his weight. With the woody security of the eaves in his grasp, Rand swung one leg, then the other over the suspended gutter and the edge of the roof, and scrabbled once again for footing.

This time his head was down, and his body paralleled the eaves, which gave protection from the wind. It was much safer, but it was also the wrong direction. He grinned and began to scrabble in a counterclockwise direction, until he lay flat on his belly holding mostly by strength of his widespread hands. He looked as if he had been crucified there, facedown, pointing toward the roofbeam. He could hear the gutter clanking below him with every twist of the wind. He groped for footing, and found it, raising himself until he was hunched like a four-legged spider. He was able to crab a few steps upward, slipped, regained his footing, and slipped again.

The porch roof joined the house in a low gable end. A louvered vent was set into the gable to ventilate attic crawl space under the eaves. The roof of the house, a little less steep than that of the porch, was two feet higher, an easy lift for Rand. The ridgeline ran at a ninety-degree angle to the porch roof. The worst news was that the shingles were slate, and crusted with old snow. The new snow frosted the roof erratically, and the wind continued to blow it into his eyes and ears, and down his collar, and up his sleeves, and under his boots. It was a long sweaty time before his fingers encountered the pitted copper flashing at the base of the chimney, swept clean of snow by the wind. It wasn't much to hold onto, but the fieldstone above it, crusted as it was with ice and snow, was still rough enough to provide a nearly perfect handhold. He hunched against the chimney, in the lee of the wind, cheek to cheek with the abrasive stone, and the first thin spice of smoke prickled in his nostrils. Instinctively, he glanced upward, expecting to see smoke trailing from the chimney, but there was nothing above him except white sky, and wind-puffed snow. Then, like a perfume, the smoke triggered its own name. Excitement ballooned tightly in his chest, and he looked back toward the Russells' place. Go-devils of snow veiled the vista, but it was still possible to make out evil colored tatters of smoke being sheared heavenward by the wind. He took it for a good omen.

Wedged between the walls of the passage, Liv and Travis shared each other's body warmth and waited. Tired and increasingly weak and foggy, Liv revived a little at the sound of the snowmobile. Travis shifted restlessly against her, and now and again slipped a few steps up or down on his bottom or in his stocking feet in hopes of hearing something else besides the lowing and hooting of the wind.

And they did hear noises, scraping and scrabbling. Each time, Liv squeezed Travis' hand and whispered, "Branches on the roof," and he squeezed back, to let her know he agreed and wasn't frightened.

Walter Mckenzie babied his Jeep along the backroads, dropping the plow where necessary, at a speed calculated to keep him moving through the soft patches, over the icy ones, and on the right side of the road. The blowing snow kept the visibility dangerously low. It was an ironic comfort that at least no one else seemed to be fool enough to be out on the road. He took the roads closest to the lake, and kept an eye peeled for Pat, meaning the dimmest glimpse of a human shape foundering out there on the shelterless plain of ice. And never did see him. By the time he reached the Dexter Road, Walter was telling himself earnestly that Pat had taken shelter *somewheres,* in some summer place or boathouse or *somewheres,* like any sane man would, or else had miraculously reached home and hearth by now. So intently was Walter assuring himself that Pat was safe *somewheres,* with all of his attention that was not fixed on the business of getting along the Dexter Road to the Russells', which a man of his experience in the vagaries of ice and snow did not trust to experience at all, and noticing the snow-covered shape of the Pacer at the turn and understanding at once that Liv Russell had sensibly left it there the previous evening, he did not see the smoke until he was groping his way around the turn and into the Russells' driveway, pushing the snow before him with the plow, when the snow blowing over his windshield suddenly turned dirty. Soot flicked onto the glass like snowflakes, his windshield wipers smeared them in arcs and he hunched over the wheel, punching the windshield washer button and peering through the streaks. His heart hammered wildly. He fought the instinctive urge to stop the Jeep in its tracks; on this hill, with the plow down, it would skid sure as beans make a man fart, and he would be lucky if he didn't wind up ass over teakettle in a snowbank, just like old Joe Nevers a year ago at the Christopher place. He rolled down his window one handed and craned his head out to see what he was going into. Snow and soot blew in, bringing the angry sound of fire with them. He got a good glimpse of the house, with a hellish glow in its windows, and a noseful of hot stinking housefire, an evil tragic smell of wood and plastics and human possessions, cloth, and glass, and paper and insulation, someone's life being wrecked.

The only worse smell he knew of was that of burning human flesh, which he had encountered few times, but unforgettably. He never forgot the names of the dead he had helped drag from fires, not Dana Bartlett, the Portland lawyer who had died when the old Christopher place had burned decades ago; nor Matthew and Brandy McAvoy, old Doc's grandchildren, who had perished in a trailer fire in 1979; nor Binny Porter, the Pigeon Hill hermit who had accidentally lit himself up from the inside out when he knocked back a slug of badly distilled antifreeze and then, befuddled, stuck the lighted end of a cigarette in his mouth, what was it, two winters ago. Walter's nostrils widened, drawing in the polluted air, searching for that scent within all the others, and found none.

He brought the Jeep to a stop at the first safely level spot, and jumped out.

"Miz Russell!" he screamed, but the roar of the fire drowned him out. He galloped through the snow to the back porch. Frantic as he was to get Liv and Travis out if they were still inside, he noticed the condition of the back door. The inside door was battered, as if someone had kicked at it. Holding the storm door open with his shoulder, Walter grasped the door knob carefully with his gloved hand and then snatched it away. He touched the door panels and they, too, were hot. He backed off, and then ran around the house, foundering in hip-deep snow, jumping up and down to look in windows blackened by smoke and soot, or broken by the heat. He circuited the house, even going up onto the lakeside deck where the fire raged visibly through the glass doors, and then around the other side, and fetched up, panting and gasping against the side of the Jeep. He hauled open the door and clambered in, and almost fell out again reaching out to pull the door closed behind him. With shaking hands, he turned on his CB radio and pulled the mike from its holster on the dash. Punching buttons frantically, he raised Reuben Styles at home.

"What say?" Reuben said genially.

"F-f-f-fire," Walter stuttered, and then in a rage with himself, shouted into the mike. "Russells, off the Dexter Road! They's people inside!"

Reuben, who was remarkably quick when he needed to be, responded at once.

"Fire at Russells' off the Dexter Road," he repeated. "Is that you, Walter?"

Walter cursed fluently.

"Calling it in, Walter," Reuben said, and the mike picked up Reuben's voice as he turned away and shouted to one of his boys.

Then he was back again. "That's fire road thirty-one, ain't it, Walter?"

" 'T is," Walter said.

"Can we get the trucks down there?" Reuben asked.

"I'm here, ain't I?" Walter snapped back. "I didn't fly in."

"You coulda snowshoed in," Reuben said.

"I ain't got no goddamn radio on my snowshoes," Walter shouted.

"We're on our way," Reuben said, and was gone.

Walter started the Jeep, and plowed the circle of the Russells' driveway to get himself turned around. Going up the driveway, he was still gasping for breath. His lungs burned and his head ached fiercely.

"Goddamn it to hell," he whispered hoarsely and wiped tears from his cheeks with the knuckles of his gloved hands. The knitted wool snagged a little on the stiff bristles of his stubble. "Goddamn it to hell," he said angrily, and pounded the steering wheel. Then he took himself in hand and stopped wasting energy. He widened the turn to make himself a parking space next to the Pacer, parked the Jeep to get it out of the way, but left the keys in it, because it was a rule to leave the keys in any vehicle at the site of a fire. He jumped out again and stared up the road, straining his ears for the sounds of the fire trucks, and then down the driveway, at the burning house. Finally he couldn't wait for the trucks any longer, and he hurried back down the driveway on foot, slipping and sliding as he went. He landed on his sit-me-down several times, picked himself up, and scuffled on, too distracted to even feel humiliated.

Once at the bottom of the driveway again, he paced back and forth, then started around the house again. It seemed easier this time. He had made himself a trail, huffing and puffing around it before. It was only then it struck him that there was another path. Someone else had broken a trail around the house since the snow began to fall and while the snow had filled it up some, and the wind had blurred it, it was still here, real close in, as if the trailbreaker had been hugging the walls. He followed the path he had not made to the beach, and saw that there, too, the snow had been disturbed, by at least one snow machine, and that recently. Again, it was plain that more than one machine had been on the beach for a considerable period of time. He followed the almost clear, recent track north along the shore a few yards and then, hearing the sirens of the fire trucks, turned back.

He huffed and puffed his way up the beach to the house again, and was on one foot and then the other, at the bottom of the driveway, when Reuben Styles jumped off the braking pumper.

"Goddamn it," Walter said.

Reuben was too busy shouting orders to the volunteers to greet Walter with more than a nod. First chance, he nudged Walter away from the trucks and the noise, and said, "Anybody in there?"

Walter shrugged. "Goddamn if I know."

Reuben rubbed his gloved hands together mournfully. "They ain't nothing we can do, you know," he said with a glance at the burning house.

"Shitagoddamn," Walter said. "Missus Russell and the boy was here. I don't know where they are."

Reuben nodded. "Talked to Frankie on the CB. He said Pat's wagon's abandoned at the narrows."

Walter stared at the house. "He might be in there, too." Walter looked at Reuben. "There's something you oughta see," he said in a low voice. I cain't figger it out."

Reuben looked at Walter, then turned back to his crew and shouted another series of orders. Then he took Walter by the elbow. "Better show me."

Walter led him to the beach. "Tried the back door," he said. "Somebody tried to kick in the back door."

Reuben stopped and looked back over his shoulder at the house. "Boys taken the ax to it by now," he said. "Nothin' we can do."

Walter grunted. "Same with these tracks. They'll be gone in no time. You better see'm for a witness."

"Ayuh," Reuben said. He stared at the trodden snow, the snow-mobile tracks, and hunkered down to take a closer look.

"Russells ain't got no machines," Walter said.

"Think Pat borried one?" Reuben asked.

Walter shrugged. "These is last night's tracks. There's more'n one. Now this one, this is today. This might be him, if he did. Borry a machine. There's some stored down to the marina. I didn't see no sign of break-in down there, but I didn't look too close. Mighta missed it."

Reuben stood up, and took off his cap. He scratched behind his ear and put the cap back on and sighed. "I hope he stole himself a machine and come up here and took his family out, Walter."

"If he din't, he's wandering around there," Walter said, indicating the lake. "Goddamn fool."

"Ayuh," Reuben said. "Maybe the fire'll draw him. It oughta be visible to the causeway."

"If he didn't," Walter said, "who was here? Banging on the door."

Reuben stared at Walter. "There's fellas I could name I hope to Christ wasn't here."

Walter's jaw dropped and snow flew in, little spots of cold on his tongue and gums. He hadn't ever heard Reuben Styles take the Lord's name.

Reuben turned back to the fire.

"Where'd they go?" Walter asked him.

Reuben trudged up the beach. "Who?"

"All of 'em," Walter shouted furiously. "Missus Russell. The boy. Whoever the Christ was on them machines."

Reuben looked back at Walter. "What business these folks got here this time of year, Walter?" he asked. "They don't belong here." He stared at the burning house. "We cain't do a goddamn thing for 'em. They're too far off the road. By the time we know, the fire's won. I like to puke, seeing it. What are we s'posed to do?"

Walter caught up with him. "We gotta try," he insisted. "That's the least we can do."

The two men plodded around the house to the back. They stood and watched the roof fall in.

Ansel Partridge, short and bald and looking fifty since he was fifteen, who had a university degree in agriculture and the best run farm in the township, hustled up, smearing soot across his brow. "That's the son of a whore," he said. "Nothin' left to do but wait for the frigging ashes to cool."

Reuben nodded.

Ansel hesitated. "Folks get out?" he asked.

Reuben shrugged.

Ansel grimaced. "We'll hope."

Walter turned away, fighting tears. He shuffled toward the woods, seeking privacy. Closing his eyes, he prayed not with words but with inarticulate yearning. Please don't let this be bad as it looks like being.

Something caught around his ankles. He opened his eyes and met the wide, mad eyes of The Poor, twisting between his boots. Bending arthritically he picked her up.

"Well, well," he said.

Suddenly Reuben was next to him. "Where'd the cat come from?" he asked, reaching for her.

Walter gave her to him. "Just opened my eyes and there she was."

The two men looked around their own feet, locating the cat's paw prints.

"Probably she was out all night," Reuben warned.

"Mebbe," Walter said. He was a lot more interested in the cat's tracks than he was Reuben's cautions. She had come out of the woods. And there, at the edge of the woods, she had used a path broken by people. Like the other tracks, it was blurred and partly filled up, but it was there.

"Somebody's been into these woods," Walter said gleefully.

Reuben nodded. "Today, too."

"Her studio's out there," Walter said, pointing down the direction of the path. "I'll just take a look," he said.

Reuben handed him the cat. "You okay by yourself?"

"Fit's a fiddle," he said huffily.

Reuben grinned. "Okay. I'll come lookin' for you, you ain't back in the half hour."

Walter set the cat down and crunched off into the woods. The Poor trotted at his heels.

Liv and Travis listened to the noises on the roof. Branches, Liv whispered to Travis, again. The wind scourging the roof with branches from the nearest trees. But there was too much, and it stopped suddenly. He was on the roof, Liv thought, and did not say anything to Travis, because just then he squeezed her hand tightly and she knew he knew. Something rattled down the throat of the chimney. Travis gasped. Liv clapped her hand over his mouth and hissed softly. Instinctively they shrank against each other. Liv's mouth was dry and tasted of old blood, carrion, as it had after she had had her tooth pulled. She pushed Travis away from her and began to shift herself rapidly down the steps of the passage on her bottom.

Rand heard the sirens and looked up from staring into the throat of the chimney. He grinned and returned to studying the problem at hand. There was nothing to see but blackness. She was down there, he was sure. The woman and the boy. They were hiding there, stiff as pokers with fear, hugging the sooty walls of the huge old chimney, balanced on the ledge inside. It was, he figured, a two-story drop—four foot of chimney above the roof line, six and half foot of second story, six and half of first, a little less than eighteen foot. Less than three times his height. Lowering himself from the top, his arms would give him two foot of that, making the drop closer to twice his height. He could handle that. He imagined hurtling down on them from above, grabbing them as he came, pulling them down onto the wood in the hearth. Terror would immobilize them. He could even scream at them, and the drop was short enough so it wouldn't make no difference, he would still be on them before they had time to react. Rand hoisted himself to the mouth of the chimney, and swung his legs inside. A chip of ancient mortar rattled down the chimney. He froze, and listened. He thought he had heard a gasp, a muffled hushing sound, even as the mortar bounced downward. Then there was scuffing, someone below shifting. Shit, he thought. They're leavin' the chimney. They'll hunker on the hearth until they think it's safe again. In the chimney.

He waited, staring over the woods. The sirens had ceased. The smoke above the trees was sequined with sparks. He didn't think she would try crawling across that floor again, under the wires. By the time she did, he would be perched like a hawk on the porch roof, ready to jump on her as she came down the porch steps. So he would give her time to convince herself it was just wind that had loosened a bit of mortar or a squirrel's hidden acorn and that he was gone, really gone.

After long moments of silence, he shifted again, very carefully, and lowered himself by his arms into the chimney.

At no time did it cross his mind that the chimney might not be the same width all the way down. Once he had looked up it, and seen the blue, and accounted for the height of the chimney affecting the size of the patch of sky, but he had been wrong.

Rand screamed "Here comes Santa Claus!" and let go. It was a great surprise when he dropped six feet and stopped. It took a while for him to realize that he was stuck, caught by a ledge where the chimney met the second floor.

Liv was waiting at the door of the secret passage when she heard Rand's scream, and the sound of his brief plummet. When he stopped in the narrowing of the chimney, there was a hail of soot and dry mortar on the hearth, and a series of thunks that were his boots in the chimney's throat. She opened the door a crack and crept out onto the hearth.

From above there was a cascade of soot and mortar, cursing and obscene threats. Covering her nose and mouth with her hands, and blinking to keep the fine particles out of her eyes, she backed to the door and crouched there, uncertain what to do next. Travis peeked out the door. She had only to look at his face to know it mirrored all the terror she felt. A fresh fierce rain of particles rattled on the hearth. It was clear Rand would soon free himself, even if he had to bring the ancient chimney down with him.

Liv pushed herself up against the door, forcing it closed. Slowly she reached for the matches in the brass matchbox holder. The sound of the match head scraping over the stone of the fireplace seemed very loud to her, louder even than Rand's nonstop cursing. She shielded the flame with one cupped hand and crouched on the hearth. Gently, she held the match to the kindling under the logs. The dry wood charred in the tiny flame, and then it glowed bluely, and began to burn. She moved the match to another piece of kindling, and it too quickly caught. The flame had crept down the shaft of the match nearly to her fingers but she held it out again, to a third stick of kindling. She felt its heat on the tips of her fingers and let it go, let it fall into the flames. The kindling caught enthusiastically. She wondered how long this fire had been laid, drying, on the hearth, as the flames from the kindling charred the bark of the logs and the bark began to spark and glow. From years of firing kilns, she knew exactly how it would burn, given the enormous inefficient draft of the antique chimney, the size of the firemouth, the papery feel of the bark on the wood.

Above her, the struggling suddenly stopped.

Somehow a little smoke found a way past him, blocking the chimney, and prickled in Rand's nose. At the same instant, he thought he felt warmth rising from below. For a moment he was too stunned to do anything. He could not believe she had lit a fire under him.

The smoke rose and met the blockage in the chimney and curled downward. It came curling under the stone mantel and out. There was no place else for it to go. Liv sidled back to the secret door and rapped at it. Travis opened it, and she slipped inside and closed it tightly. She urged him up the passageway, and followed him, on her bottom, but they both moved in slow motion, fearful of making the least noise that would give away their position. Travis was silent and tense. Liv wondered if he understood what she had done.

She sat in the darkness and listened. Tendrils of smoke pushed through the crack at the bottom of the secret panel. It hurt her eyes, and she began to weep.

The warmth grew and Rand began to struggle again, this time pushing himself up, instead of down.

"You fucking bitch!" he screamed.

It was all the breath he could afford to waste on vituperation.

As he loosened himself, more smoke was able to rise, and what was at first only an irritating, acrid trace, burned his eyes and then his lungs, for he could not help breathing it in. He struggled all the more fiercely, and felt, with a great leap of joy, that the ledge around him was breaking apart. With it came a greater panic for now he smelled burning rubber and knew his boots were smoldering. The mortar wasn't disintegrating fast enough, and his boots ignited, the synthetic of his snowmobile suit ignited and melted, the fire was in his vitals, and he screamed, and when he wasn't screaming, he was sucking in the toxic hot smoke in great burning lungfuls. At last the mortar gave way, and he was free. But though he reached upward, clawing the walls, there was nothing to catch, and he was only free to fall, fall into the fire, still screaming. He rolled onto the hearth a mass of flames and out into the room, the burning logs rolling with him. Somehow he gained his feet, and hurled himself into the room. He never felt the wires he broke. There was a roar of shotguns exploding, and the screaming stopped.

Inside the secret passage, Liv and Travis clung together, sobbing. They rocked back and forth. An unearthly glow seeped under the crack at the bottom of the secret door. The air had grown thick

and hard to breathe with smoke. It seemed as if they were sitting
outside the door to hell.

Walter McKenzie had tracked Liv and Travis to Miss Alden's
line when he heard the shotguns. He stopped short.

"What the Christ is going on?" he asked himself, and then hurried on.

Reuben Styles heard shotguns, too. His head came up sharply
and his nose was in the wind, like a dog pointing. He dropped the
hose he was helping roll and shouted new orders. Then he sprinted
for the woods, in the direction of the shots. So did the bulk of the
volunteers. Drivers mounted their cabs and began turning the fire
trucks in the driveway, following Reuben to Miss Alden's, as ordered.

Pat Russell heard the screaming, and disregarded it. A trick of
the wind.

Sarah tugged at his arm. "Did you hear that?" she asked, voice
trembling.

They halted, nursing stitches in their sides, panting painfully.

The cat materialized out of a snowdevil, and wrapped herself
around Sarah's ankles. She picked her up and buried her face in The
Poor's warmth. Then the shotguns went off. The cat shot out of her
hands, and streaked away across the ice.

They realized then the direction of the screaming, the gunshots.
It was closer than home.

"Miss Alden's?" Pat asked, unbelievingly.

"I think so," Sarah agreed nervously.

Only a few yards, and they rounded the bend, and saw it. Smoke
pouring from Miss Alden's chimney, and from the back porch.
There was an instant of joy in both their throats, as they thought
they had been mistaken, that the fire was here and not at home. But

when they looked in that direction, the smoke still rose there, like a signal fire, and they were plunged back into terror, and into fresh confusion. Then Pat saw Walter McKenzie's squat figure rolling like a peg-legged sailor from the woods, a second before Sarah did.

"Walter," she shouted.

And they began to run, as best they could, toward Miss Alden's house.

Walter's chest heaved painfully as he reached Miss Alden's yard. His eyes watered from the acrid smoke pouring from the house. At the corner of his eye, he picked up Pat Russell, who else could it be, stumbling toward him from Miss Alden's beach and a greater astonishment, a girl with him, the Russells' little girl Sarah, with him. Walter stopped and grabbed his knees, gasping. By the time Pat and Sarah reached him, Walter had caught a little breath.

"Walter!" Pat shouted in his ear.

Walter straightened up and gestured toward Miss Alden's, then back toward Russells'. "Fire department," he gasped.

"What about my mother and Trav?" Sarah shouted.

Walter shook his head.

Pat put an arm around Sarah's shoulders and drew her close. Her eyes welled with tears.

The wind blew smoke into their eyes and they breathed it in involuntarily. They all fell to coughing.

They moved to get away from it, looking for a patch of fresh air. Together they stumbled over the mound of snow that covered Gordy Teed.

"Jesus Christ!" Pat cried.

"Oh God!" said Sarah.

Walter sank wordlessly to his knees, brushing the snow from the dead man. He knew at once who it was, even before he cleared the snow from his face. Some terrible mischief had happened.

Pat backed a few steps in horror and then looked up at the house, seeing for the first time that the heap by the doorway was another body. Fire showed through the broken door as through the glass door of a stove.

"Stay here," he ordered Sarah.

She was shivering, and looked as if she might be going to vomit. But she nodded she understood. She hunkered down next to Walter, and took one of his hands in hers to comfort him. But she did not look at the corpse in the snow.

Pat ran to the porch and up the steps. By the time he reached the top step he was sure the body was not Liv's but that of a man. He stepped over and peered into the house. In the middle of the room was a fire. As he stared at it, it became the black remnant of a human being. The flames lit a maze of wire, tangled ends on the floor. A few lines stretched across the room, leading to the triggers of shotguns. Other guns cornered the room, or were on the floor, or dangling from mounts fixed to the walls. He backed off in shock. His heel thudded against the solidity of the corpse on the porch. He stared down at it unseeing.

Shaking, he stepped over it and went back to Walter.

Men in black rubber jackets and yellow firemen's hats were running out of the woods, crossing the yard. Come from his house, he thought numbly. He recognized faces. Local men. Volunteer firemen.

He stooped over Walter. "Where's Liv and Travis?" he asked, his voice hoarse with desperation.

Walter looked up at him. The old man's face was slick with tears and gray. He looked about a hundred and eighty. He shook his head.

Reuben Style's big hand fell on Pat's shoulder. Pat stood up and faced him.

"My wife and boy?" he asked.

Reuben shook his head. "Don't know." He glanced at Miss Alden's house. "What's this mess?"

It was Pat's turn to shake his head.

Walter grabbed the leg of Reuben's wool trousers. "Reuben," he said hoarsely. "Gordy's murdered."

Reuben stared at him. The cat bounded onto Gordy's chest from nowhere, and meowed at Reuben.

Suddenly everything he had seen coalesced for Pat. "Jesus, yes," he said. And whirling round, shouted at the men going up the porch steps, "Don't for Christ's sake go inside!"

They stopped and stared at him.

Reuben raised one hand in a stop signal. "He's right."

He turned to Pat. "Now tell me what's going on."

Inside the secret passage, the sound of Pat's voice electrified Liv and Travis.

"Daddy!" Travis said.

Liv sat up straight. "Oh God, I think so."

They slipped down the steps quickly on their bottoms, and Liv cracked the secret panel open to peek out into the room. A cloud of smoke spilled in on them, making them cough and choke. The fire in the middle of the room was burning brightly through the smoke. It showed Liv many things she did not want to see. She closed the door quickly.

"Can't we get out?" Travis asked.

"There's fire out there," Liv said.

Travis buried his head under her arm. "I want daddy," he said. She smoothed his hair. "We'll get out," she said. "You'll see."

She began to push her way up the stairs. The passage was growing warmer. The fire was eating the oxygen, she thought. Perspiration trickled from her hairline and tracked down her cheeks like tears. Her armpits were dripping. Travis was at the top before she was, and cracked the panel. The air coming in from above was a relief that recharged her.

The fire trucks followed the man in Walter McKenzie's plow-truck to Miss Alden's. They found everyone else in a subdued and puzzled group in the yard outside. Under Reuben's direction at what he considered a safe distance, volunteers took to the roof where they began to chop a good hole, and through it they turned hoses on the fire inside. Much to their amazement, they began to gain control of the fire. Even more amazingly, the weight of the water falling on the remaining wires triggered the rest of the trap. After the first surprise, it was a little like the Fourth of July, and they greeted each explosion with a cheer.

Reuben left off a radio transmission to the sheriff's office and joined Pat hunkering by Walter and Gordy's body. He handed Pat a thermos cup of coffee.

"It was a trap," Reuben said, "right? Some kind of godforsaken trap."

Pat warmed his hands around the plastic cup before he allowed himself a sip. It was wonderful. "I could see all these wires, and shotguns," he said, word for word what he had said several times before.

Reuben patted Walter's shoulder.

"Who are these people?" Pat asked.

"Walter's grandson," Reuben said shortly, indicating Gordy. He nodded toward the porch. "One on the porch was Ricky Nighswander. My guess is the fella inside was the older brother, Rand. Like to know how he caught on fire."

"Could there have been enough gunfire to set his clothes on fire?" Pat asked.

Reuben shook his head. "Don't know. State police forensic people'll have to figure that one out."

Suddenly there was another shotgun blast, and the sound of breaking glass. They all jumped, and then looked wearily at the house. Maybe that would be the last. Then someone shouted from the roof, and then another one did, and it became apparent that there was something else going on.

"That was from the back of the house," Reuben said thoughtfully, staring at the house. Then he began to run toward it, shouting new and incomprehensible orders about the ladder truck.

"Daddy!" a child screamed.

Pat looked up. He began to trot after Reuben. Then he began to run.

Two men carrying a ladder detached from a truck passed him.

"She blew the bedroom window!" Ansel Partridge shouted from the roof.

Walter McKenzie lifted his face. Gently he let down Gordy's head and struggled to his feet.

The bedraggled cat trotted across the porch. She stepped delicately onto the body at the door. She gave the bloody snow a lick, then climbed off, and sat down to look inside. Within the house, the fire was dead. An evil smoke and steam still rolled through the windows and door. But inside, a cold rain from the firehoses poured down through the broken roof. It began to freeze at once, glazing the furniture and the floor. Icicles bearded the trophy heads and their eyes were blackened. The remains of the burned man still lay like an insect in a bug-killing lantern on the floor. It would be a while before it was cool enough for the water to freeze on it, but it would.

From the roof, a cheer went up.

EPILOGUE

BEING LED AWAY by a trio of middle-aged white men, Miss Alden looked quite mad. She was wearing a plain, dark, front-closing dress that gaped over her bosom where a button was gone, and frayed tennis shoes without stockings of any kind. She wore no hat or headcovering. Her hair was a thin, crudely chopped thatch of yellow white. It looked very dirty. Her lips were cracked, and she seemed dazed.

"Professor Alden," the TV commentator said, "surrendered to the authorities after resigning her chair. She will be extradited to Maine on multiple charges of first degree murder."

Liv sat up in her hospital bed, snatched up the roses on her bedstand, and heaved them at the TV on its swivel arm.

It was her testimony that moved the jury to find Miss Alden guilty not of murder but of manslaughter, and to recommend a lenient sentence. Miss Alden, groomed and formidable again, accepted her sentence of probation, community service, and psychiatric counseling politely, told the TV cameras she felt a kind of rough justice had been served, and went home and shot herself with her father's World War One service pistol, which no one knew she still had.

A brand new will provided for the lifetime care of her longtime companion, Elizabeth Royal, and left her Nodd's Ridge property, known as the Dexter Place, and her cane, to Olivia Russell, and her army of toy soldiers to Travis Russell.

"Just what I need," Liv said as she unwrapped the cane.

Travis giggled.

Their reaction almost cheered Pat up.

Travis couldn't be got to bed nights in less than two hours. Pat would read to him for a long time, and then tuck him in and kiss him.

"I'll be right back," he would promise, and then he would go out and smoke a cigarette, and come back.

Travis would be waiting for him, tense and wide-eyed.

Then Pat would sit with him and they might talk or not, and Pat might hold him a little. And Travis would stroke the beard that Pat was growing to hide the scars of frostbite.

After a while, Pat would say, "I'll be right back," and he would go out for a few minutes, and come back.

It would go on like that for a minimum of two hours. Then Travis would go to sleep. And often as not wake in the night screaming.

Pat had to do it, because Liv was a long time in the hospital, trying to get her knee fixed. He thought Travis was getting better.

Sarah experienced a quiet hellish period of depression and free-floating guilt. She quit the basketball team, and threw herself into a flurry of housework and cooking, trying to replace her mother.

Marguerite discovered her weeping over sheets she had accidentally dyed denim blue by washing them with new blue jeans, and put an end to it. She bribed Sarah to rejoin the basketball team and let Mrs. Fuller do her job. The bribe was a promise of private driving lessons that would enable Sarah to obtain a license at fifteen.

Without saying anything to anyone, Pat went to a theater by himself and sat in the back to watch the movie.

FIREFIGHT

Strung up on a crude cross in a swamp, Denny Corriveau's face is streaked with blood and sweat.

"How did you know it was me?" he asks Court.

"Rat told me," Court says.

Denny laughs incredulously. "Come on, Rat's dead."

"And when you killed him, you admitted it," Court says.

Denny Corriveau's smile fades. "But I didn't. It was just self-protection."

"It was you and Jackson and Taurus and Rat," Court says. "But you did the killing."

"What about you?" Denny shouts, straining at the ropes that bind his wrists to the cross. "You killed Jackson, you might 's well a killed Taurus and Rat."

"They all deserved to die for what you done to May," Court answers.

"What about what she done to us?" Denny howls. "She set us up. She knew where we were going to be, because it was her village and you told her so she could save her family."

"She didn't," Court says.

"Then how'd they know we was coming?" Denny demands.

"They just did," Court says simply. "It was their village. Their home."

"And we're still killing each other over it," Denny says.

"Yeah," says Court. "Still dying over it, anyway."

"Your problem is you don't know how to live anymore. All you know is blowing people away," Denny says. It's a long shot, but this new tack, playing on Court's own guilt, looks like his only chance.

Court stands at the foot of the cross, his brow wrinkled, his eyes like pieces of coal

shiny with trouble and vexation. How many people
have died in the name of justice for May? How
many is enough?

He draws a Bowie knife from its sheath on his
belt and slashes the ropes that tie Denny
Corriveau's ankles. Denny smiles gratefully.

"Good man," Denny encourages him. "I knew you
were a good man at heart."

Court casts a cold glance at Denny, but Denny
misses it in his ecstatic relief.

Court raises the knife and slashes the binding
on the left wrist. It lets go, and Denny cries out
with pain as he dangles by his right wrist.

"Easy, man," Denny begs.

"Yeah," says Court, raising the knife. He
holds it ceremonially next to the bindings on
Denny's right wrist, and then slashes them.
Denny falls catlike to the ground, recovers, and
stands rubbing his wrists.

"Thanks, man," Denny says.

"Thank May," Court says.

Denny holds out his hand. Court stares at it
and then turns wearily away. Denny watches him,
picking his way through the swamp. Denny,
smiling, gathers up his knapsack, takes out a
gun, and fires it into Court's back.

Court turns around, holds out his hand, and
falls face forward into the swamp.

While the theater emptied, Pat sat in the shadows and wept.

Liv's light was still on when he came home, so he went in to see
her.

"How was it?" she asked, though he had not told her he was
going to see the movie.

He sat down on the edge of the bed. "I wish I could say it was
great. It isn't. It's not even very good."

She took his hand. "I'm sorry," she said and he knew she meant
it. She snuggled up to him and kissed him. "The next one will be
better."

Eighteen months later, Pat drove Liv and the kids to Nodd's Ridge. He had stopped saying out loud he never wanted to go back, on the advice of the family counselor, who thought Liv and Travis had to go back, to make some kind of peace. But he didn't have anything to say on the long drive, and he thought several times he might have to stop the car and throw up. Nobody else had anything to say, either. But in the mirror, he could see Sarah was holding Travis' hand. Her right foot was in a cast, the ankle sprained at basketball practice. She had left her Walkman at home. She had already announced *she* was staying in the car. The Poor turned restlessly in her carrier.

Liv got out of the car without help. She used Miss Alden's cane to keep her footing as she walked around the ruins of their summer house. The doctors' consensus seemed to be that her knee wasn't ever going to be just right again, and that someday, sooner or later, she would have to have a new one. Her mouth was always going to be crooked, too, because somehow a nerve had been destroyed.

The cat bounded into the woods, reveling in freedom. Travis dangled his legs out of the car, watching his mother anxiously.

Abruptly, Liv came back. "Let's go over to Miss Alden's," she said.

Pat glanced at Travis. The counselor had said not to push him. Travis nodded.

So he drove them to Miss Alden's. The cat was there before them, picking her way daintily through the mess. More of the house still stood, but it was worse to look at. Liv limped around a bit, and took deep breaths of the fresh sweet air and then climbed back in the car. Travis found a G.I. Joe, deteriorated from another year's weather, in the yard, and hooted with joy. Pat gathered up The Poor.

They were in the village before anybody spoke.

"It would be a good site to build on," Liv said. "Miss Alden's. Better than our lot. I know just what I'd like to do."

Pat was flabbergasted.

She smiled at him, and patted Travis' hand on the back of the seat. "A big fat woodstove with a cement block chimney," she told him.

"We need a place to hide out," she said and looked away, at the view of the lake, gleaming gorgeously at the foot of the Ridge under a sapphire sky. From here, there was no telling where their house or Miss Alden's had been, or that anything had ever happened. It was like a walled garden in the wilderness, you had to know about it to gain admission. You had to pass some kind of test.

"Don't you see?" Liv said.

She turned back to Pat, his hands tense upon the wheel.

"I fought for it. It's safe now. It's mine."

She looked back to the lake. "There's no place like home," she said, and smiled her crooked smile.